Praise fo

"With razor-sharp wit and vivid characters, *Robbie McNeil's Hit List* is a killer of a mystery that keeps you hooked to the very last page."

—Joanna Wallace, bestselling author of *You'd Look Better as a Ghost*

"With clever twists, whip-smart humor, and a side of karaoke, Heath's debut delivers kills and thrills from an antihero you never knew you needed."

—Marlee Bush, author of *Whispers of Dead Girls*

"Heath may have just invented a new genre…the cozy thriller! In *Robbie McNeil's Hit List*, the stakes are high, the characters are killers, and the story is a warm hug. This truly unique debut novel reminds us that even murderers-for-hire deserve a night out with friends. A delightful blend of cozy and sweet and murder-y… Three of my favorite things in a book."

—Tamara Berry, award-winning author of *Murder Runs in the Family*

"*Robbie McNeil's Hit List* is like a night out at your favorite gay bar. There's karaoke, musical theater, and the owners are slaying (literally). The 'hit list' is less about murder-for-hire and more about what songs they're going to play on any given night. It has the feel-good vibes of a holiday movie with a killer twist."

—Tasha Coryell, author of *Love Letters to a Serial Killer*

"Equal parts warmhearted and cold-blooded, *Robbie McNeil's Hit List* is a tale of loveable queer contract killers that's as inventive as it is wholly entertaining."

—Rob Osler, Anthony and Lefty Award–winning author of the Hayden and Friends series

"*Robbie McNeil's Hit List* is a totally original debut that seamlessly blends murder and karaoke into a wild mystery romp. Contract killing has never been so fun—or so queer!"

—Nicolas DiDomizio, author of *A Murder Most Camp*

Robbie McNeil's Hit List

BRIANNA HEATH

Poisoned Pen Press

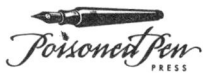

Copyright © 2026 by Brianna Heath
Cover and internal design © 2026 by Sourcebooks
Cover design by Matt Roeser
Handlettering by Erin Fitzsimmons/Sourcebooks
Cover images © MM memo/Shutterstock, Karlygash/Shutterstock
Internal design by Laura Boren/Sourcebooks

Sourcebooks, Poisoned Pen Press, and the colophon are registered trademarks of Sourcebooks.

All rights reserved. No part of this book may be reproduced in any form or by any electronic or mechanical means including information storage and retrieval systems—except in the case of brief quotations embodied in critical articles or reviews—without permission in writing from its publisher, Sourcebooks.

No part of this book may be used or reproduced in any manner for the purpose of training artificial intelligence technologies or systems.

The characters and events portrayed in this book are fictitious or are used fictitiously. Any similarity to real persons, living or dead, is purely coincidental and not intended by the author.

Published by Poisoned Pen Press, an imprint of Sourcebooks
1935 Brookdale RD, Naperville, IL 60563-2773
(630) 961-3900
sourcebooks.com

Cataloging-in-Publication Data is on file with the Library of Congress.

Printed and bound in Canada.
MBP 10 9 8 7 6 5 4 3 2 1

For Teryn.
You made a joke. I made a book.

And for everyone who needs a reminder
that home and belonging can be found
in the most unexpected places.

OVERTURE

11 years ago

ROBBIE MCNEIL DID NOT KILL A SINGLE PERSON FOR THE FIRST eighteen years of her life. After that, available records weren't quite as clear, but all in all, she appeared to have lived a relatively murder-free life.

Not that James planned to hold that against her. Everyone had points that separated their life into before and after. James didn't care about *before*. He viewed his work as being about creating *after*.

Robbie's *after* was up in the air. Of the five candidates he was considering, she was certainly not his top choice. In fact, he had quite a few reservations about her. Still, she had made his list, albeit without knowing such a list even existed. He'd been finding people like Robbie for over fifteen years now, and he'd learned to trust his instincts. She wasn't anything special, but that didn't mean she never could be. He would give her a fair shot.

It was a Tuesday, in the lull between lunch and dinner, when James walked into the Mill Creek Diner. The late March weather hadn't yet been informed that it ought to be spring, and the blast of cold air made for a rather emphatic herald of customers coming in. And yet absolutely no one bothered to so much as glance up at his arrival.

Not that there were many customers to begin with, just a handful of retirees with nowhere better to be on a weekday afternoon. The decor was so bland and predictable, he could've been in any of a hundred rural roadside diners. Vague, once-upon-a-time memories of being shiny, new, and clean clung to every worn surface.

The most recent photo he'd found of Robin Ann McNeil had been in her military file. He expected her appearance would have changed a bit in the year since she got out, but the woman ignoring him behind the counter was still perfectly recognizable. Her ashy brown hair wasn't pulled back in the harsh regulation bun but falling below her shoulders now, and her light skin had lost a bit of tan. The army fatigues from the photo had been replaced by a pale-blue polyester atrocity that he hoped was the diner's uniform and not a personal choice.

Robbie was consolidating ketchup from different bottles, which James thought might be a health code violation and also none of his business. Instead of approaching her directly, he chose a booth near the window and perused the oversize laminated menu, trying to avoid touching the sticky spot on the front. He watched in the glass as the ghost of her reflection approached his table.

"What can I get started for you?" Robbie asked, words mindlessly rolling off her tongue as if from an assembly line of preprogrammed phrases. She pulled out the order pad and scribbled in the corner to get the ink flowing in her cheap ballpoint pen.

He had assumed she would be the type to memorize orders

rather than jot them down, but perhaps that bit of his research was wrong, or maybe the notepad was a requirement of the diner, like that horrible shirt. Or, he considered, it could be entirely for show. Customers probably put up a fuss if she didn't appear to write their precious, greasy orders down.

He smiled at her pleasantly. "I will have a small house salad, Italian dressing on the side, a chocolate shake, and a moment of your time whenever it's convenient, Ms. McNeil."

James watched the confusion skitter across her face. Her first name would have been understandable; she was literally wearing it pinned to her shirt. But how would he know her last?

Most people, when he did this, asked exactly that. Robbie did not. She seemed to consider the question and then decided she didn't care—or perhaps that it simply wasn't worth the hassle of asking.

Good.

With a nod, she scribbled on her order pad—far too vaguely to have generated real words, as he'd suspected—and walked away. A few minutes later, she returned with a sad-looking salad and two far better-looking shakes, one for him and one for her as she sat down across from him in the diner booth, the peeling vinyl seat snagging audibly against the cheap fabric of her pants. She didn't say anything. She just waited.

And he didn't say anything. He just waited. This was a familiar game, one he never lost.

Robbie broke first. Of course.

"How's the salad?"

He raised an eyebrow, the amusement crinkling his eyes feeling like something of a novelty. Robbie was too young to have worn permanent lines onto her face like James had, but he suspected that when those formed, they wouldn't come from laughter either.

"Of all the questions you could ask me, Ms. McNeil, you've decided to inquire about the salad." He kept his tone soft and easy. James almost never raised his voice. Shouting tended to be rather distinctive and memorable, both adjectives he preferred not to associate with.

"It's just Robbie." She tapped her plastic name tag unnecessarily. "And it's my job to ask you about the food."

"Funny you should say that. About the job, I mean. That's what I'm here to discuss."

"You and your fancy suit came to a crappy, worn-out diner to discuss my job?" Robbie's voice notched up to a skeptical pitch.

His "fancy suit" had cost the equivalent of at least a month's worth of Robbie's wages—and less than half an hour's worth of his. He smiled again. "Well, no, not when you put it that way. Not to discuss your current job. I'm here to discuss your *next* job."

Robbie cocked her head. Despite his best efforts, James couldn't read a damn thing on her face. Maybe she was as good at schooling her expression as he was, but he dismissed that thought. More likely, there was nothing to read, no deep thoughts whirring beneath the surface. Maybe her mind was as blank as her expression. He could work with that.

Finally, she spoke, managing to cram an impressive amount of skepticism into a single syllable. "Oh?"

After waiting to see if she'd comment further and finding that was apparently all she had to say, James nodded. "Indeed. I think you may be well-suited for the work that I do."

Robbie shook her head. "You don't know me. I don't know you."

"One of those statements is correct. You're right, of course, that you don't know me. I apologize for skipping introductions. You may call me James." He reached his hand across the table. When she shook it, her grasp was cold from holding the milkshake glass but admirably firm. She didn't even ask whether James was a first name or last name as others often did.

Excellent.

"As to the latter statement, I actually know quite a bit about you."

"Seems unlikely."

"Things often do."

James took a few moments to finish his salad. He carefully blotted his mouth with a cheap paper napkin from the dispenser on the table and set his fork on his plate, tines pointed downward. Then he proceeded to lay out everything he knew about Robbie McNeil.

While James was no psychologist or profiler of any kind, his research on Robbie had painted a very clear picture. Robbie was broke, lonely, and miserable as hell.

And no, that wasn't based solely on the fact that she was working here or wearing that polyester disaster. James had done his due diligence, leveraging his connections for access to her military file and psych evals as well as taking a fruitful trip to Robbie's small, conservative hometown in Nebraska where a chatty waitress had been all too eager to gossip about her former classmate who'd been caught kissing the prom queen behind the bleachers and gotten kicked out of the oh-so-upstanding McNeil household shortly before graduation. Armed with that brief biography, James filled in extra details with the tricks of a charlatan psychic, reading between the lines, making broad statements that he narrowed down based on her body language.

Most critically, he let absolutely no judgment creep into his tone. Robbie's personal history had no shortage of rash decisions and ill-informed choices, but James was not here to criticize her past, only assess her current potential.

Robbie hadn't belonged in that rural town, and everything James had gathered about her life since seemed to point to a search for belonging. He'd found no evidence that she'd joined the military out of some overblown sense of duty or toxic patriotism or the rampant Islamophobia that drove others. James could draw a perfectly straight line from the desperate girl kicked out by her family with no money and no plan to the girl who believed all the promises an army recruiter spouted at her three days after she turned eighteen. He could see that same desperation in her multiple re-enlistments, in that blink-and-you'd-miss-it failed marriage, and in every moment his research had found where, over and over, she clung desperately to anything she could.

That was where James came in.

Just as he'd seen the obvious connections between her past actions, he could see a simple, easy path from a lost woman waiting tables for minimum wage to a woman he could utilize. She needed a place in the world, and James found that sort of need infinitely exploitable.

"Now," he concluded when his chronology caught up to the present, "you said I could not be here to offer you a job because I didn't know anything about you. I trust I've satisfied this requirement?"

She snorted rather rudely, but they could work on her manners another time. "Yeah, just a bit. What's the job?"

Not a single question about how he had possibly learned that much about her.

Magnificent.

"I won't disrespect you by assuming you'll be anything less than discreet about this conversation. Do bear in mind, however, that I cannot tolerate anyone sharing my business with others." It was the most serious tone he'd adopted, one designed to underscore exactly how unappealing his intolerance would be.

"Yeah, sure. You just rattled off my whole life story. You know everyone who's ever been in my life. Who do you think I'd tell?"

He inclined his head, considering her, and came to a decision. "Well then, Robbie, I will be direct. I will pay you two thousand dollars, in cash, if you kill someone for me next week."

"A particular someone?" She had the same bland tone as when she'd taken his order. "Or just whoever happens to walk past me on the street?"

James had come into the diner unsure, but in this exact moment, things solidified. He'd made his proposal, and Robbie didn't ask why. She didn't talk about morality or if the person deserved it.

Robbie McNeil simply wasn't curious.

Perfect.

James knew he wouldn't bother meeting any of the remaining candidates on his list.

1
Points for Effort

WHAT A PERSON LACKED IN TALENT, THEY COULD MAKE UP FOR with enthusiasm. Or try at least. Robbie had to give credit to the person currently at the mic for truly embodying this sentiment. They were absolutely in the running for "most enthusiastic performance of a song while managing not to hit a single note correctly."

"Top ten?"

The voice was surprisingly close to Robbie's ear, startling her. She didn't need to look to know who it was, but she still turned to the familiar sight of Dee Machado leaning against the wall, mouth skewed in a half smirk, gray tank top showing off a dense tapestry of tattoos flowing over olive skin. His black hair was shorter than when Robbie had last seen him a week ago, the sides shaved and only the top left longer, just enough to barely sweep his brow. It looked damn good, and she fully intended to compliment him on it, but a piercing attempt at a high note behind her obliterated every coherent thought in her head.

"I was thinking five, but I might bump that to top three," she replied in the blissful silence that followed the screech.

Dee nodded as if considering a complex issue. "Top three. All right. I defer to your expert opinion."

Expert. Robbie had a decent ear for music, sure, but Dee had never sung a wrong note in his life and they both knew it. Robbie rolled her eyes before turning back to the stage. The enthusiastic singer was flushed with excitement and possibly effort as Robbie took back the microphone. A group at a corner table was applauding and cheering the performance in a way that suggested the truest of friendships.

"Thank you for that…lovely rendition," she murmured, studiously avoiding eye contact with Dee or she wouldn't have been able to keep a straight face. Instead, she kept her gaze on the laptop screen on the desk in front of her, pretending to read the words she'd already memorized while the last performance was still going. She called up the next name in the queue.

A girl, who frankly Robbie would've thought too young to be in here if she weren't so confident that the staff at the door would've properly checked ID, approached the stage, shaky and nervous.

"Just have fun," Robbie said. Dee claimed statements like that were good customer service, so Robbie had a handful of standard mindless phrases she stockpiled for the timid ones. Giving the girl a practiced smile intended to pass as reassuring, she handed off the mic and headed back to the sign-up desk. Dee, who could always tell when she'd had enough of dealing with strangers, had already waved over Eloise, an impossibly tall woman with electric-blue hair and light freckled skin, one of only two employees Robbie had put on the schedule for tonight. Mondays rarely saw enough action to warrant more staff. Eloise took a seat at the sign-up desk, looking far happier to be sitting there than Robbie probably had—not that she disliked it exactly, but she didn't just *smile* for no reason at all—and Robbie followed Dee back to the bar.

The music started up, and after the first few bars, an absolutely stunning soprano filled the room. Robbie couldn't help but match Dee's appreciative grin. Yeah, there were plenty who competed for those coveted spots of worst singers of all time, and most fell in a forgettably average range, but then there were gems like this.

Deciding to open a karaoke bar together had been something of a whim. Neither of them had needed the money, and it turned out a queer bar wasn't exactly a fountain of profits anyway. Their primary income source had been sufficient for their day-to-day needs, at least financially, but the irregular schedule often left them with long stretches of downtime to fill.

If you had to find something to occupy that time, James had always encouraged mundane jobs. Things that involved staplers and paper cuts and interoffice memos. Probably. Robbie wasn't really clear what you did in an office job. James discouraged anything too flashy, anything that involved too much interaction with the public. He discouraged his operatives—his word—from fraternizing with one another too. Dee didn't care much for that rule, or most rules for that matter. He'd never gotten along with James the way Robbie had, the two of them frequently butting heads because Dee believed his own opinions mattered.

Which was how they came to be sitting at some nameless roadside diner in the middle of the night a few years back, both coming off jobs, when Dee had casually commented, "Bet we could start a killer karaoke bar if we wanted."

Robbie had been so certain he was joking, but something serious lay beneath his smile. Unlike with James, Dee wasn't asking

Robbie to work for him. He was proposing they build something *together*. As partners. Equals. Robbie's head had buzzed, and she had been at least 80 percent certain that wasn't just the carbonation from her soda.

The fuzzy feeling had grown as she matched Dee's smile. "Yeah, I bet we could."

So they did.

Fine, it wasn't quite that simple. They had to settle somewhere first, a decision Dee confidently and bewilderingly entrusted to Robbie. She'd picked a worn-out city in southern Indiana she'd passed through a few months prior that had inexplicably felt *right*. And of course, a good deal of paperwork and licensing was involved and many hours of manual labor renovating the little space they bought.

Dee had selected the paint for the walls, a rich shade with some food name like Cranberry Dreams or Pomegranate Paradise. Robbie had bought an obscene number of neon signs. She was particularly fond of the four-foot-tall, violently fuchsia parrot on the north wall. She'd named it Phyllis.

When all was done, they'd wound up with an open-floor plan that had a long bar near the entrance, a stage in the opposite corner, and an assorted cluster of tables, chairs, and spill-resistant couches.

More importantly, they'd wound up with a home, a concept Robbie hadn't fully understood until then. And it wasn't just for themselves but for other people looking for safety and community, whether they realized it or not. They hadn't exactly chosen an easy business to go into. Queer bars were a dying industry, practically extinct in many places. But they'd opened Coda regardless and managed to keep it running for nearly five years now.

And they still both managed to keep up with their day jobs. Which often involved working at night. Or night and day, as had kept Dee busy for the past week.

Robbie sidled up to him, poking him in the ribs with her elbow. "How'd it go?"

"Honestly, a bit of a mess."

"Figuratively or literally?"

Dee laughed. "Figuratively, thank god. Target made travel plans at the last minute, and then at the last *last* minute changed those plans. I had a hell of a time tracking them down."

"But you did."

"Of course I did. And once I found them, well, you know me. Quick and efficient."

Dee had a lot of skills. He could sing like no other. He was a decent guitar player. He could make a deliciously light soufflé. Robbie, meanwhile, was a mediocre singer, far better at guitar, and absolutely hopeless in all things cooking-related. She had no clue what a soufflé even was. The one talent they shared equally was what had brought them together in the first place: They were both quite proficient at killing people.

"Glad to hear it." They worked the bar and lived together but took contract jobs separately. She didn't mind when she or Dee was off on one of those jobs, but it just felt right when they were both home. Technically, that would be the apartment they kept above the bar, but really, Coda was home: neon lights and drunk lesbians, enthusiastic bad singing and Dee.

Dee gave her a one-armed hug. "Good to see you, Robbie. Gonna run up for a quick shower, but I'll be back down to help the rest of the night."

Robbie nodded amiably. When Dee didn't move, Robbie raised an eyebrow.

"I'm going. In a minute. This girl has a gorgeous voice and a gorgeous… Look, you can't fault me for wanting to enjoy the fruits of our karaoke labors."

Fair enough. Robbie leaned back against the counter to watch the performance too.

"Hey," Dee called casually from the bar a few hours later. When he caught her eye, he added, "Got someone needing a chat with you."

Finally. It had to have been months now since Dee last used their code phrase, but she'd been waiting. She scanned the bar, trying to see who might've come in here asking for her.

Coda was technically open for another half hour, but it was already nearly empty, only a few stragglers left to watch Georgia, a drag queen regular, swaying on stage in a glittery blue gown and deadly heels belting "I Want It All" with a passion that surely would've made Freddie Mercury proud. At the table closest to Robbie, a group of women in their forties, who came like clockwork for every half-priced drink night, oohed like middle schoolers hearing Robbie get called to the office. She flapped a hand to silence them but still cut a suitably amused smile because they were customers after all.

Robbie headed to the bar, and Dee jerked his chin to a figure at the back corner table, squeezed into the one spot that wasn't hit by some form of neon light. Great. Calling out "someone wants to hire you for a spot of murder" in a public space obviously wouldn't do, but the cloak-and-dagger type usually meant someone antsy. At least she could be confident the person already provided the pass phrase to explain why they'd come.

Despite taking jobs separately, Robbie and Dee shared the same lovely, efficient woman who'd been screening referrals for them both for the past several years. Darlene had a clever mind and a voice like sandpaper. She had also been surprised to hear from Robbie after months of Robbie saying she was closed for new jobs. But given how much she and Dee had drawn on Coda's accounts recently, Robbie needed the income. Desperately.

Dropping unceremoniously into the seat across from the shadow, Robbie set her elbows on the table and prompted, "I'll need a name, occupation, and place of residence. Then, if I decide I want to be involved, I'll tell you my fee, half of which I will need paid up front, the other half when I've concluded business."

As Robbie's eyes started to adjust to the low light, she could see the startled stiffness that took over the person's posture. What did they expect? Small talk and pleasantries? Robbie's commitment to customer service had much tighter boundaries when it came to this type of work. The customer didn't need to have *fun* here.

"I was told you don't ask questions." The voice was deep and a little phlegmy. Robbie was used to that. Nerves, knot in the throat, all common enough.

Until James, Robbie assumed everyone observed others the way she did, but he'd praised her way of cataloging details in her mind like something special. Maybe it was. When the speaker shifted slightly, just enough to inch into a patch of light, she got everything she needed in the few seconds before he shifted nervously again, dipping back into shadow. Hair that was probably some shade of blond normally but was tinged vivid purple with overlapping shades of neon signs. Expensive cut, styled meticulously with enough product that every strand fell exactly where it ought to. Someone who loved control, then, and took pride in using money as a status symbol. Dark eyes, color indeterminate, full of tension and suspicion. Square jaw, clean-shaven, thin lips pressed into an even thinner line, full eyebrows crinkled into a frown. He wasn't happy to be here, certainly not with her, but he was motivated to see this conversation through. Good. Beyond the physical details, she caught the air of someone who was used to always getting their way. Folks with that attitude could always afford to pay more, and Robbie made a mental note to add a little extra to her fee. Maybe a lot extra. She liked to think of it as a cockiness tax.

"I have to ask *some* questions," Robbie pointed out with a hint of a smile. "There are a lot of people out there. I'm going to need a little information to know who I'm dealing with."

"Right. Of course. You can call me...Mr. Clark. But I don't think my occupation or residence are any of your business."

Robbie did love the ones who didn't quite seem to know what they were getting themselves into.

"Nice to meet you, Mr. Clark, but I was under the impression that you knew what line of business I'm in."

"I do know," Mr. Clark retorted defensively. "You... Well, as I understand it, you take care of, uh, *problems* in a permanent sort of way."

Robbie nodded. In the slow, patient tone one might use to explain physics to a toddler, she said, "Yes. So unless *you* are the problem that needs to be taken care of, I don't much care who you are. What I do need is the name, occupation, and residence of your *problem*."

He shifted uncomfortably in his seat, and if he'd moved back into the light, Robbie fully expected she'd be seeing that pale face turning red. Then he shook it all off, that cockiness rolling off him in waves. "The problem is named…" He hesitated, and if Robbie didn't know better, she'd think he'd forgotten. Obviously, that couldn't be right. After a moment, he finished, "Xavier Landerman. Occupation is…something to do with antiquities? Import, export sort of thing, I believe. I don't know his address, but several nights a week, I'm certain you'll be able to find him at the card tables in the Ajax Club. It's this place in Penny Park where—"

"Thank you, Mr. Clark. I have heard of the Ajax Club." If she'd passed him on a street, she might've been surprised he'd heard of it, but he obviously didn't have anything against illegal businesses as a concept. Ajax wasn't an issue, but something still prickled up her spine. She understood clients being cagey about what they shared, but she wasn't sure she'd ever had someone this vague. Did he know *anything* about this target? Did he know the target at all?

Robbie forced her mind to pipe down. She was overthinking it. Nobody went to this much trouble to have a stranger killed. "That is all very useful. Do you have a photo of Landerman?"

A sharp "no."

She eyed him, certain he was holding out on her. Luckily, James had always taught her to work from as little information as possible. Whatever Mr. Clark wasn't saying, Robbie was confident she could pull this off without it. "Fine. I trust that you sought me out in particular because my methods will meet your needs. Anything else you feel I should know?"

"I need this business concluded by the end of the month. I will pay extra for a guarantee that you'll meet the deadline."

Not every job came with a hard deadline, but when there was, it was usually something like "you have two days." They'd just barely entered September. An entire month felt extremely generous.

She took a moment to do some mental math, trying to remember Coda's most recent balance sheet as Mr. Clark fidgeted in the shadows. For something this easy, she normally wouldn't charge as a rush job, but Mr. Clark seemed to have little to no budgetary restrictions. And as a general rule, those who hired contract killers weren't precisely good people. Robbie tallied the numbers, and then she took another moment to continue to make Mr. Clark fidget for no reason other than because she could.

Finally, she said, "Twenty grand. Expenses are included, barring anything unexpected, in which case, I will bill you as necessary."

It was a high price for such a basic job, and she'd expected to haggle until they settled on a significantly lower sum. Yet Mr. Clark nodded. "Done. How would you like the first half deposited?"

A spark of triumph danced down her spine. In the months since her last job, Robbie had started to forget the thrill of a successful deal.

After providing the requisite payment details, Robbie went to the last part of her standard hiring spiel. "I'll need some way to contact you, although I'm not picky on means. And do you have any particular requirements in terms of verifying the job is complete? I can provide you a burner phone if you'd like."

Mr. Clark stiffened again. "I will return here at the end of the month. No need to contact me before then. And I suppose if you can get a copy of a death certificate, that would be appreciated."

As far as confirmation went, that was probably the tidiest request she could get. "I appreciate the time, but this may not take a month to complete. If I'm done sooner, I will need a way to let you know."

"No need," Mr. Clark repeated. "Do whatever you see fit in whatever time you want, but you will not contact me. I will return on the thirtieth. You will provide a death certificate. I will provide the rest of your payment. That is the arrangement."

Well, fine. If he wanted things that way, that was what he'd get. She could make do with the first half of the payment for now. Hopefully. And whatever he was hiding about Landerman shouldn't matter. Robbie was a damn good hit person. She could pull this off, no problem, with plenty of time to spare.

Robbie pushed her chair back from the table and stood. "Pleasure doing business, Mr. Clark. I'll see you in a month."

2

Robbie & Dee

ROBBIE WAS NEVER THE FIRST ONE UP. EVEN IF SHE THOUGHT she was getting up early, her notion of "first thing in the morning" was an hour after Dee's, minimum.

Besides, beating him to the punch wasn't all that motivating when this way meant coffee was always ready and waiting for Robbie. Sometimes—and she never told Dee this for obvious reasons—she'd wait in her room if she woke too early and just listen. The tumbling clink as he measured out the ground beans, the slosh as he filled the water reservoir, that neat little beep as he set it to percolate.

Even this early in the morning, a humid summer heat was already threatening the air, but Robbie still couldn't resist a hot cup of coffee.

She didn't get that far.

"Robs? Who do I need to kill for a clean binder?" Dee called from his bedroom as soon as he heard her footsteps. Their agreement as roommates was that Dee cooked—and made the coffee—because Robbie didn't want to do either, and Robbie did dishes and laundry, Dee's least favorite chores.

"No need to kill. One sec." She padded down the hall in her fuzzy koala slippers and retrieved a chest binder from where she'd laid it out flat on top of the dryer. "Sorry, forgot to put them in your basket. I'm doing handwash again tomorrow if you have anything from your trip you want to throw in."

"You're a saint."

While Robbie had been raised a prude on a rural Nebraskan farm, Dee had been in theater his whole life, and if he'd ever had a sense of modesty, it hadn't survived to adulthood. He tugged off the oversize T-shirt he'd slept in and threw it in the general direction of his laundry basket, then pulled the binder on, wiggling to get it over his hips before pulling it up over his chest and adjusting it to lie evenly. He topped it with one of twenty identical gray tanks he owned. His black shorts were identical to the dozen others he had too. Robbie, who had a lot more variety in her own wardrobe, liked to tease him about his "uniform," but to be honest, she did sometimes envy how none of it required any forethought. Dee liked what he liked, simple and predictable. He also loved a good costume, of course, but if he wasn't performing, it was either his summer uniform or his winter uniform and nothing in between.

"Oh, I meant to tell you last night," Robbie said, leaning against his open bedroom door. "Love the haircut."

He flashed a grin at her as he ran a dollop of mousse through his hair. "I might have to commit to making a trip to Alabama once a month. The barber who did this was an absolute dream."

He did a quick inspection in the mirror and grinned at his reflection. Robbie couldn't help but smile at the sight of Dee being happy with what he saw, still somewhat novel. He'd had twenty-seven years of absolutely hating mirrors before that, and that satisfied grin of his was long overdue.

Obviously, his journey was his own, but she liked to think she'd helped get him to this point. Or rather, she hoped her support had mattered.

After closing one night three years ago, she'd asked, "You know I'd kill anyone who made you feel bad for being yourself, right?"

With anyone else, that would have been just a turn of phrase, but of course, Robbie and Dee were who they were.

"Yeah. Same to you," he'd replied absently as he mopped a particularly sticky spot on the floor.

"Then I think we should talk about the fact that you're unhappy being you and figure out how to fix that, because I'm not going to take out my best friend."

This was the result: Someone Dee liked being. Someone who smiled at the mirror.

As with opening Coda, it wasn't exactly that simple, of course. There were a lot of late-night conversations, a lot of trial and error to find what felt right. A good lot of talk about how they owned a lesbian bar and Dee felt being a lesbian was an integral part of his identity and how to mesh that with his gender identity and expression. The answer they had come up with was Dee could damn well describe himself whatever way he wanted, and Robbie would fight anyone who said otherwise.

By all metrics that mattered, it was an excellent solution.

While Dee finished admiring his reflection, Robbie continued her trek to the kitchen where the pot was done brewing. Dee had already set out two mugs. Taking the one covered in birds with the phrase "Nice Tits," she filled it halfway with coffee, then milk. She finished it off with a generous spoonful of sugar because she wasn't a demon like Dee who believed in drinking his coffee black.

He appeared in the kitchen doorway. His eyes widened with exaggerated shock when he saw Robbie mixing her own cup. "Who are you and what did you do with my Robbie?"

"She had to fix her own damn coffee every day. It was a travesty." It had also been the instant stuff, not Dee's freshly brewed magic. She filled his mug nearly to the brim and passed it over to him. "Also, we have that appointment with the theater manager this morning. I set four alarms and left myself an army of reminder stickies. Should I have left one for you?"

Dee shook his head. "No, I just had the one note on my calendar, but I appreciate the lengths you went to so we wouldn't miss it. But breakfast first. Omelets?"

Robbie flashed a grin and went off to dress while he cooked. While he'd politely refrained from disturbing Robbie's beauty rest earlier, he now started to sing, a distant hum at first, then gradually loud enough for Robbie to recognize it as a number from *Anything Goes*. The resonance of a song running through the apartment was satisfying in a way absolutely nothing else in the world was, especially after a week alone.

Robbie had loved music for longer than she'd known. She'd eagerly anticipated church on Sundays as a kid, not realizing until years later that hymns and choir services had been the root of that attraction, not religious devotion. During basic training and later her tours overseas, her off-brand Walkman had been a godsend. It wasn't until she met Dee that she got a crash course in Broadway.

At first, the thought of bursting into song for no apparent reason seemed absurd. But god, it was an addicting absurdity.

Why *not* break into song? Sure, spontaneous group numbers and dance breaks were still a little much, but using music to process feelings, to tell stories, to connect to others... Robbie believed in that down to her bones. It wasn't just the music either. A good musical was the culmination of a million moving parts. The more she watched, the more she picked up on the minute details someone put extensive thought into. It made a difference how the lighting hit the stage, in what color, and for how long. She noticed the choices between elaborate set design and simple and why one worked better for this show versus that. Every musical was a puzzle, and a *good* musical was one where all the pieces slotted perfectly into place.

As for breaking into song in the middle of the day for no reason, well, sharing a home with Dee had quickly shown her that some people did indeed live that way. That *Robbie* could live that way. When he finished his first song, Dee stuck with the same musical and sang through the first verses of "You're the Top" before pausing at the end of Reno's part, and Robbie picked up the next verse of the duet with him. Despite the fact that they owned a business whose entire premise was singing in front of strangers, Robbie rarely sang where anyone other than Dee could hear. Loving music was one thing; using her own voice was something else altogether.

Robbie re-emerged just as Dee was setting the plated omelets on the table. She had put on a flowing floral top over ripped jeans and heavy boots and was already rethinking the boots. If it was hot now, it was only going to get worse.

Her hair was pulled into a high ponytail, the ash-brown waves perpetually undecided whether to be curly or straight and winding up not quite either. Today was mostly frizz. It was fine, and she definitely didn't feel like cutting it all off just now when she couldn't get it to cooperate.

"What's the rest of your day look like?" he asked as they sat down. "Going to start that new job, or are you going to wait until the month is almost up?"

Rude. She met his smirk with a halfhearted glare. She hadn't exactly made a plan yet, but now that he'd brought up her general inability to work without the pressure of a looming deadline, she felt the need to say, "Actually, I think I'll get started today. Might as well get it out of the way, right? I figure I can go to the Ajax Club in the afternoon, play some cards, see if it's as sketchy as its reputation claims."

"You think this is about cards? Debt maybe?" Strictly speaking, the *why* of a job wasn't their business. They dealt with *who*. For them, the why was a payday, nothing more. But when Robbie had shared the details of the job, Dee had asked Robbie's opinion on Mr. Clark. She'd given him an honest "I'm not sure yet."

Mr. Clark was a bit of an odd duck, but the nervousness paired with a cocksure attitude matched her assessment that he was a guy with money to burn and definitive about what he wanted. Not uncommon for a contract client. The way he talked about Xavier Landerman though. Something there didn't fit, and her brain itched trying to figure out what exactly that was. Maybe the source of the discordance was that unknown *why* of the job.

"I'm not sure. It's never helpful to kill someone who owes you money, obviously, but…" She shrugged.

He knew the rest. "But the people who hire us aren't usually the type to solve their problems in a rational way."

Dee also knew as well as Robbie that they needed this. Staging a musical turned out to be an expensive undertaking. Who knew? They'd only borrowed a little from Coda here and there to start. A little more, and a bit more after that. Now things were looking bleak. Robbie wasn't great at math, but even she knew red numbers weren't good on a budget sheet. She hadn't yet figured out how to tell their bartenders *Sorry, we kinda stole payroll this week.* Now she and Dee wouldn't have to, and the weight off her shoulders left her feeling almost floaty.

"It has to be related to Ajax, though, right?" Dee continued over a bite of eggs. "Clark didn't know where Landerman lives. He didn't know what or where his work is. The only thing he knew was that the guy plays cards at an illegal gambling hall. How else would they know each other?"

"Not sure. I didn't get the impression that Clark was the type to regularly patronize that kind of place, but hopefully I'll find something out this afternoon." At Dee's nod, Robbie pulled out her phone, swiping through it. "Okay, so if that's settled, there's a small, tiny, minor thing I wanted to discuss."

Dee eyed her and then the phone warily. "Please tell me you didn't mess with anything."

"Teeny tiny thing."

"Robbie."

She sighed and gave him an apologetic look. "I rewrote a bit of the second act."

"Robbie."

"It's only one scene. And one song."

"*Robbie!*"

"Stop saying my name in that tone." She glanced back at the phone to reluctantly close out of the recording app. Dee knew the way her brain inexplicably got stuck on things, unable to move on until she found a resolution, but he still pushed—gently—back against the habit sometimes. She kept her explanation simple. "It needed to be done. It just wasn't right. I had to try to fix it."

"You don't need to change things."

"It wasn't perfect. And now I think it is."

Dee reached over and put a hand on top of hers. "It *was* perfect. Even if it wasn't, it was exactly how it needs to be, because it's not going to matter when the entire cast quits out of frustration. We're supposed to start going off book next week, and I will not hold back any rioting actors. In fact, I'd probably join them."

Robbie always had music in her head, a quiet soundtrack of catchy songs and half-remembered lyrics. Once in a while, bits of something would drift in that she couldn't place. Not long after Robbie and Dee met but well before they'd conceived of Coda, Robbie started paying attention to those bits. She'd realized how sometimes a tune would come into her brain, and if she was gentle with it, it might turn into a song. It wasn't that meeting Dee had sparked anything, she didn't think, but sometimes she wondered if meeting him and seeing his clear love of music helped open a door in her brain she hadn't known to unlock. Still, she didn't mention it to him for at least another year or two. Maybe it was *because* she knew how much Dee loved music. He knew what good music sounded like, and he'd know hers wasn't it.

But Dee had caught her humming one day, and when he'd asked the song, Robbie sheepishly admitted it was something she'd made up. Instead of laughing or telling her how terrible it was, he'd clapped. That thing people did when they enjoyed something. That thing no one had done for Robbie in her entire life.

Still, it wasn't until last year that she'd realized she could take everything both she and Dee loved about musicals and combine it with her songwriting. She could create the very thing she loved. It didn't have to be grand. It was never going to be on Broadway. But it would be *hers*. A small but unmistakable way of scribbling "I was here" on the world with an accomplishment she didn't hide away. She loved her talents when it came to her contract work, but that wasn't exactly the sort of thing you got to show off.

When Robbie first told Dee, she'd been absolutely certain that he would say hell no. Pull her back down to reality. Tell her not to rashly jump into a new hobby yet again. Remind her that she was in fact only good at one thing, just like James had always said. But the foundation of their entire relationship, the reason why they worked as partners in business and partners in crime, was an unwavering faith in each other. Dee immediately believed in Robbie's dream. He didn't need the lengthy set of arguments she'd prepared to convince him. He didn't need to wait and see how it went once she started writing. He didn't even take issue with the fact that she wouldn't technically be *writing* anything and that he would have to be the one to transcribe her recordings into a script.

She said she wanted to try. That was enough for him.

Now they were a few short weeks away from opening, but the closer this endeavor got to reality, the more her confidence wavered. Dee's belief was far more solid.

"Stop thinking of all the ways you can nitpick your own work."

"I know. Sorry. I can't always turn it off." Even after hitting pause on contracted hits for months while burying herself in show production, Robbie's brain hadn't fallen out of the habit of looking at things from every possible angle.

"You've got to at least try. We have a theater manager to meet and logistics to discuss. And then you have a man to find and kill." Dee sat back and gave Robbie a firm look. "Now finish your omelet."

Robbie definitely hadn't based her entire expectation of producing a musical on several viewings of *The Producers*—original and remake films, plus a bootleg Broadway taping for thoroughness. They'd found a choreographer entirely by accident one night at Coda, which perhaps wasn't the exact same as a collection of theatrical folks singing about keeping things gay, but really, wasn't it?

In fact, finding their production team had been one of the easiest parts of the entire process. It generally only took Robbie a minute or so to know whether someone was right for the team, whether they'd help bring out her vision or try to shift to their own, what role they'd be best suited for, and there were a lot of roles. The fact that she hadn't given up was a testament to the challenging, complex nature of the task. Through her contract work, she'd come to realize a challenge was the only thing her brain consistently found worth pursuing, and that same drive kept the fire of this new endeavor burning.

The bit that got left out of her (definitely comprehensive) idea of this process was the actual theater. Not surprisingly, if they wanted to put on a show, on a stage, in a theater, they had to rent one. For their purposes, they'd been happy to find space at the Oster Community Playhouse on the east side of the city.

Their meeting with the theater's manager today had been heavy on financial details, questions about ticket sales and run dates. Hadn't they settled all that a long time ago? Thankfully, memorizing minutiae from past conversations and lifting context clues from a person's body language were easy, even if the numbers on the page weren't. Overall, she felt it had gone decently. Dee was even whistling to himself as he and Robbie left, which admittedly wasn't exactly a metric for anything, because he'd likely be doing that no matter what.

The theater was an unassuming single-story building. The bricks had probably been a beautiful shade of red at some point, but they were covered in decades of dirt and pollution now. Major cracks crept up, splitting brick from mortar, giving the whole thing a distinct air of falling apart. The theater was bordered by a used bookstore on one side and a coffee shop on the other, both in sorry states of repair. Or at least it had been.

Dee quit whistling and elbowed Robbie with a nod to the bookstore.

It took a moment, but she sighed when she spotted the sign announcing the shop was going out of business. "I can't say I'm entirely shocked, but that's still disappointing."

"You think that'll ever be us?"

Coda was in an area of town slightly more cared for, although that was less about care and more about the fact that their neighborhood of Morningate fell right in between downtown Reevesburg and the swanky borough of the city's wealthiest citizens. Still, it wasn't exactly the beating heart of the city. Beating wasn't the right term. Staggering, stuttering, something like that.

"Of course not," Robbie answered with complete confidence. "We always find a way to keep going. You know that."

Her entire life had basically been an exercise in finding a way to keep going. Keep going in school when she just got passed along from grade to grade, never understanding how all the other kids could simply glance at a chunk of text on a page and quickly know what it said. Keep going when all the other girls talked about their crushes on boys, and she was vividly aware of yet another thing fundamentally broken about her. Keep going when she joined the army out of desperation at absolutely the wrong time and spent the next six years in hell because what else was there?

She knew Dee's experience had been wildly different from hers, but he'd had his own struggles. She was constantly impressed not just with the fact that he went to college but that he made it through despite having weeks or months when his depression was so bad, it was a miracle when he made it out of bed. She maintained a separate level of impressed-ness for the fact that he actually *enjoyed* classes when he could go, although he'd majored in music theory, and Robbie did think perhaps she would've enjoyed her education a bit more if there had been music involved.

But the fact was they were both trying to put one foot in front of the other and nothing more until James found them. He didn't care about all the things she'd failed at. He told Robbie she had a brilliant analytical mind, and under James's tutelage, she'd excelled at a particular brand of killing that left everyone assuming the target had simply fallen victim to an unfortunate accident.

And somehow, James had found Dee in the deepest part of his depression, drowning in alcohol. Robbie'd never pressed for details on what part of that equation landed Dee in jail, but she knew James had transformed that rock bottom into diligence, focus, and, with a combination of training and natural talent, someone with remarkable marksmanship. For Dee, becoming a skilled sniper had been as easy as learning to bake. A simple matter of measuring out all the right things and knowing how to put them together. He could make a damn good soufflé, and he could hit a target at one thousand yards. Easy.

James didn't eliminate Dee's moods, didn't erase Robbie's problems reading and writing, but he had given them something to focus on, a sense of accomplishment and pride in themselves that nothing else in their lives had provided. Maybe more so for Robbie than Dee, but—

"Oy." Dee punched her lightly in the shoulder. "You even listening to me?"

"Absolutely not," Robbie answered honestly. "What were you saying?"

He pointed to a flyer taped haphazardly to a lamppost and then to the dozens of others plastered to the run-down facades of the nearby buildings. "I was asking what you think of his promises to revitalize places like this."

A stylized image of Fletcher Ingram, businessman turned aspiring politician, stared out at them, a tanned face with a strong, straight nose and wide jaw, all remarkably square and chiseled, all of it seemingly untouched by age. Or at the very least touched heavily by an airbrush.

"It's a nice idea." Robbie shrugged. It wouldn't make a difference right away, but polishing up East Oster could be worthwhile. "Maybe the next time we stage a play, this area will be flourishing."

"Oh, we're staging another play, are we?" Dee smirked.

"No. I mean, we could. If we wanted. Or not. I don't know." Robbie waved a hand vaguely toward the flyer. "Fletcher Ingram already owns half the properties in the city, more throughout the state. I don't see why he has to throw himself into the political arena to make an impact. But if he's going to do anything, yes, I think it's more likely he'll champion a cause if someone else is footing the bill."

"He's a multimillionaire, Robs. I don't think he needs to run for office to get the funds to fix up some old buildings."

"He didn't become that rich by spending money on worthy causes. Philanthropy doesn't fill the coffers."

A gust of wind kicked up, a too-hot imitation of an ideal summer breeze, but god, it felt good for the air to move at all. The flyer on the lamppost fluttered, its tape making a valiant effort before the paper ripped and flew off to litter the other side of the street.

They reached the car, parked a good two blocks from the theater because Robbie hated paying for parking and this was the closest stretch of unmetered curb. Dee dug the keys from his pocket and tossed them over to her.

Pulling her phone out of her back pocket to avoid sitting on it, she swiped away notifications until pausing on a missed call, unsure how to process it. It had been at least a year, probably longer since she'd seen that contact pop up. Hell, it had been three phone numbers ago. Of course, the fact that she'd never given James her current number wasn't a deterrent for someone like him. Why would he bother though? Had thinking about how he'd found her and Dee somehow summoned his attention like the big evil eye from that time Dee made her sacrifice hours of her life to marathon *Lord of the Rings?*

"You coming or what?" Dee grumped from inside the car.

She'd call James back. But not right now. Not while there were things to do, not while Dee was around to make opinionated comments about James. She had a job, and James would understand the job always came first.

And while they did the actual hit parts of their jobs separately, Robbie and Dee were both well-versed enough in the prep steps that they occasionally tagged along with each other when it suited their schedules. As she slid into the driver's seat, Robbie asked, "Since we're frequenting the less illustrious parts of town today, any chance you want to get lunch, then accompany me to check out what are sure to be some unsavory characters?"

"My favorite kind of people."

Robbie started the car, and Dee started whistling again.

3

Bad Luck

THE AJAX CLUB WAS UNREMARKABLE IN DAYLIGHT. IT WAS ON the opposite side of the city from the theater, but it was situated in a neighborhood that was just as run-down, if not more so. Penny Park was quite literally on the wrong side of the tracks, a sprawl of warehouses and industrial buildings spilling outward from a spine of freight train lines. Even miles away at Coda, Robbie could sometimes hear those trains sounding their horns in the dead of night, running on their own schedule without a care for anyone sleeping.

The club itself was a squat, unexceptional cinder block building painted a dull matte black. No sign of any kind. Robbie had never been, but when she'd moved to this city five years ago, she'd done her due diligence finding all the illegal operations nearby.

"How do you want to play this?" Dee asked as Robbie pulled into the small parking lot, making her best guess at a parking space between the various faded lines.

"Split up. Observation only. All I'm hoping for today is to get a sense of the place, the clientele, that sort of thing."

Dee, through his own consortium of murky connections, had

gotten them each a glossy black poker chip embossed with the white clover outline of the clubs symbol. He went in first, flashing the token at the tank of a guard at the door before successfully disappearing into the building.

After waiting several minutes, Robbie did the same, saluting the tank with the token held between her index and middle finger. The tank nodded. The door opened.

The plain black building had a lot more going for it than its lackluster exterior. The floors were a deep burgundy that Robbie appreciated as a shade that could probably mask both wine and blood rather decently. Even midafternoon on a weekday, there were a good twenty or so people there, scattered across an orderly arrangement of table games. A handful clustered around roulette games that flanked the entrance, several more making noise by a long craps table toward the center of the room. But most of the patrons leaned heavily on the green baize of the card tables—baccarat near the bar, poker toward the east wall, and blackjack along the back. The dealers were dressed in black button-downs with suit vests the exact same shade as the carpet.

All in all, it was a rather decent place. Straightforward, tidy, clean. At least clean enough. She really did think that carpet was probably hiding a multitude of sins. Still, the place didn't entirely look like it lived up to its reputation as a dodgy gambling hall. Sure, she'd kind of been envisioning something out of a 1940s noir film, but that was a perfectly reasonable expectation, wasn't it?

She wandered closer to the roulette table, pausing near where Dee stood watching the red and black spin.

"Not sure this is all it's cracked up to be. Bit…dull," she murmured, keeping her complaint low enough that only Dee could hear.

Dee coughed. "You sure about that?"

Robbie cast another quick glance at the room. "Probably?"

"You're slipping, Robs. Pay attention. Maybe this is a boring little place to play cards, but let's say Landerman were here right now. Take a look around and tell me you'd be willing to do the job here."

Robbie swept a casual glance around the room. Two doors on the back wall were flanked by employees dressed in the same uniforms as the dealers, with the notable difference that they were all carrying visible firearms. Some had more than one.

Now that she was scanning the room with a more critical eye, it was clear the dealers and even the waiters circulating with trays of drinks were all carrying concealed. As she walked, she counted without even thinking. There were at least nineteen cameras watching every angle of the room, including dedicated cameras aimed at those back doors. Where was her mind? She should've noticed all of that the instant she walked in. Instead, she'd been busy thinking about the choice of carpet colors—something that would've been relevant if she were recreating this set onstage, but she needed to switch her brain from musical producer to contract killer.

She was a bit curious what lay beyond the well-monitored back doors, but it wasn't the point of today's excursion. She didn't need to know the inner workings of this place. Robbie's plan was to simply observe. She wasn't going to bring any attention to herself by asking about Xavier Landerman. Mostly, she figured she'd let herself be seen to the precise point of not being considered a stranger but unnoteworthy beyond that. In another day or two, she'd return and do the same. A third trip was the earliest she'd risk dropping a name, something made up to carry them off any scent. Fourth trip, perhaps sometime next week, would be an acceptable time to bring up Landerman if she hadn't found him via other means by then.

The night before, after Mr. Clark had left, Robbie did a quick search for Landerman but hadn't found anything useful. That was fairly uncommon these days, but it happened. Robbie and Dee took strides to keep information about themselves off the internet. And if she couldn't find anything about Landerman online, she was plenty capable of doing things the old-fashioned way.

Robbie slowly made her way toward a blackjack table at the far end of the room, surveying each gaming table she passed, a quick glance for each player. That college-aged redhead had to be here for the first time, still figuring out how roulette worked. The middle-aged man in the slightly wrinkled suit fidgeting his hands as he lost at craps was, to Robbie's eye, obviously going through a divorce, presumably his spouse's idea, because he clearly didn't know when to quit. The leather-clad group at the bar looked like they should belong to the Harleys in the parking lot, but she'd put money on them being dads who drove the minivans out there. She spotted a rich kid slumming it at the same table as an elderly couple funding their retirement via baccarat. No one with the vibe of "a jumpy man with nice hair and a lot of money wants me dead," but the day was young.

Dee had slipped into a seat at a poker table close to the entrance. Robbie had made it almost all the way to those back doors, so she took a spot at one of the farther tables. It didn't give her a great view of the room, but she stayed to play for a bit anyway.

After playing a few bad hands of blackjack, she sighed and pushed her chair back. "Guess this isn't my lucky table."

If she were here to make money, poker would've been her game, something that relied on figuring out a person's tells, but the blackjack tables gave her a better view of the room. A few of the dealers rotated out, leaving through the back door on the left, replaced by new dealers in black and burgundy. The guards remained unchanged, straight-backed and solid, eyes surveying the room without moving their heads. Not ex-military but a decent imitation.

She'd circled back toward the front doors to spend a bit of time throwing away money on roulette and was about ready to call it a day when a white man with messy blond hair and a dark blue hoodie flew past her. With a nervous energy, he sped past craps and poker and baccarat, not giving any of the games so much as a glance. Who came to a gambling club and didn't care about the gambling? Robbie lost the current spin of the roulette wheel but was too distracted to place another bet.

He kept going, hurrying past the blackjack table where Dee had amassed a sizable pile of chips, directly to the door on the right, the one that hadn't opened the entire afternoon. He said something to the guards. One of them knocked, a four-rap pattern, then murmured when the door cracked open an inch. It swung open farther, revealing a thick black curtain. The man disappeared through it. Whatever was through the curtain, the door closed again before Robbie could catch a glimpse.

That alone was notable. And then Dee immediately cashed out and left, setting off an alarm in Robbie's mind.

Robbie stayed for two more spins, trying not to fidget in anticipation, then made her own graceful exit. When she got outside, Dee was already sitting in the passenger's seat, waiting.

"Well?" she asked before she'd even climbed into the car.

"The blond. He told the guards, 'Let him know Xavier's here. I'm expected.' And it did seem like he was."

Well, shit, she'd found him. Or Dee had. A burst of adrenaline spiked through her, the flush of success. She hadn't expected to get anything nearly that useful today.

"Did he say Landerman?"

"Nah, just Xavier."

Her pulse slowed a bit. More than one Xavier existed in the world. All the same, a possible lead was better than none.

"You see anyone else back there by the doors?"

As Robbie started the car and backed out of the parking spot, Dee said, "Nah. I couldn't stare without being obvious. Was more interested in eavesdropping, and that seemed to yield the truly useful information anyway."

"Definitely," Robbie agreed. "Now I'm glad I brought you along."

"Oh?" Dee raised an eyebrow. "And if I hadn't found your target for you?"

"I would've left you there and never spoken to you again."

"You think it's that easy to get rid of me?"

Robbie laughed, and Dee's face split into a smile. "I guess we'll never know."

He fiddled with his phone for a minute, connected it to the car's aux cable, then settled back in his seat as Blondie came on with "One Way or Another." A bit on the nose maybe, but Robbie wasn't going to call him on it. It took all of two seconds for Dee to start singing along and no more than two after that for Robbie to join in.

Dee was going to die.

Or maybe he'd be calm and relaxed and handle everything beautifully.

Robbie ran a hand over her face. Dee was definitely not going to handle this beautifully. She wasn't even sure she was managing to handle this, but it helped to focus on Dee's potential reaction rather than allowing a reaction of her own.

She'd waited until Coda was in full swing for the night, Dee dancing as he tended bar and sang along with whoever was at the mic. At present, that was three people who were doing more laughing than singing as they made their way through something resembling No Doubt's "Don't Speak." Dee was grinning too.

Maybe there would be a better time.

"How long are you going to lurk over there trying to talk yourself into saying whatever it is you want to say to me?"

Goddammit.

"Honestly, was kinda hoping I could do it indefinitely," Robbie answered miserably.

Dee waved to Marisol, the bartender officially on shift tonight. She was a little shorter than Robbie, her skin and hair and eyes all made up of shades of warm browns. Although it wasn't technically required all the time, she wore a Coda T-shirt, as she did every night she worked. When they'd hired her, it had still been early days, and Robbie had discovered the company who made their first batch of T-shirts didn't run sizes that fit Marisol. Marisol had been utterly polite about the whole thing, but Robbie was furious with herself for not catching the problem sooner. Coda was supposed to be for everyone. She'd immediately canceled her outstanding order and switched to a manufacturer that ran their sizes into a range that fit Marisol, who took a great deal of pride wearing them and representing Coda. And Robbie took a great deal of pride in having Marisol on their team.

They only had three employees, but Robbie figured they all enjoyed getting the shifts when Dee or Robbie decided to drop in and do most of the work themselves. Marisol had gotten to spend at least half the night flirting with a very giggly woman in the corner. She took the time to wait for the woman to scribble a phone number down on a bar napkin and hand it to her before sauntering over to relieve Dee of bar duty.

With that sorted, Dee edged over to where Robbie had propped herself by the staff room door. Robbie was pretty sure just about every difficult conversation they'd ever had had been like this. Shoulder to shoulder, Robbie on the right, Dee to the left. Face-to-face was never their style. Who wanted to make eye contact with someone while having open, emotional conversations?

"It's about the theater," Robbie started after several moments of silence.

Dee's posture drooped, but he didn't say anything, just waited for Robbie to go on.

"They've been struggling. Everything over there is, you know. Like the bookstore. It's just, well, apparently the manager ran some numbers after we met the other day."

"I take it the numbers did not run in our favor?"

Robbie shrugged. "The numbers apparently didn't run in anyone's favor. I'm not even sure they ran. The numbers walked. Or just...lay down and refused to go on."

"Please don't make me listen to you try to drag this metaphor any further." Dee groaned. "Just tell me. What's going on with the theater?"

Well, she had to say it eventually. "They're closing."

Dee tensed beside her. "But they're closing *after* we run our show, right?"

"Not to drag up the metaphor again, but…running? Not really a thing apparently."

Robbie held her breath as she waited for it to sink in. It had been a bit impulsive when they decided to actually *stage* the musical she wrote, and it may have started as Robbie's dream, but it belonged to both of them now. Partners in crime. Partners in business. Next up was supposed to be partners in musical theater.

Except, it would seem, that wasn't entirely accurate now.

"*Fuck!*"

Several heads whipped around to stare back at the dim corner where Robbie and Dee stood. Robbie waved a hand and gave what hopefully was a reassuring smile. They all turned away, only to stare again as Dee produced what may have been the most inspired assembly of profanity Robbie had ever heard.

Robbie elbowed him in the ribs.

"Hey, I'm pissed, okay? Let me be pissed." After a second, though, Dee deflated. "Come on, Robbie. If I'm not angry, I'm probably going to cry, and you know how I feel about that."

"Never outside the apartment. Yeah, I know. But your options aren't just split between crying and scaring off the customers with your vocabulary. I'm sure their mothers are perfectly nice people who don't deserve to be drawn into this."

That at least elicited a snort of laughter. "Yeah, my apologies to nice mothers everywhere."

"It's…it's not so bad, right?" Robbie had cracked when she got the news. Yes, they'd been working hard on everything up to this point, but she wasn't sure she realized how much she wanted this dream to succeed until it came crashing down. Still, she'd calmed down after a bit. Surely, he could too. "Other theaters exist. We can figure out how to move the show."

"With what money, Robs? We *just* got the payroll account fixed. We can't keep draining things here, or there will be no Coda."

Not an option. The show was her dream, sure, but Coda was her heart.

"We'll have the rest of Mr. Clark's payment coming at the end of the month. That'll be enough for a deposit on a new place, and we'll figure out the rest. We can figure it out. Can't we?"

What she wanted was a clear, unwavering *yes*. What she got was a halfhearted shrug. Dee was obviously still processing.

"I've taken the liberty of signing you up for a spot." Robbie waved toward the stage. "Name your tune."

Dee reached over and punched Robbie's shoulder. "You monster. You planned this, didn't you? When did you find out about the theater?"

Robbie rubbed the spot on her shoulder. The punch was playful, but it was certainly more than a tap. Despite that, it felt good, like everything was fine for the two of them. For now, if not forever. "Noon-ish?"

"Seriously?" It was a little after ten now. "I don't know whether to be mad, impressed, or sorry for you that you kept it in this long."

"Due to the quality of your punching skills, I would vote either impressed or sorry. Pity me. But first, pick your song, good sir."

It had been a long day, but as Dee headed to the stage, Robbie was glad she'd waited until now. They'd chosen to create a business built around music for a reason. Sometimes—okay, *frequently*—that entailed terrible, off-key, overly enthusiastic music, but still, a place where people found joy in that. The two of them made their actual living killing people. They did it exceedingly well, but it most certainly was not about *joy*.

Robbie didn't spend a lot of time thinking about what she considered chapters one and two of her life. Ignoring her entire childhood was easy enough. Pretending her years in the military never happened generally suited her just fine. Except for the one okay thing she'd brought back with her. During her third tour, someone in her unit had taught her to play guitar, and she was *good*. This bright, almost drunk feeling welled up when she perfected a new chord or made it through an entire song without a single mistake. Sometimes it even stayed bright when she did make mistakes, because at least then she was still playing. And it was so pure. Nothing else existed while she played. She didn't have to think, just let herself sink into that brightness.

It was an embarrassingly long time before she figured out that sensation was the elusive, mythical feeling other people referred to as happiness.

A significant chunk of her first paycheck from James had gone toward buying herself her own guitar. Piano came later, first with a keyboard and then as she dropped a frankly obscene amount of money on the baby grand that was situated in the apartment upstairs. When she'd gotten the phone call from the theater this afternoon, she'd spent over an hour on that bench.

Then she'd waited until she could break the news to Dee in here, where the music was waiting.

The last singer finished, and Dee took the mic from them as he input his song choice into the machine.

Dee positioned himself, turning his right ear toward the speaker. Years ago, a job had gotten what Dee termed "messy," which Robbie felt was a very polite way to describe an explosion that had resulted in Dee losing a significant amount of hearing in his left ear. For day-to-day things, he'd accepted the need to adapt, and he was plenty happy wearing a hearing aid for all that. But music was different.

Robbie understood disability, but hers had always been there, her brain always being the way it was. She had no grasp of what it would be like to experience a sudden change. She'd watched as it took hard work and long practice to relearn how to match his voice to the notes in his head, but an alternate path to joy still got there in the end. She'd navigated her own winding path to the joy of this place and her life with Dee. The idea of losing the theater, losing the show, was crushing, but maybe there would be an alternate path for that too.

The diminished E-flat chords, chords it had taken Robbie ages to master, and distinctive strumming of "Don't Dream It's Over" started playing. Robbie heard someone near her grumble, "Hey, I was going to sing that."

Too damn bad. If they wanted it that badly, they could open their own karaoke bar.

Dee began to sing. Robbie grinned. They'd figure the show out. Solve the theater problem.

For now, they still had this: Coda and music and hard-won joy.

4
Good Luck

ROBBIE HAD STAKED OUT THE AJAX CLUB FOR TWO NIGHTS with no Xavier, and after breaking the theater news to Dee, she returned for a third round of slumping in her car across the street from the gambling joint. It wasn't exactly the same as sitting at home watching TV, but all three nights provided some entertaining viewing. It certainly helped take her mind off the theater problem. Cataloging the clientele had proved especially engaging. On the previous nights, she'd identified several members of city council, a police chief definitely not there in an official capacity, and two judges. Tonight, she glimpsed a familiar face that made her do a double take.

Fletcher Ingram. *The* Fletcher Ingram. Face plastered on practically every vertical surface in a hundred-mile radius Fletcher Ingram. Robbie couldn't remember a time when she hadn't known the name. He'd made his first million through remarkably savvy investments as a nineteen-year-old wunderkind. An investigation into allegations of insider trading should have been damaging to his image, but instead, his cocky brand of charisma and his penchant for witty sound bites had made him a media darling before Robbie was even born. In the forty-something years since then, he'd continued to amass both wealth and public favor, weathering multiple scandals and investigations, always coming out on top.

It hadn't come as a total surprise when he decided to take up politics as his latest hobby and run for senator of the great state of Indiana. Robbie liked several of his policies but hadn't decided whether she'd be inclined to vote for him. Either way, she certainly hadn't expected a dodgy gambling den in Penny Park to even be on his radar.

But fine. Say that he knew the place, knew the right people to get him in. All those other notable visitors had after all. She still didn't expect this would be his style. And she absolutely didn't expect him to leave his two bodyguards at the door, although from their body language, they clearly hadn't expected to be left either.

Huh. Fletcher Ingram.

That was enough revelation for one night, and she didn't have high hopes for more, not when she'd arrived so late after breaking the theater news to Dee. She was about to pack it in when a flash of blond hair caught her eye. In the low light, she couldn't quite tell whether that was the same blue hoodie as before, but the urgent, hurried air was unchanged.

Xavier was back.

Figuring out whether he was Landerman was still on her to-do list, but spotting him was a decent start. If he repeated his previous performance, it would only take him a minute or two to vanish into the back room. Shit. It would take her longer to get from her car to the entrance. She wasn't about to do something as suspicious as running after him either. The adrenaline buzzing through her would've loved that, but she forced herself to wait.

"Your brain is more sophisticated than some dog madly chasing a scent," James had told her once. "Use it."

Even if he went straight to the back rooms, he had to come out eventually. She could be there when he did. No need to rush. Two full songs on the car radio later, she shrugged an air of indifference over herself and followed him inside.

Late on a Friday night, the place was significantly busier than it had been on a Tuesday afternoon. The tables were full up with players, and even more people crowded around to watch. Robbie had been through enough safety inspections at Coda to know this definitely wasn't within a fire marshal's occupancy limits.

Robbie wove her way between tables, eyes skimming over countless faces. She didn't see Fletcher Ingram—she figured at least part of the back rooms had to be for high rollers, and nobody in this city rolled as high as him—but Xavier Possibly-Landerman was in the main room this time, playing blackjack.

Her core process for hits was essentially the same for everyone. Observe, plan, act. Her observations gave her a picture of the target, their habits and routines, the risks they took. Everything she needed to concoct an informed plan on the best way to take them out.

She moved slowly through the large room, doing her best to avoid the press of bodies. Four blackjack tables lined the back wall, and Xavier had chosen the one closest to the back door. Plopping down beside him was far too direct. Instead, Robbie snagged a spot at the nearest table, her back nearly touching his. Not ideal for observation, but the club was packed, and besides, this way no one would get the impression she'd come for him. She played three hands before putting on an air of boredom, glancing around at the other tables as if any of those would prove to be greener pastures.

One more hand and she gave her seat to an eager man with a shaved head and remarkable number of facial piercings. Robbie hoped never to be that memorable. Shifting around casually, she turned to watch Xavier's game.

The tidiness of his play struck her first. When cards were dealt in front of him, he carefully straightened them so the edges were precisely parallel. His chips were neatly arranged in piles of either five or ten, all set in a perfectly straight line.

He played well too, which she hadn't expected, although where that assumption had come from, she wasn't sure. He was quick and decisive. Smart rather than intuitive. After watching for several hands, she felt confident he'd studied blackjack strategy, whether that meant understanding the math or simply being very, very good at memorization. Robbie fell into the latter camp with a lifetime spent perfecting memorization skills, something she'd learned very young could prevent people from realizing the other skills she lacked.

Then his betting shifted. Eyeballing it, Robbie guessed the shoe was down to maybe three decks' worth of cards. Xavier didn't overbet, didn't do anything to raise suspicion, but he quietly increased his bets and the rate at which he won. Robbie had learned the principles of card counting in an effort to best James in games on long stakeouts while he was still training her, and she was okay at it, but it had taken her a couple years to be able to keep the math right in her head. Xavier looked like a natural. She was going to kill this man at some point, but for the time being, she was suitably impressed.

His game started to slip after a half hour or so. When the dealer reshuffled, Xavier had adjusted accordingly, but even as enough play passed across the table for him to get a confident count again, he wasn't winning like before. He lost track of the cards as his gaze repeatedly drifted toward the back door.

But he didn't get up, and he didn't stop playing.

When another player bowed out, Robbie snagged the spot, finally getting a clear view of Xavier. Up until now, she'd been focused on the player, not the person. But after getting a straight look at him, Robbie was...confused. How was this the same guy keeping everything so tidy and holding all the information in his head to play strategically? If she hadn't been standing there the whole time, she might've thought he'd been swapped out for someone else entirely. Or perhaps that this version had been the one who'd been losing the last several rounds while someone else played the role earlier.

He looked young, really young, although he was probably at least in his early twenties. His blue hoodie had presumably been slung over his stool before he sat, but now it pooled on the floor, hanging by a single arm. The black Joy Division T-shirt he wore had clearly sat crumpled for a long while before he put it on. He'd probably never even listened to Joy Division and just bought the T-shirt to look cool. He did not, in Robbie's humble opinion, do that successfully.

His pale skin was sunburnt across his nose, with a distinctive curve showing where sunglasses had been, overlapped now by regular glasses, rectangular frames of lightweight silver. Behind them, he had what Robbie would definitely be describing to Dee later as puppy-dog eyes. Big, round, with gorgeous deep brown irises, framed by long pale lashes. Robbie had brown eyes too, but hers sure as hell didn't look like that. If Mr. Clark got what he wanted by money and sheer force of arrogance, she'd bet Landerman got what he wanted by wielding his puppy eyes. His hair was that whitish-blond that children tended to grow out of, rather in need of a cut. Based on the level of tidiness, Robbie had to assume it had never met a comb in its life. She glanced down to confirm his neat chip piles and perfectly aligned cards were still as they were. Irritatingly, she wasn't quite sure how to interpret the discrepancy. Carrying out a hit on a meticulous person required an entirely different kind of planning than a messy one. So which was Xavier?

As she tried to figure it out, Xavier lost six times in a row. He rubbed his hand through his hair in frustration, setting it into a fresh state of disarray. If that were a regular nervous tic of his, she did see how he could curate that perpetually disheveled look.

The losses gave her an opening though. Not that she ought to take it, anonymity being a far wiser choice, but she couldn't resist. She had to figure him out. For the sake of the job, of course.

"Rough run," she said with a sympathetic smile. "Lucky streaks always turn on you eventually."

Xavier glanced to either side of himself before turning back to Robbie with almost comical surprise when he realized she was addressing him. Then his surprise turned into a little frown. "Gambling doesn't work like that."

"Doesn't work how?"

"On luck or the lack thereof."

Thereof. How pretentious. Robbie opened her mouth to reply, but he apparently hadn't finished.

"The concept of luck is the human mind attempting to ascribe meaning to patterns that aren't readily comprehensible," he said, as if that were a perfectly normal sentence to utter. He wasn't exactly zealous about it, but the words tumbled off his tongue as if they'd done so many times before. Was this a conversation he'd had frequently, or was he quoting something he'd memorized? "But wins and losses are simply subject to mathematical principles. Every bet is independent of all previous and all subsequent bets. A winning hand doesn't have any effect on whether or not the following hand will win."

He was…almost right? If they'd been over at craps or roulette, sure, but they were here with the cards. But she didn't argue. The two other players still at the table were now staring openly at Xavier. When he noticed, his entire demeanor shifted. His shoulders, tensed while he played and even more so when talking to Robbie, dropped. The little frown he'd had for her melted into a warm smile.

"How's your night been going?" he asked in what sounded like a genuinely friendly tone, and they responded in kind.

No way he could know who she was or why she was there. No reason not to be friendly with her, so…what? She'd accidentally pressed on a hidden trigger that set him off? She didn't get it. She didn't get *him*. The warmth had to be an act. Probably? No one took out a hit on a golden retriever. If Mr. Clark was willing to pay twenty thousand dollars for this guy to die, surely he had his reasons.

The dealer cleared her throat to draw everyone's attention back to the game.

As the cards were dealt to each player, Robbie lifted her chin toward Xavier and murmured, "Good luck."

Then she winked. Just for fun. Just to see how he'd react.

He seemed torn between annoyance at her disregard of his lecture and confusion about…well, presumably about her general existence. Instead of deciding, he settled his attention to the cards.

He won.

One of the other players cashed out, and Robbie took the opportunity to take the open seat next to him.

"So, Rain Man, you feeling a lucky winning streak coming on?" she asked with what Dee had once dubbed her disarmingly cheeky smile. It was a useful sort of expression.

He blinked a few times. Come on. Did kids these days not watch classic movies?

"It's not luck. It's chance," he huffed after a moment, as if those words didn't mean exactly the same thing.

And okay, she'd tried to not say anything before, but come on. He wasn't the only one who could parrot fancy-sounding shit. "No, roulette is chance. Dice are chance. One spin or roll doesn't affect the next. But we're playing cards. So if I'd already seen five face cards come up since the deck was last shuffled, I know my odds of getting another face card would not be the same as they were before those other five were played." If he'd been counting, he ought to realize she wasn't stating a hypothetical. "That does affect things in a way that I'm sure someone could take advantage of to win. Not luck, perhaps, but something better."

He blinked at her with, once again, a look of surprise. Did he frequently look that way, or did she bring it out? Maybe a bit of both. Those wide puppy eyes did surprise particularly well, and the confused blinking was an effective act. Then his eyes narrowed with suspicion. Defensively, he said, "The average player can't be expected to keep track of all those cards."

"All right, I'll give you that. The *average* player cannot. It would take a significantly more skilled player to rely on winning that way." Without giving him time to fully grasp her meaning, she stuck out her hand. "Veronica Werner, by the way."

He hesitated a moment before letting out a little sigh and shaking her hand. His palms were uncomfortably sweaty. "Xavier."

He didn't give his last name. He hadn't the night Dee had overheard him either. There was still a slight chance that this wasn't Xavier Landerman.

She remembered Mr. Clark's hesitance, the way he seemed unsure of everything to do with Xavier. Maybe Xavier didn't seem like someone Mr. Clark would want dead because he wasn't. Maybe this odd, contradictory man wasn't her target at all. Or, she considered, Mr. Clark had seen the same contradictions as Robbie and hadn't been sure how best to describe him.

"Pleasure to meet you," Robbie said while she surreptitiously wiped her hand off on her jeans. "And to play with you. Always nice to find someone else who thinks about the game and not just the chips."

As they kept playing and the club started thinning out for the night, Robbie finally felt like maybe she could get an accurate sense of the guy. Even after getting his head back in the game, he still kept an anxious eye on the back door, which hadn't opened to let anyone in or out. Xavier kept up the friendly act. The few times it started to slip, he was always quick to pull the chipper persona back on. Robbie knew an actor when she saw one. She just couldn't nail down who he was acting for.

"You local?" she tried after a while.

"For now."

Yeah, she was going to need a bit more than that. "Oh, where are you from?"

"Here and there. I've done a lot of traveling, checked off some places on my bucket list. I've been in Reevesburg for a bit. Got a place in Keyton Heights." His jaw twitched, like he hadn't meant to share that last detail but hadn't been paying enough attention not to, his eyes trained on the door.

"Not sure where that is." She didn't want him thinking he'd overshared and censor himself. Let him believe he hadn't really spilled anything. "I do a fair bit of travel myself. Well, it's not like I go vacation in the Bahamas all the time or anything. It's mostly for work. I'm just down from Indianapolis for the week, actually. Business trip. Do you like living here?"

"If this is the kind of place they send you to, I'm not sure that counts as nice," he said, all smiles. "The only people who like Reevesburg are the ones who grew up here. They like the idea of a hometown, and that matters more than the reality of the place. But I'm sure your work sent you here for a reason. What is it you do?"

Robbie would've argued that she chose this city. She hadn't grown up here, but she'd found it and fallen in love with its reality, potholes and crumbling infrastructure and all. But she wasn't Robbie at the moment, and Veronica Werner was here on business.

"Shipping industry," she decided. The sort of thing that someone who did imports and exports might talk shop about for a bit.

"What kind of shipping? Like supply chain management? That always sounds so mundane, but it's one of those behind-the-scenes things I bet is more complicated than people think."

"Sounds like you have some experience with that?" She certainly didn't, not enough to expound on the virtues of supply chains.

He didn't take the bait. "Nah, I like straightforward stuff. What you see is what you get. Life's a lot easier that way, you know? But I guess easy isn't always the most important thing. Do you enjoy what you do?"

Damn, he was good. His demeanor didn't come off as intentionally evasive, but he managed to casually talk his way around most topics and always, without fail, steered the conversation back on her.

That, like his card counting, was a well-practiced skill. James had helped Robbie hone that ability. Even people who weren't prone to sharing let little bits of personal information slip into their conversations without even realizing it. It was human nature. The utter absence of any personal details, especially in reply to the generous oversharing of Veronica Werner's imaginary life, was strategic.

Puppy Eyes had something to hide. Something worth killing over?

A little after one in the morning, Robbie cashed out. Xavier was the last person left at their table, but he showed no signs of calling it a night.

"Nice playing with you, Xavier." She meant that, despite having been paying far more attention to Xavier than the game.

"You too." He actually sounded like he meant it as well. "Maybe we'll meet at the tables again sometime."

"Yeah, maybe."

Probably not. She'd likely gotten all she could from him tonight. He wasn't going to spill all his secrets over their next hand of cards. Whatever else she needed to learn wasn't going to come from him directly.

As she walked away, she flagged down a waiter walking past with a tray and handed them a folded bill. "Mr. Landerman's next drink is on me."

They nodded, and as Robbie walked slowly the rest of the way to the door, the waiter headed directly to Xavier and murmured something to him. He glanced back. Catching Robbie's eye, he gave a little wave of gratitude.

So.

That was definitely Xavier Landerman, and by this time next month, he would be dead.

5

Your Place, Not Mine

YAWNING, ROBBIE RETURNED TO HER CAR. EVEN THIS LATE AT night, the air was still warm and muggy. Had summer always intruded this much on September? Surely, they were due an autumn at some point. But wishful thinking didn't stir the air, so she cracked her window, listening to the swoosh of cars speeding down nearby streets, a passing siren, some kind of insect scratching out a mating call with admirable dedication.

It wasn't an entirely unpleasant place to be, but nobody was around to care about a thirtysomething woman loitering in her car in the pre-morning hours.

Her main focus was keeping an eye out for Xavier, who she hoped would leave sometime soon so she could follow him home and still have time to make it back to her own bed for a few hours of decent sleep. With her attention narrowly awaiting her target, it took her a good twenty minutes before she registered the fact that the bodyguards who had accompanied Fletcher Ingram earlier were no longer skulking around the club's entrance. The car he'd arrived in was gone too.

Unlikely he'd be left there alone, which meant he'd been taken out some back exit. But if a back door were an option, why go through the front in the first place?

She yawned again. At some point in her life, she'd have to admit that her body and brain just wouldn't be able to handle all-nighters forever. But she'd rather that point not be tonight. Instead, she pulled out her phone to find some distraction and started to text Dee, do u think we could try the show again next. She stopped and held down backspace until all the words vanished. She did want to talk to him about the future of their musical, whether there was still any hope for that dream, but that ought to be in person. Or maybe she didn't want to ask at all, because she wasn't sure how she'd handle it if the answer was no.

Instead, she sent, bored. entertain me?

No response. Robbie turned her phone back on to check the time. After a minute, she did it again, because she hadn't processed the numbers on the first go. A little after two. Coda would be closed. Dee could be helping with post-closing chores or sleeping or taking over the empty stage in the bar singing his ass off or occupied with someone he'd brought up from the bar. All were perfectly valid decisions on his part but rather unhelpful for Robbie's need to pass the time.

She had other friends, sort of. Casual acquaintances, mostly. Certainly, none who knew about the kind of work she did that required spying on sketchy gambling clubs in industrial parks late at night. And she knew other contractors, but none who were on friendly enough terms with her for casual texting. Her and Dee's dynamic aside, James hadn't been wrong about people like them being better off not associating with one another. If someone else in this business went down in flames, the greater the distance between you and that fire, the better.

Robbie harrumphed and slouched down in her seat.

Her phone buzzed in the cupholder, the insistent sound of a phone call. Dee would've texted back. Unless something terrible had happened at Coda. Scrambling, she grabbed the phone. Shit, maybe her evil eye theory was right. Think about James and now…

"Yeah?" she answered.

"Your manners are as appalling as ever, Robbie," James said in his clipped, professional tone. He always sounded like he thought he was better than everyone around him, which to be fair, was often true. "You didn't return my call."

She tried for casual. "I meant to. Got caught up. Stuff and things, you know."

"I'm not calling for my own amusement. If I call you, there's a reason."

"I know. Sorry, sir." Dammit, the *sir* just slipped out. Her old military habits had still been deeply ingrained when she started working for James, and calling him sir never wore off. Dee absolutely hated whenever Robbie did it. "So why are you calling?"

"I have a job for you."

"I'm already on a job. And I don't work for you anymore, James. I'm independent, and you're retired."

Retired-ish at least. Not that retirement had been his idea. He'd had a heart attack, then bypass surgery, and he couldn't keep up with it all anymore. But of course, he never fully let go. Robbie didn't blame him. Retirement, as a concept, sounded like the most boring thing she could possibly imagine.

"Retired is a relative term. I don't spend my time knitting these days. I may not be recruiting, but I still manage my people."

As far as Robbie had been able to tell, James had essentially moved from managing an arsenal of dangerous people to managing managers of such arsenals. If nothing else, she had to admire the fact that he'd effectively turned contract killing into a pyramid scheme.

"I still hear from old contacts when something notable comes up. This is from a very important old friend to whom I owe a favor."

"Like I said. I'm not available."

"Robbie, I need you on this job. You know I could call anyone. I know plenty of professionals. I'm calling you because the job requires your expertise. No one else will do."

James wasn't begging, wasn't even slightly pleading, but this was the closest approximation he'd ever pull off. And she did have a whole month to take care of Xavier Landerman. Besides, any extra bit of income right now wouldn't hurt. She could make this work.

"All right. Fine. Do you have the details, or is someone else going to be in touch?"

"I knew I could rely on you," he said confidently, without a trace of relief or surprise. He'd known she'd cave. Of course he'd known. James always knew. "I can give you the details now if you can spare the time."

At her underwhelming "yeah," he filled her in on everything she needed to know: a name and a location. Anything beyond that was unnecessary. As James had always taught her, the more you knew about your target, the more likely you were to mess up—or worse, start to humanize the person you were hired to kill. That would never do.

You sure as fuck weren't supposed to play blackjack with them. What had she been thinking?

"Thank you for taking my call, Robbie," James said, as if she'd had any other choice. "I hope you're well. You and D—"

"We're fine." Oh, Dee would hate knowing James was thinking of him. "I gotta go, James. Job'll be done as soon as I can. I'll text you the payment details."

She hung up and closed her eyes. Should've said no. Should've told him she couldn't take on a second job when she already had one and then stood her ground. But it was *James*. She owed him, would always owe him. He believed in her, saw something in her no one else did. He supported and trained her and knocked down the first dominoes in the chain that led her to Dee and Coda. She'd make this work. Somehow.

She'd nearly dozed off when a flash of blond caught in the strobing flicker of a dying streetlight outside the club. This was her first glimpse of him without anyone else around. No one to perform for. And she was too damn far to see anything worthwhile.

Landerman checked his phone, glanced around, checked it again. After a moment, he visibly sighed and started walking up the street. He couldn't possibly be planning to *walk* to Keyton Heights, could he? It wasn't exactly a nice neighborhood for a stroll, and depending where exactly his apartment was, that would be a good three or four miles. No way was Robbie going to follow on foot. She was already very, very done with tonight.

To her relief, Landerman approached a silver sedan loitering at the top of the block with multiple stickers for rideshare apps in its window. He got in the front seat, so either he was feeling incredibly sociable or was a control freak. She thought of his chip piles and his friendly attitude. Both maybe?

A problem for another day. Despite her drowsiness, her heart kicked up a notch as she started her car. She'd successfully confirmed his identity, and now she'd find out where he lived. One more corner piece to this puzzle, and it was always smooth sailing once the corners were in place.

She didn't need to follow all that closely to keep an eye on her quarry. The neighborhoods slowly morphed, warehouses giving way to shabby houses with the light-dark-light-dark pulse of streetlights. Shadowy tufts of crabgrass pushed their way out of cracked sidewalks. Then houses became duplexes became slumping apartment buildings wanting to collapse in exhaustion as much as Robbie.

This city wasn't glamorous. Most of it was barely hanging on. Robbie and Dee probably could've set up shop in any number of other places. Maybe a not insignificant part of her secretly loved setting up a queer business not so far from the place that threw her out for her identity. Besides, glamour and shine wasn't really their vibe anyway. This weary, crumbling city fit them far better.

Within a matter of minutes and wandering thoughts, the rideshare pulled up in front of a cinder block apartment building. That was all Robbie needed. She pulled over long enough to watch Landerman let himself into the building, saved the address in her phone, and finally headed home.

When Robbie came out of her room in the morning, bleary-eyed and functioning only enough to shuffle her way to the coffeepot, a stranger was sitting at her kitchen table.

The girl had dyed firehouse-red curls falling loosely in that annoying way some people had where they managed to look good with bedhead. Her makeup hadn't fared quite so well, but the smudging wasn't terrible.

She was wearing Robbie's robe.

One of her robes anyway. A sky-blue terry cloth that Robbie tended to forgo in the hottest months when any fabric thicker than a whisper was just too much to bear. The redhead seemed to be bearing it just fine.

"Good morning." Robbie's voice had that early morning phlegm sound.

The girl—okay, to be fair, she did look at least somewhere in her twenties. The *woman* jumped.

"Oh. I didn't know anyone else was here. I'm so sorry. Am I in your way?"

"There's a clear path from me to the coffee, so no. You're not in the way."

The woman stood. "I should go."

Robbie was inclined to just nod and go back to her own business, but Dee came out of his room wearing just boxers and a ragged T-shirt, whistling softly to himself, steaming coffee mug in hand. He smiled as he noticed Robbie.

"Good morning, sunshine. I didn't hear you come in last night."

"Got home a little before three." Robbie went through her routine, filling her mug halfway up with coffee and the rest with milk before dumping in a heaping dose of sugar. Extra heavy on the sugar this morning.

Dee held his mug out, and she topped it off. He flashed her a grateful smile.

Curious to see where the pseudo redhead would fall on the good versus black coffee debate, Robbie raised the pot to their guest, but she waved a hand to decline.

"Saw your text. You end up doing something that kept you sufficiently entertained?" Dee asked.

Robbie nodded. "I did indeed. Relaxed a bit, made a new friend. Made sure he got home at the end of the night, then came back and crashed."

"Glad to hear it."

"I see that you had a good night too? And that you raided my laundry basket."

The woman's face flushed as red as her hair. Oh, she was adorable. Good on Dee.

"Ah, right. She was dressed for a night on the town. Not the sort of thing that's comfortable in the morning. I figured you wouldn't mind lending some clothing for a worthy cause."

Robbie rolled her eyes affectionately. She turned her attention over to the woman. "Since he's apparently forgotten his manners, hi, I'm Robbie."

"Sorry. Right. Robbie, this is Ayako. Ayako, Robbie. Robbie lives with me. As you probably figured out. Ayako is a graduate student studying, uh, public policy, yeah? She's also a bridesmaid who attended her friend's bachelorette party last night."

"Nice to meet you," Ayako said. After a brief pause that may have been her working up the nerve, she asked, "You two just live together, right?"

"Live together. Work together. Own the bar downstairs together. Commit murders together. Normal stuff." Dee loved that joke way more than it deserved.

"But you're not *together* together," she pressed with a little undercurrent of worry.

Robbie snorted. "Not like that."

"It was a fair question," Ayako said defensively. "Dee told me he was available."

Dee squeezed her shoulder. "It was fair, and Robbie clearly had no right to accuse me of forgetting my manners when evidently she's never heard of the notion."

"Sorry," Robbie said genuinely. "Common misconception. Dee and I… We're soulmates, yeah? But not in a romantic way, and not in a sexual way. It's a queerplatonic sort of deal, if you're familiar with the concept."

They'd talked about it once, late one night in the early days of the bar. Even then, they'd agreed quite thoroughly that they considered themselves soulmates, just not in the romantic way people liked to use the term. Queerplatonic soulmates, although that language came later. Robbie hadn't yet had the words to understand herself as an aromantic lesbian. Dee didn't have the words to understand himself as a transmasc lesbian. What they did understand was that they had a deeper bond than the word "friendship" covered and that they were fantastic versions of themselves when they had each other for support.

Robbie offered the girl the politest smile she could muster before the caffeine hit her bloodstream. "I know you were asking out of worry for having done something wrong. You haven't. If it weren't a hundred percent okay with me, Dee would never have brought you up here."

"Oh. Okay. Yeah."

Dee met Robbie's eyes and mouthed a *thank you*. Then his eyes flicked toward the door.

Of course.

"Dee and I have to meet an electrician for the club this morning, so I'm going to go hit the shower. It was lovely to meet you, Ayako."

Hopefully that made it clear enough that Robbie expected Ayako would be gone by the time she finished showering. Dee gave another nod of gratitude, and Robbie left the two of them to sort out their goodbyes and determine who was going to call whom. (Dee wasn't going to call.)

Robbie disappeared into her room, then into the bathroom, although she didn't bother starting the water running. The door to the back patio softly clicked as it closed. After a few minutes, the sound of Dee's footsteps on the outside steps clanked back up, and by the time he was back in the apartment, Robbie was waiting at the kitchen table.

"Don't say anything," Dee said by way of greeting.

"I wasn't going to."

"Maybe not with words, but your eyes are definitely saying a lot. Stop that."

"All I'm going to say, Dee, is that if you can't get a girl to leave in the morning without my help, she's probably not one you should bring home in the first place."

"Go back to just saying stuff with your eyes." Dee gave an exasperated sigh. "Ugh, I know. She seemed different last night. It wasn't until this morning that she started talking about a second date and brunch and did I want to be her date to her friend's wedding."

"No."

"Yeah. She asked. Three times."

"Oof. Should I have lied and said we were actually '*together together*'?"

For obvious reasons, neither of them could ever allow dating to turn serious. There were standard milestones expected in a committed relationship—swapping apartment keys, meeting the parents, probably that whole saying "I love you" thing—and while the details of those might vary from person to person, at no point did they include explaining a career in wet work.

Robbie didn't mind. On her twenty-first birthday, or at least the next leave after it, she'd met a guy in a bar, and three weeks later, they were on a road trip to Vegas, which admittedly had been a mistake for no other reason than the fact that she'd never been attracted to men and had married him out of an unhealthy need for emotional attention. She'd technically still been married, although she hadn't spoken to him in over two years, when she met James, but James helped her sever that tie neatly. Since that mistake, though, she'd spent more time figuring herself out, having a lightbulb moment when she discovered the term aromantic. Even if she hadn't had a secret illegal job, she wouldn't have been happily coupling up with anyone in a romantic capacity anyway. Once she had the words, she found it a lot easier to explain to interested parties—a lot easier for her at least, but that was sufficient. It didn't matter if other people understood the ins and outs of it all as long as she did.

Dee, on the other hand, loved connections of all kinds. Without their contract work in the way, Robbie was pretty sure he would be entirely happy having more serious romantic relationships. But he was also perfectly happy going Robbie's route: skipping the complicated emotional parts and just entertaining whoever caught his eye. His sex partners understood the limitations of the arrangement. Usually.

Dee drained the last of the coffee from his mug. "Nah. She

would've felt absurdly bad in that case. She was a nice, smart woman, and in an alternate universe, I wouldn't entirely mind knowing her in the non-biblical sort of way. But oddly enough, direct wasn't working for her, so I thought perhaps subtle hinting would be more her style. I wanted to make her go home, not upset her."

"And they say chivalry's dead."

Rolling his eyes, Dee asked Robbie for the actual details of her night. When she filled him in, he was appropriately shocked by the presence of the various characters—the judges, the police chief—but reserved his highest level of intrigue for Fletcher Ingram. She hesitated to fill him in on the other event of the night, but keeping things from Dee wasn't exactly her strong suit.

"Out with it, Robs."

"Yeah, so James called me."

Dee nearly dropped his coffee mug, fumbling before managing to balance it out at the last minute. "I'm sorry, what? He called you. James. Like *James* James. Controlling, persnickety, *retired* James."

"Mentor James. He, uh, he has a job he wants me to do."

"And you said no."

"Well… It shouldn't take long. I'm sure I can be done in the next week or two, and all the money can go toward the show."

She'd hoped the money would be a selling point, but he breezed right past it. "Seriously, Robbie? Why did we go independent? We wanted choice. What jobs to take, how often. Taking only a few jobs a year—and never more than one at once—keeps us safe, gives us time to run Coda. You're not a murder machine that James can aim and fire at his convenience. You're a professional with a life of your own. Call him back and tell him no."

Robbie got it. Really, she did. It wasn't that Dee had anything against the profession. In fact, the decision to specialize as a sniper had been entirely his own. It required focus and precision, and according to him, when he was looking down a scope, calculating distances and angles and wind speeds, there wasn't room left in his head for anything else. No, what Dee had a problem with was that he felt James had taken advantage of the whole situation. Robbie could recite whole tirades from memory about how James should've worked to strengthen them but instead chose to press on their weakest points.

It sounded all righteous when Dee ranted about it, but it wasn't Robbie's experience. James *had* strengthened her. He'd given her skills, something to be proud of, and, perhaps most importantly, the confidence to fit into that pride instead of eyeing it warily like a set of oversize boots. And yeah, she had other things now. Dee, Coda, even the show, hopefully. But she only had those things because James had found her and built her up. If she let go of him or what he'd taught her, how could she be certain she wouldn't be letting go of everything else?

"I took the job, Dee. I didn't tell you so we could discuss it. I just told you because I thought you'd want to know."

Dee slumped, all the aggression in his posture vanishing with the steam off his coffee. "All right. I appreciate you telling me. Don't like it, but I'm not going to fight about it. You matter more than him. I'm not granting him the right to get between us."

"Thanks," Robbie mumbled.

Silence wrapped around them for what was steadily inching toward an uncomfortably long time. What else was there to say?

Robbie shuffled over to the coffee maker and poured herself a second cup. Dee drained his mug in an ambitious gulp and idly spun it in circles on the table.

With the silence getting stale, Robbie opened her mouth.

Dee beat her to it. "So, uh, you going to set up Landerman in his apartment?"

"I still don't know about his work." Robbie shrugged. "Might be that a workplace accident is better. I'm going to tail him for a bit. See if something inspiring comes up. You can ride along if you're bored."

"Nah," Dee said. "I'm going hunting for another theater venue today. I know we wanted to stay in the city, but I'm going to drive down to Owensville. Their community college has a theater program, so I'm going to start there."

His suggestion wasn't ideal. Owensville was forty minutes away, closer to an hour with traffic. It would be a huge ask for their cast and crew and production team to be expected to make that commute, but as they currently had no other options, Robbie supposed it was worth a shot. It meant everything that Dee was still fighting for this dream with her. "In that case, good luck. I hope your search is productive."

"Same to you."

Robbie finished off her coffee and went to get ready for her own day of hunting.

6

A Bit of Light Stalking

WHEN ROBBIE HAD FIRST BEGUN WORKING FOR JAMES, SHE'D expected things to be rather straightforward. You had a target. You took out the target.

As it turned out, things were considerably more complex. James found the word "murder" to be beneath him, but he still taught that the principles were the same: motive, means, and opportunity. While motive—for them at least, not their clients—was a paycheck, the other two were still variable. Everyone had a different style. Some people liked variety, mixing it up regularly. More opted for a specialty, like poisoning or shooting. Dee, for instance, was a sniper.

Even with the most basic of methods, though, opportunity was still crucial. When was the best time to slip something deadly into a person's food? When would the target be somewhere that a gunshot wouldn't draw attention?

James, ever-patient James, had allowed Robbie to find her own preferences. He still trained her, of course, and ensured she didn't do anything to endanger herself or his operations.

As it turned out, the straightforward methods didn't feel right to Robbie. Obviously, they worked: The target ended up dead, and she ended up with a paycheck. But doing a job successfully didn't mean it couldn't go *better*. With James, Robbie began to recognize how much her brain craved having something to solve, a puzzle to challenge it.

She'd been channel surfing one night when she came across a news story about a man who'd slipped on an unfortunately placed patch of black ice in front of his house and fallen in the way of an oncoming bus. A terrible accident, the anchor said. It probably was, but Robbie's first thought was how it would be relatively easy to create a patch of ice to ensure someone would fall. The bus part might take a bit more planning. Obviously, the timing had to be just right. But still, someone with enough creativity and thought could theoretically have arranged this man's death.

After, she'd called James and asked him whether that sort of thing was possible. Specifically, whether it was possible for *her* to try. Up until then, James had helped her plan every hit, trying to find the right fit. Her most recent had been staging a mugging gone wrong. She hated it. It'd been crass and unsophisticated, reminded her too much of combat and her time in the army. She'd gotten a spattering of blood on her leather gloves, and she'd spent over half an hour scrubbing her skin raw in the shower when she got home just to get the feeling off her. But accidents—those could work for her. She could have more distance and more control. No blood, no guns, no memories of explosions and sand and people screaming. Besides, it barely even counted as killing someone. The accident killed them. Robbie just made the plan.

James had agreed and immediately seen promise, something worth investing in. His only concern was for her.

"Are you sure that's the route you want to go? It's popular among clients, but it's hard to pull off."

"I'm sure I want to try," she'd answered.

After that, he'd hooked her up with all sorts of useful training, from scuba certification to free climbing. He met with her in anonymous cafés and parking lots and movie theaters and let her talk through her ideas, giving suggestions and guidance whenever she got stuck. Wherever she needed to go, whatever the job required, Robbie was covered.

When she was a kid, her habit of analyzing people's appearances and demeanors had been a problem. Nobody liked it when a nine-year-old could look at Mrs. Dufflin from the hardware store and Mr. Levi the band teacher chatting at the church social and know something was going on between them, and they certainly didn't like when that nine-year-old insisted on asking questions, trying to understand what she saw, until their affair was uncovered. The desire to ask questions had vanished over time, but that way of reading people had gotten sharper too.

James didn't tell her to stop or even dial it back. He encouraged her to lean into this gift.

It was immensely satisfying to be able to identify just the right kind of accident for the right person, to organize events to set that accident in motion. Every job became a puzzle, novel and unique.

Robbie parked in front of Landerman's apartment complex, cracking the windows before getting out and heading toward the building. It had been a hulking shadow of concrete the night before, and the daylight didn't do it any favors, exposing years' worth of grime discoloring the walls and fissures stretching up from the foundation. Some kind of climbing vine had halfheartedly started to scale the south face of the building, but even that was withered and yellow, like it couldn't be bothered. Over the entrance, a rusted metal frame jutted out. Robbie assumed at one point there had been fabric covering it, but as awnings went, it was particularly ineffective now. No sign of security cameras, although if there had been any, she would've had doubts whether they even worked.

By her count, it was about six stories, and the building's managers had seen fit to bless Robbie with the handiest feature of multiperson residential units: names on the buzzers.

She spent a long minute running her fingers over the labels. There. *Landerman, X.* was handwritten in tidy lettering next to the button labeled 5F. Lovely. And *Czajkowski, K.* was right below that in 5G.

Robbie pressed the button for 5F.

A groggy but familiar voice crackled out of the speaker. "What?"

She pitched her voice up a bit, although she doubted Landerman would connect her with the woman he'd met at the Ajax Club the night before. "Yeah, I got a delivery here for, uh, Mr. Kuh-zuh-juh-kow-skuh?"

While she intended to butcher the pronunciation horribly, she had no idea how far off she was. She was fairly certain it was one of those words where all the letters weren't supposed to be pronounced.

"Wrong apartment. Read the damn names," he griped. "Even if you can't pronounce it for shit."

That shouldn't have stung. Landerman didn't know the number of times she'd been teased for reading something wrong. She had to take a breath before replying. "Sorry about that, man."

If Landerman hadn't been home, she would've taken the opportunity to scout out his apartment for any advantageous hazards.

People were fascinatingly oblivious to how dangerous their homes were, how close to accidental death they were all the time. Since he was there, though, she returned to her car to wait for him to leave. At which point she'd hopefully be able to find out where he worked too. Between work and home, most people had at least one significant means of encountering a tragic accident.

It was an hour before Landerman exited the building. Cracked car windows had long since proved inadequate, and Robbie lounged with all the windows down and vents blowing warm but at least moving air. God, she'd taken a shower right before coming here, and already she'd sweat enough to cancel out that overpriced jasmine body wash she stole from Dee.

When Landerman hopped into another rideshare—did he not have his own car?—Robbie turned the ignition, the prospect of running the AC beyond thrilling.

To her mild disappointment, it didn't seem that Landerman was headed to work—at least not toward anything that would qualify as the sort of import-export business Mr. Clark mentioned.

He was dropped off at a coffee shop at the corner of Northcote and Wilden, one of those hipster places with the exposed brick, dangling Edison bulb lamps, and handwritten chalkboard menu that graced every gentrified neighborhood. It was nice and all, but it also wasn't the sort of place she'd expect a person who lived in a crumbling apartment in Keyton Heights would go. Maybe someone else picked it for him.

Robbie parked but stayed put, lingering in the residual chill of her car's AC while Landerman went inside. He was still visible through the shop's front windows, glancing around as he stood in line. She watched the tilt of his head, the way his gaze swept across the inside of the shop. Idle glances, not the searching look of someone looking for a specific meetup. Robbie searched for the shop on her phone. She very much understood going well out of your way for an exceptional cup of coffee, but the reviews mostly praised the aesthetics and friendly baristas. The coffee, as far as she could tell, was mediocre and overpriced.

Her speculation was interrupted when Landerman reappeared with his drink and crossed the street. No rideshare this time, so he must have another destination within walking distance in mind. Robbie ventured out, sullenly paid the meter, and followed him up two blocks, keeping a safe distance. God bless flat cities and straight streets. There was nothing so frustrating as trying to tail someone who could quickly vanish around a bend in the road or the crest of a steep hill.

Tossing his coffee cup in a trash can, Landerman dug his wallet out of his pocket and headed into the Reevesburg Museum of Arts and Culture, a broad, curving two-story building of glass and sandstone that probably counted as a work of art and culture itself. Robbie could not imagine a building that was more the polar opposite of the Ajax Club if she tried. She paused a moment to check that she hadn't made a mistake, that he was going in and not passing on his way to somewhere more his vibe, but nope. Not a mistake.

Midmorning on a Saturday meant the place was bustling. Tour groups pouring off buses, parents pretending not to notice their tantruming child, sulking teenagers who'd rather be sleeping, artists carrying notepads. Plenty of crowd to blend into. Robbie paid the frankly exorbitant price of admission and headed inside.

When Mr. Clark said he thought Landerman worked in some sort of import-export business, maybe that meant acquiring and selling art for the museum?

Except this was a nice place, and Landerman was dressed in cargo shorts, a *London Calling* T-shirt—was that good taste or another failed ploy to look cool?—and sandals coming apart at the soles. Bare minimum, based on the appearance of all the employees she'd seen handling the crowds, this place had a business casual dress code. If acquisitions included meeting with wealthy art donors, the casual part of that probably didn't even apply.

But it was also Saturday. Landerman hadn't struck her as the Monday to Friday, bankers' hours sort, but Robbie had to admit there was a solid chance this was his day off.

As Robbie drifted after him from gallery to gallery, that seemed the most likely option. He didn't head toward any "employees only" door. He didn't meet with anyone. He just looked at the art, head periodically tilting in a contemplative way, as if considering some deeper meaning.

After half an hour, Robbie headed back to her car. Hell if she knew why he'd come here, but it would keep Landerman occupied for a while.

♪

This time, when she walked up to Landerman's apartment complex, she pressed the buzzer for *Czajkowski, K.* in 5G. After a long moment that had her heading toward the conclusion no one was home, a man's tired voice came on, slightly drowned out by the sound of a screeching baby in the background.

"Yeah?"

"Delivery for Landerman in 5F. He's not answering and—"

"Whatever."

The door buzzed open. Top-notch security.

If the outside of the building was run-down, the inside was worse. Paint chipped and peeled from the walls in a shade of grayish-brown that Robbie suspected had once been white. A brown water stain took up a large part of the far wall. The lobby's fluorescent lighting flickered and hummed obnoxiously. Crumpled food wrappers and cigarette butts were stomped into the dirty linoleum. She didn't even want to guess what color that was supposed to have been. A mildewy scent tarnished the air. Toxins in the environment weren't her favorite way to fake an accidental death, but she could work with that if she had to.

Landerman had been distracted the night before, but when he was focused, he'd won a decent amount. Maybe imports and exports didn't pay well, but if he played like that a few nights a week and cashed out at the right time, he could potentially make enough money to afford somewhere a little nicer than this. Perhaps Landerman was terrible at knowing when to quit.

Cautiously, she pushed the cracked button to call the elevator. A chorus of clanging started, quickly joined by a cringe-inducing grind of metal. On second thought… Robbie came to figure out how to kill Landerman, not herself. She pivoted and located the doorway to the stairwell.

The fifth-floor hallway wasn't much better than the lobby, although several of the lights were burned out, which at least made the grungy appearance less visible.

No one was in the hall. The baby in 5G was apparently still very unhappy, and the walls were clearly very thin.

Landerman's door had a standard key and two bolts. Robbie unzipped the flamingo-print makeup bag she'd brought from her car. On one side, a little pocket held two flavors of lip balm, a couple hair ties, and a tube of cheap mascara she'd bought a few years ago and never used. On the other side were neat little slots intended for, she assumed, various makeup brushes. From one of the slots, she pulled out her tension wrench, then selected a standard lock pick from another.

She got to work, glancing up every so often to make sure no one approached. Honestly, though, she had a feeling that if anyone saw her, they wouldn't much care what she was up to. Someone breaking into an apartment here was probably a weekly, if not daily, occurrence. Still, she hoped Landerman had several more galleries worth of paintings to admire.

When she finally got the locks open, she pushed open the door with her gloved hand. Inside, the apartment was…nice. A little shelf near the door held a pair of boots and two pairs of sneakers, with an empty space that presumably was for the sandals Landerman currently wore. The entryway had a clean blue rug covering most sins of the floor, even if the door did snag on it.

As she walked in, the space opened up into a studio. Directly across from the door, a mattress and box spring sat with no bed frame, topped with a pale-green blanket and light-yellow decorative pillows. The bed being made at all was a little surprising, but far more so were the sharp hospital corners of the thin blanket and sheets. She knew why her own bed at home looked like that, but if Landerman had a history in the military, Robbie would've clocked it that first night she met him. Wouldn't she?

The colors were an interesting choice too, making for a far lighter, airier vibe than she had ascribed to Landerman. Maybe the fact that both times she'd seen him, he'd been wearing T-shirts of old punk bands had been a fluke, because this? Not very punk.

She could feel the pieces of the Landerman puzzle in her mind, her brain itching to make them fit together. Except instead of slotting neatly together, she kept getting new, disparate pieces.

A small white dresser was pushed up against the wall, a sharp contrast to the bed as several drawers sat half-opened with wrinkled T-shirts spilling out in dark shades of blues, grays, and blacks. That felt far more in line with the Landerman she'd seen so far.

Next to it sat a squat bookshelf. Robbie crouched down and found an assortment of thrillers and horror novels, all alphabetized by author and title. Those were the kinds of stories she loved too. She smirked. Don't try to lure him into a creepy basement or an abandoned cabin in the woods, because he'd know better. Noted.

Three little pots, two with succulents and one with a fern, were set atop the bookshelf in perfectly spaced intervals. The plants were all impressively alive. The green curtains covering the windows didn't match the bed and yet didn't exactly *not* match. Shit, did Landerman have a roommate? That would explain why only half this place aligned with what she'd seen of him so far. An in-home accident was far harder to arrange when someone didn't live alone.

Robbie turned to assess the small kitchenette. The fridge was probably a good forty years old, the gas stove not much younger. She loved a good old plausible-to-leak stove. On the counter, the microwave had both a small toaster and a stained, old coffee maker balanced on top, all three making for an unsafe number of appliances daisy-chained to an extension cord leading to what clearly wasn't a GFCI outlet. No dishes in the sink, just one plate, one fork, and one cup set on a dish towel to dry in the single square foot of counter space. Nothing more in the cupboards. She let out a small sigh of relief. No roommate then.

She didn't even bother checking the bathroom. Since entering this building, she'd identified at least half a dozen ways an accident might befall someone here. Frankly, she wasn't sure she even needed to *do* anything. If Landerman lived here for the next month and did nothing else, there seemed a solid chance he'd die all on his own.

Carefully looking around to make sure she hadn't left any traces of her presence, Robbie headed out. A little table by the door caught her eye. It had a few envelopes, all bills and junk, nothing of interest, other than confirmation they were addressed solely to Landerman. But there were several smaller scraps of paper too.

Robbie reached into the back pocket of her jeans and pulled out the ticket stub from her museum admission. Exactly the same.

Xavier Landerman lived in a squalid apartment building in a disreputable part of town. He spent a lot of time in a gambling hall in an equally sketchy area. While there were modest little touches in the apartment and he clearly tried to keep it tidy, it was still a very spartan space, and the decor was made up of cheap, bargain-bin sorts of things. Nothing about the apartment made her think of him as a wasteful person.

So why did he have a pile of at least ten ticket stubs from the outrageously expensive art museum, all dated within the past two weeks?

She cringed at the abrupt metal-on-metal clanking coming from... Oh shit, the death trap elevator. The museum question would have to wait for another time. Now, she whirled in a circle, a quick inspection of everywhere she'd been in the apartment. All perfect, except the curtains had been closed half an inch more. She darted over, setting them precisely as they'd been when she entered. Slipping out of the apartment, she pulled her pick back out and set to work relocking Landerman's apartment.

She had just finished when the excruciatingly slow elevator screeched to a halt on the fifth floor. Robbie darted to the stairwell as the elevator doors opened and Landerman stepped out. Thankfully oblivious to her presence, he walked right past the doorway to the stairwell and headed to his apartment.

Robbie made her way down the stairs, back into the oppressive heat and her oven of a car. At least now she knew it would be very easy to carry out the hit on Landerman. In a few weeks, Mr. Clark would return and give her the second half of her payment. Simple. Straightforward.

Straightforward like a guy who, for unfathomable reasons, frequented both an illegal gambling hall and the city's classy art museum. Who decorated with pastels and made his bed with military precision and yet wore crumpled punk T-shirts and seemingly had never brushed his hair. Who was perhaps a bit snarky but overarchingly friendly and yet had apparently managed to upset the uptight, arrogant Mr. Clark so much, he was willing to pay twenty grand to kill him.

It wasn't her place to wonder what exactly a person had done that made someone pay an obscene amount of money to have them die. Focusing too much on why someone wanted a target dead was a surefire way to screw things up.

She'd let herself get curious once. A woman in North Dakota in her late fifties. No political connections, no wealth or businesses in her name. Robbie knew within a day or so of following Arabelle McGeorge that an accident involving garden tools would be the woman's end. Except Robbie kept digging, pun not intended but wholeheartedly endorsed. Who wanted this quiet woman dead? What was it about Arabelle that could've offended someone so much that they'd contacted James to solve the problem? She was kind, well-liked by her neighbors, cordial with her coworkers.

"What if it's just a misunderstanding?" Robbie had asked James. "We should go back to the client. Confirm everything, get more information."

James, sitting across from her in a roadside diner not unlike the one he'd found her in, had cut her his sharpest glare. "Curiosity is not the role of a contract killer."

"I know, but—"

"But nothing. You're off the job."

"Hey, that wasn't what I meant," Robbie protested. "It's fine. I have all of it planned. A whole thing with a rake and pruning shears. I'm not letting that go to waste."

"Perhaps you shouldn't have wasted time poking around in her life then. I didn't hire you to ask questions. You're off the job. It's done."

She'd never seen him so devastatingly disappointed in her. His tone was an iron security grate crashing down. No room for arguments. It wasn't until later that she found out when he said, "it's done," he really did mean the job was done. He'd sent someone else. Within a day, another of James's operatives had shot Arabelle McGeorge—whose name turned out to be Moriah Arden, former accountant in witness protection. Robbie hadn't known Dee then, so to her, it was just some anonymous sniper taking her job. She'd been utterly replaceable. Nothing special in the least. Robbie had to be better than that. Needed to be.

James knew best, far better than her. He'd been doing this work since Robbie was toddling around the farmstead in Nebraska. If James said curiosity wasn't her job, it damn well wasn't her job.

But she was just so very curious about Xavier Landerman.

7
Power Moves

DESPITE DEE'S SEVERAL ATTEMPTS TO GET ROBBIE TO CALL James back and decline the job, Robbie was still on the hook for taking out one Kyle Lynch. James had given her the general details: name, city, vague description. When she'd asked him to be more specific than "white, blond hair, tallish, fairly fit," he'd laughed—the dry, singular "ha" that was his equivalent of a hearty chuckle—and hung up on her.

Because James didn't operate on convenience, the job was out of town. Not too far at least. She took the nicer car she had for daily use, not the junky one she used for local surveillance. Sunday morning traffic wasn't as nonexistent as she'd have liked, but it wasn't terrible either.

The minimalist approach to information wasn't something she missed from her days with James. In fact, it had been one of her reasons to start working solo. Direct contact with the client meant Robbie could feel them out, ask for more information when she needed it, and decline work if she didn't think she was the right person for the job—and perhaps more importantly, if she got the sense the job would risk endangering her, Dee, or the life they'd worked so hard to build. With James's brief call, Robbie hadn't been able to get all the information she normally liked to ask a client—not even basics like the target's address and occupation as she'd asked of Mr. Clark.

Still, unlike with Landerman, a simple search pulled up a wealth of information on this target. God bless the internet. How did hit people function before it?

Much to her surprise, Kyle turned out to be a woman, although Robbie supposed she was the last person who ought to be making assumptions about gender when it came to traditionally male names. According to the blessed internet, Kyle Lynch worked at a highly successful finance company called Thatcher, Lynch, and Boone. Sure, women got their names on things, but a lot less frequently and with a lot more effort than men. Unsurprisingly, Thatcher and Boone were both men.

In any case, Lynch was a powerful woman with a lot of money, and everything always came down to money. Someone else, also with money to burn, disliked her enough to want her dead. Being rich seemed an awful lot of work, but with Robbie's help, at least Lynch wouldn't have to do it for much longer.

In under a minute, Robbie had the woman's current and last three home addresses, along with numbers for her personal and work cell phones and her office line. The current address was a light-blue town house in a classy district. Enough trees had been planted along the street to keep it from looking like it was smack in the middle of a city, but according to Robbie's phone, the offices of Thatcher, Lynch, and Boone were less than ten minutes away. Workaholic then.

Even without seeing the woman, Robbie could piece together a life. She figured Lynch's weekday routine probably consisted of long hours at work, an expensive restaurant at least twice a week, and jokes to friends with phrases like "wine o'clock." Weekends, Robbie reckoned occasional brunches, some kind of indoor exercise like Pilates or yoga that could be done rain or shine, and a strict hair and nail salon regimen.

She parked down the street from the town house and settled in. When she'd first started with James, she'd been surprised by how much of this job was just waiting. Waiting for people, waiting for opportunities.

At a quarter to ten, her waiting paid off. Lynch—who was indeed white, blond, tallish, and fairly fit—stepped out and slid into a cab parked at the curb. This was no Keyton Heights. This was the sort of place where people actually cared what happened around them. No way was Robbie getting into that house in the middle of the day without a well-prepared cover. Instead, she tailed Lynch's cab to a posh yoga studio. Nailed it. It wasn't as interesting as an art museum, but maybe that was for the best. She wasn't in the business of "interesting." She batted aside the mental jigsaw that was the disparate aspects of Landerman. She was *not*, she repeated to herself, in the business of interesting. And especially not while on a separate tail.

When she could see people bending themselves into triangles or whatever through the studio's front windows, she headed inside.

"Welcome," the woman at the front desk said in the sort of soothing tone you'd use to put a baby to sleep. Probably. Robbie wasn't entirely sure how babies worked. "Can I help you?"

Robbie cast a quick glance around. Along one wall of the

orange lobby were cube storage shelves painted earthy green and stuffed full of, well, stuff. She spotted the black-and-white striped handbag Lynch had been carrying when she left the town house.

The receptionist emanated people-pleaser energy, which Robbie figured made her a good front desk option for any business. And convenient for Robbie's current needs.

She nodded to the woman. "Has anyone turned in a wallet?"

"Not that I'm aware of."

"Oh." Robbie did her best impression of being crestfallen. Her eyes darted over to the shelves, then back to the receptionist. "I think I might've left it in one of the cubbies. Would it be okay if I go check?"

"Of course."

Taking two steps, Robbie paused. "Um, do you think it's okay if I move some people's stuff out of the way? I won't mess with anything, I promise."

"I'm sure no one will mind."

Unsuspicious people were Robbie's absolute favorite.

She headed to the cubbies and made a show of digging around, and the receptionist quickly lost interest, pulling out her phone and playing some colorful game. Robbie angled her body to block the woman's view just in case, then unzipped the striped handbag and fished out a phone with a polka-dot case.

She slipped it in her pocket and pulled out her wallet.

"Found it," she stage-whispered to the receptionist. Pointing down the hall, she added, "You mind if I use the restroom real quick?"

The receptionist didn't mind at all.

Ignoring the overwhelming scent of incense that saturated the walls, Robbie shut herself into the first stall and pulled Lynch's phone out. Locked. Of course.

Not the end of the world though. The lock screen showed the grid of nine dots awaiting the right pattern. Robbie wasn't a tech genius, but people weren't security geniuses either. And not to speak ill of an entire gender, but statistically, women chose less secure passwords and patterns than men. She started with the good old classic square, the lock pattern equivalent of using "password" as a password. No luck. She tried a few more of the classic shapes, then turned to letters. Drawing a K with a single line would be difficult, but L for Lynch was straightforward. Ta-da! The lock screen dissolved into a home screen full of icons.

She scrolled through Lynch's browser history for the past month as well as her calendar, taking photos on her own phone as she went along. Probably she could get more, but Robbie didn't want to risk spending too much time here.

In any case, she'd struck gold. There were few things in the world Robbie loved more than a target who took risks. Lynch had a rafting trip this upcoming Saturday. Sure, lazing on the water in a giant inflatable doughnut didn't seem inherently dangerous, but water was always a risk. Robbie saw the word "river," and a thousand possibilities went spinning through her brain. Already, she was thinking through weight shifts and water flow rates and rope.

According to James, these sorts of things didn't play out in other people's heads. Others could figure out the things Robbie could, but it would take time and math and a lot of scribbled notes.

"It's a gift, Robbie," James had told her time and again. "Just because no one else saw the potential in you doesn't mean it was never there. I see it though."

Nobody *had* ever told her she had potential before James. No one ever treated her like she was valuable. Now she had Dee and Coda, but lots of people owned bars. Plenty of people wrote musicals. What James had honed in her though? That was still special, still uniquely hers.

Robbie headed back to the front, pausing to slip the phone back in the bag before passing the receptionist and giving a little finger wave.

"Namaste," the woman said, like that meant something.

"Sure," Robbie replied with a shrug.

She could head home. The rafting trip was a good enough opportunity. When James trained her, though, she'd learned to always cover her bases. Lynch had the trip planned, but Robbie doubted she was doing that solo. Finding out who else was in her life, who else might be present on that trip and how they might affect Robbie's plans, was critical to doing this right.

Pulling out her phone as she reached the car, she sent Dee a courtesy text: going OK but might be home late.

Dee replied almost immediately with a simple OK.

Time for more waiting. Robbie cracked the windows of the car and watched the yoga class through the window. All things considered, a view of women in tight pants wasn't the worst way to pass the time.

Kyle Lynch appeared to be having an affair. Not on the bingo card, but it felt in line with the profile Robbie had built. Robbie watched the woman's honey-gold hair fall gracefully as Lynch tilted her head back in the perfect laugh. The man sitting across from her, ostensibly the source of the humor, appeared to be a life-size cutout from a men's magazine. Sporty and professional and suave, all rolled into one unrealistic human being. Who Magazine Man was not was Richard J. Lynch III, who, according to the research Robbie had done, was legally married to Lynch.

Lynch laughed again, a perfectly poised and controlled display.

"No one's that funny," Robbie muttered to the half-empty glass of pop she'd been nursing for a good twenty minutes now. She absently grabbed one of the room-temperature fries beside the glass and popped it in her mouth.

The restaurant Lynch and Magazine Man were in was an exclusive place, and Robbie hadn't had the time to bribe anyone to let her in. However, as expensive places often did, the restaurant had giant windows. In fact, it didn't have walls at all. It was exclusively window, all the way around. Conveniently, this allowed Robbie to sit at the much cheaper café across the street and watch her target perform the art of flirtation like she'd read it from a textbook.

The affair was irritating. Not that Robbie was judging or anything. Everyone was free to do whatever and whomever they wanted. All fair. It was just that Dee's voice kept popping up in her head, grumbling about how leaving James meant more choice in the jobs they took. Robbie hated domestics. James had never let her make the distinction, never let her even ask the question.

Since she'd gone independent, though, she'd been able to choose for herself, and that meant she simply wouldn't take out anyone's spouse for them. It was sloppy and risky. The spouse was always the first person cops looked at, and come on, who wouldn't give up the information about who they hired in exchange for a reduced sentence or the right to have a pet hamster in prison or whatever it was people got out of plea bargains? Frankly, it had always surprised her that James allowed those jobs, but then he likely never asked for those sorts of details. Maybe he did, though, and that was how he decided which of his arsenal of professionals was best for the job. Of course, if Robbie did things right—and she took pride in her ability to do so—then the spouse wouldn't be suspected, because there was nothing to suspect.

Oh, and lunch was over. Magazine Man paid the bill and walked Lynch out front where their kiss goodbye was bordering on public obscenity.

"Gotta hand it to her," Robbie told the remaining ice cubes in her glass. "Bold move carrying on like that in public, in the middle of the day, where anyone could see."

The ice cubes offered no opinion.

As Magazine Man tucked Lynch into a cab, Robbie dug some crumpled bills from her pocket to pay her own tab. No credit cards while on a job, of course. Nothing concrete to link her to this time and place.

Lynch's cab drove off across the street, and Magazine Man hailed another. Despite it being Sunday, Lynch's phone calendar had shown her taking a meeting at work this afternoon. Workaholic, just like Robbie predicted. She considered following her to her office. See any opportunities for an accident there. She'd looked up the building. Thirty-two stories. Robbie had always wanted to stage an accident involving an elevator shaft... But no. Rafting would do just fine.

One thing was still bothering Robbie, though, as she walked the five blocks back to her car in the muggy heat that had set in midmorning and gotten oppressively worse as the day wore on. She didn't care about Kyle Lynch. Not a problem per se, but she still had the museum admission stubs in the cupholder of her car reminding her of the stack in Landerman's apartment. Why was it that Lynch didn't inspire even the tiniest smidgen of curiosity in her, but Landerman did?

Getting in her car, she cranked up the AC and basked in the air flow.

Lynch was exactly who she seemed. Rich, accomplished, into yoga and generically attractive men. After lunch with Magazine Man, she would go back to her office and sit at her desk telling people how to spend money or whatever it was financial consultants did. When she finished there, she'd go home to Richard Lynch III. Maybe she'd head back out for dinner with a friend or stay home to sit at her end of some absurdly long dining table while Richard sat far away at the opposite end. Tomorrow, she'd go to her morning yoga, work, lunch, work, home. Rinse, repeat. Season with river rafting or other adventures from time to time because her life was frankly very dull.

Landerman though. Every time Robbie learned something new about him, she was hard pressed to fit the new information in with the old. Was he the disheveled anxiety ball who'd barreled through Ajax that first day or the clever, meticulously organized card counter who befriended everyone at his table? Pastels and hospital corners or punk and wrinkled clothes? Too poor to live somewhere better than a crumbling building literally full of trash or well enough off to buy frequent admission to an expensive, upscale museum despite having no job as far as she'd been able to discern? Those were pieces of different people. They didn't make sense together. Paired with Mr. Clark, who frankly seemed more likely to take a hit out on someone like Lynch than Landerman, the pieces of Xavier Landerman's puzzle made even less sense.

Her day spent following Kyle Lynch had been a wildly different experience than her time following Xavier Landerman. And Robbie kind of wanted to go back and follow Landerman a little more. How much could it hurt to indulge just the tiniest wisp of curiosity? And seriously, what was it about that museum that he liked so much?

8
Everything Is Totally Fine

"SO," DEE SAID AS HE FLIPPED A CHAIR AND HUNG IT OFF THE edge of its table, "what you're telling me is you haven't finished the Landerman job because the man likes art?"

Robbie reached with the broom to sweep the flotsam out from under the table Dee had just cleared. Eloise and Gabriella had handled the bar for most of the night, but Dee had let them go home early, instead committing himself and Robbie to closing and cleaning. Yeah, it was probably a nice thing for him to do for their employees, but Robbie definitely would have preferred Dee choose a way to be nice that didn't involve having to see the gross things people felt entitled to leave on the floor of a karaoke bar.

"Well, not if you put it that way. That sounds terrible and weird."

"Yeah, because it is."

"*Landerman* is weird. He's like this sketchy little enigma. It's like when you assemble furniture and you think you've got everything all put together and then you find five more screws in the box and have no idea where they go."

"So you haven't finished because…your target is furniture?"

Robbie snorted. "I don't know, maybe. Who wants to kill art-loving furniture anyway? Mr. Clark was serious and uptight and secretive, and I don't think I'm surprised he'd hire someone like us, but I'm not positive he knew what he was getting into. Hell, until I found Landerman, I wasn't sure he was a real person and not someone Mr. Clark made up. How weird is that?"

Dee disappeared into the back room, returning with a spray bottle and rag. He set to work wiping down the bar before replying, "I'm not sure why you're still trying to convince me. You told me from the start that something about Mr. Clark felt a little off-kilter, and I believe you. But your brain is clearly getting stuck, and I know how that can go for you. That's why I think you should stop fussing around with all this extra stuff and be done with it."

When it came down to it, Mr. Clark being a little off-kilter didn't bother her so much. In this production, Landerman was the star. Mr. Clark was simply a supporting player. Chorus member almost.

"I'm not saying any of this stuff is relevant. Maybe it's just a bunch of odd, unrelated things and nothing deeper. But I don't want to dismiss them and have something turn into a problem later on. My gut says something's off. James always said trust your gut."

Dee made a grumbling noise of reluctant agreement. While Robbie and James had gotten on well and parted on good terms, Dee's relationship had been considerably rockier, and his few attempts to move to independent work had resulted in a series of stolen clients and sabotaged jobs—something Dee attributed to spite on James's part and Robbie figured was James just having a very strict noncompete strategy.

But regardless of who said it, that advice was solid, and Dee knew it.

"I still have three weeks left from Mr. Clark," Robbie pointed out. "I'm in no rush. I just want to check things out, make sure there aren't going to be any loose ends or messes."

"You know I'll certainly never argue in favor of messes. What's next then?"

Robbie dumped the dustpan into the garbage and began tying up the trash bag to take out. Next was probably tailing Landerman a bit more, but this conversation seemed to have run its course. She considered Landerman's museum trip, the pivot from crumbling apartment to beautiful art, and decided to pivot to her own artistic endeavors. "What's next is we have the space at the rec center booked tomorrow for choreography practice."

They'd gone back and forth on what to do with the show's cast. It felt a little futile to keep preparing to perform a show that no longer had a performance space. At the same time, everyone had worked incredibly hard, and Robbie and Dee wanted to keep an optimistic vibe, even if Robbie wasn't always feeling optimistic herself.

Their compromise had been they would still have rehearsals on the days that had been originally designated, but the content would shift. Tomorrow should've marked their first run-through with everyone off book, but the cast might as well get some extra time to get their lines down. Instead, they'd shifted to dance practice, which frankly Robbie felt needed more work anyway.

"You don't technically need to be there." Dee waved a hand. "You can skip if you need to go chase down information on Landerman."

Robbie narrowed her eyes at him. "I resent the fact that you even suggested such a thing. I—Here, can you get the door for me?" Dee propped open the back door, keeping it from automatically locking behind Robbie as she carried the trash out to the dumpster in the alleyway. "Thanks. I just said how I have plenty of time. Yes, I know I don't *have* to be at rehearsal, but it's my music you're all dancing to. I like watching everyone bring the songs to life."

"That's a terrible line." But he was laughing anyway as Robbie flashed him a smile.

One Friday night several months back, a woman had gotten up on Coda's little stage to sing Jamiroquai's "Canned Heat" while three of her friends fulfilled their obligation to cheer her on. She hadn't been great. Not top ten worst but on the downhill side of mediocre. On her own, her performance would've been entirely unmemorable. In fact, Robbie couldn't remember much about that woman at all.

What she *did* remember was one of the friends dancing. It was a stifled sort of thing, the moves of someone who didn't intend to dance but was powerless to remain completely still. Even without trying, though, it was clear that moving their body to music was as inherent to the person's being as Dee's singing was to him. Robbie knew, an unshakable gut instinct, that was someone she needed if she wanted the show to live up to her dreams.

The next time the person came to the bar to get a round of drinks, Robbie struck up a conversation. By the end of the night, she had a meeting set for the following week with Nadine Raad, choreographer.

Previously, Robbie had thought of choreographers in terms of ballet, imagining them to either be lithe, willowy ballerina types or cranky old women past their dancing prime, beating a tempo out on the floor with a cane. Nadine was neither.

Nadine was compact, with a blocky, muscular build that wouldn't have been out of place on a rugby player. They were just shy of forty, and okay, Robbie didn't know exactly what age constituted being past one's prime in dance, but Nadine clearly hadn't hit it. They danced with an unparalleled energy and sharp, bold movements.

Today, their dark hair was tied up in a scarf the color the water had been when Robbie went to the Cayman Islands once. Waters in which a banking executive had encountered an unfortunate accident with his scuba equipment, but really, a beautiful shade of blue to die in if you had to go. They had a loose gray shirt and black leggings that blended with the black prosthetic of their left leg and ended in contrast with the brown skin of their right.

The whole company had been running through dance moves for nearly an hour straight. Nadine called out a break, grabbed an enormous water bottle, and came to sit next to Robbie on the floor, back pressed up against the wall.

"Well, what do you think?" Nadine had been fairly young when their parents had emigrated from Lebanon, but their accent was still distinct and lovely.

"I think I'm not even remotely qualified to judge professional dancers on their technique," Robbie said.

"Oh, definitely not." Nadine laughed. "But it's your music, your show. How is this comparing against your vision?"

"I..." Robbie trailed off, not even sure what she could say.

Nadine took a long swig from that unwieldy bottle. "I will consider 'rendered speechless' as a compliment. It's either that or the worst sort of insult, but I have at least enough confidence in my work to know, objectively, it doesn't entirely suck."

"That's definitely her impressed face," Dee said, walking over to them. Instinctively, Robbie shifted to her right to make room, her body moving before her brain processed why. If he'd taken the spot to Robbie's right, the ear on Robbie and Nadine's side would've been the one currently lacking the hearing aid he took out during dance rehearsals. "Give her a few minutes. I'm sure she'll find something nice to say."

"A nice thing to say would be that you have a venue for us."

Robbie groaned. Dee took a monster bite of the protein bar he'd just opened and shrugged at Nadine.

"The search is going that well, is it? You said you're going to try checking out some stuff in Owensville. Still planning to do that?"

"Dee went this past weekend," Robbie answered as Dee continued to chew far slower than was probably necessary. "There were two spaces that would've been suitable for our needs." She held up a finger as Nadine perked up. "Each are booked up at least a year out. One is actually closer to two."

Nadine wilted. "You couldn't have told me this before I just spent an hour whipping everyone into shape?"

"We're not giving up," Dee said firmly, having washed the protein bar down with a sip of water.

"The sentiment is lovely and all, but people can't dance on optimism. I need a solid floor. Preferably sprung, but I'll take what I can get." They sighed heavily. "Have you told everyone else?"

They didn't mean the cast currently in various degrees of lounging and sprawling around the room, although Robbie and Dee would have to tell them eventually. "Everyone" in this case consisted of the production team: the show's director along with the leads of each individual component—music, set design, lighting, sound, costumes. All the people who'd been in this longer than pretty much anyone other than Robbie and Dee themselves.

She shook her head.

"It's all well and good that you two are feeling optimistic, and maybe some of the others will feel that way too, but not letting us each decide for ourselves isn't fair to anyone."

"We know," Dee said, sounding about as miserable as Robbie felt. Nadine was entirely right. It just felt like the more Robbie and Dee shared of their failures to get this problem solved, the more real the problem became, and it was nice pretending otherwise.

"Team meeting this weekend?" Robbie suggested. Enough time to figure out how best to break the news to everyone that, realistically, all their hard work was going to go to waste, and this entire endeavor was over.

Nadine nodded and stood up. "I'm free Saturday. Can you coordinate with everyone else and figure out a time? Meanwhile, I have some disappointment to burn off, so I might as well put everyone through Charlie's dream sequence again."

Nadine had turned a musical number near the start of the show into one of the most challenging dance routines of the whole production. The hardest parts fell to the actor in the starring role of Charlie. Dee groaned in protest.

"I suffer, you suffer," Nadine told him cheerfully before clapping their hands and calling for everyone to get off their collective asses.

Dee dragged himself to his feet. Looking back down at Robbie, he said, "Hallway's pretty quiet. Nadine's not going to let us go for a while, so no one will be coming out any time soon."

It wasn't that she couldn't manage typing a quick text inviting people to meet on Saturday, but everyone would be texting back, and their director, Julia, tended to write incredibly long-winded responses to even the simplest of questions. In here, with the music blasting as the company danced, Robbie couldn't exactly use speech-to-text or her reader apps. She nodded to him and flashed a grateful smile.

"Dee!" Nadine called. "Get over here. Your presence isn't optional."

With an exaggerated expression of terror, Dee shuffled to the center of the room. Robbie stayed just long enough to watch them through the first verse of Charlie's dream before she reluctantly slipped out to arrange the meeting to end her own dream.

By the next morning, the looming production team meeting was as oppressive as the muggy summer heat. She got why they needed to have it, and yes, it probably was for the best to keep everyone informed about the brutal reality of their dying dream and let each person decide for themselves whether to jump ship, but she'd really let herself think everything would work itself out before they got to that point. *This* point. The imminent point where she'd have to speak aloud the fact that she'd failed at this too, like she'd fucking failed at so many other things in her life.

Shit. She slammed the brakes and swung her car in an illegal U-turn. She'd driven right past Landerman's apartment without even noticing. "Get your head in the game," she muttered to herself.

On her second pass, she parked down the street from Landerman's apartment building. From this angle, she could see a faded outline of lettering she'd entirely missed before labeling the complex as the Deacon Arms, which wasn't fancy per se, but still a classier name than she'd expected. Aspirational, perhaps. She left the radio on and settled in to wait. The air was still humid enough for fish to breathe, but the temperature was at least a little lower than it had been the last time.

Still, sitting in her car was starting to get uncomfortable, and she was relieved when a rideshare SUV pulled up to the curb and Landerman got in. It was Tuesday. Since he hadn't worked over the weekend, she hoped at least this time she had a better chance of following him to work. She'd already decided her own job would take place in his apartment, but if she knew where he worked, she'd have a better idea of his schedule—and critically, when he'd be out of his apartment for long enough for her to work.

But a sense of déjà vu hit her as the driver turned north on Wilden. This might be the first predictable thing Landerman had done. Robbie headed to the art museum and waited in the car, thumbing through a set of links Dee had texted her of affordable theater venues with unreasonably long commutes while singing along with the radio. After fifteen minutes, she turned down the music, her singing becoming halfhearted as she scanned the passersby. She'd been certain this was where Landerman was headed. Had she missed something? Driven past where she should've been, like she'd driven past Landerman's apartment?

Another ten minutes. She tapped her fingers against the steering wheel. Her best move would probably be to return to his apartment, arrange an accident, and be done. But she had to be sure he'd be out for long enough. That was why she needed to follow him. Certainly not because of this feeling of "god, why can't I figure him out?"

Sharp relief crawled through her at the sight of messy blond hair to her right. Landerman dropped a coffee cup in the trash as he approached the museum. She had no reason to be suspicious about his coffee habits but it was interesting that he had his rideshare drop him off three blocks from the museum, especially in this hot weather.

Focus on the job, she told herself, the voice in her head sounding remarkably like James's annoyingly unplaceable accent. *Your target's life isn't what really matters. Your job is simply to bring it to a neat and tidy end.*

Focus. Yeah, she could do that.

She gave Landerman a five-minute head start before heading into the museum. She expected to have to, once again, pay an arm and a leg for admission, but since it was midmorning on a weekday, she was heartened by admission now only costing an arm.

Landerman wasn't in the lobby, so Robbie cautiously wandered into the first gallery. The museum had perhaps five or six other patrons, not the crowds that had easily hidden her presence before. It was, of course, also much easier to spot Landerman's blond chaos of a hairstyle as he disappeared around the corner. Robbie followed him slowly, stopping just shy of going into the second gallery where Landerman was the sole occupant.

She was fairly confident she hadn't yet given herself away, but Landerman was looking around, peering at the doorways at least as often as he looked at the art. A museum employee passed through, giving Landerman a polite smile. He waited, casually checking something on his phone, until the employee was gone before walking into the next gallery.

As she moved to follow him, she paused. This wasn't what she was meant to be doing. But oh, that infernal curiosity already had her feet moving again. She half expected her phone to ring any second now with James magically sensing her unreasonable feeling.

A security guard strolled past her and through the gallery where Landerman was engrossed in a moody-looking painting of a woman in a garden. Maybe his reasons for being here weren't as complicated as she tried to make them. Maybe he was simply really into art, the way Robbie was into music.

His right index finger was idly tapping a steady pulse against his thigh. He had that constructed expression of contemplation she'd seen before. When the guard exited, Landerman's hand stilled, and he casually wandered into the next gallery.

Oh.

Robbie turned and headed back to her car. She'd seen enough. The emptiness of the museum worked in her favor, allowing her to catch the blatant signs that had been drowned out in Saturday's crowd. The frequent visits, the metronomic tapping, the ever-so-casual observation of people's comings and goings. Robbie was quite familiar with it all, had certainly done her fair share.

She'd been wrong about Landerman being here simply to enjoy the art, wrong about him not going to work today. He *was* working, although not as an employee of the Reevesburg Museum of Arts and Culture. Landerman was a criminal—probably a thief, given the location—and he was currently casing the place.

9

Falling in Love

ROBBIE COULD RECONCILE LANDERMAN THE CRIMINAL WITH both his presence at the Ajax Club and the Museum of Arts and Culture. It felt like the key to that question she'd absolutely not been asking or thinking about in any way: *why*. Mr. Clark—or any client—wouldn't go to the effort and expense of hiring her to kill some random guy for no particular reason, but a criminal? Yeah, she got that.

It all fit together like one of those cheap jigsaw puzzles from the dollar store where the pieces weren't cut quite right. She could smush them all in, but sure would be nice for them to fit a little better. This didn't entirely explain Landerman's inconsistent personality or the way his apartment had looked like two people lived there, although she could shoehorn those into a sweeping explanation that with criminals, what you saw wasn't always what you got. Hell, if someone followed her around, wouldn't they find a few oddities in the way she lived her life?

Not that she was anything like Landerman. Unfortunately, they did have one thing in common: irregular schedules. It would help to know just a bit more about him. For the job, of course.

Landerman did regularly leave his apartment to come to the museum, but she had no way of knowing when he planned to pull off his theft. She wasn't happy about the prospect of relying on one of his museum trips giving her enough time to set things up in his apartment. Alternatively, she could stake out Ajax, then head to his apartment once she was certain he was busy gambling. Breaking in places was always riskier at night than during the day, but she wasn't overly concerned about that with this place.

She was almost back to her car when she registered the marquee on the building across the street from the museum. Not any words—the marquee itself was blank—but simply the existence of a marquee at all. The building was clearly a theater.

She dashed across the street, not bothering to go up the half block to a crosswalk. Jaywalking wasn't even a crime in her book. All right, so she thought that about a lot of things, and such a book would probably get banned by upstanding folks everywhere.

Two sets of glass double doors lined the front of the building. On either side and in between each set, display cases showed off vintage posters for big-name musicals—*My Fair Lady*, *Chicago*, *42nd Street*. Cupping her hands near her eyes, she peered through the glass doors into the dim space beyond, shuttered box office to the right and stairs on either side of the lobby. The crimson carpeting was clean and not too worn. Actually, everything appeared to be in pretty good shape.

Robbie checked the poster displays again. Definitely all reprints of original Broadway runs. Nothing that indicated a current production. The marquee was blank. There was a very, very slim chance the wild notion in her head could come to fruition, but a slim chance wasn't the same as no chance.

Pulling out her phone, she looked up her current location and called the number listed. After a few rings, it went to voicemail. A woman's voice told her to leave a message, but little else.

At the beep, she told the machine, "Hi. My name is Robbie McNeil. I have a few questions about your theater's operations. If a manager could call me back, that would be much appreciated."

She left her cell number and hung up. With one last glance at the glass doors and the dark interior, she dashed back across Northcote Boulevard toward the museum. Her phone started buzzing as she was backing out of her parking spot, and she pulled right back in to answer.

"Hello?"

"This is Janelle Alston from the Gillespie Theater. I'm calling for Robbie McNeil."

Shit, that was fast. "This is Robbie. Are you the theater's manager?"

"I am, but if you are from any media outlet, our press coordinator would be better suited."

"Oh, no, not media. I was just at the theater in person and noticed it didn't look like there are any productions going on."

"Not at present, no." Janelle sounded a little hesitant, as if she expected something negative to come next.

"Cool. So I guess what I'm calling about is whether it might be possible to rent the space."

Janelle's tone was considerably more relaxed as she replied, "Renting isn't... Well, it's not *not* an option."

What the hell was that supposed to mean?

"Would it be possible to arrange a tour at least? My business partner and I would be interested in seeing the interior. Our schedules are pretty flexible, so whenever is convenient."

The rapid rattle of typing was audible. After a moment, Janelle said, "Is tomorrow afternoon at three too short of notice?"

"Not at all. We'll be there."

As she hung up, Robbie filled the car with a scream of excitement. Once she finished dancing around in her seat, she sent a text to Dee.

> ROBBIE
> Tmrw 3pm cancel any plans asap

She'd save the rest of the details to tell in person so she could enjoy Dee's reaction. Backing out of her parking spot once again, Robbie cranked up her stereo and joyously belted out every single song on the way back to Coda.

Dee was fussing with his tie. Again. It had taken fifteen minutes to drive from Coda to the Gillespie Theater, and in that short time, Robbie had seen him mess with his tie eight times.

"It's fine," she said. Again. "You look absolutely fine."

They both did. Dee wore a long-sleeve button-down in a mossy-green shade that Robbie was certain had been made specifically for people of his exact warm, olive-brown coloring, an absolutely fine skinny black tie, and dark slacks. He'd gone back and forth on whether to wear a jacket, which was a bit absurd given the summer heat. Even his long sleeves seemed overkill, although his concern about having armfuls of tattoos deemed "unprofessional" was understandable. Still, in her opinion, he'd made the right call, leaving the jacket at home.

Robbie'd also gone with her most professional clothes—at least in the traditional sense of the word, not her own specific profession—with a blue chiffon blouse and gray dress pants. She did own a pair of nice heels, or at least she was pretty sure a pair lived somewhere in her closet, but in the interest of comfort, she'd gone with simple, glossy black flats. In a fit of annoyance at the summer heat lasting far beyond sundown, she'd given into temptation a little before midnight last night and lopped off a couple inches of her hair. Now the not-straight-but-not-curly chaos barely reached her chin. It wasn't the neatest cut and maybe didn't entirely go with her attempt to look professional, but hell if it didn't feel amazing right now to have the faint whisper of an afternoon breeze kissing the back of her neck.

With Dee along to make sure Robbie didn't wind up being late, they arrived at the theater at 2:55. A Black woman in her twenties with a pale-pink maxi dress and ombre braids reaching down past her waist was by the front door holding a clipboard.

"You Janelle Alston?" Robbie asked hesitantly.

The woman smiled brightly. "That would be me. Don't worry, you're not the first person to expect me to be older. I appreciate you not assuming I must just be an assistant."

Robbie had been thinking the alternative was "random stranger who's not an employee of the theater" rather than "assistant," but good enough.

"I take it one of you must be Robbie and the other is Dee?"

Robbie nodded, and there was an exchange of names and handshakes.

Janelle pulled the door open, then paused. "Just a heads-up. I got here about half an hour ago and turned on the air, but it's still pretty uncomfortable in there."

"The theater's not in use regularly?" Dee asked as they followed Janelle inside.

"Not in quite a while. To be entirely transparent with you, the owner has asked me to sell the place. It's a registered historic building, though, so there are some tedious logistics involved in getting it ready for sale, and we just haven't gotten around to working through all that."

It was a rather significant building to have sitting around without generating revenue. Robbie and Dee had bought rather than rented the building that housed both Coda and their apartment, but they still had years of mortgage payments left. Then there was the upkeep: electricians, plumbers, the new roof they'd needed put on last year, not to mention the unexpected costs of things breaking. All of it added up to a lot of money that the bar needed to bring in. More often than not, the bar operated at a loss. How anyone ran a successful small business without also killing on the side was beyond Robbie. Between the two of them, their contract work allowed them to be financially stable and independent in a way they couldn't be otherwise. But for the most part, those finances were kept separate, with the money laundered through the bar running through in a thin but steady stream. Anyone looking at the records for Coda and its owners wouldn't find a single thing amiss. Usually. Best if no one looked at their books right this moment, when they still hadn't fully repaid the most recent funds they'd siphoned off for the show.

While her brain was too wrapped up in finances, her body had followed Janelle and Dee inside. It was a well-maintained space, even in its disuse. The lobby had the rich red carpets she'd seen the other day, the color somewhat reminiscent of the Ajax Club floor, although this was brighter and had a geometric design that made it look much bougier. It could probably still mask a wine stain but likely had never been called upon to conceal blood.

Intricate paneling in cream and gold covered the walls. Deep coffered ceilings were done in the same cream tone. It certainly wasn't a modern style—the whole aesthetic wouldn't have been out of place in the home of French aristocracy—but it was still beautiful. And clean. That type of molding had a lot of tiny spaces for dust, but as she surreptitiously ran a finger over the walls, she found them perfectly spotless.

"Oh, Robbie, you have to come here," Dee called rather breathlessly from somewhere farther inside.

Robbie followed the sound of his voice, stepping through a set of double doors to—Oh.

To her right, rows of seats with plush red cushions climbed upward. A balcony jutted out above, the face of it done in a simplified version of the molding from the lobby. Individual boxes lined the sides of the space.

To her left, Dee stood with his eyes wide with a mix of excitement and disbelief. The tasseled curtains were pulled open to a huge hardwood stage.

"There's an orchestra pit," Dee murmured.

"We don't need an orchestra pit." The band was part of the show itself, with their setup at the back of the stage. Robbie didn't want to be a buzzkill, but… "We don't need any of this. This is too much."

The Oster Community Playhouse was run-down and small, seating maybe a couple hundred people. It was the kind of place for beginners to stage a goofy little musical written after hours in a karaoke bar. It was campy and old, and no one expected much of it.

This was the type of theater for Broadway tours, for professional ballet companies, for people who knew what they were doing. People who could draw an audience to fill all these seats. All. These. Seats.

Dee was apparently thinking the same thing. He looked over at Janelle. "How many does it seat?"

"Between the floor, balcony, and boxes, it's about nine hundred, all counted."

Shit.

"Robbie tells me you said on the phone that it was available to rent. Or that it wasn't not available? Can you clarify that?" Dee had on his extra professional voice.

"Given that the owner asked me to look into selling it, it doesn't seem fair for me to say it's completely available. But as long as we have it, there's no reason it's not rentable until it goes on the market. It would just be a matter of negotiating a suitable time frame. What would you be looking to use the space for?"

Robbie shrugged. "Oh, it's nothing. I don't think this would be the place for us."

Dee punched her. Hard. She was pretty sure there would be a bruise on her upper arm tomorrow.

"Robbie's being modest," he told Janelle. "She writes. I sing. We're staging an original musical, and we unfortunately lost our theater space, so we're trying to find somewhere new."

Janelle's whole face lit up. "Oh, that sounds amazing!"

"It's cool and all, but it's not the sort of thing this space deserves." Robbie studied the shiny gloss of her shoes.

"Nonsense. I'm sure it's a lovely show. When were you due to open before you lost your space?"

"Little over three weeks," Dee answered.

"That's a bit short notice—"

"Which is why we understand that this space wouldn't be available."

"Robbie," Dee hissed quietly enough that Janelle couldn't hear. "Stop being a fucking downer."

She didn't mean to be. The Gillespie was an incredible and beautiful theater. She already loved it, and they'd been there less than ten minutes. But she knew better than to expect great things.

Janelle cleared her throat. "I meant it was very short notice for your other theater to give you. I imagine that was frustrating."

"Absolutely." Dee cut a quick glare at Robbie as if daring her to continue on her train of pessimism.

"I can't promise anything, but if we got you into this space, do you think you'd still be ready to open then? I don't know how long you'd want for adjustments. I'm sure sets and choreography and all that would have to be modified to match the space."

"We would love to still have a show ready quickly, but honestly, we've lost some time, so between transitioning to a new space and catching up on rehearsals, I don't know that three weeks is realistic. But hopefully not too much past that."

Nothing in that statement for Robbie to argue with.

"Let me pitch this to the owner. Frankly, I think he's going to love the idea. He absolutely adores musicals, and he's an avid supporter of local arts endeavors."

"Could you give us pricing?" Surely, that was a practical enough question and did not constitute "being a fucking downer." Dee's refreshed glare told her he'd interpreted it otherwise. But she knew their budget, and no matter what Janelle answered, this wasn't within their means. It didn't matter how desperately she wanted this dream to keep going. Even with the money from Mr. Clark's and James's jobs, adding something this grand to the dream was impossible.

"Of course." Janelle flipped over the top page on her clipboard and handed the board and a pen to Robbie. "Jot down your preferred contact info for me. I'll get pricing details over to you as soon as I get back to the office. But do keep in mind that if the owner is on board with this whole endeavor, I'm certain he'd be open to reducing the rates if they're too steep for you."

Robbie scribbled in the corner of the page to make the ink flow. God, she hated handwriting things, or more specifically, writing things for someone else to read and potentially judge. Dee reached over and took the clipboard from Robbie without a word.

As Dee dutifully wrote down each of their email addresses in his neat, rounded cursive and passed the clipboard back to Janelle, Robbie let herself cast another glance around the theater. She'd never realized it was possible to be in love with a building. Coda was special to her, but that was more about the ideas—karaoke, a queer bar, hard-earned joy, running a business with her best friend—than the building itself.

Janelle walked them out, chattering with Dee as Robbie trailed slowly behind them and let herself believe, just for a moment, that they could have and deserve this place.

10

Killer French Toast

"SO YOU EVER PLANNING ON KILLING THE GUY OR WHAT?"

Or at least that was the general gist of what Robbie heard. The sheer volume of popcorn interfering with Dee's enunciation left a lot open to interpretation, and the box fan running full blast on top of the coffee table didn't help.

They sat in their living room, sprawled out on their respective couches. Dee's, pushed up against the wall, was a long three-seater sofa with fabric he claimed was a subtle blue and Robbie was fairly certain was just gray. His overabundance of throw pillows included some that were actual blue, and the difference was very clear.

Because they'd bought things for the apartment piecemeal, nothing was part of a set. Robbie had a love seat positioned at a right angle to Dee's in an inoffensive beige color that, while it didn't match Dee's *gray* couch, had probably never clashed with anything in its life. As with all their standard places in the apartment, the two couches were positioned so that when they were in their respective spots, Robbie was to Dee's right, ensuring he could hear her optimally even when he wasn't wearing his hearing aid.

For the billionth time, Robbie tried remembering why she'd ever thought leather was a good idea as just about every inch of exposed skin stuck to the seat. She should've gotten a different couch. She should've put on pants. Either option would suffice, and yet she'd gone with neither.

"Don't rush me, Dee. You're cramping my style."

"Your style is currently lazy as hell."

Robbie grabbed a throw pillow and slung it at Dee. It made it less than halfway there, landing with a soft plop next to the coffee table. Damn it. Now she didn't have a pillow for her thighs. Her thighs, which were now sticking to the couch. Gross.

"I'm an artist. My work is elegant and refined." Robbie sighed dramatically. "You couldn't possibly understand."

A piece of popcorn bounced off her nose. Dee was much better at aim and distance than her. Robbie was fairly certain when James had gotten Dee trained as a sniper, he never intended those skills to be used to assault anyone with items of food.

"Yeah, yeah. You're a murderous Michelangelo. I take it that makes Landerman what, the Sistine Chapel?"

Robbie couldn't remember what exactly that was, as was the case with a good number of references Dee made. He never made her feel bad, just sometimes forgot the two of them had different ideas of what constituted common knowledge. Even without recalling the details, though, she did know for sure that a Ninja Turtle wouldn't have been named after a guy who didn't make fancy art.

"Yeah, that."

"Okay, well, it took him, like, four years. I seem to recall you were given closer to four weeks—two of which you've spent putzing around indulging your curiosity." Another piece of popcorn hit Robbie, this one striking her chin.

Robbie picked the piece up and tried to throw it back. It landed near the pillow on the floor. "You have to admit it's interesting. Do you think Landerman robbing the museum is the reason Mr. Clark took out the hit? Maybe that's why he said the job was time sensitive."

"You think he's paying you twenty thousand dollars to stop an art heist?"

"It's possible." Though Robbie had to admit, not probable. It had been her latest in a line of theories with highly variable quality and plausibility, but her brain refused to stop spinning new ideas. At some point, one of those ideas had to be right. Or maybe she was creating complexity where there was none, because to her mind, simple was boring.

"Why would he do that? Stealing anything from the museum is a crime. Mr. Clark could stop that easily. He doesn't need to commit his own crime to do it. He could literally just turn Landerman over to the actual authorities."

Yeah, she'd come to the same conclusion. It hadn't resolved the way her brain stuck on Landerman, like an earworm karaoke song.

"Landerman doesn't make sense," she said with a huff.

"*You* don't make sense," Dee shot back automatically. More deliberately, he added, "He doesn't need to, Robs, and you know it."

Robbie did know it. But despite Dee's joking attitude, the first part of what he said hit her full force. A professional criminal who counted cards one night and dove wholeheartedly into art the next day. An apartment with hospital corners and horror novels. She thought of the chaos of sticky notes that always blanketed her room with reminders for all the things her mind couldn't hold, and yet in her work, she was precise, making sure everything lined up just so, no detail overlooked.

Popcorn stuck in her throat, and she rolled to the side to cough and gasp for air. She flapped a hand dismissively at Dee's concerned head tilt. Fine. She was totally fine. It wasn't at all disorienting for the contradictory profile of Landerman she'd pieced together to overlay so neatly on her own. But it was an illusion. She could use the same four chords on her guitar to play dozens of songs. Just because they had overlapping parts didn't mean they were the same song.

She did not, absolutely would not, find anything relatable about the man she was hired to kill. Best to shove any hint of that thought into a box in her mind, clamp a padlock on it, and bury it under assorted other mental debris.

"You good?" Dee asked as Robbie rolled back into the well-worn spot on her couch.

All the contradictions and similarities shouldn't matter. *Didn't* matter. Landerman could be the same four chords. He could be a never-as-good-as-the-original cover song for all she cared. He was still going to end up dead. That was the job after all.

"Yeah. I'll go kill him in the morning."

"Brunch after?"

"Oh, we could try that new place in Elkmont that Marisol was raving about the other day. Killer French toast, she said."

"It's a date. Kill Landerman, followed by killer French toast." Dee nodded approvingly. "Okay, now open your mouth a bit. I want to see if I can land a piece of popcorn from all the way over here."

She was absolutely certain Dee was going to throw popcorn at her regardless. With a resigned sigh, Robbie tilted her head back, opened her mouth, and tried not to choke laughing at the excited screech Dee let out after succeeding on his very first try.

Robbie had decided on the stove. It was gas, it probably hadn't been maintained in her lifetime, and despite Dee's pushing, Robbie felt there was a solid chance she didn't even have to go tamper with anything; that stove could kill Landerman for her well before the deadline. She watched from her usual spot down the street from the apartment to keep an eye on it before she'd head in. Dee thought maybe—*maybe*—it would be possible to get the Gillespie if they borrowed money from Coda accounts one last time. What Robbie would get from her two current jobs wouldn't cover the entire rental price, but they would have enough to put a deposit on the theater, and later they could—

A flash of blond in her periphery cut off her thoughts. Shit, how long ago had Landerman come out of the building? Couldn't be long, surely. He tapped his phone. Summoning his rideshare, presumably. Right. She had a job to do, and it wasn't mental accounting.

He looked almost antsy this morning, darting little glances around, twiddling his fingers, shifting his weight back and forth, so even when he was standing still, he wasn't really *still*. Though, to be fair, maybe that was normal for him. This was the first time Robbie had seen him come out of the apartment building before a car arrived for him. She'd never witnessed what it was like for him when he had to wait. He sucked at it.

Not that she was judging. God knew she'd never managed to sit still in her life. Even now, she was absently tapping one hand against the bottom of the steering wheel in time with the radio. She could do just about anything, including being reasonably patient and still, as long as she had something to listen to. At present, the Black Keys were doing the job quite well.

A black SUV pulled up, and Landerman climbed in.

Robbie waited for "Sinister Kid" to finish playing, then got out and headed to the building. She didn't bother with buzzers this time. When she'd been inside before, it had been clear the exterior door was mostly for show. It took her under a minute to jimmy the lock.

Since the person who was supposed to die today wasn't Robbie, she once again skipped the elevator. She really was going to do a job involving an elevator shaft one of these days.

Instead of going straight up to the apartment, she took the stairs down one level, cautiously making her way through the basement, where the vague mildewy scent from the lobby fully saturated the air. At the far end of the building was a plain door. A piece of duct tape was stuck at roughly eye level, and someone had written JANITORIAL in blocky permanent marker. She'd been anticipating maintenance, not the least because this building didn't look like it had ever even met a distant cousin of a janitor. It didn't look like it'd ever seen any maintenance either, but of the two, that had seemed the more likely pretense. Still, she wasn't here to complain.

She knocked. After a minute, she knocked again. Satisfied, she tried the doorknob, and—bless this wreck of an apartment complex—the door just swung right open. There wasn't even a proper lock, just the push button kind.

The room itself contained wire shelves that had been stocked with cleaning supplies by someone not particularly committed to the effort. On the wall behind the door, Robbie found what she came for: a set of hooks, each with a pair of keys hanging off. Okay, so it would've been nice if they were labeled, but obviously, that was expecting too much.

Presumably, they went in order, but she wasn't sure where that order started. She ran through the possible configurations in her mind and, for each, plucked what ought to be apartment 5F. When she'd finished, she had four keys, the rings looped over each finger of her left hand.

Closing the door gently behind her, she headed back the way she'd come. Too many flights of cement stairs later, she exited the stairwell into the empty, grungy, fifth-floor hall. The baby in 5G was still screaming, and who knew if it had ever stopped or if it had been crying nonstop for nearly a week now. She couldn't blame it, but surely, it had to get bored of hearing itself at some point, didn't it?

The key on her middle finger successfully let her into 5F.

The door didn't snag on the blue rug. That was the first thing.

The second thing was the light. It was too bright. It only took a quick glance to see there were no curtains blocking the windows. Not just that the green curtains were pulled back. There were no curtains at all.

Fuck.

Her gaze fell on the rest of the room. Fuck, fuck, fuck.

The entire apartment was empty.

No bed, no bookshelf, no three little plants. Even the damn microwave was gone from the kitchenette. She wanted to kick something, but even with the baby to cover the sound, she still didn't want to risk attracting attention. She aggressively cracked her knuckles instead, continuing to squeeze her hands together even after every joint popped.

She opened a few kitchen cabinets without much hope, and unsurprisingly, they were completely bare. Bathroom? Nope. Empty.

Landerman clearly didn't live here anymore. And he'd moved out at some point well before today, since he hadn't been carrying so much as a bag when he walked out earlier.

Her phone buzzed.

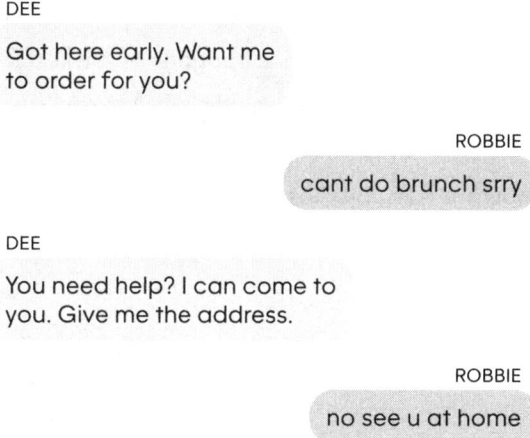

Robbie shoved her phone back in her pocket and ran a hand through her hair aggressively. Several strands snagged and continued on with her hand as she dropped it.

Goddammit. *I have plenty of time, Dee. Don't worry about it.* Those words had been so believable, so confident when she said them.

She'd procrastinated. Her curiosity had gotten the better of her, even though James had absolutely taught her better than that.

Locking back up, Robbie clattered down the stairs and back to the janitorial closet, replacing each set of keys exactly where they'd come from. As she got back to her car, a droplet of water hit her face, then another. Ah, so the humidity had given up all pretense and conglomerated.

The storm was to the east, and she drove right into it. Her windshield wipers swept aggressively and mostly effectively, although she definitely needed to get the blades replaced. Hadn't she just done that though? No, maybe that was Dee's car. Yeah, she'd gotten new wiper blades when he was out of town, and she took his car for an oil change, and—

Not important. She was giving every stray thought free rein in her mind, because that was easier, but none of it was relevant.

Landerman. Landerman was relevant. He was the *only* thing relevant.

And now she'd fucking lost him.

11
Falling Apart

ROBBIE WAS STILL IN A TERRIBLE MOOD, ALTHOUGH IT HAD been mitigated significantly by the fact that Dee had brought home pancakes and they had been absolutely delicious, even if they weren't the French toast she'd been looking forward to. It was also helped by Dee not even once saying "I told you so." The look didn't even cross his face. Instead, he'd walked in and simply asked, "Commiserate or problem solve?"

Robbie chose problem solve. Dee immediately began brainstorming ways to find Landerman. The tightness in Robbie's rib cage didn't let up, but it loosened an appreciable amount.

When Robbie had looked before, Landerman didn't seem to have a digital footprint, but he clearly had a physical one. He had lived in that apartment at one point. His name would be on the lease, and presumably he would have mail forwarding set up.

After twenty minutes on hold, during which Robbie wondered what they could possibly have better to do, the receptionist for the property management company, in a tone that expressed she thought absolutely anything in the world would be something better to do, asked, "Right, what'd you want?"

"This is Detective Malloy from Reevesburg City Police, badge number 60356." Robbie was 99.9 percent certain the receptionist would not be verifying that or probably even know how. People liked authority though. "I'm calling in regard to one of your tenants at Deacon Arms, Xavier Landerman."

"Oh. Yeah, all right. What'd you want?" While the words were unchanged, the question was delivered with significantly more respect this time around.

"Mr. Landerman may have information that can help us in an ongoing investigation. However, we have been unable to get ahold of him. Could I get any contact information you have for him as well as for any emergency contacts or personal references he provided when applying for the apartment?"

"Yeah, yeah, sure, Officer Molly."

"Detective Malloy."

"Right. That. You said Landerman?"

Robbie confirmed, and her mood did not improve at all when the barely competent receptionist put her right back on hold. This time was under ten minutes though.

"I don't got a lot. No emergency contact. One reference for a previous rental, one personal. And I got a phone number for him. You want that?"

"Yes," she said through gritted teeth. It was a miracle they had any information at all. Absolutely nothing about that apartment building indicated to her that management put any amount of effort into screening the people they rented to. Or the people they hired. "That's exactly what I asked for."

"No need to get huffy." But the receptionist went ahead and read off all the information to Robbie, who'd put the call on speaker so Dee could write everything down.

Robbie managed a barely polite "Have a good day." A thank you was too much for anyone to expect of her.

The tightness loosened a little more. They had a phone number. They were making headway.

Dee took the number of the rental reference while Robbie tried Landerman's cell and personal reference. After a few minutes, she turned a desperately hopeful eye to her partner, but he shook his head. "Number's been disconnected. I looked up the name and can't find any information about it. Not even sure it's a real place. I take it you didn't get ahold of anyone?"

"Also disconnected."

This was something Robbie imagined plenty of people experienced with herself and Dee. The two of them went through burner phones like candy. She spent a few minutes letting her mind fill up with blissfully irrelevant distractions again. Her brain was very good at that. A brief reprieve while the tension around her ribs and the abyss of doubt still lurked around the edges.

"Yeah, it's me," Dee was saying to someone on the phone as Robbie snapped herself back to the moment. "Calling in that favor. Can you run a Xavier Landerman for me?"

Dee went through a series of mm-hmms and okays and several nods that the person on the phone couldn't see. After several minutes, he hung up and frowned at Robbie.

"What?"

"That was my guy in vital records." Dee knew all the most useful people. Closest Robbie had was a contact at the DMV, but that was less helpful at the moment, especially to track down someone who never drove himself anywhere.

"Oh, brilliant idea. And?"

Dee's sigh said it all before he even put it into words, the vise crushing all the air out of Robbie's lungs. "I'm sorry, Robs. As best I can tell, there's no such person as Xavier Landerman."

Fuck.

For the most part, the different domains of Robbie's and Dee's lives were relatively easy to keep compartmentalized. They tried to never take contracts at the same time as each other, which allowed them to keep one person reasonably available if anything happened at Coda. While they laundered money through the bar, they didn't otherwise let their two sources of incomes officially touch. Since deciding to embark on this whim of turning a collection of songs Robbie wrote into a full-blown musical production, they'd done reasonably well keeping that separate too, recent finances aside. They'd even hired a new person to work nights at Coda so they could attend rehearsals without worrying about leaving their staff short-handed. Each side of their lives was designed to remain functional even when they had to step out of it.

Robbie didn't really want to step out of the Landerman issue. If she had her way, she would've liked to either spend the next few days wallowing face down on the couch or finding a magical yet-undiscovered lead that would point her right at Xavier Landerman or whoever he really was. Not an option.

They had a meeting with their production team scheduled at noon, and then Kyle Lynch had a river adventure the next day that wasn't going to sabotage itself. Robbie couldn't let herself get stuck on Landerman.

"You want me to cancel?" Dee asked an hour before the team meeting.

"What? No. Why would you do that?"

"Because I've been talking to you for ten minutes now, and you're clearly somewhere else entirely."

"Shit. Sorry. It's just Xav—Landerman, and I have James's job I want to get wrapped up. Assuming that target actually exists and isn't also some fake person about to vanish off the face of the planet."

Dee had stiffened the second Robbie mentioned James. "Seriously? Right now, when you have so much to deal with, you're still going to go out of your way to do a favor for him?"

"It's not a favor. It's a job."

"A job that's a favor. Just call him and tell him he can fuck off and find someone else. We're hardly the only people in this business. You're good, Robs, you really are, but you're not even the only one who specializes like you do." He held up a hand and began ticking off fingers. "Inez Torres does accidents too. They're in South Carolina, last I heard, but they do anything east of the Rockies. Val Solheim has that whole deal with household poisons, which basically still falls under the accident umbrella. Plus, he lives in fucking Winnipeg, so I'm sure he'd love any excuse to travel, even if it is just to Cincinnati. Who else? Oh, Sylvia Endicott, she's great with accidents."

Robbie shook her head. "I'm not passing this off to Sylvia or Val or Inez or anyone else. James gave me the job. I'll see it through. And you know we could use the money."

Robbie hadn't realized how aggressive a sigh could be until Dee demonstrated in this moment.

"Dee? I'm low-key panicking about Xavier. I have my usual production team 'they're going to all decide the show sucks and back out' panic going on today along with the 'we don't have a theater' panic. Could we maybe argue about James some other time?"

Immediately, the defensive set of Dee's shoulders softened, his grimace fell away, and this time, his sigh was sympathetic. "Yeah. Absolutely. Want to go downstairs and blast some music until everyone gets here?"

Dee had the best ideas.

Several loud power ballads later, the production team arrived, taking their seats on a set of couches around a low, hexagonal table in the middle of Coda's large, open space. She and Dee hadn't figured out how to make the Gillespie Theater a realistic prospect for them, but the team had generally sided with Dee's optimism. Nadine, unsurprisingly, had seemed more inclined to believe Robbie's multiple warnings that they not get ahead of themselves. Overall, though, the mood of the meeting was far better than any of them could have anticipated when Robbie had issued the invitation earlier in the week.

Rather than focusing on the glaring problem of not having anywhere to perform, the team worked through their agenda as if that were simply an obstacle they'd clear later. Robbie kind of liked that approach. She could take a page out of their book when it came to her big, glaring Xavier problem. Even if no one by his name existed, he still existed as a person somewhere. She knew at least two places he frequented, so she made a mental agenda and added Ajax and the museum to it. He had to live somewhere, so she could try finding recently closed listings for shitty apartments. That went on the agenda.

When she'd apparently zoned out too much with her imaginary agenda, Dee pulled her back to the real one by snapping his fingers at her. "Robs. You with us? Julia was just throwing out some ideas for that rapid scene change in act two."

Robbie snatched at the fraying edges of her attention, trying to hold them together. "Yeah? What's currently your top choice for a solution?"

It was the right question. Julia's blue eyes lit up, and Robbie felt bad for letting her mind wander. Julia didn't deserve that. She'd been working as an assistant under a highly acclaimed director for years prior to this. Dee had originally found her. Robbie met with the woman, and something about the combination of Julia Vogel's passion, pride, and posture told Robbie that a good deal of the acclaim for that other director's work was actually due to Julia. Dee trusted Robbie's instincts, and they'd been rewarded with a woman who was an absolute delight to work with. Robbie hadn't thought anyone could love this show as much as she and Dee did, and it still amazed her every time someone else on their team had this much enthusiasm.

"Losing the Playhouse is terrible, but it's given us more time, and I think I can fix that transition. All the set pieces need to change there, basically the entire company needs to switch costumes, even the lighting's going to be radically different, although I'm not worried about that because Summer is a genius." Julia nodded toward Summer Miao, the show's incredibly talented lighting designer and also her wife. Summer's round cheeks dimpled with Julia's praise. "But having a break between those two scenes has always felt choppy. Everything around him is different, but for Charlie"—a nod to Dee, as their lead—"it's all just the continuation of everything falling apart."

Maybe that was how Robbie needed to think about this whole Xavier fiasco. Everything was falling apart, but in the show, that point was early in act 2, with a whole third act left to go, one where the show's lead character, Charlie, managed to get his shit together. Robbie just needed there to be another act after this Landerman fiasco.

"—thinking we leave Charlie where he is," Julia continued, and Robbie drove all her effort into paying attention. "We bring him down center, and the lights get low on everyone else. The cast members move the set. They change costumes on stage. The audience is experiencing this shift happening around Charlie as he's singing about wanting things to change."

Honestly, Robbie hadn't needed Julia to explain. Everything Julia had come up with so far had been absolutely perfect. The story and music had come from Robbie's head, but turning that into a vision of an actual show? One hundred percent Julia.

"I think that's brilliant."

Julia grinned. And then her face fell. "It doesn't matter how brilliant my ideas are for the show if we don't have anywhere to put it on."

"We're figuring it out," Dee said confidently.

"The Gillespie?" This was from Nadine, of course. "You keep talking about it like it's a sure thing, but you've had a bunch of other leads already, and nothing panned out. Be honest with us. How realistic is it that we actually get a place like that?"

Robbie opened her mouth, then closed it again as Dee cut her a look that clearly was instructing her to not be a fucking buzzkill. Or just not to say anything at all, because *fucking buzzkill* was probably her only mode of being today.

The fact was they weren't going to get the Gillespie. They weren't going to put on this show. Even if they went ahead with their plan to siphon off more Coda funds for a deposit and replace those later with contract money... What contract money? Robbie wasn't going to get paid for her complete and utter failure at the Landerman job.

Dee turned to Nadine. "There's no guarantee, but I'm optimistic. And even if the Gillespie falls through, we'll find something else. You know how much Robbie and I love this show, and we know how much work you've put into it. We're not going to let all that go to waste. This show is happening. Now, what's next on the agenda for today?"

12

The Great Outdoors

ROBBIE'S SKIN WAS ITCHY AND TOO TIGHT, LIKE A SWEATER that shouldn't have gone through the dryer. After several hours tossing in bed, she'd given up on sleep around three in the morning and gone to the music room to pound away on the piano. Her brain itched too. No, not quite that. It was more like a room full of radios all tuned to different stations, constant overlapping noise she couldn't parse into individual thoughts.

She had no idea where or who Landerman even was. She had no idea if her theatrical dream was going to crash and burn before it ever got off the ground or if they'd manage to find a theater to perform in. What she did have plenty of ideas about was river rafting. She couldn't tune out everything else, but she finally managed to turn the volume down on the rest just enough to focus on this one thing.

So many things in her life felt like they were falling apart right now. The least she could do was make someone else's life fall apart.

She spent Saturday afternoon sorting through her own supplies. Hopefully, she wouldn't need to go in the river, but she liked to be prepared for any possibility, so she dug her wet suit out from beneath a heap of winter blankets she'd shoved in the top of her closet. Her grip gloves had suffered the same fate as so many socks, one of the pair lost forever in some unfindable liminal abyss. She drove to three stores around town before she found a new pair.

Was Landerman still in the city? Or had he headed elsewhere—another city or an untraceable cabin in the woods? She made it halfway home before turning around to head right back to the last store because she hadn't been paying enough attention to get the right gloves on her first try. Off to a great start.

Loading everything up along with several bundles of paracord and her favorite utility knife, Robbie cranked up the playlist she maintained for when she was on the job, which she hadn't been able to resist calling her Hit List. She let it play on shuffle, the smooth, bluesy voice of one of Delta Rae's singers belting out "Bottom of the River" as Robbie pulled out of Coda's back alley and headed south toward the Cumberland River where Lynch would be going tomorrow.

It was near dusk by the time she arrived at the spot where Lynch and friends would launch from. Robbie parked on the side of the road, grabbed a flashlight out of her glove box, and hiked down toward the water, relieved to be out of the car and moving. She followed the shoreline downriver, cataloging where the water sped up, where the eddies swirled, where rocks seemed to come out of nowhere. Bats chittered in the air above her, swooping low over the water before flapping away again. Robbie kept swatting away insects, annoyed with herself for not bringing bug spray. Fucking nature.

About twenty minutes into her hike, she found what she was

looking for. Several elm and ash trees were close enough to the riverbank for her purposes, and a handful of them so far had branches stretching out over the water. This one, though, had some form of brown rot and a heavy, dead branch in just the right position.

Enough moonlight illuminated the area for Robbie to mentally catalog everything. The branch, the rapid flow of the surface, the rocks causing eddies to form. Perfect.

Opening her backpack, she pulled out two neat bundles of black paracord and set to work. The branch needed to break naturally so the broken edge would be rough and splintered, not cleanly cut by an axe. But she'd also need control over when it fell. Dee and the production team all praised how creative Robbie was for coming up with the show, but long before she'd used that creativity for musical numbers, she'd honed it in a far less jazz-hands-y way.

Pulling the branch down only took ten minutes or so. The complicated dance of hoisting, counterbalancing, and securing the branch back in its original spot took nearly an hour. Covered in a sheen of sweat, Robbie was nearly tempted to take a dip in the cold river, but who knew what lurked in rivers at night? Robbie didn't want to find out.

She patted the critical tumble hitch knot with pride before shimmying down from her perch in the tree. For the next few minutes, she tossed various items into the river—twigs, leaves, a plastic inflatable buoy from her bag, a crumpled-up Coda bar napkin from her pocket. She left it at that. Murder was fine and all, but she didn't love the idea of littering.

Satisfied with her setup, she turned and hiked back to the car.

After another restless night, this time on a lumpy mattress in a questionable roadside motel, Robbie got up early and returned to the river. With the muggy heat already setting in, the riverbank was full of people preparing to spend their day on the water. Lynch and her friends arrived not ten minutes after Robbie. Thank god Lynch hadn't also vanished and ceased to exist.

She stayed only long enough to watch the first of Lynch's friends pull a black inner tube off the top of their station wagon. As they began carrying that down to the water's edge, Robbie slipped away to hike down to her dead-branch masterpiece. Shit. The branch hung precariously, nowhere near as secure as she remembered leaving it. She'd double-checked the knot last night. Or, well, she'd looked at the knot twice. Had she actually *checked* to make sure she'd tied it correctly? She couldn't remember.

Scrambling up the tree, she adjusted the cord and its knots to get everything back into its proper place. She cast quick glances upstream every few seconds. It would take time for Lynch and her friends to unload their car and get onto the water, but Robbie hadn't counted on needing any time to fix her setup.

A set of submerged boulders beneath the tree altered the water's flow, forcing anyone coming downstream into the fastest part of the river. The bottom dropped right after, so even as the top layer of water slowed, the undercurrents kept racing. Robbie could see it all in her head, playing out like a movie scene. Yeah, this would be good. The knot was tied properly. Back on track now. She could do this.

It wasn't too long before a group of teenagers went past on an inflatable raft. They flowed right through the way Robbie expected. She let out a sigh of relief that at least that had gone right. Their parents weren't far behind. Then came Lynch's friends, ahead of her, just as Robbie had expected too. The relief she felt seeing that surprised her. Normally, success came with pride. When had she lost confidence in this plan? "Here, I'll go first and show you how it's done" was a reasonably predictable strategy when the two companions had done this at least once before and Lynch hadn't. And despite presumably launching more or less together, they'd become somewhat spread out. Best of all, none of them were wearing life vests. Robbie fucking loved people who eschewed safety devices.

Lynch was still a ways upriver when the first friend bounced past Robbie, the edges of their tube bumping against the rocks. They shouted garbled instructions over their shoulder on how best to navigate, although most of their words probably didn't make it back as the river shot them rapidly downstream.

As the second friend smoothly entered the riffle, Robbie's heart lurched along with the branch as her hand holding the cord instinctively went to pull. She stopped herself just in time to avoid taking out a person no one was paying her to kill. Robbie focused on steadying her breathing. Lynch was left to go last, to follow their examples. Except things would be going rather differently for her.

This was the part Robbie could never articulate. It was the one thing in all the world her brain truly excelled at, and she couldn't for the life of her explain how. Not for lack of trying either. James had, on multiple occasions, asked her to narrate her plans and tell him exactly how and why those plans would work. But the why didn't matter, so Robbie didn't put much effort into it. It just worked.

She'd seen each of the previous people—the teens, the parents, Lynch's friends—pass by this spot. She'd felt the weight of the branch as she'd hoisted and positioned it last night. Sure, someone could do a lot of complex math or physics or whatever for this next bit, but for Robbie, that wasn't necessary. She knew exactly when to pull the tail end of her quick-release knot.

It would've been the same with Landerman. She would've known how much she needed to turn the valve to time the gas leak so it wasn't detected while Landerman was awake but would build up enough while he slept. Maybe that plan would still hold. Surely, if she found him again, he would be in an equally dumpy place with convenient disregard for building codes and safety standards.

Robbie startled as Lynch floated into her line of sight, headed toward the boulders. She could've sworn Lynch was still farther upstream. Robbie yanked her knot loose. The branch fell free and crashed down just in time to—shit, nearly miss Lynch's head. That was supposed to land squarely across the woman's eyebrow, not glance off her temple. Robbie's stomach dropped clear out of the tree. One edge of the inner tube still went up against a boulder right as the weight of the branch pushed the other edge, like it was supposed to, but she held her breath, watching it teeter, unsure whether it would flip the way she predicted, but there—yes, it toppled over, and Lynch was tumbling unconscious into the water.

Fuck. Spots danced in Robbie's vision as she gulped air into her burning lungs. She couldn't see Lynch's inner tube as she blinked away the mirage, but that was fine.

Robbie never watched the next bit. Setting up was fine. It made for a fun, intriguing puzzle. The critical moment itself was pure adrenaline, an absolute festival of chemicals in her brain buzzing around. And she didn't mind checking later to confirm a death. She had a job after all. A mission. An objective. That was what James had taught her. That was what she'd excelled at under his mentorship. That was what made her good, and she was proud of it.

She just didn't love watching that moment when the objective went from one state of being to another.

More cautiously than she had the night before, Robbie climbed out of the tree, making sure the foliage kept her out of sight of those downstream. She wound the paracord lines back into neat hanks and tucked them into her pack. With everything tidied away, no evidence of her presence anywhere, she looked back out at the river.

Lynch hadn't surfaced. Relieved, Robbie began the hike back to the car.

The burner phone for the trip was in her trunk. Even after all this time, she still knew the number. She texted the green circle emoji, just like she used to, then tossed the phone on the ground. She didn't even feel the crunch when she backed over it, nor when she hit it again pulling forward out onto the road.

There. Job done. Even if she was massively failing on the Landerman job and the whole theaterless show was looking doomed, she'd accomplished something today. Barely. She was good at this—the accidents, the contracts, everything James had taught her. Sure, she was fairly good at co-owning Coda with Dee, and everyone kept saying she was good at writing music and putting together the show, but in her entire life, her contract work was the one thing she'd never doubted herself on.

The concept for this job had been clever, even if the plan nearly fell apart when she'd fumbled the execution. Yeah, technically it wasn't a failure. It just felt like it wasn't her win. It was James's job, James's win. Robbie was just a tool. Fuck, that was what Dee always said.

Robbie pushed away the thought. She flipped on the radio, fiddling with the dial to find whatever stations existed out here. She managed to get an oldies station playing a slightly staticky version of "Take Me Home, Country Roads," which was apparently the best she was going to get. Allowing herself one heavy, dramatic sigh, she set all her annoying feelings aside and drove back toward all the other things that were falling apart.

13

The Fletcher Ingram

ANY LINGERING FEELINGS OF SUCCESS FROM THE LYNCH JOB had melted away by the time Robbie made it home midafternoon. The Landerman failure overshadowed everything. Fucking Landerman.

She spent the remainder of the day alternating between lying face down on her bed grumbling incoherently and continuing to try to find leads on her missing target. She probably could've done that for significantly longer if Dee hadn't come up from the bar around ten that night and physically dragged her down.

If there was irony for Robbie owning a karaoke anything when she hated singing in front of people, there was an equivalent irony in Dee owning a bar. Dee had been sober nearly the entire time she'd known him. She hadn't known him well before he got sober, and the two of them didn't talk about it much, other than him giving her a heads-up when he was leaving to go to a meeting. Although he'd always been clear he wasn't bothered if she had a drink around him—the problem, he said, wasn't other people but with where his head went when it was him alone with a bottle—she hadn't really expected him to want to pursue opening an entire business centered around alcohol.

Instead, he'd countered that with a *lesbian karaoke bar* was surely a business centered around the first two words more than the last, something he had presented in a thoroughly convincing manner that involved singing a very cheesy and yet impassioned rendition of Starship's "Nothing's Gonna Stop Us Now," substituting a rapid-fire "lesbians who like karaoke" for the word "lovers" in the chorus and sending Robbie into fits of laughter.

Dee was remarkably good at convincing Robbie of things, which was why, when he'd dragged her away from her Landerman pity party and used a combination of wheedling, death threats, and shoving on his part and a decision on her part to supplement with tequila shots, he had gotten Robbie onstage with him to sing "I Got You Babe" with Robbie doing Sonny and Dee doing Cher. She was pretty sure they'd also gone on to do "You're the One That I Want." Those memories were a bit hazier though, and perhaps best they stayed that way. She didn't really want to remember the embarrassment of not only having sung in front of people but, oh god, having sung something from *Grease* of all things.

The tequila shots were what did her in. Drinking at thirty-five was nothing like it had been when she'd been twenty-one. Robbie woke up thoroughly convinced she'd been run over by a freight train; Dee was probably onto something with the whole sobriety notion. It took her foggy, aching brain a minute to realize why she'd woken up at all.

She pawed around under her pillow until she found her vibrating phone. Her finger hovered over the Reject Call button. It was probably spam, right? But it was a local number.

"'Ello?" Even to her own ears, her voice sounded miserable.

A crisp, polite voice said, "Fletcher Ingram's office calling. May I speak with Robin McNeil?"

Her mind scrambled, and her limbs did a similar sort of flailing. It felt like one of those moments that should've snapped her right out of her hangover, but presumably that sort of magic didn't happen in your thirties either.

"This is Robin. Uh, Robbie."

"Please hold for Mr. Ingram."

Robbie cringed as an orchestra began to play loudly in her ear. Frankly, it seemed a little rude to put someone on hold when you were the one calling them, but she could handle that. And if she was on hold... She muted her microphone and shouted Dee's name over and over.

He came in wearing boxers, a ratty old T-shirt, and a bemused expression. He still looked better than she felt. He, of course, had the advantage of not being hungover.

"Wha—"

Robbie waved a hand and put her phone on speaker. Sitting down on the end of her bed, his face changed into a different flavor of confusion.

After a few more seconds, a deep, pleasant voice came on. "Hi, Ms. McNeil? This is Fletcher Ingram. You may know my name from my political campaign."

Dee did a round of flailing not unlike Robbie had earlier, barely managing to keep himself from falling off the bed.

What?! he mouthed.

No idea, Robbie mouthed back. Out loud, she said, "Um, yes, Mr. Ingram. I know who you are. And it's just Robbie."

"Then it's just Fletcher. I insist." Somehow that didn't feel all that much less formal. "I understand you have a business partner named"—there was a shuffle of papers—"Dee Machado?"

"Yeah. He's here with me. You're on speaker."

"Hi, Fletcher Ingram," Dee squeaked out.

He laughed, a surprisingly warm sound. "Lovely to meet you both."

"What, uh, what can we help you with, Mr. Ing—Fletcher?"

"It's actually what I can do for you. I understand you're interested in renting one of my properties. My building manager Janelle told me a bit about your project, but she said she sent you some rates and hadn't heard back."

His property. The Gillespie Theater was owned by Fletcher Ingram? *The* Fletcher Ingram? And he was personally calling because Robbie hadn't replied to an email for a few days?

"We just needed to look over our finances before replying to her."

"I completely understand looking over your finances. However, I'm very interested in your project. I'm told you had a previous theater booked and that fell through. I would be willing to rent the Gilly to you for whatever amount you were planning to pay for your previous place."

Robbie had no idea how to even respond to that. No way was this real. There had to be a catch. She stared at her phone, stunned.

After a moment, Fletcher asked, "Robbie? You still there?"

Picking up the phone, Dee took over. "Hi, Mr. Ingram. This is Dee. Robbie's a bit shocked at the moment, and I have to admit, so am I. I'm not sure you know what you're offering. We were renting the Oster Community Playhouse. I'm sure you know the property values in East Oster compared to the Gillespie's area."

"You are quite correct there, Dee, but I'm afraid you're wrong that I don't know what I'm offering. I know exactly what I'm offering. A chance for two local artists to give back to their community, promote the arts, and give a purpose to one of my favorite historical buildings in this city." He sounded almost wistful. "I do have one condition."

There it was. There was always a condition. No such thing as a free theater.

"What's that?" Robbie asked, having managed to pull herself together.

"I'd like to know what I'm investing in. My assistant informs me I have a half hour opening at one this afternoon. Would you be willing to meet me for a late lunch to tell me about the show you're proposing?"

It was a little after ten now. Robbie was pretty certain she wouldn't recover from her hangover by then, but damned if she was going to let this chance be ruined by the minor issue of feeling like death had vomited her out into the day. She gave Dee a small nod.

He answered for the both of them. "We'd love to do lunch."

"Excellent. I'm usually at my campaign headquarters during the week, but today I happen to be at home. I'll have my assistant give you directions to the estate."

Estate. Of course he lived in an estate.

They both murmured the appropriate gracious pleasantries, and then he was off, and his assistant was rattling out an address.

When Robbie took her phone back and ended the call, she fell backward onto the bed, cursing softly at the pain of her pillow's impact. Dee crawled over and flopped down beside her.

"What the fuck just happened?"

Robbie shrugged. "No clue."

"You gonna be human before one o'clock?"

"Absolutely not, but I might be able to fake it by then."

"Good enough for me."

They both fell silent, staring at the ceiling in bafflement.

The Ingram estate turned out to be…well, an *estate*. Like the kind you saw in movies. Robbie wouldn't have been surprised if it had actually been used as a filming location at one point or another.

She was familiar with the wealthy homes in Sheridan Hills, a neighborhood on the far eastern side of the city, but only those visible from public streets. Even those were wild in terms of the discrepancy with the shabby vibe found nearly everywhere else in the city.

Ingram's house was set well back from the road, down a long drive lined with elm trees that stretched toward one another to form a sort of tunnel, the leaves a deep summer green. Between the trees, she could see golden, grassy fields spotted with shrubbery and even more trees and what looked like it might be a sizable pond.

When the trees opened up at the end of the drive, the house sprawled into view. It was constructed in an older style, but the building itself had no cracks, no years-old ivy scaling the walls. Some academic would probably call the architecture a something or other revival, although hell if Robbie could say what style was being revived. It was by far the fanciest rectangular box she'd ever seen, lined with more windows than there'd been in every place she'd ever lived put together, and even more in each of the peaked gables popping out of the roof. Each was framed with tidy green shutters set against the stark-white siding that someone was presumably paid generously to pressure wash on a regular basis. On the side closest to them, there was a covered patio—no, probably it was called something like *veranda*—with the roof being its own broad balcony.

"Wow. We're for sure going to let him give us the theater for super cheap, right?" Dee asked, face pressed against the passenger window to stare at the house, clearly having the same train of thought as Robbie. "Because he definitely doesn't need the money."

Robbie nodded mutely and pulled up along the drive as it curved in front of the house. As she and Dee walked up to the door, she fully expected a butler or those other ones on stuffy British shows—a footman?—to open it and greet them.

Instead, Fletcher Ingram himself opened the door. Shock crashed into her nearly as hard as it had when she received his phone call that morning. In part because he was greeting them directly, and an entire other layer of shock came from his appearance. He looked…normal? He wore jeans and a blue polo shirt, and he was a lot thinner than he appeared on TV. A lot more gray in his hair too.

"Ah, welcome, welcome. Thank you for coming on such short notice." He sounded just as genuinely warm as he had on the phone, although it was hard to tell if that was from years of practice honing a particular image in the public eye or due to something more innate. It was certainly effective. She found herself instinctively liking the man. Not exactly trusting though. His public image always seemed a bit too clean, and she wasn't sure she could fully trust that sort of cleanliness.

"Yeah, of course, no problem. I'm Robbie, and this is Dee."

Ingram shook Dee's hand, then Robbie's, a firm, well-practiced handshake. He even did that politician thing where he laid his other hand on top of their clasped ones.

The interior of the house had that casual sort of opulence that spoke of wealth that the owners no longer even saw. It was also immaculate. No casual knickknacks, no forgotten bills left on a side table, no stray pieces of popcorn swept against the baseboard from where someone had thrown it too far past their target. Robbie would take a messy home full of personal touches over something like this any day.

He surprised her again by leading the way not to some sort of living or dining room or even a professional conference room that she was certain had to exist somewhere in this expanse but into the kitchen, where he produced a loaf of whole-grain bread and began pulling out sandwich fixings from the fridge. It was as odd to see as his casual clothing. Robbie vaguely suspected Fletcher Ingram might in fact be an actual, real human being.

"I guess we should tell you about the show?" Dee ventured.

Ingram glanced over. "If you'd like. I was going to start with perhaps tell me a bit about yourselves. Most of my life is in the public eye, so I'm not sure I have a lot to share about myself that you couldn't find out with a quick internet search, but I know very little about you. Just the bits Janelle told me. Your names, your interest in the theater, and such. Is your theater work what you do full-time?"

Robbie knew Dee had been enthused about Ingram's plans if elected, and she recalled agreeing with several key parts. Only she couldn't for the life of her remember, in that moment, what a single piece of his political platform was, but damn if she wouldn't vote for him. He was warm and personable and focused, like this was the only important thing he could possibly imagine doing right now.

But he was a politician, which was basically an actor on a different stage. Landerman had fooled her. She wasn't about to let another man do the same.

"No," she answered. "Dee and I actually own a bar."

He grinned with actual delight, a perfect smile that advertised thousands of dollars in orthodontics and whitening and possibly veneers. "In the city? What's it called?"

"Coda."

"Coda. Like in music?"

"Exactly." Dee nodded, smiling. The pun had been his idea. Coda, the part that brings a piece of music to an end, for a place owned by two people whose other work was about bringing things to an end. Including the musical notation for a coda—a circle with sniper-like crosshairs—in their logo still made Dee grin with a goofy sort of pride on a regular basis. "It's a karaoke bar."

Ingram laughed. "Clever. So theater is a side project, but music is still a significant part of your life then."

"Oh, very much," Robbie said, trying to figure out what answers he wanted from them. She didn't believe for a second all he wanted in exchange for thousands in lost rent revenue was to hear about their lives, but sure, she could play along. "I'm pretty sure Dee is made of music. He sings constantly and magnificently."

Despite this being absolutely nothing new, Dee ducked his head almost shyly. "Yeah, I sing, but Robbie is the one who wrote our show. The whole thing. Just—poof! Appeared from her brain like magic."

Pausing slathering Grey Poupon on the bread—because of course the man didn't have normal, plain yellow mustard—Ingram motioned between the two of them with the knife. "How long have you two been together?"

"Five years," Dee answered right as Robbie said, "We're not."

Their host raised an amused eyebrow. "If my wife, Cynthia, were alive, I would be in major trouble if I answered something like that."

"We've owned Coda together for five years," Robbie explained. "But we're business partners, nothing else. Well, obviously very good friends too."

She didn't want to sidetrack the conversation by getting into the concept of queerplatonic relationships. She had no clue if Ingram's nod meant he understood or he was indulging them while still thinking otherwise, but it didn't matter, because the next words out of his mouth were "All right, so two very good friends who love music decide to put on a show. Tell me about your musical."

Maybe this was it. The catch. He'd want something particular, like a show that espoused the key points of his political platform or some such, and when they didn't fulfill that, he'd have the perfect out to rescind his offer.

She looked him over, trying to read him the way she did everyone. Give her a few seconds and she'd have him figured out. Except they'd been here a couple minutes already, and all she'd gotten was that he was so rich he'd become oblivious to his own decadent surroundings, and he had a warm smile. Maybe she could read something in his proud-but-relaxed posture or the confidence of his movements as he assembled sandwiches as efficiently as any line cook. A few weeks ago, she probably would've come to several conclusions about him by now.

But she'd concluded things about Landerman. Look where that had gotten her.

Dee elbowed her sharply. "You gonna talk about the show or should I?"

"Oh, yeah, okay." She had no idea what Ingram wanted to hear in order to give them the theater, but saying nothing wasn't an option. She'd just have to wing it and hope it got them what they needed to keep the show alive. "All right, so there's this guy Charlie—that's who Dee plays—and he gets mistaken for someone else."

14

An Actual Human

COMPLETELY MISREADING LANDERMAN HAD RESULTED IN making an utter mess of the job, but thankfully, not being confident in her read of Fletcher Ingram hadn't stopped them from getting him to commit to everything she and Dee asked for: a test rehearsal of the Gillespie to ensure it met their needs, followed by—Dee had done the quick math to figure out their ask—*seven* weeks of renting the space for rehearsals and the show, all at the low cost they'd originally budgeted for the Oster Playhouse.

Riding that high, Robbie dove back into finding Landerman. Well, perhaps waded rather than dove. The waters were shallow. Her best hope was that Landerman would make an appearance at the Ajax Club.

He never showed.

She even went so far as to ask about him one night, just a casual, "Hey, my friend Xavier said he might join me at the tables sometime this week. He been in yet?"

No one had seen—or at least admitted to seeing—him.

Finally, Dee had convinced her to take a break long enough to attend the first rehearsal at the Gillespie Theater, insisting it would do Robbie some good.

Dee was right.

Of course.

Dee was always fucking right.

Just returning to the Gillespie—the Gilly, as Ingram apparently called it—lifted her mood. Sure, she'd messed up a job incredibly badly, and not only was her target still alive, but he was entirely in the wind. Still, life couldn't be *that* terrible when this gorgeous building existed.

Technically, this was a test rehearsal so they could decide whether they really wanted to put on the show here. As if they had any other options. If Ingram asked for something in return right after they accepted his offer, though, Robbie had wanted an out. Test rehearsal or not, the team was giving it their all trying to adapt to their new setting.

From a plush red velvet seat in the front row of the balcony, Robbie watched as the cast ran through the choreography that Nadine had revised to take advantage of the larger stage. It really was going to look spectacular when everything was ready.

After a half hour of increasingly improved practice, everyone dispersed for a break before they started on the next number. Dee, in his basketball shorts and sweat-stained tank, took a long swig from his water bottle, then walked to the center of the stage, inching slightly forward, then left. And then he found just the right spot.

An old theater like this had been built long before wireless microphones and the speakers now mounted on the walls. It had relied on the power of the performer's voices and carefully planned architecture.

Robbie leaned forward, arms on the balcony's railing, as the acoustics filled the theater with Dee's voice carrying the richness of "The Music of the Night."

Dee did love the classics.

The seat next to her made a slight metallic creak as it was folded down, but she didn't turn her attention away from the stage. Whoever had come in didn't say anything either, just sat silently as Dee sang a few more verses. He didn't do the whole song, just enough to appreciate the sound; then he stopped and grinned up at the arched ceiling fondly, like a proud parent whose child did something spectacular. Several cast members who'd sprawled over the first few rows of seats during their break clapped.

The sound of clapping next to her made Robbie finally turn to see Fletcher Ingram, possible, actual human, sitting next to her.

"I'll say, the Gilly is no Palais Garnier, but Dee would make a fantastic Phantom."

She didn't know the French name he'd spouted, but she did at least know the musical Dee's song was from. "If you say there's an underground lake beneath your theater, I'm sure you could convince him to take up residence."

Ingram laughed. "Alas, beneath the theater is just solid earth. I'm sure I could get a nice chandelier in here for him to break though."

Robbie had always found that scene in *Phantom of the Opera* inspiring. Now *that* was a brilliant way to take someone out. A chandelier crash, like an elevator shaft, was on her staged accident bucket list. Maybe someday.

"I hope you don't mind the company," he said. "I've been traveling the past few days, campaign duties and all that, but I got back this morning, and Janelle mentioned your troupe would be rehearsing today. I'll admit my curiosity got the best of me."

Once again, Robbie was struck by how incredibly charismatic the man was. Something about his demeanor could set her at ease in an instant if she wasn't careful. It was a dangerous and powerful trait. She could see how he could easily get anything he wanted in life. That could be the problem, not Robbie. It wasn't that she couldn't get a read on him, but the volume on his charisma was turned up so much, it overwhelmed the rest.

"It's not much today." Robbie shrugged. "Mostly blocking. We have to adjust everything to fit this theater. People first, so we're getting them good to go while we work on trying to convert the existing set pieces as well as redesigning the ones we hadn't started. Redoing the lighting plans. Adjusting the audio setup."

"That sort of thing isn't cheap."

Oddly, he reminded her a bit of James then, something in the way he could make a perfectly neutral comment, free of expectation. It was kind of alarming to have Fletcher Ingram exist in the same mental space as James. But the latter had taught her just how a smile could mask a cunning, vicious mind. Best not to forget that.

"No, it's not cheap. But it's worth it to be able to have the show here."

"I'd like to help if I can. The sets or something else. Pick some expenses you need covered, and I'll take care of it."

Robbie shook her head. "No, we can't do that. You're already renting the theater to us for a third of what you ought to. We can't make you pay for our adjustments too."

"You can," he replied firmly. "As you perhaps may have heard once or twice, maybe in passing, I have a bit of money." She laughed, and he smiled with satisfaction that his joke landed. "I'm an investor, Robbie. It's what I do, what I've been doing for my entire life. I'd like to invest in your show."

"Why?" She desperately needed to know what the cost of his patronage was. She hadn't been able to figure it out at lunch, and perhaps he subscribed to a "first taste is free" approach, letting them have the theater while genuinely expecting nothing in return, only to then up his offer and tack on some quid pro whatever. "Is it a PR thing? Politician donates money to the arts, politician supports local business, that sort of thing?"

He was silent for a long moment, blue-gray eyes staring down at the stage where the actors were walking through a scene. Maybe he was offended by her question, but if he was going to throw money at them, surely it wasn't unreasonable to ask whether he was using the connection for some sort of personal or political gain. Being used was fine. She just couldn't stand the thought of being used without knowing it.

When he spoke again, his warm charisma wasn't gone exactly, but it was tinged with something raw. "I was never much for musical theater growing up. Not much for theater at all, I suppose."

"What changed?"

"My daughter. She loved it all when she was little. The costumes, the singing. She'd watch bootlegs of Broadway shows with stars in her eyes. She'd play the cast recordings at full volume, dancing through the house. Sometimes she'd create her own little shows. Write playbills. Enlist the household staff for various roles. Always cast herself as the lead actress, of course. She'd invite us all to her opening night in the living room." He sighed. "Not that I saw many of them. I meant to. I always meant to. But inevitably some business deal would need reworking at the last minute, or I'd need to go out of town to inspect some property or program, and I'd always tell myself, 'Well, it's okay if I miss just this one.' Of course, it was never just one."

He sounded genuinely remorseful at having been a shitty dad. Robbie could give him credit for at least recognizing that. Her own certainly never had. Still...

"You have a daughter?"

She knew Ingram had a son, Nicholas. He wasn't a media darling like his father, but he didn't manage to avoid the spotlight altogether. If Ingram won the election, he would be handing complete control of all his business dealings to a third party to allow him to focus on his political work—and supposedly avoid conflicts of interest. But no one cared about a third party. Talk shows loved to bring up that plan during interviews—more specifically, the fact that Ingram appeared not to trust his son to take over the company. Most of the time, Ingram's son wasn't present for those segments, but he couldn't fade into obscurity either.

And although Robbie didn't know the details, she'd known Ingram's wife wasn't in the public eye either. Based on the man's comments over lunch, that was presumably because she wasn't alive anymore. She couldn't exactly follow him around on the campaign trail. Death did have that effect on people.

"Had," Ingram replied. "Alexandria. I'm surprised you don't know what happened. There was a time when it seemed everyone in the world couldn't stop talking about her. The media ate us alive."

"Recently?"

"No, no, it was years ago now." He paused, as if trying to recall how many years, but it was clearly something he'd never forgotten.

"Sixteen years. It was the end of a rocky second quarter." Belatedly, he clarified, "Middle of summer."

Robbie, who did not measure years by financial quarters, appreciated the addendum. Discretely counting out the years on her fingers, Robbie nodded. "Ah. Yeah, I'm afraid I didn't watch much TV at the time. I spent that whole summer on a breezy vacation in Kandahar."

A look of alarm crossed his face before he understood her meaning. "Military?"

"Army." She didn't elaborate. She never liked to elaborate. It was a thing she'd done, a chapter of her life long over. That was all.

"Right," he said after a long pause waiting for her to continue. "Long story short, Alexandria was kidnapped. We were given a ransom demand—exorbitant, but I would've robbed Fort Knox if that was what it took. I got the money together, and we paid."

"And yet I take it this story doesn't have a happy ending?" she asked as he paused, then cringed. Was that insensitive?

He didn't seem to care about her manners though. He shook his head, blinking away tears as he focused his gaze firmly on the stage below. She was pretty sure the tears weren't part of his performative persona. If they *were* an act, he deserved to be down on that stage next to Dee. "It does not. The exchange went…poorly. They ended up with the money. They… I mean, there was… I just…" He gave up his parade of unfinished sentences and shook his head. "I ended up losing my child."

"I'm sorry." She didn't know what it was like to lose a child, didn't know what it was like to have a child in the first place, but she did understand losing family. Understood trying to make the best choices you could and still winding up with nothing. She resisted the urge to pull her phone out right in front of him to look up news stories that would fill in the blanks between his words. That would probably be seen as rude, and she was making—well, not a friend exactly, but she was making some sort of acquaintance here.

Clearing his throat, he gave her an apologetic smile. "And I'm sorry for bringing the mood down. I believe this tangent was a roundabout way of me saying I'd quite like to invest in your production, and I won't take no for an answer."

Nostalgia and misty-eyed feelings were all well and good, but Robbie still didn't trust that Ingram wasn't going to ask for something in return. That didn't mean he had to set the terms though.

"How about in exchange, we let you use Coda—our bar—for a campaign event, no charge?" She flicked a glance at the grandness of the Gillespie. He didn't need a dark karaoke bar and a neon parrot. A trade had to mean something he needed. "Did we mention it's a queer bar? It might help you connect to a voter demographic you don't normally have access to."

Ingram's startled look lasted a split second before it turned calculating and then back to his warm charisma. He stuck out his hand. "You have a deal, Robbie. Please let Janelle know what you need for the show, and she'll route it my way."

Already she regretted bringing Coda into this. What was she thinking, offering up her and Dee's sacred space to a guy she knew nothing about? But she shook his hand and said, "Sure. Thanks."

He stood. "I have to leave for a meeting across town now. Thank you for allowing me to impose on your time."

"You're throwing boatloads of money our way. Impose anytime you want." Robbie heard her own words and kind of wanted to wince. Instead, she added, "Even without the money, it was nice talking to you. You're not what I expected you to be like."

"Oh?"

"I mean, I know your name. Everyone knows your name. I see your campaign posters, your TV spots, your radio ads. You've built an image."

"You think that image is false?"

"No, not exactly. But it turns out you're...human, for lack of a better word." She shrugged apologetically, but she didn't know how else to phrase it.

Ingram smiled. "I'm fairly certain that's a compliment, and if it's not, please don't disillusion me. It's been a pleasure speaking with you. Please convey to Dee my highest praise for his voice. I'm looking forward to seeing what you two create here."

Robbie nodded her thanks and watched him pick his way down the row of seats toward the exit. The second Ingram vanished through the doors to the stairwell, Robbie tugged her phone out of her pocket and ran a search for "Alexandria Ingram ransom drop."

"Oh shit," she muttered as she skimmed a news article, trying to pick out key words here and there without having to read the whole long-ass wall of text. She skimmed the missing persons description—age, hair color, eye color, along with details like a birthmark on the right shoulder, last seen in overalls and a pink T-shirt—before skipping further in the article until the word *blood* jumped out at her. She highlighted the paragraph and copied it to her text-to-speech app, keeping the volume relatively low so she didn't disturb the rehearsal below.

"Officials say they believed two kidnappers were involved," the app read out in its robotic monotone. "On the ransom call, Ingram was instructed to bring cash to the St. Charles overpass, where he was to drop the bag off the edge. He was told his daughter would then be left at the southeast corner of Sheldon Park. Undercover FBI and local police were in place to capture whoever dropped off Alexandria in the park. However, an FBI spokesperson reports that Ingram received a second call after dropping the bag of cash. In this second call, he was told the presence of law enforcement changed the situation and that he should go to the north end of the park instead. Upon arriving, Ingram and law enforcement found blood and a handwritten missive. The exact text has not been shared publicly, but the note is described as scolding Ingram for 'not following the rules.' In a press conference held the following day, an FBI spokesperson stated that in light of evidence found in the park, they are now treating the case as a homicide, and their investigative efforts will now include a search to locate the body of Alexandria Ingram."

Some more digging yielded a long-form article written on the five-year anniversary of Alexandria's disappearance. Robbie was fundamentally opposed to the entire concept of long-form journalism, but she scrolled through and used text-to-speech on the pull quotes and captions on the photos. Eventually, it had been leaked that they didn't just find a bit of blood in the park. Estimates were in the range of a couple pints, and Robbie how no idea how much blood a child had, but a couple pints would leave a full-grown adult worse for wear.

Robbie was glad she hadn't jumped right into searching for this when Ingram was still here on the balcony with her. Even that little bit of a news article seemed like it would be pretty traumatic for him to listen to, especially since speaking about it in even the vaguest of terms had been so hard for him. In her searching, she'd found his wife had died a few years after his daughter, his big happy family rapidly dwindling to just him and his only son.

She still wasn't sure how she felt about Ingram overall as a person, but she did have sympathy for this one piece of his life. He still got to be rich and successful and powerful, so she didn't feel totally sorry for him, but even with his very high highs, he'd clearly hit some pretty rock-bottom lows in his life too. It really did make him seem like a real person. Robbie didn't know what kind of person or whether she could trust him, but with him involving himself in the production of their show, she suspected this hadn't been the only opportunity she'd get to form an opinion.

15

FML

MR. CLARK WAS DUE TO RETURN IN JUST OVER A WEEK. ROBBIE had run down every single lead she or Dee could think of and still had absolutely no clue where to find Landerman.

For the moment, Ingram's generosity had gotten the show off its deathbed, but finances were still tight. Even before the show, they'd begun to rely more on contract money to keep Coda afloat over the past few years. Both Robbie and Dee had gotten swept up in the show, though, taking fewer jobs than normal. She couldn't afford to pay back Mr. Clark's deposit. It had been enough to resolve their payroll issue, but their staff had picked up and cashed their paychecks promptly.

She should've refunded Mr. Clark the moment she lost Landerman and couldn't finish the job. James always said a good contractor never took money for failure. But she'd been so determined to fix it, to find Landerman and get back on track. All she needed was a little more time. Which she'd now had and still gotten nowhere.

That wasn't entirely accurate. Yesterday, she'd gotten a hit from the news alert she'd set up. A theft at Reevesburg Museum of Arts and Culture. Details had been sparse, the word "forthcoming" used a lot, but she knew. It hit like a gut punch. It had to be him. Before, she could make excuses to herself that Landerman could've fled anywhere. He might not be in this state or even this country anymore. No, instead, he was in the city, probably had been the whole goddamn time, and she still couldn't find him.

For a minute, her spirits had gone up. She'd had Dee ask around his shadier contacts for information on thieves involved in the museum heist. So far, either nobody knew anything or nobody was willing to talk. Another failure, surprise, surprise.

Robbie needed to find Landerman in the next nine days, or she needed to figure out a way to talk Mr. Clark into letting her keep the ten grand he'd already given her. Neither problem was solving itself, and no, that wasn't driving her absolutely up the walls. She was great. Five by five.

"You could've just given Marisol the night off. It's Saturday night. She's worked, like, five Saturdays in a row. I'm sure she'd love to have the night off. People love time off."

Robbie was on a yoga mat on the living room floor, medicine ball held in front of her chest. With a deep breath, she started her next set of sit-ups. She was in nowhere near as good a shape as she'd been when she left the army, but she hadn't entirely slacked off for twelve years. She'd just slacked off for the past three weeks or so, and dear god, it was definitely showing. Her abs were already displeased, and she wasn't even halfway through her standard routine.

"She needs the money, Robs," Dee said wearily as he lounged comfortably on his couch. "If she wanted the night off, she knows she just has to ask, and we'd say yes. But people who have jobs… They do that for a reason. Let her work."

Focusing on her breathing instead of replying, Robbie kept going until she finished off the set. One more set to go. But first: "Yeah, but I could just pay her for her hours anyway, and she wouldn't even have to show up. Everybody wins."

"Robbie, you've already cleaned the entire bar top to bottom twice, the entire apartment once. You alphabetized the liquor downstairs by brand name, which I'm sure absolutely no one will thank you for. I don't know what you did to the pantry—"

"Also alphabetized."

"—but I spent twenty minutes trying to find a jar of peanut butter today. I'm sorry this whole Landerman-Clark thing has you stressed, but I just need you to chill."

"Chill? I'm fine. I'm totally fine, Dee. I just had some free time."

Dee snorted, but he gave up trying to argue, instead settling back into the battalion of pillows on his couch and waiting for her to finish her last set of sit-ups. When she was done, she set the medicine ball off to the side and rocked upright, hugging her knees.

"Oh, by the way, I saw you hadn't finished putting away your laundry, so I did that for you and also washed another load. I'll put that away when the dryer goes off."

"So chill," he murmured.

A knock sounded at the door—the internal one that led down to the bar rather than the private entrance out the back of the kitchen. Robbie scrambled to her feet. Far more slowly, Dee stood and strolled after her with an air of lazy curiosity rather than any actual urgency.

Marisol, who could have had the night off, stood on the landing in her Coda T-shirt and black sweatpants. For about six months after opening, Robbie and Dee had required their employees to follow a somewhat fancier dress code, but Robbie had argued that as long as they wore something decent on the upper half of their body, it didn't matter what was going on behind the bar. Everyone got to be comfortable, and Robbie got to be a really nice boss.

"You want to cut out early?" Robbie asked hopefully. Saturday nights in the bar were hectic, the kind of noisy bustle that drowned out the noise in your head reminding you of the utter lack of ideas on how to resolve your multiple failures.

Marisol raised an eyebrow. "Um, no? There's not one but two bachelorette parties plus some sort of birthday shindig going on. I'm absolutely rolling in tips, and I've had five different women slip me their number."

Damn. Robbie wasn't about to ruin *that* for her.

"I do need you to come down though."

Dee sighed dramatically behind her as Robbie perked up. "Yeah?"

"There's a guy here. He's, uh, asking for the manager."

"*You* are a manager," Dee pointed out. Marisol was their most senior employee.

"Yeah, but he's specifically asking for Robbie."

Fuck. Was Mr. Clark back this early? That wouldn't do. Or maybe it would. Maybe she could at least get everything over with so she could stop feeling so restless.

Dee asked, "By name?"

"Well, no. But he described her pretty accurately. Said he's not leaving until he speaks with her, and he's willing to stay all night." Marisol sighed. "He's really harshing the vibes. Can you just come deal with him?"

Mr. Clark knew Robbie's name. If he was here asking for her, he could have specified. Describing her by appearance alone was odd.

She glanced back at Dee, who shrugged. "Maybe put a shirt on at least, but I suppose you should go check it out. I'll come with."

Robbie glanced down. All right, so their dress code was casual, but it wasn't hot pants and sports bra casual, even if those were entirely appropriate for her planned evening of working out in the late summer heat and humidity that refused to dissipate. A piece of fabric hit her face. A black T-shirt, just like Marisol's, with the Coda logo on the front in electric blue. She tugged it on and gestured to Marisol. "Lead the way."

The bar was absolutely packed, even for a Saturday night. But people loved fall weddings, so there was no shortage of bachelorettes this time of year. Someone was on stage doing a passable Shania Twain rendition.

They shouldered their way through the people dancing in every open space and made it to the safety of the bar. Eloise and Gabriella were engaged in an impressive tango, moving fluidly back and forth between taking orders and mixing drinks. Eloise wore a half apron overflowing with cash from tips. Marisol waved a hand toward the far end of the bar before throwing herself into their dance, smoothly taking a highball glass from Gabriella's hands and turning to fill it with ice.

Robbie and Dee squeezed past and made their way to where Marisol had directed.

"Fuck me."

Robbie stopped dead in her tracks. Dee ran smack into her. He peeked around her to see what caused her reaction.

"Oh, shit, is that…"

"Xavier Landerman," Robbie finished. Her target, the man she was supposed to have killed by now, or at least no later than next Monday, sat at the last seat at the bar, back against the wall, wearing a yellow Sex Pistols T-shirt and casually sipping what looked to be an appletini. His still messy white-blond hair glowed from one of the black lights, and the bustle and motion of the bar were reflected in blurry duplicate in his glasses. A half-amused smile curved pleasantly on his lips as he watched the girl finish conveying Shania's thoughts on feeling like a woman.

Dee shoved Robbie forward. Landerman's attention shifted as they approached, and that smile completely died in an instant.

"Can I help you?" Robbie said stiffly.

"This wasn't what I was expecting."

"That makes two of us."

"Three," Dee mumbled.

Landerman gestured out toward the bar. "No, I mean this. Lesbian karaoke bar. I was expecting maybe some sort of shabby little office, but not this."

"Well, I wasn't expecting to see you at all."

He shrugged. "What can I say? Curiosity got the best of me."

"Definitely should avoid ever letting that happen," Dee said dryly, elbowing Robbie in the ribs. She wasn't sure if this was better or worse than Dee taking over the stage and singing "I told you so, I told you so" for five minutes straight, which seemed a viable option at this point.

"Am I correct in assuming your name isn't Veronica Werner?"

"Seems likely, doesn't it?"

"But my initial assumption that you were some sort of detective or PI was wrong. I can tell that much. Yet you obviously do more than just listen to drunk ladies belting off-key."

Robbie opened her mouth to answer—not *everyone* was terribly off-key, and they had some very talented regulars—but Dee cut her off. "Why don't we talk somewhere private?"

Landerman eyed them suspiciously.

"This is our business," Dee pointed out. "We're not going to do you any harm here, all right? Just find your way to the back door, and we'll talk."

With a nod, Landerman finished his appletini and stood. He began maneuvering his way through the crowd, and Robbie and Dee pushed their way past the chaotic flurry of their three bartenders.

Given that they had far fewer people to get past, they pushed their way out into the back alley well before Landerman.

"What are you doing?" Robbie hissed. "We aren't here to make friends."

"He found you, okay? We can't just leave him in there and pretend he doesn't know about us. We need to sort this out, and that's certainly not going to happen in the midst of some forty or fifty drunken customers."

"You could've just told him to leave. You didn't have to invite him to hang out."

"I didn't *have* to do anything, Robbie. Landerman is your problem. Whatever he's up to, whatever he wants from you right now, it's on you."

Robbie threw up her hands. "It's not like I invited him here!"

"No, but you did putz around playing detective. You know how much I absolutely hate to invoke his name, but what would James say? If you'd just killed Landerman when you were supposed to, none of this would be happening."

Robbie opened her mouth to reply with some sort of retort she hadn't yet come up with, but she and Dee both froze, eyes locked on each other, at the sound of the door latching closed.

Very softly, in a wavering voice, Xavier Landerman said, "You're going to kill me?"

If this disaster of a situation had any silver lining, it was that at least Dee had now fucked up too. Robbie always felt mildly better in any situation where she wasn't the sole fuckup in the room. Or dimly lit back alley, as it were.

Robbie turned and faced her target, this twentysomething who now *really* looked like a kid as he stared at the two of them in horror. His gaze darted around the alley, lingering on the lamppost with its flickering light, then on the dumpster pressed up against the back wall. His hand hovered against the handle of the back door, presumably because he'd been too distracted on his way out to notice the sign warning the door was an emergency exit only and would automatically lock behind him.

"No," she answered. In a fit of honesty, she added, "Definitely not tonight at least."

Unsurprisingly, he didn't seem reassured.

Dee pointed at the door behind him. "Our business." He shifted to point toward the top floor of the building. "Our home. We're not that sloppy."

This also didn't seem to reassure him.

Robbie did a quick inventory of the alleyway's contents, spied an old five-gallon bucket, and flipped it upside down to serve as a seat. Dee followed her lead and perched on a stack of wood pallets.

Landerman didn't move.

"You know anyone named Mr. Clark?" Robbie asked.

He shook his head. "I don't think so."

Of course not. It was obviously an alias anyway. "Right. Things are a bit unbalanced, but of the two of us—three of us—only one has committed a crime so far." By "so far," she meant recently, like very recently. On her part, she was going with "so far tonight." Landerman, she went a little further back. "I'm sure the Museum of Arts and Culture would love to know who was behind their recent theft."

He stiffened. It was a good thing his game was blackjack and not poker. Given her current track record, there had been a solid possibility she'd been wrong about the museum heist, that it had been pulled off by someone else entirely. But her initial instinct was right. She'd obviously hit her mark. Well, poor choice of words there.

"I'm not intending to turn you in or anything. I'm just saying I've got something on you, and I'd like you to keep that in mind as I tell you a few things."

"Is this a good idea?" Dee murmured, voice pitched just for Robbie.

"I think we left good ideas behind a while ago. This is what I've got. And maybe he knows more than he's telling." To Landerman, in a regular tone, Robbie said, "A man calling himself Mr. Clark approached me a few weeks ago. He offered a large sum of money in exchange for me killing you."

"Why?"

"I didn't ask."

Landerman pressed his back against the door and slid down to sit on the rocky pavement. His shaking hands were tangled up in that haystack hair of his. But he looked up at her with something surprisingly fierce in his eyes. "A random stranger, someone you don't know at all, approaches you and offers you money to kill another random stranger, who you also don't know at all, and you just say yes and never ask why?"

She knew he meant to describe the current situation and that it could describe pretty much her entire contract career, but she was struck by how much his description reminded her of that very first day that James had walked into the diner. A man she'd never met approached her. He offered money to kill someone else she'd never met. And she absolutely never asked why, not then, not ever. More than once, James had alluded to that being one of the main reasons he picked her. Not being curious made her not just good at this job but truly excellent. Until now.

"That's about the sum of it, yes."

"How much?"

Robbie blinked. "I'm sorry?"

"How much were you going to get paid? Like, was I at least expensive? I'd be pissed if you were going to kill me, and it wasn't even for that much money. More pissed than I already am, I mean."

Dee cackled loudly, and Robbie cut him an annoyed glance.

"Twenty."

Landerman's eyes widened. "You were going to kill me for *twenty dollars*? What the fuck, man."

The wooden pallets clattered as Dee nearly fell off, doubled over in silent laughter. At least someone was having fun.

"Thousand," Robbie clarified. "Twenty *thousand*. Actually, I already got half. I get the other half when you're dead. To be honest, kinda poor life choice, you showing up here. I'd lost you entirely. I was going to have to refund Mr. Clark."

The kid scrambled to his feet. His gaze cut to Dee. "You said you wouldn't kill me here."

"Relax. She's not going to kill you tonight. She'll probably just follow you home and then kill you in a couple days. It'll be fine."

"It will *not* be fine," he retorted.

"It's not like you're going to know the difference," Dee pointed out.

"Look. Ten grand is what you get if you finish the job, right? What if I give you that much?"

Robbie raised her eyebrows. "You just…have that lying around?"

Landerman held up his hands and waggled his fingers. "Thief, remember?"

"Right."

He seemed to gain back some of the smooth confidence he'd had earlier in the bar. "Okay, how's this? I'll pay you ten thousand to not kill me, at least for a little bit while I try to figure out who your Mr. Clark is and why he wants me dead."

"He's supposed to meet me next Monday, and I'm supposed to show proof that you're dead."

"Just don't kill me before then, all right? If I haven't learned anything about him by then, I'm fair game. Not that I'm going to make it easy on you. I already shook you once. I can do it again."

How was Robbie supposed to resist a challenge like that? She could keep track of Landerman's whereabouts, get the money from him, and still take him out after, winding up with both his and Clark's money added together. A win for everyone. Except Landerman, obviously, but as Dee had pointed out, it wasn't like he'd know any different.

Standing up from her bucket stool, she walked toward him, rolling her eyes as he flinched, and held out her hand. "You're on."

He hesitated before he reached out and shook on it.

Then he turned, bolted down the alley, and disappeared onto the street beyond.

From behind Robbie, Dee remarked, "Well, I for one think you're making absolutely stellar decisions lately, and I can't wait to see how this plays out."

16

World Peace

ROBBIE WAS FULLY CAPABLE OF MAKING STELLAR DECISIONS. She even used that capacity most of the time. Or at least some of the time.

All right, so her deal with Landerman perhaps wasn't one of them. Taking Ingram's offer and moving the play into the Gilly apparently wasn't either, she learned, as Priya Nayak, their set designer, took over the production team meeting with an impassioned rant about what exactly it meant to change the entire venue and expect the sets to magically adjust.

Dee had a look on his face that told her he wasn't even going to try to wade into the fight, not the least because Priya was his ex, or the closest approximation he had of an ex. Things hadn't ended badly, but Dee did put extra effort into not pissing Priya off. He and Robbie wanted the best people for this show, and it wasn't like you could expect to assemble an entirely queer production team in this city—couldn't assemble any large group of queer people in any city, probably—without someone being someone else's ex.

Robbie waited for an opening and finally managed to get in,

"We don't expect magic, Priya. I know this is a huge ask. It doesn't need to be perfect."

"Of course it needs to be perfect. I'm not letting my name get printed in playbills and be associated with some half-assed production. And I've put too much work into this not to have my name there. You see my problem?"

"Absolutely."

"Are you patronizing me?"

Holding up her hands in surrender, Robbie said, "Really not trying to. I know you weren't here at last week's meeting, but I'm going to tell you the same thing I told Julia then. I trust in your vision."

"Hear, hear," Julia chimed in, clinking a fork against her mimosa glass. If they were all going to be working on a Sunday morning, Robbie and Dee had felt serving up free drinks from the bar was the least they could do. Which was incidentally also why they were sitting in a corner of Coda instead of around the kitchen table upstairs. Robbie had a strict, unspoken rule that absolutely no alcohol entered the apartment. She believed Dee without question when he said owning a bar wasn't a threat to his sobriety, but the apartment was supposed to be the one place both of them were safe. Untouchable. Better to keep everything down here, solidly on this side of the boundary between their home and their business.

Priya dropped back into her seat, picking up her own mimosa glass from the table. "It's not my vision that's the problem. I'm sorry I was out of town last week—"

"You have a life. It's totally fine."

"—but I did finally have a chance to do a walk-through at the Gilly yesterday. I've done work there before, but it was years and years ago. I forgot how fucking grand the space was. It's a nice place, you guys, don't get me wrong. I just… I spent so much time on the ground plan for the Oster Playhouse, you know?"

Summer reached over and squeezed her hand sympathetically. "I feel you. The new theater is so nice, but god, I've got an entirely new tech system to try to map my previous work onto. Pretty sure that's an actual nightmare I've had before opening nights in the past."

"Aw, shit, Summer. I didn't know you felt that way," Robbie said.

"Oh, everyone feels this way a bit. I'll bet even Dee does, a little."

Robbie turned her head to where he sat on her right. He shrugged reluctantly. "It's fine, Robs. It's a bit of a hot mess right now, changing so many things all at once, trying not to push the opening further back than we already have, adapting to the new space. Everyone's had some frustrations."

"You never said." Robbie tried to mask the twinge of hurt, but it was Dee. Dee always knew.

"It's not a big deal," he repeated. Priya coughed, but he ignored her and continued. "The fact is everyone was absolutely killing it with the preparations before, and if everyone had been a bit less competent in their jobs, things wouldn't have been so well-developed and perfectly fit to the Playhouse. Everyone's too good at their jobs. So let Priya rant all she needs to. Let Summer have whatever frustrations she has going on. We'll get the show together. We will. And because they're working on it, it will wind up being perfect, one way or another."

Oh, he was good. Julia clinked her glass again. Summer lifted her own. "I'll drink to that."

Everyone leaned in to tip their glasses together. Even Priya looked mollified.

Maybe Robbie could take lessons from Dee in the art of pep talks because *damn*. Where mere minutes ago, Priya had been a few seconds away from nuclear detonation, she now had a spark of excited anticipation in her eyes.

"Wait, I totally forgot to mention something," Robbie cut in. Dee wasn't the only one who could save the day.

All eyes turned to her, like they were all expecting her to be an absolute buzzkill. That light, bubbly sensation fluttered in her chest. She was *not* going to be a buzzkill. She was going to be a…whatever the opposite of that was. Buzz-giver? Buzz-maker? Oprah?

"You all know the theater is owned by Fletcher Ingram, right? He's giving us a discount on renting the space because he wants to support the arts."

Julia nodded. "Dee mentioned. Seems wild. A guy that rich and famous being interested in our little show?"

"But he is. In fact, he dropped in on Friday night's rehearsal for a bit. Very impressed with everything. And you know how rich people show their appreciation for things?" Robbie grinned. She fixed her gaze on Priya so she could enjoy the woman's face as she said, "He told me he's 'investing' in the show, starting with funding all the changes we need to make for the sets. Those ideas Summer mentioned? Any of them that were off the table because they were too expensive? Put them the hell back on the table."

Priya's delight was perfect. Not only was she no longer about to go nuclear, but she was now grinning with a smile bright enough to bring about world peace. She leaned in and began throwing out ideas, pulling a notebook from the bag slung over the back of her chair and starting to sketch things out, getting input from the rest of the production team on how to integrate her new set pieces with everyone else's vision.

There. Robbie *did* make stellar decisions sometimes.

After a moment's thought, she casually stood and did a lap around the table, refilling everyone's glasses. Dee caught her eye as she passed and leaned over to whisper low enough only she could hear. "You didn't tell me Ingram committed that much. He really said he'd pay for everything?"

"Well, no." Robbie chewed her lip. "Actually, he said to choose one thing and he'd cover the costs, but I can try asking for more if it comes to that"

"Uh-huh. Not going to crash this moment for everyone, but you probably should've asked him *before* that speech you just gave everyone."

Well, all her decisions couldn't be great. She shouldn't have overpromised, but come on. Look how happy they all were now. Excited and enthusiastic about her dream again.

Maybe she wouldn't have to ask Ingram for more anyway. After all, she'd have the double payout of the Landerman job to bridge the gap between what he'd offered and what she'd just promised.

In the music room, Robbie sat idly plunking out a tune on the piano while the recording app on her phone kept track of anything she might want to remember later. Sometimes a tune came together, a few notes or maybe a bit more, but Robbie had found it hard to predict when those moments happened, so she recorded everything. The recording automatically paused as her phone started buzzing with an incoming call.

"Yeah?"

"Manners, Robbie," James said coolly.

"Sorry, sir." It came out more reflex than anything. She tried to think of the polite way to phrase her next bit. "Uh, so what can I do for you?"

Seemed better manners than "What do you want?"

"The job, Robbie. Is it done? It's been over two weeks. I taught you better than to drag your feet."

Yet she'd dragged her feet long enough on Landerman to turn the job into an absolute shit show. She had no idea how to explain that mess to James. Losing her target? Having her target find her? Making a *deal* with her target? Where was she even going to start?

Oh right. She didn't have to start anywhere. He wasn't calling about *that* job. He was calling about the Lynch job. Tree, river.

Her stomach dropped. She did finish it, didn't she? Yeah, the timing had been a little off, but the branch hit Lynch. She did go under. Any number of things could've happened when Robbie wasn't paying attention, though, and focus hadn't been her strong suit that day.

Normally, Robbie would've confirmed the death the next day, but Fletcher Ingram himself had called her first thing the next morning. It had been a weird couple of days.

"The Lynch job is done. Last weekend. No complications." It was most likely true, right? She needed it to be true—needed the Lynch job to remind her what success looked like at the same time as she was staring down the barrel of the biggest fuckup of her career.

"Yes, I saw the newspaper."

Thank god. Somehow the relief felt even tighter than the worry though. He only ever called when he wanted something.

"Not the point," he continued. "I know you're independent now, but this job was a favor to me. I expected to be kept informed."

Robbie cocked her head. "I sent you notice right after it was done. Same as always."

"Ah. The number you used to use is no longer in service."

Well, how was she supposed to know that? No point arguing with James though. It wasn't even something she'd considered or tried before meeting Dee, but when she did get around to attempting to argue, James had shut her down so fast, she never bothered again. "Sorry about that then."

"Not to worry, Robbie. Your mistake is understandable."

"I guess that's why I haven't gotten paid?"

He clicked his tongue in that irritated way of his. "Your cut will get to you soon enough."

"Thanks. Anything else?"

If she had to stay on the phone any longer, she wasn't sure she'd manage to avoid confessing to the whole Landerman fiasco. This was James. At one time, he would've been the person she asked for help if things went wrong on a job. Went wrong at all in her life, probably. But as James had reminded her, she was independent now. She didn't rely on him. If she made a mess, she'd clean it up. If she needed help, she had Dee.

"No, that's all. Thank you for your assistance on this. I knew I could count on you."

"Yeah, all right."

"Manners, Robbie," he scolded. "Have a good day."

Dee popped his head in as Robbie hung up. "Did I hear you talking?"

"James." Robbie wiggled the phone as an explanation.

Frowning and scrunching up his nose as he always did at the mention of James, he gave a curt nod. "Didn't tell him about the Landerman deal, did you?"

"Of course not." The temptation had only lasted a few seconds.

"Good. You don't need him nosing in. You're smart, Robs. You can sort this all on your own."

The vote of confidence meant a lot. Robbie might not have believed someone else saying those words, but Dee never sugar-coated things, never lied to spare her feelings. Neither did James, of course, but it was different.

"So, uh, if you're done in here, what're your thoughts on picking up Thai before we head over to the Gillespie?" Dee asked.

Robbie pushed back from the piano bench and shoved her phone in her pocket. "I'll get my boots."

17
Nobody Asked for This

THE REST OF SUNDAY WAS SO FULL OF PREPARATIONS FOR THE show, Robbie barely had a moment to dwell on the unusual and frankly rather questionable deal she'd struck with Landerman, a welcome relief after spending every day worrying over the fact that she'd lost him. Enthusiasm carried the team meeting two hours past its planned end. Then on to costume fittings in the afternoon, an orientation meeting with the band in the evening, and around eight p.m., Dee arrived with the truck carrying all the existing set pieces he'd picked up from the Oster Community Playhouse. By the time he and Robbie finished unloading everything, inventorying each piece against Priya's newly made list of what was fine as it was and what would need to be remade or modified, Robbie was exhausted.

When they arrived home, she made a gourmet dinner for herself and Dee, which entailed dumping some tortilla chips on a plate, throwing shredded cheese on top, and microwaving for thirty seconds. It was a masterpiece.

And then she went to her room and fell face-first into bed fully clothed and didn't move for nine hours.

It took her probably a solid minute—although it could've been five seconds or five minutes or anything in between—to register the sound of polite knocking. She sat up stiffly, back aching from her ill-advised sleeping position, and cocked her head. It wasn't the inner door down to the bar. Someone was knocking on the outer door, the one that led to the back patio and the steep metal stairs outside.

She dragged herself up. By the time she made it to the kitchen, Dee was shuffling out of his room too. He tilted his head questioningly as he tied the sash on his lightweight robe, but she just shrugged.

"Yeah, yeah, I'm coming," she told the knocking as it resumed after a brief pause.

After punching the code into the alarm keypad on the wall, she undid the chain, the two dead bolts, and the knob's regular lock and pulled the door open.

Xavier Landerman stood before her.

"Oh good. I was beginning to think this was the wrong place." Robbie wasn't convinced he'd been incorrect. "But your friend did say you lived above the bar, and I saw the stairs, and it didn't look like there was more than one place up here, so I figured this had to be it."

All this was delivered in the bright, friendly tone one might use with a good friend. It was not the tone you used to speak to the person you were paying to not kill you some thirty-six hours after they admitted to being paid by someone else to kill you in the first place.

"Can I help you?" She tried to make her own tone imply that the answer ought to be no, but he didn't take the hint.

"Yes, actually. I'd like you to tell me more about Mr. Clark."

"I don't know anything about Mr. Clark."

Landerman shrugged. "Well, you've met him, and I haven't. Obviously, your knowledge, however small, trumps mine. So I'd like to ask you some questions."

"I..." Robbie wasn't even sure where to take that sentence. She wasn't sure what to do with any of this.

"Come on in," Dee said from behind her in a voice that sounded suspiciously like it contained laughter. "I'll make us some coffee."

Landerman pushed past Robbie. "Thanks. You need help with anything?"

"You're very sweet, but no. I'm entirely capable of making a single pot of coffee all on my own."

Robbie shut the door slowly. Turning around, she watched the absurd scene: Dee moving through his practiced morning routine, pulling out a bag of beans and the coffee grinder while Landerman set a messenger bag on the dining table and plopped down into one of the chairs. Into *Robbie's* usual chair. He pulled a laptop out and ping-ponged his gaze between the two of them. "Can I get your Wi-Fi password?"

She should've killed him when she had the chance.

Dee, goddamn Dee, rattled off the password. Robbie was pretty sure he was being overly nice to get a rise out of her, a form of subtle teasing for fucking up this job so badly. Landerman didn't notice a thing, just thanked him and then looked over at Robbie.

"Care to take a seat?" He gestured at the chair next to him like this was his home and she was the guest.

Reluctantly, she sat, leaving a chair in between them because, all appearances to the contrary, this was her house, and she was *not* going to let him tell her where to sit. "Fine. Why are you here?"

"What can you tell me about this Mr. Clark? Anything at all. What did he look like?"

Robbie shrugged.

"Please tell me you did at least meet the person who paid you to kill me, right?"

"Yeah, but it was in the bar. It was dark. He intentionally sat in the darkest corner in the place. I know that he was a little taller than me, at least while we were seated. Um. Light hair, kinda boring-looking. I don't know. I don't really pay much attention to men's faces. They aren't my thing."

Dee snorted.

That ridiculous, eager light in Landerman's eyes dimmed a little. "All right. Anything else distinctive? An accent?"

"Nope."

"Clothes?"

"He had some."

"Aw, come on, give the kid something." Dee came over and ruffled Landerman's hair like they were old friends. "He's trying here."

Landerman turned a vivid shade of pink.

This was painful.

He cleared his throat. "Okay, how about the money? How did he pay you?"

"Wire transfer."

The kid made a triumphant sound. "We can trace that!"

Even Dee seemed surprised, glancing at Robbie with an unspoken question. She shook her head. It wasn't an avenue she'd pursued. To be entirely honest, the effort she'd put into finding Mr. Clark had primarily consisted of a quick call to Darlene, who said Mr. Clark had been referred by a forger who Robbie and

Dee and many other contractors worked with. Darlene hadn't dug much further.

Instead of digging deeper in that direction, Robbie had dedicated most of her time to trying to identify and locate Landerman. Well, she'd located him. In her own fucking kitchen.

"What's your name?"

He looked up. "Xavier Landerman. But you knew that, or you wouldn't have found me."

"Xavier Landerman doesn't exist. What's your *real* name?"

"Can we leave it at that? It's a name I've been using for a little while now, so I'm fine if you just stick with that."

Robbie shook her head. "Nope. I want to know who I'm working with."

"Seriously? This from the person who has so far managed to tell me that Mr. Clark—not his real name either—was boring-looking and wore clothes." Fine, so he had a point there. "And might I also call attention to the fact that neither of you has given me your name."

"I'm Dee. She's Robbie."

"Dee!"

"What? He's literally in our home. It's not like him knowing our names is going to tell him anything more personal about us at this point."

Fine.

Robbie resumed her baseline glare in the general direction of Landerman, who nodded a brief acknowledgment of the introduction "My name… You can call me X. Or Xavier. Either is fine."

She glanced down at his T-shirt, which today had the letter X going up in flames. Seemed apt.

He was busy typing away with remarkable speed. Something about him was familiar, like she'd seen him in a different context, but she couldn't place it. He'd looked young when she'd seen him at the Ajax Club. The rest of the time she'd followed him, she hadn't been so close. The club had been relatively low light, nothing like the bright morning sun streaming in from the window and illuminating his face.

"How old are you?" she asked.

He glanced up from his computer. "Um, like twenty-five?"

"Very convincing."

"I'm twenty-five, okay."

Sure he was. Robbie bit back a retort that he looked closer to twelve or some other overexaggeration of his youth. His face still had a bit of residual softness he hadn't yet grown out of, and she would bet he couldn't grow a beard if his life depended on it. Everything about him felt out of place in their kitchen. Everything about him felt out of place period.

Dee set mugs of coffee in front of each of them, then brought the milk and a half-full, two-pound bag of sugar to the table as well, pushing a vase out of the way to make room. See, Landerman—Xavier—didn't belong in the same space as the bright sunflowers Dee had bought at the farmers market over the weekend. It just wasn't right.

Though to Xavier's credit, he reached over and dumped a mountain of sugar into his coffee and a bit of creamer. Good choice, but Robbie didn't like knowing her target's taste in coffee was similar to her own. She didn't want him to be similar at all.

She couldn't imagine what James would say if he'd ever seen her sitting down for coffee in her own home with a target. He would have a heart attack. Which, to be fair, he'd already had once, but at least that time wasn't her fault.

Xavier swiveled the laptop around to face her before leaning forward so he could still see some sort of form up on the screen. He pointed to two of the fields. "I need your account number, the one that received the money, and down here, the date when the transfer went through." After glancing up and seeing the look on her face, he sighed. "I'm not going to steal your money or anything. This doesn't give me access like that. It'll just let me trace the transfer itself."

That account didn't have any money left to steal anyway. If she wanted to fix that, helping Xavier was her best way to do so. Reluctantly, Robbie pulled out her phone and copied the information onto his computer.

"This'll take a bit." He typed and clicked and muttered to himself for another minute after that. He sat back and cast a far-too-casual-to-actually-be-casual glance around the room. His gaze landed on Dee, where it paused, and then Robbie, where it stayed. "Why would some random stranger approach you like this? Seems super risky, if you ask me."

"I did not."

"Yeah, but still. Seems if you picked someone off the street, they'd be far more likely to turn you in to the cops than take you up on your offer. Why would he think the manager of a karaoke bar would be a good choice for this?"

"Owner," she corrected. "Owner of the bar."

"Co-owner," Dee said, smirking. "And do tell, co-owner, why *would* someone approach you to take a hit out on someone?"

"You can go to hell, Dee."

"I'd miss you terribly if I got sent elsewhere."

Xavier was watching them with a bemused expression. "Is this some weird lover's quarrel?"

"No," Robbie and Dee said together. Robbie followed up with, "Not everyone who gets along well is romantically involved. Not everyone in the world even wants to be romantically involved—ever."

"Literally everyone asks, though, so don't worry about it," Dee added. "We're used to it. What we've got going is a queerplatonic thing, and that's not a dynamic people are often familiar with."

Robbie rolled her eyes. "And not one I feel like explaining to some baby-faced straight kid right now."

"If that kid is straight, I'm Cher," Dee muttered.

Xavier had sunk very low into his seat, face about as red as was humanly possible. Well, all right then. She glanced at Dee and shrugged.

They all fell silent for the next few minutes, Xavier occasionally reaching over and tapping something on the laptop. The quiet was abruptly shattered as he sat up quickly with a shout, nearly spilling his remaining coffee. Would've probably made Robbie spill hers too if she hadn't already aggressively chugged the whole thing, ignoring the sensation of her entire throat catching fire.

"Nothing that says Clark, but do you know anything about a company called Victory Holdings?" When Robbie shook her head, he frowned at the screen. "It looks like that's who actually paid you. It's a subsidiary of... Okay, have you heard of the Kolen Fidelity Group? Some sort of investment firm."

Once again, Robbie shook her head. Xavier bit his lip as he looked back down at the laptop, and his eyes got kind of watery. After a split second of panic, Robbie uttered a silent thanks to the universe that Xavier did not cry. He was in their apartment, at their table, fine, but she wasn't about to deal with some maudlin display of emotion.

After a moment, he looked up and sighed. "It's a series of shell companies. I hit a dead end. Maybe some professional financial person could get further, but this is the best I can do. We're not going to identify Mr. Clark this way. But you never answered my question earlier. Why did he pick you? Maybe if we can figure out his connection to you, we can figure out who he is."

"The deal was for you to figure out why he picked *you*. You're the one he wanted killed."

"Yeah, but I don't know who he is. Obviously, you must somehow. What about when you've worked together before?"

"Look, I'm not sure how many more times I can say it. I don't know the guy. I'd never met him before."

Xavier shot her… What was that? A judgmental look? Skeptical? She didn't like it.

He hit a few keys on the laptop. "What about in April?"

"Nope, didn't know him in April."

"January?"

"If I knew him in January, I would've known him in April. That's how time works," Robbie snapped. "Do you want to keep picking random months, or have we established that I don't know him?"

"They're not random." Xavier frowned. "So if not him, then who else wired large sums of money in January and April, each of those split into even halves paid in relatively short succession?"

Oh shit. "You said you didn't have access to my accounts."

"No, I said I wasn't going to steal your money." He blinked at her, all guileless charm. The kid could act. She'd give him that. "I still had to look at the account."

"Well, stop looking!" Too late now, she supposed. She should've acted casual when he asked. She'd been so fixated on his irritating presence when she should've remembered that behind the baby face and wrinkled T-shirts and unkempt hair was the sharp mind she'd seen at work in the Ajax Club. How the hell did she let herself get fooled by Xavier Landerman *again*?

Of course she knew what he'd found. January had been a lawyer slipping down a flight of icy stairs. April had been the head of a construction company meeting an unfortunate safety violation on one of his sites. Half the payment up front, half when the job was done.

"So." Xavier nodded like all the pieces had slid into place in his picture of Robbie. Must be nice. "You've never met Mr. Clark before, but you have met people like him. People willing to pay a tidy sum for someone else to wind up dead." Xavier sighed deeply. "A random stranger didn't just happen to approach another random stranger and ask to have me killed, did he? He hired a professional hit man."

"Hit person," Dee noted in a tone that unfortunately made him sound very impressed by Xavier's alarming conclusion. "It's more inclusive."

"You're also free to leave that part off altogether and refer to me simply as a professional," Robbie added.

Xavier didn't seem to hear Robbie. He was instead staring in horror at Dee. "You know? What she's done? Are you—"

"Dee knows what I do," she interrupted, "but he has nothing to do with my work or the hit Mr. Clark took out on you." It wasn't technically a lie. And fine. Xavier knew her secret, and it was her fault for being careless. She'd need to assess how much danger his knowing put her in. But she would rather die than let her mistakes—starting with not killing Xavier weeks ago—endanger Dee.

She badly needed his money, but Xavier didn't look as uncomfortable being in the home of a contract killer as he ought to. "If you're thinking about telling anyone, you should know, I could just kill you right here and be done with all this."

She got to treasure one whole second of Xavier looking alarmed before Dee retorted, "Not in my kitchen you won't. Who's cleaning up that mess?"

"Fine." She turned back to Xavier and tried again. "I could follow you home and kill you in *your* kitchen."

No alarm at all this time. Xavier shrugged. *Shrugged.* "Will you though? No offense, but you did try following me before and weren't so great at it. All I have to do is slip you again, and you're right back where you were."

"I'd—" She also couldn't afford to lose him again. Saying she'd know better and would find him this time around would be a lie, and they'd both know it. Eventually, she would kill him when they were done with their deal, but before that, she'd need more information on him than anything she'd gotten today. A tiny bit of civility wouldn't be the worst thing she could do. "Fine, no killing in anyone's kitchen."

Xavier's smug satisfaction of having figured Robbie out melted away. "What now? I had exactly one idea on how to find Mr. Clark, and that didn't pan out."

"Honestly? Now, you go on with your life until you don't." Although Dee clearly used a tone intended to soothe, his words finally succeeded in freaking Xavier out.

When Xavier pulled his bag up and put away his laptop, surely that was a sign progress was being made. But he didn't seem like he was going anywhere. He just stared morosely at the empty table instead of at his computer.

"Look, you wanted to know why Mr. Clark approached me, so I told you. But like I've been saying, the question is not and has never been why Mr. Clark picked me. The question is why did he pick you?"

"I don't know."

"Yeah, you've made that pretty clear. I meant let's figure it out." She held up a hand as he leaned forward enthusiastically. "Not right this second. You showed up at my door unannounced. Dee and I do have a life that extends beyond your existence. You can come back later when you are *invited*, and then I'm going to need you to tell me everything there is to know about Xavier Landerman."

After several rounds of thanks from Xavier and a follow-up meeting begrudgingly scheduled by Robbie, the kid was successfully shooed out the door. Robbie didn't scramble to try and follow. He'd be back.

As Dee started doing up the locks, he asked, "What was that about? You actually going to help him?"

"I don't know, but I do know he desperately wants that and is willing to pay ten grand for it. We wouldn't even have to borrow from Coda again to keep the show going." Robbie was getting more enthusiastic. They wouldn't have any more unknown debt to Ingram over their heads. This could work. "Besides, as long as Xavier thinks I might have answers, he's not going to disappear again before I can finish the job."

That and her damn curiosity was flaring up again.

18

Problem-Solving Skills

THE MAN ROBBIE WAS SUPPOSED TO KILL ARRIVED AT HER door for dinner on Wednesday evening wearing jeans, worn-out purple Chucks, and a skinny pink tie over a black T-shirt featuring the album cover for *London Calling*. The same T-shirt she'd seen him wear to the museum in fact. His hair was shockingly somewhat combed. Somehow that made the nagging feeling that she'd seen him somewhere even stronger, but she still couldn't place it.

She waved him inside and set the locks behind him. As she turned around, she found him staring at a framed picture on the side table near the door. In the photo, she and Dee were behind the bar, both wearing matching Coda T-shirts. Dee—considerably more feminine-presenting but still clearly recognizable—held an overflowing bottle of champagne with a surprised smile on his face. Robbie had her head thrown back, laughing. She couldn't remember who took the photo, but it was just after closing on Coda's very first night.

When the two of them had met through James a few years prior, they'd immediately hit it off. Robbie had finished a loose-carpet-at-the-top-of-the-stairs job in Virginia before driving up toward central Pennsylvania to rendezvous with James for a check-in. She'd been working for him for three years by then, and most of the time, he accepted updates via phone. But periodically, he liked to meet face-to-face. Something about nonverbal cues helping him gauge mental state, blah, blah. A multicar accident on the highway made her over an hour late, and when she'd arrived, someone else was sitting across the twenty-four-hour diner's Formica table from James, arms folded, posture sullen.

"Ah, Robbie. I wasn't sure you were going to make it."

"Traffic."

"Of course. Would you mind giving us a few more minutes? I'll be right with you."

She sat a few tables away, trying and failing to eavesdrop on the furiously whispered conversation. Then the other person had stood abruptly and stormed out. Robbie moved to sit across from James, who revealed absolutely nothing, immediately shifting the conversation to focus on her. But later, after James had paid their tab and left, Robbie and her to-go box of fries headed to the parking lot to find that same person perched on the trunk of a gray sedan, head down. The car's back right tire was very, very flat.

"Hey, um, you work with James?"

With an exaggerated startle, the person looked up, eyes so dark they were black in the evening light, meeting Robbie's gaze defiantly. "For. Not with."

Same thing. "Okay. You need a ride? I'm Robbie, by the way."

"Da—actually, Dee. You can call me Dee. And if it's not too much trouble, I wouldn't mind a lift to a motel. We're in the middle of fucking nowhere, so tow truck said they probably won't get here until tomorrow morning."

"Sure. I'm too tired to drive much more tonight, so I need to find somewhere to crash too. Come on. I'm parked just around the side."

Dee followed Robbie, not saying a single word until they were both in Robbie's car. Out of habit, the same sort of automatic muscle memory as putting on a seat belt, Robbie plugged the aux cable into her phone and let her playlist pick up wherever she'd left off. For the first time, Dee's sullen expression vanished, replaced with an infectious grin as the Grateful Dead started up with "Ripple."

"I love this song."

Robbie matched the smile. "Yeah, me too."

When Robbie dropped Dee off at the diner the next morning, they swapped numbers. Just in case they wanted to get in touch.

James had frowned on it, but he'd never done anything to interfere with their friendship. Although she'd left his employ to work independently a year before his heart attack, Robbie could've easily gone back and run his operations while he recovered. Instead, she let it go to another of his "utilities" and helped Dee strike out on his own. And she and Dee began working on this absolutely harebrained idea about opening a lesbian karaoke bar.

"You're not what I'd expect from, uh…a professional," Xavier said, looking up.

"It's a job. Still just a regular person."

"I guess. But your job is, well, it's death. And this"—he waved a hand around their bright-yellow kitchen—"is all so lively and happy."

"Gotta have balance. My job may involve death, but *I'm* not dead, so why shouldn't I be lively and happy?"

He shrugged.

"Exactly. Now come on. We're in the comfy chairs tonight." She walked past the table where they'd sat previously and led him down the hall to the living room.

Dee was sprawled out on the long couch, head near his turntable, eyes closed as he sang along with the spinning record, his voice harmonizing with the rich tones of Nina Simone as she sang about new days and dawns. Out of the corner of her eye, Robbie could see Xavier had come to an abrupt stop.

"Holy shit," he whispered. Not an unprecedented reaction to hearing Dee sing for the first time.

Robbie smiled. "Yeah, he gets that a lot."

"Does he know we're here?"

"Dunno. Doesn't matter. He'll be done when he's done. Have a seat. Enjoy."

She gestured to one of the two mismatched armchairs they had for guests and took the love seat for herself. Xavier fell into the navy wingback chair more than actually sat, his eyes not leaving Dee. Which, Robbie knew, was mostly due to the singing, but Dee looked sharp too. He'd come out of his room this evening in nicely pressed charcoal-gray chinos and a black button-down, the sleeves cuffed short enough to show off the tattoos that wrapped around his forearms: musical notes and piano keys, guitar frets and vinyl records, an entire love letter to music inked onto his skin.

"Are you dressed up?" Robbie had asked.

"I do look good, don't I?"

"You're aware that we're having Xavier Landerman over tonight so I can interrogate him about why someone wants him dead."

"Yes, I seem to recall something like that."

Robbie had leaned against the fridge, folding her arms. "Are you dressed up *for* Xavier?"

"I'm not saying I am, but I will say that every time he looks in my direction, he turns pink and gets flustered." Dee smirked. "It's precious. I enjoy it."

"I'm supposed to kill him in five days. Please tell me you are not getting attached to my target. He isn't even your type." Dee's type being broadly defined as "not male."

He'd shrugged. "Sure. I'm not getting attached to your target. I'm just having a bit of fun. He's not *my* target. Besides, if you do your job right, does it matter whether I dressed up tonight and made him blush? Outcome's the same either way. Except this way, I get some entertainment out of it." Robbie hadn't argued further.

Now Dee was lounging in his lovely clothes, his dark hair in a neat faux-hawk combed up from a freshly done fade, singing in a voice like rich chocolate, and his mission was fully accomplished. Xavier looked like he'd just found God on a couch in Morningate.

And dammit, it *was* a little bit precious.

The song ended. The orchestra started up with the next track, but Dee sat up and reached over to lift the needle and stop the record. He turned and flashed a smile at Robbie and then took in Xavier's expression and *winked* at the poor boy. Much more from Dee, and Robbie wouldn't have to do anything; Xavier would topple over dead all on his own. Death by furious blushing.

"Nice to see you again, Xavier. Congrats on the whole still-being-alive thing."

"Thanks," Xavier whispered, or at least Robbie was pretty sure that was what he tried to whisper. It came out as breath and a sibilant hiss, with something vaguely resembling the hard K in between.

Robbie cleared her throat, and both Dee and Xavier jumped. "How about we get down to talking before that still-being-alive time ends?"

"Right." Xavier nodded. "What do you want to know?"

"How long has Xavier Landerman existed?"

He slumped a little.

"What? Everyone in this room is aware that Xavier Landerman is not a real person. You don't want to tell us your actual name, fine. But Mr. Clark hired me to kill Xavier Landerman specifically, not whoever you actually are."

That seemed to cheer him up. "Well, I set up the identity a little over a year ago, but I didn't become Xavier until maybe nine months back."

"Why'd you create Xavier?"

"The museum job."

"It took you nine months to steal a single painting from the museum?" After they'd struck their deal, Robbie had dug around local news sites more and learned he'd stolen that painting he'd been admiring when she caught him timing the security rounds. A Pre-Raphaelite according to the news clip, which Dee explained did not have to do with Raphael at all for some reason, but yes, it did still constitute "fancy art." There had been no alarms, nothing caught on camera, just a big blank spot on the wall the next morning when museum staff arrived. It was very nice work.

"No, it took me nine months to do a series of smaller jobs to prove myself as Xavier to the person who hired me to get the painting. I knew there was a job and that it would pay incredibly well, but for that type of work, you don't just hire the first schmuck who walks in off the street."

"You were auditioning," Dee said approvingly.

Xavier, to his credit, only turned a light bubblegum pink instead of the full crimson. "Yeah, exactly."

"Obviously, the audition process went well for you." Robbie paused, then made the connection. "Ah. The Ajax Club. It's where you met with the person holding these auditions."

"Lucky Ace Tivoli. He's part owner."

Lucky Ace. Sure. She bet his real name was something like Joe or Fred, but she kept her comments to herself as Xavier continued.

"He runs the backroom games. Despite the name, the club's main money isn't from the blackjack tables or anything else in the front. It's the private stuff Lucky has going on. Exclusive card games, and he uses the bets as a cover for selling things he's had someone steal."

Both Dee and Robbie nodded.

"Makes perfect sense," Robbie said before Dee could open his mouth and fluster up Xavier again.

"Does it? I never quite got how he was going to make it so that the person buying the item would win the game. I suppose he fixes the cards."

"He may not have to. Cash-heavy businesses like gambling halls or"—she waved a hand toward the floor to indicate Coda below them—"bars are ideal for laundering money. His customers probably buy an item outright, and he masks the deal within any number of other transactions taking place the same night."

"Is that why you…" He repeated Robbie's vague gesture at the bar beneath them.

Dee laughed. "Nah, it's just a convenient perk. We would've opened this place no matter what. Do what you love and all that."

"Oh." A darker shade of pink.

Robbie would've preferred Dee not say "we" when describing the illegal side of their business, but after Xavier left the last time, Dee had told her that while he wasn't planning to tell Xavier outright that he was a contract killer too, he wasn't going to go to a lot of trouble to hide it either. Robbie and Dee came as a set, he'd said. If all this blew up and Xavier knowing meant Robbie went down for it, Dee would go down with her, and that was just fine by him.

"All right, so Landerman has existed for a year, you said? Walk me through that year. Every person you've met, every audition you did. At some point, you had to have met Mr. Clark and done something to piss him off."

Dee held up a hand as his phone buzzed. "Hold that thought. Pizza's here."

He disappeared, Xavier's eyes following him out. The best way to handle the awkward silence was obviously not looking at each other. After a minute or two, Dee returned with two pizza boxes, a liter of pop, and a bag of red Solo cups.

"All right. Let's begin."

They ate a solid pizza and a half, and the remaining half had long gone cold by the time Xavier finished his detailed accounting of the past year of his life. He started with coming here in response to a call for freelance thieves. That smugness of his returned as he detailed how he'd successfully stolen from art galleries, private residences, and museums both local and throughout the state as part of the audition process. With some prodding, he described the handful of other thieves he knew of who had also been auditioning for the Pre-Raphaelite job. After the first day in the kitchen, Robbie had gone to the security room and rolled back footage to Mr. Clark's visit. He had a professional's ability to casually angle himself away from the cameras. Robbie had Dee go back to his contacts to ask whether any knew a thief matching Clark's description, but no luck, and Xavier's descriptions didn't sound like Clark either.

Xavier even listed out in excruciating detail every coffee shop he remembered going to, where he bought groceries, where he went to weekly spin class before he had to hide from Robbie—she had not pegged him for a spin class person, but who fucking knew what he was really like.

Not one bit of it seemed to tie him to Mr. Clark.

Finally, Robbie called it for the night. "This is going nowhere. Dee and I have to be at the Gillespie early tomorrow to go over set pieces with the building manager and our set designer. Go… wherever home is for you right now, which I hope to god is nicer than your last place."

"A bit." Xavier stood. "Did you say Gillespie? Like across from the Reevesburg Museum?"

Dee grinned. "I guess we have you to thank for that. If Robbie hadn't been following you, she might never have found the place, and we never would've rented it."

"Renting? What for?"

"Robbie wrote a musical. We're putting it on at the Gillespie. Opening's in a few weeks."

Xavier broke into a wide smile. "I *love* musicals. I'd love to come see your show whenever it opens."

"Yeah?" Dee stood. "Here, I'll walk you out and tell you the gist of it."

As Robbie watched the two of them head down the hall, she

had to admire how neatly Dee had sidestepped the statement. By the time they opened the show in a few weeks, Xavier wouldn't be around to see it.

It was at that bright-and-early meeting that the show really hit Robbie. Priya had worked absolute wonders, transforming the Gillespie's plain stage into a 1920s speakeasy, a recording studio, an apartment. Every setting from the play was there, life-size and real.

Priya led a long, very thorough discussion with Janelle about the logistics of storage, backdrops, set changes, and a lot of details Robbie didn't even know were a thing. Janelle, who also did not seem to know all those details needed discussing, listened attentively, taking copious notes.

After a bit, Robbie drifted off, leaving Priya, Janelle, and Dee to wrap up the conversation. She wandered between the set pieces, fingers trailing over the exquisite details. There was a bench seat, the corner table in the speakeasy, and the seatback had a delicate geometric art deco pattern painted in gold. No way the audience would be able to see closely enough to catch that, but it was there all the same.

"Fletcher Ingram's money at work," Priya said from close behind Robbie, startling her.

"It's excellent work." Robbie hadn't expected that to come out as reverent as it did, but the tone wasn't wrong. "I saw everything you had in East Oster, and it was great, but this… You've outdone yourself."

She did her best not to add up how much this must've all cost, how much she now owed Fletcher. It might be a tad over the ten grand she was counting on from Xavier, but hopefully, that would reduce her debt and whatever Fletcher might ask in return otherwise.

"You may absolutely print my name in the playbills now."

"Well, the order's already gone to the printers, so bit late to make any changes."

Priya started to say something else when Dee materialized at Robbie's side. "Sorry, Priya. Can I borrow my other half for a moment here?"

"Have at her. I need to go check a few things backstage anyway."

He waited until she disappeared into the wings, then turned to Robbie with a rather urgent look.

"What's wrong?"

"Apparently, the Oster Playhouse had a leaky pipe. Poor maintenance and all that. Not significant enough for anyone to notice, but just a slow drip over time."

Robbie waited for the punchline.

"We were storing stuff there," Dee said, as if that explained his concern.

"Yeah, but I thought we finished moving everything here last week. Didn't we?"

"Sort of. Not entirely." He sat down on the detailed bench seat and intently studied the stage floor by his feet. "Liz still has her whole setup over there, so she's been carting stuff back and forth. After fittings on Sunday, she took things back to work on this week. The thing is, the leak… It was near the costumes she'd taken over."

Oh. Panic clawed its way up Robbie's rib cage. "How near?"

"Right above."

She dropped onto the seat beside him. "It's fine though, right? I mean, it's just water. Things dry."

Not that she believed that. He would not be this upset if that were the case.

"The Playhouse isn't exactly in great shape. Lot of rust in those pipes." He leaned into her, and she put an arm around his shoulders. "Bottom line, seventeen costumes got destroyed."

Wonderful. Right when the show finally felt like it was coming together. Of course.

"We'll fix it," she said confidently. "We have time."

"Not today we don't."

Robbie tried to remember if there had been any other colored sticky notes on her calendar at home. Or on the fridge. Or on the corkboard in their hall. She was pretty sure this morning's meeting with Priya and Janelle had been it for the day.

"I took a job." Dee sighed. "Got the call from Darlene right before I heard about the costume fiasco. Shouldn't be long, but it's got a tight deadline, and I need to head out of town this afternoon."

Yeah, that whole compartmentalizing their lives thing was going fantastic. "All right, so I'll deal with it. Obviously, it's not a solve-in-an-instant sort of thing, but I can get gears moving and all that."

"You have a job too."

Robbie wasn't sure whether he meant killing Xavier or working with him to find Mr. Clark, but she waved a hand. "Don't worry about it. I'll get everything done. Go home. Pack your stuff. Go do your thing. I've got everything under control."

She wasn't sure if she'd made that sound as convincing as she intended or Dee just wanted very badly to believe it, but he nodded and stood up. He'd taken a few steps toward the wings before turning back to her. "Thank you, Robbie."

"You don't need to thank me."

"No, I don't need to, but I'm doing it anyway. You have my back. I appreciate it."

Robbie smiled. "Always, Dee. You know that."

He returned the smile and headed out. Robbie tilted her head back against the seat. Yes, helping Xavier figure out the Mr. Clark situation was important. Some of his money could even go toward covering any new costume costs. But this was her show. It was important too.

No reason she couldn't do it all, but this whole costume thing—it had to be the priority right now. As soon as she dealt with it, she'd get back to working with Xavier.

She pulled out her phone and dialed their head costume designer.

"Hey, Liz, it's Robbie. I heard you have a problem. What can I do to help?"

Everything would be fine. She'd have this sorted by the time Dee returned. She still had four more days to work with Xavier before Mr. Clark was due back. What was the worst that could happen by putting things off for one more day?

19

Look Who Showed Up

ROBBIE HAD ENTIRELY FORGOTTEN FRIDAY WAS '80S NIGHT until she walked down the back stairs and out into a line of women in neon leggings and side ponytails waiting for the bathroom. In her gray T-shirt and denim shorts, she stood out far more than if she'd chosen to wear, say, a bright pink tutu that glowed under the black lights, as apparently all her bartenders had done.

Dee was still gone on his last-minute job, having called her earlier to reluctantly say he'd be missing tonight's rehearsal for the show. Robbie's heart had squeezed. The only reason he'd accept a job right now was to help with their financial mess, which meant either the show was costing even more than she realized, or Dee wasn't confident Robbie could fix the Xavier-Clark tangle. She didn't love either possibility.

Someone on stage had already broken out the Cyndi Lauper. Most nights, there were limits about repeating songs someone had already performed, but they did occasionally relax the rules to keep customers happy, which on '80s night could mean the difference between a fun evening and a full-on riot.

With only a few days left until Mr. Clark's return, Xavier was supposed to be making a list for Robbie of other freelancers like him who worked for Lucky Ace at the Ajax Club. Dee's inquiries about rival thieves hadn't been fruitful, but Robbie got the impression that didn't necessarily mean they didn't know anything. They'd also said they didn't know Xavier when she'd been trying to track him down, but Robbie was pretty sure it had been a case of protecting their own. Xavier, it seemed, had no such qualms spilling all the details about his criminal peers. It could help identify Mr. Clark and get her her money, but a knot had developed in her neck at the idea of someone who knew *her* criminal identity being so willing to overshare.

Hopefully, whenever Xavier sent his list, it would give enough of a lead to satisfy her end of the bargain—namely why someone wanted him dead. All she needed was to meet up one more time, follow him to wherever he lived now, and start scoping out the area for possible accidents to arrange for him, preferably something quick. In the meantime, she might as well be useful. She washed her hands, squeezed in among her tutu'd employees, and started taking drink orders.

When Robbie next pulled her phone from her pocket, it was somehow nearly midnight. She headed to the stock room to get more bottles of blue curaçao, the star of tonight's featured cocktail. When she returned, Marisol grabbed her arm. "A man's here asking for you by name. Different man than last time. I think he retreated to the patio to get away from all this, but pretty sure he didn't leave."

"Thanks, Mari." She handed over the curaçao bottles, trying to mask her frown. Different one than last time meant it wasn't Xavier. Who else did Robbie know? Fletcher Ingram? He wouldn't come here. The only other man who might come to Coda asking for—oh shit.

Robbie's pulse pounded in her ears, out of sync with the beat of the music as she made her way through the crush of bodies to the patio. Mr. Clark wasn't supposed to come back until Monday. She was supposed to have gotten Xavier's money and killed him by then. Not only was he not dead, his habit of showing up here unannounced meant, at any minute, he might walk right into Coda, all gangly limbs and inconvenient aliveness.

The patio ran along the front of the building but was enclosed by a tall, bronze-swirled privacy fence, so the only access was from inside the club. Someone's decent rendition of "Smooth Criminal" was being pumped out from the outdoor speakers but not as loudly as inside. Although the air still had a bit of that lingering summer warmth, it still felt far fresher and cooler to not be crammed in with quite so many bodies.

She didn't see Mr. Clark as she stepped out, but this end of the patio was crowded and fairly well-lit. He wouldn't want that. She walked down the length of the patio, pressing close to the building.

Reminiscent of the cloak-and-dagger vibes of their initial meeting, a figure was crammed into the farthest, darkest corner of the patio, back pressed up against the fence like a cornered animal.

"Mr. Clark," she said amiably as she approached. Best not start by pissing him off. "I hope you're having a nice evening."

"Is it done?"

Yeah, she hadn't figured him for small talk. "Straight to business then, is it?"

"Yes. Let's make this quick."

No. She needed time. With his presence alone, things were already moving too quickly. She plastered on a wry smile. "Oh, come on, Mr. Clark. If you wanted quick, you didn't have to give me a full month to take care of this. Why the sudden rush?"

He shifted uncomfortably. With her eyes adjusting now, she could see he'd grown a thick beard in the past month, a few shades darker than his close-cropped hair. And oh, good lord, the man was wearing sunglasses. At midnight. It was like he'd looked up "how not to appear suspicious" and then done the exact opposite.

"It's not sudden. You've had plenty of time. This was always the deadline."

"Fair point, although strictly speaking, the end of the month isn't until—"

Abruptly, Mr. Clark tensed and cocked his head sharply. "You're stalling."

"Why would you say that?"

"Don't deny it. I can tell. We had a deal."

That was it then. He knew. They were seconds away from everything falling apart. But they weren't there yet. Robbie shrugged in her best imitation of casual dismissal, calculating. "All right, so I'm not *not* stalling. And you're right. We did have a deal. One where you only supplied me with a fraction of the information I needed and asked for."

"I gave you his name. I told you he frequents the Ajax Club. That should've been plenty."

"Yes and no. The bit about the Ajax Club was good. I did in fact find the person I was looking for there. But you told me very little about Xavier Landerman."

"I don't know much," he countered, but Robbie caught the

slight shift of his shoulders, the hint of a waver in his voice. Not everyone was as hard to read as Xavier.

She exaggerated her confidence by cocking a finger gun at him. "See that right there? That's my problem. It strikes me as highly suspicious that you would go to the trouble of finding me, agree to my fee, and pay the deposit, all for a man you know so little about."

"My reasoning is none of your business."

"But it is my *concern*. Makes me think you're up to something, and I don't want to be in the middle of whatever it is." She didn't have high hopes for this conversation, but if she held onto the hope of Xavier's payout, it couldn't hurt to learn what Mr. Clark *did* know. Before Mr. Clark could say anything in response, she asked, "I understand it's not a lot, but tell me, what *do* you know about Xavier Landerman?"

He shrugged. "Landerman's not who he claims to be."

Oh. That was more than Robbie expected him to know. "Is his name even Landerman?"

"No."

Far more than expected. This opened up so many possibilities to fulfill her side of the deal with Xavier. And okay, fine, she was intrigued. Mr. Clark's hit on Xavier had become an even more complicated puzzle.

"I think you've stalled enough. Confirm the job is done, I'll send the rest of your payment, and you can get back to whatever...this is." He gestured dismissively at the revelers. Someone in a jazzercize costume had climbed up on one of the picnic tables to dance to "Hit Me with Your Best Shot" and was actively trying to get several friends to join her. Robbie would've liked to leave them to their fun, but after several years in this business, all she saw was an insurance liability in lime-green spandex.

Before she could deal with that, she had to get Mr. Clark off her back. Her mind scrambled for a way to spin things. "You hired me to take out Xavier Landerman, and Xavier Landerman is no more. Job's done."

Not even a lie. She'd need to tell Xavier to pick someone else to be so it *stayed* not a lie, but that seemed fair enough to her. She fulfilled the terms of Mr. Clark's job to the letter.

"I refuse to pay for a loophole. The job is *not* done. You're not getting paid until you finish."

It had been worth a shot. She drew in a deep breath, which didn't calm her one bit. Unless she produced a genuinely dead Xavier Landerman, she had a feeling she wasn't going to talk him out of this. Long before Xavier made her lose confidence in her own skills, Robbie had sized up Mr. Clark. A man used to getting what he wanted. Best she could do was deny him the satisfaction of begging. "Fine. Then I'm not getting paid. I don't appreciate being played, Mr. Clark."

"I want the rest back. What I already paid."

Shit.

"That actually was my plan," she said, trying to channel James's most condescending tone.

This was nowhere close to the plan. Losing the second half of the payment hadn't been in the plan either. The costume crisis had set them back again, as had getting all the playbills reprinted with the Gillespie's information. They could cover it by dipping into Coda's accounts one last time, but without Mr. Clark's money to refill it, that was off the table.

Bare minimum, she had to talk him out of her giving back money long gone. "That was when I thought you'd unwittingly sent me to take out someone who doesn't truly exist. But you *knew*. So no, there will be no refund. Consider it payment for time wasted."

"You'll regret this." He did a fair imitation of an aggressive tone, although he could definitely learn something from all the actors Robbie had been spending time with lately.

"I already do." In more ways than he could possibly know. "Now, if you'll excuse me, I have something I need to take care of." She gestured to where there were now three women on top of the table.

"I know you own this bar, Robin McNeil. You and your *partner*." He paused for effect, then dropped Dee's deadname, pronouncing it completely wrong and yet still filling her veins with ice. "Maybe you think you can brush me off, but think about what you stand to lose. I will come after you. I will come after her. I will tear down your business faster than you can blink. You have no idea who you're crossing."

All the air left the patio at once.

"Mr. Clark," Robbie said, forcing a calm, steady breath even as her fists trembled at her sides. "You're right that I don't know who exactly I'm pissing off here, but as you've made quite clear, you sure know who I am. So I'm going to walk away now, and before you waste another second's thought on doing anything to hurt me or Dee or this bar, please do recall that I have been killing people for a living for over a decade now. I would have absolutely no qualms about adding you to my list."

"You can't—"

"I can. I will. Now get the fuck out of my bar."

She'd hoped he'd run scared. Instead, he muttered, "We'll see."

He pushed past her, shoving his shoulder into hers, and headed for the door briskly.

When he vanished into Coda, Robbie sagged against the fence, all the adrenaline and bravado leeching out of her. So much for Mr. Clark being a background member of this show. Yeah, Xavier was still the star, but damn, she had miscast Mr. Clark.

Maybe her attempted big scary speech would make him hesitate before acting, but it wasn't going to hold him off completely. James had taught her she should have no roots, no friends. No vulnerabilities. But she didn't live by James's rules anymore. Dee and Coda did make her vulnerable, but the answer wasn't to not have them in her life. It was fighting like hell to protect them.

This whole week that she'd been helping Xavier, she'd been so focused on the money. Suddenly, genuinely helping Xavier for the sake of figuring out Mr. Clark felt a hell of a lot more important. If she knew who he was, maybe she could find an effective way to threaten him right back, like the thing with nukes. Mutually assured destruction. That was it. She needed that. Otherwise, what stood between him and tearing down Coda and this precious, joyful life she and Dee had built?

When Dee was gone, Robbie found the apartment was often unnervingly quiet. Maybe they ought to get a cat. Not that cats made a lot of noise, she was pretty sure. Although Eloise was always calling her cat "chatty," so there had to be some cats who made noise.

She didn't need a cat.

She was fine.

Robbie glanced down at her phone, hoping Dee had texted that his job was done, only to see a message from Marisol. Apparently, she'd seen the same man multiple times as she ran errands. From Marisol's description, it could be Mr. Clark or any number of average-height, average-build men with light hair and a suit. Could be a coincidence. Could be nothing related to Robbie's mess at all. Still, she asked Marisol to try to covertly take a picture if she saw the man again. After last night, better safe than sorry.

The silent apartment seemed even more unnerving now. Dee had described his latest job as being a quick one—although Dee's jobs were always a bit quicker than Robbie's. She could handle this. He would be back soon enough and most likely wouldn't appreciate being replaced by a cat.

Instead, Robbie was rummaging through his vinyl collection with the idea that putting something on would help with the quiet.

"I'm gone for forty-eight hours, and you're already stealing my things?"

She stood, whirling around. "Not stealing. Borrowing."

"Only because I caught you." Dee had on generic bro clothes: khaki cargo shorts and a blue T-shirt with some sports team logo on it. Robbie wasn't sure which one, and she wasn't positive Dee knew either. It was just the sort of thing he wore when he didn't want to stand out. In winter, that could be achieved with plain black clothes, but it was fall, and a summery one at that, and someone dressed like a cat burglar was rather notable. Over one shoulder, he had a small duffel bag. A guitar case covered in souvenir stickers was propped against his legs, although if Robbie were to open it, she wouldn't find a guitar.

"I should've gone with the cat," Robbie muttered.

Dee raised an eyebrow. "Should I know what that means?"

"It's nothing. How was your trip?"

"Lovely. Efficient. Not at all messy. How was '80s night?"

"Oh, it was a wild adventure."

Dee tossed the duffel bag onto the couch and picked up the guitar case. As he headed toward the studio door, he asked, "Highest sign-up?"

Robbie drifted after him. "'Don't Stop Believin'' got twenty-four. Barely edged out the twenty-one for 'Girls Just Want to Have Fun.'"

The apartment technically was a three-bedroom, but since it was just the two of them, they had converted the largest into a music space. A piano and guitar for Robbie. Dee's own guitar, not in his case. They'd soundproofed the walls when Robbie bought recording equipment in an estate sale, and a long table sat occupied by more knobs and dials and faders than was probably healthy.

Along the right-hand wall were a pair of bookcases. Most were an assortment of nonfiction titles related to things like music theory, recording, or Broadway history. One section was full of mixology books along with dry tomes about running your own business. Dee had tossed in a slew of fantasy novels and travel memoirs. He'd even made sure they had space for Robbie's old collection of audiobooks, squat little packs of CDs from the days before downloading a whole book onto your phone became a thing, because Dee said those counted as books too. All in all, the bookcases weren't overflowing, but they were clearly in use. As they ought to look. The left one just happened to be on casters.

Dee knelt and pulled the latch near the floor, then easily swung the bookcase outward. Sure, Robbie could admit it was absolutely a cliché to have a secret passage hidden behind a bookshelf, but she and Dee had been entertained beyond reasoning at the idea. Their contractor had smiled indulgently as if they were small children when they asked her to make it happen, but she did it, and Robbie and Dee definitely thought it was very, very cool.

He stepped into the narrow corridor beyond the bookshelf, taking the guitar case with him. It wasn't a lot of space, maybe four feet wide or so, and almost half that width taken up by a set of industrial shelves. Further down, the hall ended in a crawl space directly above Coda's entrance. When they weren't actively on a job, everything related to their contract work resided on those shelves or in that crawl space. Robbie nudged a bin with her bare foot. Definitely needed to restock the burner phones soon.

"Not that Journey isn't fun, but what exactly made the night an adventure?" Dee asked as he opened the guitar case and began transferring the pieces of his disassembled rifle to one of the lower shelves.

"The bit where Mr. Clark showed up early."

Dee's head snapped up, his eyes widening slightly. "Please tell me he at least came dressed for the occasion."

"I mean, I guess technically he was. He was doing a solid attempt at the Unabomber... *Sunglasses*, Dee. Sunglasses on the patio at midnight."

Dee laughed. "Subtle. Did—"

They both froze at the sound of someone knocking at the apartment door.

"You expecting anyone?"

Robbie shook her head.

Leaving the half-emptied guitar case on the floor, Dee followed Robbie out. She waited for him to clear the doorway, then slid the bookshelf back toward the wall, pushing until she heard the click of the latch falling into place.

Another knock, this time a bit louder.

They walked briskly down the hall toward the kitchen. Robbie paused a moment in the living room to get the handgun they kept in a drawer of the coffee table. After leaving the army, Robbie never handled a gun unless she absolutely had to—a point of contention and the only thing she absolutely put her foot down on when she started working for James—but when Dee raised a questioning eyebrow, she just shrugged. She'd hoped her counterthreat to Mr. Clark would last longer, but she wasn't taking chances.

Robbie positioned herself with her back against the wall and cocked the gun. Dee punched in the alarm code before undoing the dead bolts, the chain, and the regular lock. And then he swung the door open.

She hadn't been sure what to expect, but the look on Dee's face certainly wasn't it.

"Xavier?"

The hell?

Robbie ejected the magazine, then released the round in the chamber. She tucked the unloaded gun into the back of her pants and dropped the magazine on the side table, partially hidden from view by the framed photo of Coda's opening night. Dee, who'd been watching her out of the corner of his eye, now pushed the door open wider so she could see Xavier Landerman, frowning and slightly flushed, hair once again a disaster, this time wearing a Bikini Kill T-shirt. Briefly, she wondered if it was his own interest or if this persona of his was into a wildly uncurated assortment of punk music.

Dee cocked his head at Xavier. "How come you're not dead?"

"Should I be?"

"Robbie said Mr. Clark came by. I assumed that meant your time was up."

Robbie scrunched up her face. "Yeah, I was about to explain that to you before we got interrupted."

"As long as you're going to explain it to me, you might as well explain to him too." Waving Xavier inside, Dee set the locks again, then gestured for them all to head to the living room.

When Robbie sat down, she pulled the gun out of her waistband. Xavier watched with wide eyes as she reloaded the loose round into the magazine before placing the gun and magazine back in the coffee table drawer.

"Were you…planning to shoot me?" he asked with what Robbie figured was probably a reasonable amount of concern.

"Not you specifically. Whoever was at the door if it happened to be someone who needed to be shot."

"I don't know that anyone *needs* to be shot ever."

Robbie shrugged. "You just haven't met the right person."

"Isn't that what people say about finding love?"

"Yeah. Love isn't my thing, as it turns out. But I know plenty of people believe if they search long enough, they'll find The One. In my opinion, if you search the world long enough, you're also bound to find someone you absolutely think could do with a bullet or two." She'd figured the latter out long before she figured out her aromantic ass wasn't failing at the former.

Dee cleared his throat. "Whenever you're ready, feel free to explain why he's still alive. And I hope it's better than 'he wasn't The One' nonsense."

With a sigh, Robbie related the events of '80s night and her encounter with Mr. Clark. She didn't bring up the text she'd gotten from Marisol. She wasn't sure what to make of that yet. Until she knew more, Robbie wanted to focus on the facts she knew were relevant.

Throughout the retelling, Dee didn't say anything. Xavier made a lot of indignant noises.

"So," she concluded, "Xavier isn't dead, we still don't know who Mr. Clark is, and I have a perfectly valid reason for being prepared to shoot an unexpected visitor."

"Damn right you do," Xavier growled with surprising force.

Up until last night, Robbie would've been happy giving Xavier anything that satisfied his curiosity about Mr. Clark. False information would've been fine, as long as it was convincing. All she needed was him to pay up. To keep Dee and Coda safe, though, genuine answers had jumped way up on her priority list.

Flopping back onto his armada of pillows, Dee propped his feet up on the coffee table. "Where does this leave us?"

"It leaves me permanently alive, right?" Xavier brightened considerably.

"Nobody is *permanently* alive," Robbie retorted. "You're still going to die. Just probably not quite so soon and not because of me."

The silence that fell over the room was a bit uncomfortable, but after a moment, Dee shoved a topic change in to break up the tension. "You check the security tapes already?"

She'd slept well past noon. Eighties night had been tiring, as had Mr. Clark. "I have done absolutely nothing."

"Which includes not killing me nor planning to," Xavier pointed out. "Can I just say, thank you so much for that."

"I'd really rather you didn't."

"Oh. Well. Still."

Dee stood up. "I'll be in the security room. Either of you want to join me?"

Robbie opened her mouth, but Xavier stood up before she could say anything. At Dee's glance toward her, Robbie waved a hand. "I've got some things to do downstairs. You two go enjoy a tiny room together."

As expected, that turned Xavier a shade of red she was certain would meet Dee's criteria for "precious." Robbie headed down to the bar to do inventory, contemplating the fact that while Dee's expression upon opening the door and seeing Xavier had primarily been one of surprise, Robbie hadn't missed the fact that there absolutely was some relief mixed in there too.

20

Sense and Logic Need Not Apply

XAVIER LOVED MUSICALS.

That was what he'd said.

That was what *Dee* had said. Only Dee had said it like it was an excuse or a reason, and somehow, Robbie ended up sharing her plush red balcony seating with an eager twentysomething in an absolute lie of a T-shirt that read "Minor Threat," who had opinions about literally everything.

She glanced down at the notepad in her lap, which was more for appearances than anything. So far, it contained a single scrawled word to remind her about a lyric everyone kept stumbling on—she planned to tweak that for them—and an extensive doodle of a flowering vine. She added another swirling tendril shooting off from the central stem.

Robbie hated that she'd failed the job, but right now, not getting the rest of her payment stung more. Without Mr. Clark's money, Robbie had reluctantly asked Ingram to help cover the costs of the new costumes and an addition to one of Priya's backdrops that needed to fill the stage better. He'd been delighted to help. She was still waiting for the other shoe to drop, but she couldn't keep spending so much of her time juggling finances. Not when Mr. Clark's threat against Dee and Coda wouldn't stop playing on a loop in her mind.

After Dee and Xavier tried, Robbie had gone to the security room to watch the footage of '80s night herself. Like when he'd first come, Mr. Clark angled himself away from the cameras, and even when a bit of him was visible, his ridiculous hoodie and sunglasses combo obscured his features. Dead end.

"Can I ask you something?" she said, interrupting some ramble that seemed to be about incorporation of dancers into set design.

"Yeah, yeah, whatever you want."

"The night I met you at the Ajax Club, you were nervous about something. You kept messing up your count."

He'd been leaning forward onto the balcony railing, but now he sat back, his enthusiasm waning. "You caught that?"

"The counting or the mistakes?"

"Well, both, I guess. I thought I was doing decently at not making it too obvious. I'd just finished the last audition for Lucky a few nights before that, and he'd finally agreed to let me in on the museum job. Didn't want to piss him off by having him realize I was cheating."

"First of all, it's not cheating. It's just smart playing."

Xavier laughed. His laugh surprised her. It was higher than she expected and lighter too. "I'm sure Lucky would be more than happy to debate the finer points of card sharkery with you."

"He why you were nervous then? You were worried he'd catch you?"

For a long moment, he was silent. She wasn't sure if that was intended to mean yes or no. Finally, he said, "A lot of people pass through the Ajax who don't belong there. They go for some sort of lark. You can always spot them. Most ditch their fancy suits, dress in their best impression of common people, all the while forgetting there's still a Rolex on their wrist. Even without that, though, it's still there in the attitude. It's obvious when someone thinks losing a couple grand a night is chump change."

"Here I was bothered I lost four hundred there over the course of several nights when I was trying to find you. After you disappeared."

"Yeah, I know. I'm friendly with most of the dealers. They'd text me if you showed up so I would know not to come."

That explained a lot. She shook her head. "Dick move, but I get it. Setting that aside, though, you were saying about that first night?"

"Right. Well, there's this guy Lucky's been meeting. Political type, one of the dealers said." Xavier scrunched up his nose. "He doesn't belong there any more than the others, but he doesn't sit at the front tables like they often do. Goes straight to the back and everyone else gets kicked out so he and Lucky can talk. Thing is I can't tell who's playing whom. Can't tell if Lucky's dragging the political guy into some scheme, getting some dirt on the man to leverage later, or if the political guy is trying to clean up Lucky's house."

Ah. "Ingram?"

"Who?"

"Tallish white guy, gray hair, sixtysomething, kind of wiry. Is that who was meeting with Lucky?"

Xavier nodded. "Yeah. That sounds like him. You know who he is?"

"You don't?"

"I'm not much for politics." He shrugged. "I've always had more immediate concerns."

Maybe Robbie had been spending too much time in places where Ingram had influence, but it was hard to believe anyone could exist in this city, or even this state, without knowing who he was. "I know he was there that night."

"If Lucky was doing the dragging, I didn't have too much to be worried about, you know? But if this Ingram guy was there to try to warn Lucky off or get him to stay out of trouble, that could mean the heist getting called off. I needed the money." He pushed his glasses up on his nose. "I was sort of running out of what I had stacked up from my last big score. It's why I was at the Ajax Club so much in the few weeks before the museum job. Blackjack's a decent enough income if you know what you're about and you don't have that many expenses to cover."

In person, Ingram was different from who he presented as on TV. The acting was impeccable. To the press, he said just the right buzzwords, talking about support for local businesses or the arts or homeowners or whatever the topic of the day was. But it was away from all that where Robbie found him most believable.

It was a bit of a leap from that to him making any sort of deals with a criminal boss up in Penny Park. In truth, though, she didn't know enough about him to know how unusual that might be. Yes, he supported their show. Yes, he'd practically donated this theater to their production. Yes, he made a fantastic turkey sandwich on rye. But Xavier had recently reminded her just how contradictory a person could be. Ingram's support of Robbie and Dee didn't mean he wasn't also meeting in shady back rooms with people like Lucky at the Ajax Club.

"You were worried he'd mess with your revenue stream?" she said to Xavier, trying to recall his point as her thoughts wandered.

"Pretty much."

"All right. Fair enough."

The rehearsal taking place below tugged her attention again, all the actors sitting in a lopsided circle going through lines and musical numbers without blocking and choreography. Nothing fancy, but it was in preparation for their first run-through off book, and they were killing it. It was wild listening to these talented actors singing her music, songs that she wrote sitting at her piano in the studio above Coda.

"You ever see someone, and you're sure you've seen them before, but you don't know where?"

Robbie raised her eyebrows as her chin lifted sharply in surprise, both at the fact that apparently talking time wasn't over and at how specific his question was.

"I guess." She'd felt it that first morning Xavier had shown up at the apartment, but she chalked it up to having seen him in so many other contexts but never like that. Never as an ally instead of a target.

"Well, that was the other reason."

"Reason for?"

"That night at Ajax. When I kept getting distracted and messing up my game. When the political guy walked through to get to the backroom door, I just had this feeling I'd seen him before, and my brain kept getting stuck trying to figure it out."

Robbie laughed. "The guy is famous, has been since, I don't know, the seventies or eighties. He's a household name. He's on TV at least twice a day, minimum. Honestly, I was surprised when you said you didn't know him."

"I don't. Really. Not his name or what he does at least. But that must have been it."

He sat in silence after that, letting her focus on the rehearsal. Still, he was *there*, and that made her too self-conscious to actually write anything in her notebook, so instead she doodled idly as she made mental notes on things to fix or tweak and the things that were going well too.

He stayed quiet all the way until Dee and Julia wrapped up the main portion of the rehearsal, sending everyone on break before it was time for Robbie to go down with her notes.

"Robbie?"

"Xavier?"

"Dee's kind of amazing, isn't he?"

Despite herself, Robbie grinned. This poor kid. Across all the years she'd known Dee, she'd seen plenty of people have this reaction, although it never really led anywhere. Still, it was a common sentiment for good reason.

"Yeah. You're absolutely right."

Robbie loved nothing more in the whole world than being woken up at five in the morning by her phone buzzing violently and loudly on the nightstand. She didn't bother checking the caller ID. Bleary-eyed, she vaguely located the green circle on the screen and swiped to answer.

"What the fuck is so goddamn important you're calling me now?"

"Good morning, Robbie." Aw shit. James. Perfectly composed James. "I have a question."

Great. "And it couldn't wait at least a few more hours?"

"No, it could not. What did I train you to do? Tell me, what were the basic principles I taught you?"

He woke her up for a pop quiz? Fine. "Never ask why, don't get emotional, do it right the first time, and don't make a mess you can't clean up." The four pillars of James's mentorship.

"Oh, so you do remember that last one. Here I thought perhaps you'd forgotten."

"James, I don't know what time zone you're currently in, but it's five a.m. here. Can you just tell me what's up?"

"Don't make a mess. Don't make a fucking mess, Robbie McNeil. How hard is that?"

Robbie was fully awake now, sheets falling away to leave her sweating skin chilled. James had a very subtle way of expressing himself. He was never angry, just disappointed. He never raised his voice but used a cutting, dry tone that conveyed unmistakably that his opinion of you had gone down a few notches. This? This was the closest to genuine emotion she'd ever heard.

"I'm sorry?" She didn't know what for, but she was genuinely sorry to have set him off like this.

More evenly, he asked, "What have you gotten yourself into?"

"Nothing, as far as I know." Well. There definitely was shit going down. Nothing in the world was going to make Robbie admit the whole Xavier fiasco to James though.

"Explain to me why someone contacted one of Alma's folks to put a target on your back."

Goddamn Mr. Clark. "Shit."

"Precisely. Now Alma was kind enough to let me know." Alma had presided over James's operation for the period of time when his health prevented him from running things effectively himself. While James had fully rebounded from that, Alma remained a sort of lieutenant in his pyramid scheme. "I've sorted things temporarily. I'm effecting a ban on anyone taking a job with you as the target. Anyone breaking the ban will have me to answer to."

"Thank you."

"Don't thank me. This is all you get. I've only put out that this ban lasts a month. If you haven't managed to clean this up by the time that month is up, I'm not granting an extension. After that, whoever you've pissed off is free to hire whomever they please, and I'll do nothing to stop them. Understood?"

"Yes, sir."

"I care about you, Robbie." His voice was back to his typical calm neutrality. "Always have."

He didn't have to say the rest. Robbie had learned it long ago. There was no such thing as unconditional affection. Caring about her only extended as far as she managed to earn it. Past that point, she was on her own.

"I know. I'll get this all taken care of."

"Yes" was all James said in reply before hanging up.

Robbie flung herself sideways to crash into her pillows. Wonderful. Mr. Clark was making himself a nuisance, and they still had no idea who he really was or why he wanted Xavier dead. She did at least understand why he wanted *her* dead.

James was right though. This was her mess. She was responsible for cleaning it up. She just had to figure out how.

Well, she certainly wasn't going back to sleep now. She rolled out of bed and padded down the hall. Dee was tangled in this mess.

Even if he weren't, he'd still be the person Robbie would want on her side.

She raised her hand to knock on his bedroom door. No, she could do this right. She dropped her hand and headed to the kitchen. It wouldn't be as good as his, but if she was going to bother Dee this early, she could at least bring him some coffee first.

The summer heat broke in a beautiful thunderstorm that filled the air with an earthy, autumn scent of fallen leaves and wet cement. Robbie hadn't liked fall much prior to moving here. Maybe wet cement shouldn't be considered a seasonal smell, but she associated it with this place. It smelled like home in a way nowhere else ever had.

She stood on their back porch watching flash after flash of lightning in the distance, counting the seconds until the thunder—although she never could remember what you were supposed to multiply or divide that by to figure out distance. Her clothes were soaked through within minutes, but she stayed until the gusts of winds finally chilled her a bit too much for comfort.

The apartment was empty when she went inside, which was probably good. Dee would've definitely made some sort of remark about the way Robbie was leaving a watery trail behind with every step. As she changed into dry clothes, her phone buzzed. Digging it out from the laundry basket and blotting the screen with her new dry shirt, she swiped away several junk notifications, the kind from apps she kept meaning to uninstall and never remembered to, then saw a missed call from Dee, followed by a text.

> **DEE**
> Are you home? Can you come here?

> **ROBBIE**
> ?

> **DEE**
> Security room.

> **ROBBIE**
> im like 15ft from u

> **DEE**
> FFS. Just get over here.

Fine. Robbie stepped out of her bedroom and crossed the living room. From the landing of the stairs that led down to Coda, the door to the small security room was open enough for Dee to be visible sitting at the desk, head wavering back and forth slightly in front of the wall of monitors.

There were regular cameras, infrared sensors, motion detectors, all keeping track of everything that happened in and around Coda. Did a karaoke bar really need all that? Probably not. Did Robbie and Dee? A bit more so. It was the same with all the locks on the doors and the bulletproof glass in all the apartment windows. It had been a calculated risk allowing potential clients to occasionally meet them at Coda, a risk that relied on Darlene pre-screening and not disclosing that the location was anything more than a random choice. They did their best to mitigate that risk, but tracking dirt in the door wasn't entirely impossible.

Dee was jumping through the recorded feeds Robbie had already watched from the bar on '80s night. As she walked in, he paused, then began scrolling more slowly, the time code running backward. He queued up one of the patio cameras with a time stamp reading just before midnight, but before explaining himself to Robbie, he pulled up Coda's Instagram page.

"First of all, god bless social media. Our Mr. Clark is in the background of multiple photos. The problem is that most of the time, he's not in focus."

"Figures."

"Ah, but have hope, my dear. In a few shots, at least part of his face is visible. Most importantly, see these shots with the trees off to the side?"

On either side of the patio door, they had yucca cane growing in huge white planters. The distinctive fronds were visible in the pictures Dee pointed out.

"He was about to go inside, right? It wasn't bright on the patio, but we do have plenty of lamps out there. But to leave Coda, he had to go inside and exit out the front."

Robbie nodded. The bar only had one way out, or at least only one available to customers. From her first time watching the footage, she knew Mr. Clark didn't speak to anyone, didn't stop and linger, just kept his head down and booked it toward that door. "So?"

"So inside, especially near the front entrance, it would've been extra dark compared to the patio." Dee clicked through to another picture. Mr. Clark still wasn't entirely in focus but…

She should've noticed it herself. "He took his sunglasses off to go inside."

Dee snapped his fingers. "Exactly. That got me an exact point to start combing all our cameras for a good angle."

"You got something?"

Instead of answering, Dee hit play on the video he'd queued up. Robbie watched as the man she knew as Mr. Clark angrily shoved his sunglasses in his pocket and walked straight toward the camera above the door. The moment lasted only two seconds.

"Play it again."

Dee did, and a third time at Robbie's request—well, more like demand.

"You plan to tell me what you're seeing here?" Dee asked when Robbie requested a fourth run-through.

"I'm not sure." It was like Xavier had said at the theater about seeing someone and not being able to place them. She could swear she knew those eyes. Had she met him elsewhere? Couldn't be since their first meeting, or she would've spotted him. Maybe she'd seen his picture? The details had to be in her brain somewhere. "Play it again. Better yet, keep it on a loop."

The moment it clicked brought only a fleeting sense of triumph. At their first meeting, she'd clocked him as being around her age. Midthirties. Even if she were off by a decade, he still wouldn't be old enough, because the picture she remembered seeing had been when she was in fifth grade. Report cards had come in the mail. Her father had lectured her for twenty minutes straight about how poorly she was doing in school, and she'd refused to look him in the eye. Instead, she'd fixed her stare on a glossy magazine on the kitchen counter.

Robbie pulled out her phone and ran a search. Man of the year. The name of the magazine escaped her, but how many could there be? More than she expected, but there. Sandy hair, square jaw, thick beard. The beard had been throwing her.

Dee tapped her arm. "Care to share with the class?"

Okay, so this couldn't be the same man from fifth grade, but the resemblance was there. She ran another quick image search. Lots of hits. All clean-shaven, but so was Mr. Clark at their first meeting. She'd only caught glimpses of his features, but she could match those now. She pulled up a clear shot and held it out to Dee.

He nodded, looking mildly impressed. "Definitely could be the same guy. Who is that? I feel like I've seen him before."

The man must have gotten a fair amount of his looks from his mother, but the resemblance was quite clear. That square jaw, the long straight nose, the thick brows. It all looked different on someone over twenty years younger, but she was surprised Dee didn't see the resemblance.

Still, that was understandable. It barely made sense to Robbie as the answer crossed her lips. "It's Nicholas Ingram."

Dee's head whipped around sharply, eyes wide with disbelief. "You can't be serious."

"Wish I wasn't."

For a very long moment, the two of them sat in silence, completely at a loss for words. Finally, Dee managed to ask the obvious question that was running through Robbie's head too.

"Why the hell would the son of Fletcher Ingram want to kill Xavier Landerman?"

21
A Little Light Interrogation Between Friends

"I NEED TO TALK TO XAVIER," ROBBIE MUTTERED FOR THE THIRD or fourth time as she paced the width of the living room. They needed a bigger living room. The pacing distance was not sufficiently satisfying.

She'd tried sitting still, and she'd been successful for nearly a whole minute. In the time since identifying him, Robbie's mind had helpfully spun half a dozen ways Nicholas Ingram could be connected to Xavier. Her least favorites, and therefore the ones she couldn't stop dwelling on, were where all this was orchestrated by Fletcher Ingram. The notion came in two flavors.

In one, Fletcher had gotten in bed with Lucky or someone else at Ajax. Xavier knew or overheard something he wasn't supposed to. Bam, contract hit, problem solved.

In the other, Fletcher didn't care about Xavier but Robbie. He'd known exactly who she was that first day he called because he'd had his son hire her. The hit, the cheap theater, the investment in production costs, all to get leverage over her and... It fell apart there. Leverage for what? What could any Ingram possibly want from Robbie McNeil?

So she went back to the first one. She didn't like either version, but the one centered around Xavier was marginally better, because she'd made an absolute mess of everything, gotten Dee involved, and had Nicholas threaten Coda, but the show was the one thing she had left that wasn't completely entangled in this mess.

She needed Xavier to tell her it was the first version.

Dee had mostly been ignoring her, but he finally looked up from his phone. "Tonight?"

"I don't know. Whenever I can find him, I guess. I never did find out where he's living now. He said somewhere that's a step up from his old place, but that bar is practically underground, so it's not like that's a lot for me to go on. I suppose—"

"You could go meet him at the Ajax Club tonight around eleven."

Robbie stopped the unsatisfactory pacing to turn and look at Dee in his familiar sprawl across his couch. "Maybe. But it's a Monday, so he might not be there. And he finished the museum heist. I'm not sure if he has outstanding business with 'Lucky Ace.' God, what a ridiculous name. Maybe we could—"

"Robbie. He'll be at Ajax at eleven." Dee held up his phone, pointing to what looked like...a text chain?

Robbie cocked her head. "I'm sorry, are you *texting buddies* with my target?"

Shrugging, Dee dropped his phone onto his chest. "Technically, I was never texting your target. But *after* he stopped being your target, yeah, we talk. Don't look at me like that. If you have a problem with it, consider whose fault it is that he's alive. Dead guys don't text."

Difficult to argue with that.

She glanced at her watch. It was about half past eight now.

Although she didn't want to get there at the exact same time as Xavier, this was pushing it a bit too much on the early side. Still, maybe—

"Being antsy and impatient isn't going to get you answers any faster," Dee said with annoying sagacity.

"Being calm and patient won't get them any faster either."

"Touché." He sat up. "Given that time will be going at the same rate regardless of what we're doing, what are your thoughts on walking down to the corner and picking up some Chinese food to soothe your impatient little soul?"

Not a bad plan. The sweet and sour pork from the restaurant at the end of their block could soothe just about any ailments. "Great. Let's go."

Dinner had indeed done wonders for the tension coiled up in Robbie's bones. She was in a considerably better mood two hours later as she and Dee drove to the Ajax Club.

It was as slow as it had been the very first day they'd gone. Without the need to be undercover, Robbie and Dee sat down at the same blackjack table at the back.

They'd gone through several hands when a blond mess dropped into the seat between them. Sure, he *said* he was living somewhere better than the Deacon Arms, but as far as Robbie could tell, it must not have had space to hang up his clothes. Today, he'd gone with a Ramones tee, a solid choice on his part in Robbie's humble opinion. There were more pressing questions to get to tonight, but did he own any shirts that didn't have album covers screen printed onto them?

"Wasn't sure I'd see you here again, Veronica," he said to Robbie. Ah, so they were doing aliases then.

"Wasn't sure I'd give it a go, but if you're here, obviously there's plenty of luck at the table." She met his eye roll with a smirk, then gestured to Dee. "Have you two met?"

It was up to them what they wanted to say. Dee shrugged indifferently. It fell to Xavier, who reached his right hand over. "I don't know that we have. Xavier."

Dee shook his hand. "Nicholas."

Xavier didn't even blink at the name, although that didn't necessarily mean anything. It wasn't like Ingram's son had a monopoly on it. Instead, Xavier nodded to the dealer. "Theresa. Lovely to see you. Anything new with you since we last talked?"

There was just a hint of flirtation in his tone, which was a hint more than Robbie would have thought him capable. Theresa, who was surely closer to Robbie's age than Xavier's, smiled sweetly. "Nothing major. Heard you did some good work recently."

"I do my best."

"I'll bet you do," Theresa said as she began dealing. "If you're looking for work in a week or two, you might get lucky."

Robbie wasn't sure whether that was regular lucky or Lucky Ace. It did seem a terrible choice of a nickname for someone who worked in a gambling club.

Robbie checked the cards. Nine of hearts and seven of clubs for her, a pair of queens for Dee, seven of spades for Theresa, and a goddamn natural blackjack for Xavier, although she supposed she couldn't resent him for what was actually pure chance. The son of a wealthy businessman-slash-aspiring-politician wanted Xavier dead. Clearly, he deserved some sort of win. Not that she and Dee didn't after tonight.

A few more hands left Dee down by one hundred dollars while Robbie and Xavier had each roughly broken even.

Xavier smiled at Theresa and jerked a thumb toward Dee. "I think our friend here could use a drink before he can't afford to buy a round. Give us a few minutes?"

"Yeah, I'm due for my break. Don't get into trouble while I'm gone, Xavier."

"I would never."

"Uh-huh." Theresa took the cards, closed out the table, and left them there alone.

As soon as Theresa was gone, the carefree demeanor Xavier had been performing since he arrived melted away. He took a deep breath, closed his eyes, and got straight to the point. "Dee said you found something. Apparently, something big enough that you actually came here to find me. How much trouble am I in?"

"It's not *terrible*," Dee said, attempting a reassuring tone just as Robbie answered, "A helluva lot."

Xavier glanced toward Dee as if maybe he could choose which answer was true, but with a sigh, he looked over to Robbie. "All right. Lay it on me."

"You said you saw Fletcher Ingram here one night."

"The political guy."

"Right, and you're sticking with your story that you had no idea who he was?"

He made an indignant squeak. "It's not a story. I didn't know."

"Are you absolutely positive on that?" Dee asked, surprisingly gently. "Or did you maybe speak to him? Interact in any way?"

Robbie tacked on, "Or overhear him talking?"

Xavier shook his head at each question, and Robbie mostly

believed him. She stood slightly to pry her phone out of her back pocket and pulled up a photo of Nicholas Ingram to show Xavier.

"How about this guy?"

"Nope." Was that a flicker of something in his eyes when he first looked? Not recognition exactly. Perhaps just connecting the person in the picture to the politician he claimed not to know.

"You're positive."

Xavier looked at the picture again. "Yeah, positive."

"Are you absolut—"

Dee elbowed Robbie. "He's sure, okay?"

The jittery anticipation that had filled her ever since they identified Nicholas fizzled. Instead of confirming the explanation she preferred, Xavier had killed it as effectively as Dee sniping a target.

"What does he want with me?" Xavier asked.

"He wants you dead, obviously."

"I know, but *why?*"

Dee had a little line deepening between his brows. "We were kind of hoping you'd be able to tell us."

"I really don't know anything. I'm sorry." Both Xavier's tone and his expression were truly apologetic, like he actually felt bad for not having answers about why someone wanted to kill him.

Robbie folded her arms on the blackjack table and crashed her head into them. She'd expected this lead to blow things wide open. Xavier would have answers. Robbie would find leverage to keep Nicholas away from Coda and Dee, and then she could, as James eloquently put it, clean up her fucking mess.

Instead, this was all wildly unhelpful.

"We'll keep digging," Dee told Xavier. "Maybe something will come up. If you think of anything, even if you're not sure it's relevant, let me know, okay?"

He didn't look particularly reassured. "Yeah, all right."

Robbie stood to leave. They'd gotten what they came for, more or less. Okay, just less. And Dee probably didn't need to lose any more money.

As she turned toward the door, though, she caught Dee looking up at her over Xavier's head. "I'll meet you in the car, okay? Just need a minute."

She wasn't sure what to make of that, but she did as she was asked. It was only five minutes or so of waiting until Dee slid into the passenger seat without a word. Robbie started the engine and pulled out of the Ajax Club's parking lot before asking, "What was that about?"

Dee shrugged in a way that most people would probably see as indifferent or nonchalant. Except that Robbie knew her partner. That wasn't what nonchalant looked like on Dee. It was definitely very chalant.

Robbie waited.

Two stoplights later, Dee still hadn't spoken. Robbie wanted to make some teasing remark to lighten the mood, but that didn't seem right for the moment. Instead, she went with a more careful, neutral tone, trying her best not to sound judgmental. "The other day, you said how it was entertaining to see how flustered you can make Xavier. I believe the exact word you used was 'precious.' This whole business with him… I know you were relieved when you got back from your trip and he showed up at the apartment in a not-dead capacity."

Dee snorted.

"You actually care about him, don't you?"

Dee didn't reply.

That was an answer.

Shit.

It seemed entirely possible, even likely, that sometime soon, even without Robbie involved, Xavier would turn up dead. Hell, Robbie couldn't rule out the possibility that she might still have to finish the job herself. But Dee would know that as well as Robbie. There was no need to throw it at him with words.

Still. "I really didn't think Xavier was your type. You know, the whole being male thing."

Dee made an exasperated sound. "But Xavier—Never mind. Can we not talk about this?"

"Sure. It was just idle curiosity. Not trying to tell you your business. You know I would never."

"I know, Robs, and I appreciate it."

They fell into silence for the rest of the ride, and that, more than anything, told Robbie that something was truly off. He didn't turn on the radio. He didn't sing. At one point, he did pull out his phone, and for a moment, she thought he might connect it to the car's Bluetooth, but instead he typed something and dropped the phone back on his seat.

When Robbie pulled into the alley behind Coda, the silence followed them out of the car and up the steep metal staircase to the apartment's back door. She expected they'd call it a night and head to bed, but Dee went straight past his bedroom door and on to the living room.

She followed, folding herself up on her couch, watching Dee carefully. He didn't have on his "irritated by something Robbie did" face, which was a small consolation. Had Xavier said something after she'd left Ajax? Or was it some news about the show he was holding back?

Maybe the problem didn't make a difference. She knew the answer. Music had always helped them both when their heads weren't where they wanted to be.

When Robbie still had nightmares and would wake up, heart pounding, thrashing in her sheets, Dee always came in. Nothing he could do to fight a nightmare in her head, but he would curl up on the other side of her bed with his MP3 player, gently handing one earbud to her and keeping the other for himself. They'd lie ear to ear on the pillows, listening until her heart slowed and the world became solid again.

On days when Dee couldn't get out of bed, Robbie used to feel incredibly helpless. She didn't know where his mind went when that happened, but she hated seeing him in that state. It had taken her a while to realize she was never going to find a way to magically turn his brain into sunshine and rainbows. His depression wasn't a demon she could fight. What she *could* do was sit in his doorway playing music on her phone, not saying anything, just being there.

This wasn't that familiar sort of bone-deep, exhausted sadness, but she figured the principles were the same as they'd always been: Play music. Be present.

She unfolded herself from her couch and went over to kneel by his turntable. A Brandi Carlile album was already in place. She set the needle and let "Wherever Is Your Heart" fill the room.

As the record moved on to the next track, Dee reached over and turned the volume down. "Got in a bit of an argument with Xavier."

In an instant, Xavier went back on Robbie's hit list.

"Nobody needs to be killed," Dee added dryly, reading her mind.

"Fine." He could get moved to standby. "What was this argument about?"

He crinkled his nose. "You. Kind of. And about Xavier too."

Robbie didn't say anything. Dee spoke when he was ready.

"So that whole thing with us being 'texting buddies,' as you called it, started after I got back from my job, and *your* job had gotten difficult with Mr. Clark showing up early. We got talking when we were looking at footage in the security room, ended up exchanging numbers."

"By talking, do you mean that thing where you say something even vaguely flirty and he blushes so hard he might set something on fire?"

Dee snorted. "No. A real conversation. Questions about me, my background, all that."

"So he wanted to confirm you were a hit person too." Robbie knew Xavier had probably figured that out all on his own, but she could see him trying to get Dee to confirm it.

"Actually, no. More the difference between current me and past me, if that makes sense?"

"It does not."

At least Dee was feeling better enough to sigh dramatically. "Okay, look, he told me stuff in confidence and wanted it to stay between him and me. But he doesn't get that me includes you, y'know?"

Robbie nodded. A lot of people didn't get that. "When you were arguing tonight, it was about me in the sense that you want to tell me whatever it is you're dancing around, and he doesn't?"

"Exactly."

"Does it endanger you, me, or Coda?"

"Oh, not at all."

"The show?"

He shook his head again, although with slightly less confidence this time.

"Does it affect our ability to find out what's going on with the Ingrams?"

Just like that, Robbie could read Dee again. That slight tightening of his cheek where he bit the inside, the way his eyes flicked away from hers, then back again because he realized looking away was suspicious. She stared and didn't stop until he threw a pillow at her.

"It might not affect anything," he said. "I just think everyone should have all the information in case it does happen to make a difference. But I said fine, I still wouldn't tell you yet—emphasis on *yet*. I'm sorry I sulked on the way home. That wasn't your fault."

"Of course not. Nothing's ever my fault." Everything wrong in their lives was her fault, but who was counting?

"But then you said something in the car about how Xavier wasn't my type, and it was such a minor, offhand thing, but, Robs, if I can't even have a simple conversation with you, it's not okay." He gestured at his phone, teetering precariously on the edge of the coffee table. "So I sent a text taking back what I'd agreed. Haven't gotten—"

The phone buzzed itself off a cliff. Dee grabbed for it, and a second later, an avalanche of tension crumbled away. He flopped back against the couch, swiveling so he could stretch his legs out comfortably.

"He said yes?"

"Yeah. Well, actually, it just says 'fine' with a period at the end, but I'll take it. All right, so Xavier has been living as Xavier for months now. And you know how theater lets people step into roles and identities they wouldn't experience otherwise? It's like that. So we've talked a lot about, y'know, how I figured out my identity and—"

"Oh my fucking god, Dee, you know his real name, don't you?"

"You're ruining my dramatic reveal."

"Screw your dramatic reveal. Spit it out!"

"Fine, her name is Cassie Whitaker."

"Her. Her name. Is Cassie."

"That's about the sum of it. Playing the role of Xavier unearthed some gender feels, which is why she shared with me in the first place, but yeah, being Cassie is her truest self right now."

Robbie had expected finding out Xavier's true identity would be a moment of triumph. Instead, the bottom had dropped out again. How the hell had she missed that?

One look at a person and she could know everything about them. That was how it was supposed to be. How it used to be.

She'd had all the pieces. The inconsistencies in who Xavier seemed to be. Hell, she'd thought two people lived in that Deacon Arms apartment. Two people basically had. She just hadn't been able to connect the dots.

Still, she'd known from the beginning Xavier was holding something back. Even after their deal, when she'd asked questions about the past in hopes of finding a connection to Mr. Clark, he still hadn't shown his cards. At least she'd been right about that.

"You think that makes a difference with the Nicholas thing?" Dee asked, almost hopeful.

"I don't know. It's a piece to the puzzle I didn't have before, though, so who knows?"

The record finished, and Dee's sigh sounded even louder in the quiet room. "I'm grasping at straws, I guess."

"Those particular straws, yes. But there *is* an answer to this all somewhere. We'll figure it out, okay?"

"Yeah." Dee ducked his head. "If we could do that before anyone else kills Cass, I'd appreciate it."

It wasn't an unreasonable request, although Robbie wasn't confident in her ability to deliver on that promise. All the same, it was clearly what he needed to hear, so she simply said, "I'm sure we can manage that."

22

Useful Things to Know

THEY HAD NOT FIGURED IT OUT.

But time had also not stopped to wait for them to do so. They had their first fully off-book rehearsal awaiting their attention, and Robbie desperately wished her dream show didn't feel like an inconvenient distraction.

Robbie sat up in her balcony—well, the Gillespie's balcony, but she'd become rather possessive of her perch now—doing her best to pay attention to the rehearsal below. That attention was immediately knocked off course as she saw the tall apartment facade now gracing the stage, paid for by Ingram's money.

She still couldn't figure out if Ingram—Fletcher—had anything to do with the Xavier mess. Her brain was overlapping radios again: Fletcher's involvement on one station, the role of Cassie's true identity on another. A blaringly loud station was set to the text she'd missed from Marisol last night while she and Dee were distracted, saying they'd had four different underage college students attempting to order at the bar last night.

Thankfully, staff had all carded exactly as they were supposed to, but four incidents in one night? The state had a whole program where cops recruited underage kids to check bars for compliance with liquor laws. Robbie did not believe for a second that Coda just *happened* to be subject to one of those covert inspections mere days after Nicholas threatened her, after it had likely been him who had freaked out Marisol by following her.

But was it only him coming for Coda, or had his politically minded father pulled the strings with the state to target their bar?

The noise in her head was interrupted by noise outside it: the cast applauding themselves for a successful run of act 1. Robbie clapped belatedly, dragging her attention back to the show. *Her* show.

She'd spent hours and days and weeks and months crafting something, then another eon revising, polishing, and working hard to accept Dee's valid critiques as constructive and not a commentary on Robbie's abilities. That had gotten easier as she realized that Dee would never offer anything short of his full support, and genuine support didn't take the form of cushy words and empty praises; it was pushing and shoving and offering a solid hand up.

It worked.

God, it worked. Maybe this whole endeavor would flop. Maybe they'd run the show one night and not sell a single ticket after. Maybe they wouldn't sell any in the first place—no, that wasn't true, because apparently, they already had. But regardless of how it turned out, Robbie had accomplished this.

"You created something you're so proud of that you want to put it out into the world, and that in and of itself is incredible," Dee had told her.

Damn right it was.

And she wasn't getting to enjoy a second of that pride. Her brain had already started spinning again as the company began act 2 and a velvet seat creakily unfolded next to her.

"I don't mean to impose on you again," said a warm, familiar voice, "but I found myself once more having a small bit of time freed up in my schedule."

Oh, she had not been prepared for this.

She glanced over at him to see what she'd come to think of as his human smile rather than his political one.

"Nice to see you again, Fletcher."

He'd said to call him that, and she never had. But she couldn't get the name *Ingram* to cross her tongue right now, so *Fletcher* it was.

He watched the rest of act 2's opening number in silence, applauding politely but enthusiastically at the end.

"It's coming together quite nicely," he remarked as the next scene started. "I rather think you and your friend undersold the whole thing when you pitched it to me."

She flushed a bit with pride before her stomach flipped. A part of her brain whispered, *compliments are an excellent diversion tactic*, and it sounded uncomfortably like James's voice.

"Thanks," she murmured, because what else was there to say?

"I know I've said this before, but I'm impressed with the two of you. When I go out and do all my stumping and handshaking and what have you, a good deal of it is inspiring, but it's very easy to get lost in the rhetoric."

Robbie had no idea what he was talking about and said as much, which got her an easy sort of laugh.

"Here I am proving my point, saying words without actually saying anything. What I meant is that I've appreciated being involved in this project. The two of you…local business owners, creative artists, innovators. You are the absolute picture of the type of person I want to work on behalf of, the reason I decided to get into politics."

Given the intent of the statement, Robbie went ahead and stifled her snort of incredulity. Business owners. Creatives. Killers. They really did look picture-perfect—if you ignored that last bit.

She didn't ignore it though. That was who she was. As much as she tried to compartmentalize, being a contract killer had now spilled out over every aspect of her life. How much had this charismatic, smiling man had to do with that? And if the answer was anything other than zero, why? What did he want? It had to be political, surely.

"It's a big change for you, isn't it? This whole campaign."

"Oh, not as much as you probably imagine. It's been something on my mind for a long time. You know how I got my start, right?"

She'd reviewed his Wikipedia page for the umpteenth time this morning. "Insider trading at nineteen, right?"

"Just trading," he corrected. "The insider part was speculation on the part of the media and the SEC."

"Speculation means they couldn't prove it. Doesn't mean it wasn't true."

"I like the way you think, Robbie." He smiled like he meant it. "The point is I was nineteen. I didn't care about much then. Live fast, die young. That sort of mentality, you know? More like get rich, die young, I suppose. I thought the world owed me something, and I decided not to view that in the abstract. I took every penny I could and then some."

Dryly, she remarked, "Seems to have worked out well for you."

"It did, it did. But it got old. *I* got old. Now this isn't a plight toward which I expect anyone to be sympathetic, but I got tired of all the money."

Her cynical laugh was so abrupt, it turned into a cough as the air stuck in her throat. "Not relatable in the least, no."

"I didn't think so. All the same, with enough money, I stopped thinking the world owed me, and in recent years, I spent a lot of time wondering if perhaps I don't owe the world something. Or if not the world, some small piece of it."

It didn't make a *lot* of sense, but it made some sense, she supposed. He viewed himself as the hero of his narrative, painting himself in a quite flatteringly philanthropic light, but at the heart of his story, he was rich, got bored, and decided to play a new game. Understandable.

"But it means leaving behind everything you've built, right? You have to surrender all your business interests and whatnot."

He waived a hand like his billion-dollar companies were a minor detail. "I will. I'm not concerned about that."

"Does it all go to your son now?" she asked, mind flicking over the half dozen press interviews she'd watched of Fletcher saying that wasn't the case.

"Ah, Nicholas. He's… He could do quite well with all of it." The confidence in his tone picked up as he finished his sentence, but Robbie hadn't missed the hard dip in the middle. "He's got an excellent head for numbers. Excellent at making deals to our advantage."

Wasn't he just. "Good, levelheaded sort then?"

Fletcher hesitated, which answered Robbie's question far more than the words he flung out after. If he was in on the Xavier hit, he could not be happy with how Nicholas handled it.

"I'm sure I'm not supposed to be this honest, but—well, Nicky's not a perfect man." Understatement. "I did briefly consider handing him the keys to the kingdom, but he still has some growing to do, and that's difficult when you have that much responsibility. He understands my decision, but I'm sure he feels the loss. He's suffered a lot of that. He wasn't quite twenty when we lost Alexandria, and my wife passed only a few years later. It's been just him and me for a long while. All this has been his dream his whole life, stepping into my shoes. Used to do it as a child. Literally wear my shoes, put on one of my ties, and clomp around the house with a head full of ideas on how things ought to run."

"Gotta start honing those skills early."

"Yes, I suppose," he said, although it didn't seem entirely directed at Robbie. He shifted topics as the next musical number began. "Oh, I believe I heard a portion of this one at a previous rehearsal. My god, it looks marvelous all come together like this."

It did, and Robbie let the attention center back on the stage below them, or at least Fletcher's attention. Her own mind was turning over what he'd said—and what he'd clearly not said—about his son.

The underlying lack of trust seemed key. If Fletcher didn't trust his son to take care of his business, would Fletcher trust him enough with a murder? Every single thing he did now, however small, had to be calculated, weighed against how it would affect his political aspirations. Supporting local theater, a good look. A botched contract hit, not so much.

The two of them could still be in on a scheme together, but if so, Nicholas had contracted Robbie without his father's approval. Maybe *that* was where she'd get leverage. Blackmail wasn't her thing, but she could make an exception. She'd gotten good at exceptions in the past few weeks.

Fletcher watched in silence a bit longer, then took his leave, walking slowly across the balcony, absently running his fingers along the railing. He wasn't totally in the clear. He'd invested heavily in the show, and Robbie was always going to be wary of his motives. For now, though, she had to prioritize working out her next move against Nicholas.

Robbie awoke to more phone notifications than she'd ever had in her life.

"Dee! What happened?"

"Get out of bed," he called back, his voice closer than she expected.

She rolled out of bed and shrugged on a robe, shuffling out to find Dee on her couch, not his own. Their rarely used TV was on. He patted the seat next to him without tearing his eyes away.

A reporter sat beneath a "Breaking News" banner talking about—

"The fuck happened to Fletcher Ingram?"

Dee flipped the channel. Another reporter, another banner. This one was at a different point in the story, though, and soon cut to footage of a crowd of frenzied, panicked people.

"Campaign rally in Fort Wayne. Sniper." Dee scoffed. "Sloppy work."

Robbie's heart was doing a full-on sprint while she sat frozen. "That's your issue? A sloppy sniper? What about how the person financing a critical portion of our show just got shot?"

He waved at the TV. "He didn't get *shot* shot. Got him in the arm. Barely even counts. Hence, sloppy work."

In Robbie's book, getting shot anywhere seemed like a problem, but she could see why Dee was annoyed. While it was rare, Robbie did occasionally stumble on news of someone dying of suspicious circumstances intended to look like an accident. Their work was a finely honed craft. Seeing people who couldn't be bothered to get it right was irritating.

The craftsmanship of the sniper wasn't Robbie's first thought though. Even her question about show financing hadn't been first. No, her mind went straight to Nicholas. It couldn't be a coincidence, Fletcher getting shot at while Nicholas was embroiled in his own messy scheme.

"Coffee for your thoughts?" Dee held out a mug, already doctored exactly the way she liked. Not steaming hot but warm enough.

"Are Nicholas *and* Fletcher both involved in something shady, maybe to do with the business at Ajax, and this is a byproduct? Or just Nicholas, but someone's trying to get to him through family?"

"Or Nicholas is behind it," Dee suggested.

Robbie nodded, chewing at her lip. Yeah, that could fit.

"Or it has nothing to do with Nicholas and is a genuine politically motivated assassination attempt."

"Or," Robbie countered, still spinning through possibilities, "Fletcher himself is behind it to get sympathy votes."

"I like that one. Not a sloppy sniper. Someone paid to miss." Dee hummed contentedly, as if this possibility had solved everything.

It certainly had not. Robbie pulled her phone from the robe pocket. Within a minute, she'd pulled up shaky footage from four different bystanders. She handed it to Dee. "Do you recognize anything that might tell you who the sniper is?" There was an easy way to answer their questions and find out who was behind this: Ask the person who did it.

Dee looked at the videos she'd found. When those apparently held nothing, he got his own phone out and began searching for more. They kept going, from official news to social media—Robbie didn't think anyone would bother taking the time to post while fleeing the scene of an attempted assassination, but she turned out to be wrong. After an hour, Dee made the same clicking sound with his tongue as he did when he finally opened a peanut butter jar with a tricky lid.

"I think I've got it. Here, look." He was holding her phone and she his. They swapped back and Robbie squinted. Dee pointed at something blurry in the background. "There. See? That blue thing."

"I think that's the T-shirt of someone running."

"Could be, but I'm pretty sure it's a scrap of a grocery bag."

"You're awfully excited about some piece of trash."

Dee rolled his eyes. "It's supposed to appear that way. Nobody pays attention to trash, but someone put it there."

He was already scrolling the contact list in his phone. He dialed, but when someone answered, all he said was "Dee. Monty. Squid."

Snatching Robbie's phone, he typed something into her notes app. The process repeated three times, switching only the last word each time: pineapple, clock, ember. On the fourth call, Dee put the phone on speaker and held it between them.

"What?" The voice was gravelly and accented. Australian maybe? Robbie was terrible with accents.

"Monty. Dee."

"Yeah, I know. I heard you've been making calls." That was fast. "What do you want?"

"Blue wind marker. That was you."

A note of caution crept into the voice. Monty's voice, Robbie assumed. "Jesus, Dee. How?"

Dee shrugged, even though the other person couldn't see. "Guess I'm better than you."

He said it in a friendly, almost teasing way, like this was part of a longer running conversation than Robbie knew. Monty grunted.

"Listen, I'm gonna need to know who hired you."

Monty's laugh was deep and full-bodied. Genuine amusement. "Good one. Why are you actually calling?"

"No, really. I need to know who hired you."

"Dee." The laugh was gone without a trace. "You trained with James. You know better than to ask that."

Robbie couldn't quite tell whether Monty was saying he'd also trained under James or only knew him by reputation. She didn't recognize his name, but that meant nothing. He could've been James's best friend in the world, and James would still never have shared the details with her.

"Come on. You owe me for Miami."

"Good to hear from you, Dee. Have a nice day."

The call ended.

Robbie had to respect his professionalism—everyone knew you never talked about a client—but disappointing all the same.

"Well," Dee huffed, dropping the phone. "I had hoped that would go better, but we can rule out a random politically motivated bystander at least. Someone hired Monty."

"Is Monty good?"

"Are you asking me if he missed?" At Robbie's nod, Dee wavered his hand in a so-so motion. "He's not the very best, but he does know what he's doing. Conditions weren't tricky, so I'm inclined to say it was probably a scare tactic or publicity stunt, not a true hit."

Of course he wasn't the very best. Dee was, and Robbie didn't have to know a thing about sniping to know that.

Dee wasn't wrong about the possible reasoning though. Robbie grabbed her phone to look up other threats to Fletcher's life. If this was a stunt to earn him sympathy among voters, maybe the same tactic had been used before. Not another sniper, of course, but even "leaked" news of a death threat could be used to manipulate the board of a company toward a preferred decision.

Unfortunately, if that had been a strategy, Fletcher hadn't used it for himself, as far as she could tell. The closest she could find was the death of his wife, which had certainly garnered him plenty of public sympathy. She frowned at the official obituary. *Cynthia, only child of August Wright, former head of the Wright-Foster Shipping Company, used her inherited fortune to further her philanthropic works.* Robbie had thought the woman was, for lack of a better word, a normal person. She'd come from money though. Nicholas was in his early twenties at the time, old enough to inherit. Her death had been described simply as an unexpected illness. James had included poisons in his initial broad training before Robbie chose her specialty. Plenty of poisons looked like unexpected illness.

Without more information, this was nothing but speculation, but it didn't seem out of character for Nicholas to kill to get money. Maybe he'd intended the same with Fletcher, or simply creating a big enough scare to get his father to drop out of the Senate race. Succeeding in that would mean not losing his role in the family business—and the income that came with that. She didn't know what else Nicholas had his hand in, but perhaps another one of his schemes had been upset, and he saw a hit as a means of correcting that. Too many maybes for her liking.

She sighed and hauled herself off the couch, snagging her mug and Dee's to take for refills. This gave her more puzzle pieces, but hell if she knew what to do with them.

Best she could do was focus on the one piece she could question.

"Call Cassie," she told Dee. "Ask if she wants to chat."

He raised his eyebrows. "Ask?"

"I was trying to be polite. Call Cassie. Tell her she's coming over to talk."

23

Imaginary Creatures

IT WASN'T THAT ROBBIE WAS EXPECTING SOMEONE DIFFERENT to show up at her door when Dee invited their dinner guest, but… She was expecting someone different to show up at her door. Instead, the person standing on the back porch, nervous foot-tapping audible against the brick, looked exactly the same as all previous visits.

Mostly.

It was less a difference in appearance and more a difference in expectation. The baby face that made a twenty-five-year-old man look like a teenager could be the youthful appearance of a fem-presenting person in her midtwenties. Robbie could still see it either way. Maybe both ways were true at the same time. It wasn't like there were traits exclusive to any specific gender, just ones that people expected or didn't expect based on what they knew—or thought they knew—about a person.

What *was* a bit jarring was the fact that the person at her door was wearing a *Star Wars* T-shirt.

There were probably better greetings she could have gone with, but instead, she blurted out, "That's not a punk album."

Or maybe there wasn't a better greeting than that. The nervous tapping stopped. Cassie Whitaker actually smiled.

"No, it isn't, is it?"

"I'd been wondering about that. I take it the album-cover wardrobe was part of the persona you created for Landerman?"

"Would you believe that all my music-related shirts are in the wash?"

"I barely believe you live somewhere with a washing machine."

"Hence my current outfit."

Robbie returned the smile as Dee materialized by her side, nervous tension coiled in every limb.

"You're here." It was unclear who that was directed at. "Okay, well, Robbie, this is Cassie. Cassie, Robbie."

"Yeah, kinda got that already," Robbie remarked dryly as she waved their guest inside.

When they'd all settled into their seats in the living room—a relative term in the case of Dee, who couldn't seem to stop fidgeting his entire body—Robbie turned to Cassie and said, "So. Xavier Landerman then."

"Xavier Landerman. It was an identity that was supposed to last me longer than it did, to tell the truth."

"Yes, let's do that."

Cassie flushed, but with a much more miserable air to it than when she turned red under Dee's gaze. "Sorry about that. It's just that you came after me as Xavier Landerman, and then you said Mr. Clark was looking for me as Xavier, and it seemed like nobody knew who I actually was. As dangerous as it seemed to be to stay Xavier, I was scared switching back would alert everyone to my real identity."

"I'm not sure I agree with the logic, although I do get where you're coming from. But apparently, pretty much everyone knows you aren't Landerman. Even Nicholas Ingram knew that when he hired me. But it's clear to me that he could have wanted me to take out Cassie Whitaker and was pointing me to you as Landerman was simply the most expedient way to do that."

"Yeah, but why me at all?"

"That's the twenty-thousand-dollar question," Robbie said. Dee and Cassie both made similarly unamused soft chuckles. "Why don't you tell me about yourself? Your actual self."

"I don't know what to tell."

"Xavier Landerman was a thief. Let's start there. Is Cassie Whitaker also a thief?"

"Oh, well, yeah," Cassie said as if it were an absurd question. Her voice seemed to maybe be pitched a little different now that she wasn't Xavier. Though that could be Robbie's interpretation and expectation running off again.

She gestured for Cassie to continue. "Care to elaborate? For how long? Ever steal anything from someone who shouldn't have had it in the first place?"

Cassie, to her credit, seemed to think hard about the question, leaning forward in the armchair and putting her elbows on her knees, frowning at the blue damask rug. Finally, she said, "I'm not sure."

"To which question?"

"All of it. I don't know if I've taken anything like that, because I don't pay much attention to where an item's been, just where it is and where it's going. And I'm not sure the best way to answer how long I've been a thief. Always, I guess?"

Dee laughed. "I know you're talented, but I have a hard time picturing a toddler wandering into the Louvre and making off with a Caravaggio."

Someday, Robbie was going to get all Dee's references. For now, she was at least glad to see him look a little more relaxed, a hint of a smile lingering on his face.

Cassie just shrugged. "Obviously, that's a bit of a stretch, but my dad was a thief. My earliest memories tend to jumble together, but I remember learning very young how to…well, how to deceive people. Misdirection, subterfuge, prevarication. The lines between what was real and what was an act were always so fuzzy for me. My dad was gone a lot when I was little, but I was maybe ten or so when he first took me out with him. Nothing major. Shoplifting, really, but it was how I got started."

Great. That didn't even come close to narrowing things down as much as Robbie had hoped. A few years of stealing would have been enough to sift through, but a decade and a half? And it wasn't as if Cassie would know the rightful owner of everything she stole. Something could link back to Nicholas, could mess with some moneymaking scheme of his, with Cassie none the wiser.

"Does stuff from way back then matter though? Maybe there's nothing to worry about anymore," Cassie suggested with admirable optimism. "Nicholas's deadline for the job passed, right? Maybe there's no need to kill me now. Maybe he'll give up entirely."

Robbie opened her mouth, but Dee was the one who replied, stopping his fidgeting long enough to ask, "Are you willing to literally stake your life on that?"

Cassie looked down at the carpet again, her "no" barely audible.

"What about your dad?" Robbie asked to nudge them back on

track. "It may not be about you at all. Maybe *he* stole something recently, and Nicholas is taking you out as a way to get to him?"

"He died about two years ago."

"Sorry," Robbie and Dee both said automatically.

Cassie shrugged. "It's fine. We weren't close in the end anyway."

"What about other relatives? This sounds like a family business. Did your siblings get into it? Aunts or uncles? Cousins?"

At each question, Cassie shook her head. "My dad was an only child. My mom left when I was nine. The whole process of adopting me was taxing on their marriage, which I think was already on the rocks. Besides, we moved around a lot, so even if there had been relatives, I probably wouldn't have seen them much."

Not a family business then. Not much of a family, in Robbie's opinion, if Cassie's purpose in life was simply to be her father's convenient accomplice. Robbie didn't have any right to judge family dynamics though. She hadn't spoken to her own biological family in seventeen years. James had been more of a father figure to her than her actual father, and he had run an international collective of contract killers. If she thought about it, her purpose in James's life had been as something of a convenient accomplice. She preferred not to think about it.

"Anyone?" Dee asked. His tone wasn't exactly pitying, but it wasn't far off. "Anyone else who might care enough that taking you out would hurt them?"

"No." The rug in the living room had never gotten so much attention in its life. "Maybe Lucky would've noticed if I didn't finish the museum job, but even then, he'd just hire someone else for the theft. I mean, it's why I've been having the hardest time understanding why someone would pay so much money—any money, really—to have me killed. If I died, frankly, no one would notice at all."

Well, that was an abysmal sentiment. Robbie opened her mouth to say at least someone cared about Cassie enough to kill her, which was better than no one caring at all, but somehow, she didn't think Cassie would be cheered by that.

Honestly, she wasn't sure what to say now. Dee, on the other hand, got up and went to crouch by the side of Cassie's chair. His voice was pitched very quietly, not intended for Robbie, but she heard anyway as he said, "I would notice if you died, so I would really rather you not."

Cassie's lips moved in what Robbie was pretty sure was the shape of a thank you.

Dee gave a curt nod and stood up. "Right. This has, once again, been spectacularly unhelpful. Robbie, we need to be at the theater soon to run through lighting cues with Summer, so if we want to continue to get nowhere, we'll have to do so later."

Cassie hesitated in the hallway before turning back to Robbie. "I know I still owe you the rest from our first deal."

Eh, Robbie had drawn a line through that debt the moment Dee asked her to keep Cassie safe. Plus, Ingram had come through with the funding, and while still suspicious, it took care of any immediate financial threat to the play.

"But just wondering," Cassie continued, "how much would it cost for me to hire you to take out this Nicholas Ingram?"

"You don't want to do that," Dee said from farther down the hall. "Takes a certain type of person to take out a hit, and I promise, you are not that kind of person."

"I could be," Cassie said in a halfway decent imitation of confidence. "How much?"

"It's not a matter of cost. I shouldn't be anywhere near Nicholas Ingram's death. Even if it looked like an accident, there's still a chance the death of someone that rich and influential would have an investigation. I'm tied to him. We've met. He came to Coda. He gave me a significant sum of money in a difficult but not impossible way to trace." Taking him out to protect Coda and Dee seemed an easy out, but not if the act simply endangered them in a different way. Robbie spread her hands. "I'm sorry. If you really want to do that, best I can do is give you some referrals."

Cassie slumped. "I can't. Dee's right."

"That he is. With annoying frequency."

As Dee walked Cassie out, Robbie headed to get dressed. They had gotten nowhere. Dee *was* right. Except Robbie couldn't help but feel like every piece of information they had and the shapes of every gap still unfilled were telling a story, one she could use to counter threaten Nicholas, if she could just fit them all together.

Of all the things Robbie expected to have to do in order to stage a musical, settling a screaming match between two actors was not on her list. The show was due to open in two weeks, and good god, Robbie did not know tensions were going to get this high.

Dee had been onstage before, had been through this whole process various times in varying capacities, but he wasn't entirely unaffected. Sure, he didn't appear to care one way or another about these two fighting over missing each other's cues, but Robbie could still see tension in the way he moved, hear a tightness in his voice as he sang. Probably nobody else noticed, but she knew his voice as well as she knew her own.

"Take ten," Robbie told the fighting actors firmly. "Go sit and speak to each other like the fucking adults you are. Sort this out, figure out a way to work together, and don't you dare set foot on this stage again until you've put this behind you. Am I clear?"

They both nodded and shuffled off.

"It's a full moon tonight," Julia said from somewhere behind Robbie. She turned around to see the director pinching the bridge of her nose and sighing heavily.

"I wasn't aware we'd included werewolves in the cast."

"And yet here we are, full moon, everyone going wild."

"Dee says this is normal at this point in show prep."

Julia shrugged. "Sure. It's normal. Doesn't mean they're not all animals."

"Anything I can do to help?" Aside from coming up with the entire show, most of Robbie's contributions since production started had consisted of raw physical labor, getting money from Fletcher Ingram, and wearing out the balcony seats. And she'd been so lost in her head lately, she hadn't even realized they were less than two weeks out from opening. She felt useless.

"Are you aware that my lead actor is currently lying on his back in the center of the stage, staring up at the battens and mumbling to himself?"

Robbie followed Julia's gaze to Dee. "Ah. That doesn't look good."

"No, it doesn't. If you want to help, please go work some magic on your better half so I can have a functional lead again. And if you can get him off the stage while you do that, I can at least run scenes with his understudy, because they need to rehearse too."

With a nod to Julia, Robbie went over and lay on the ground

next to Dee. Out of the corner of her eye, she saw Julia throw her hands up in exasperation before stalking off. Full moon indeed.

From this perspective, Robbie could see all the assorted pipes and rigging that held curtains and ropes and Priya's newly and magnificently redone backdrops. All of it lovely. All of it hovering ominously over them. She'd never seen it from this perspective. Sure would be easy to fake an accident that sent all that crashing down.

The chances of someone else with her specialty getting the job and pulling it off tonight weren't zero, but they were small enough that she could take a moment to listen to Dee speed reciting his lines like it was some kind of race. If theater and murder didn't work out, he could probably find a fallback career as an auctioneer. He was somewhere near the end of act 1, and she let him keep going. It took maybe five minutes for him to reach the break, and as he took a deep breath to presumably launch himself into act 2, Robbie slipped her hand into his and squeezed.

He exhaled.

"Few more times with that, yeah?" Robbie said softly. "The deep breath and the exhale."

He did as instructed, and she was certain he was more relaxed for it, even though she couldn't spare a glance his way as she kept an eye on the totally safe rigging above them.

"Julia said she'll buy me a unicorn if I get you to move off her stage." It seemed more likely Julia was going to somehow gift her a werewolf at this point, but Robbie liked this version better.

"Where are we going to keep it?"

"I'm thinking the Coda patio. It's enclosed, so it couldn't get out. It's either that or tie it up to the dumpster out back, and I feel like the patio is classier."

"Yeah, but a unicorn could really class up the back alley."

"Fair point. What do you say we get out of Julia's way? I don't think I've ever shown you where I hide out when I'm watching rehearsals."

Robbie stood to pull Dee to his feet, then into a hug. Neither of them said anything, but she felt him take another deep breath and let it out slowly. As she led him offstage, she caught Julia in her periphery mouthing an exaggerated "thank you" to her.

Robbie needed to get back to solving their Nicholas problem, but keeping Dee in sight as much as possible was one way to keep him safe.

She led the way up the back stairs to the balcony, and Robbie took her usual seat. Dee dropped down next to her.

"It's nice up here," he said softly. "I get why you like it. Good, powerful vibes."

"Well, perhaps you may have heard, I'm actually the creator of this entire musical, so I'm basically the god of this show. And a god needs a solid place to look down upon the mortals."

"Forget the back alley. Obviously, you need to keep your unicorn up here."

Robbie made a vaguely agreeing sort of noise. They watched as Julia waved a hand and Dee's understudy stepped onto the stage and began speaking lines from act 1, scene 5 or maybe 6. Robbie was blanking on the numbers. It was a good scene, though, and while Robbie had a bias toward Dee's way of performing, the understudy brought nice vibes to the stage too.

"Is it just nerves about the show?" she asked after the scene progressed a bit.

Dee sighed, and Robbie almost regretted breaking the moment. Almost. He'd needed that bit of levity before, but he needed this now too. "No."

"Talk to me, Dee."

"You should've killed Xavier Landerman when you were supposed to."

That wasn't even in the ballpark of what Robbie expected. Not even the same country. She couldn't manage a response, just a choked cough.

"I'm not saying I want Cassie dead right now. But if you'd done your job and killed her when she was Xavier, I wouldn't have gotten to know her. And I wouldn't be concerned about why the Evil Ingram has it out for her, and I wouldn't be bothered by loose ends and frayed threads. I would just have the show to worry about, and it would be plenty."

"I'm terribly sorry." It sounded sarcastic, but she meant it. Dee may not have intended to say it, but he was right this was all her fault. "Sorry I didn't kill Landerman, and sorry we didn't get to do a proper brunch after."

Dee's laugh was almost a happy sound. "That's absolutely the worst part of all this. You owe me brunch."

"Brunch with killer French toast. When everything is over and done. I promise."

"She *knows*, Robbie."

She glanced over at him, trying to puzzle out his meaning from the look on his face. That didn't work, so she went the direct route and asked.

Dee sighed. "About me. About us. What we do. She knows, and it definitely freaks her out, but she still turns pink when I look her way, still replies to all my texts instantly, still wants to help out backstage with the show."

"Oh."

"Yeah."

It wasn't something either of them had experienced before. Both Dee and Robbie were good at truly keeping their one-night stands actually limited to one night. Even seeing someone more than once always ended when he couldn't share enough of himself to make it worth the other person's time. The only people they trusted with their full selves were each other. Robbie didn't know what to make of the idea of someone else.

"Is it serious?" she asked, because she didn't know what else there was to say.

There was something relieving in Dee's laugh. "Hold the U-Haul, Robbie. It's been, like, two weeks. Most of that time, she's been trying to figure out why someone wants to kill her. I've been up to my neck in rehearsals and show preparations. Of course it's not serious. It's friendly and it's flirting, but that's it."

"Still."

"Yeah, still. I don't know. I don't know if after all this is over, either of us will want to see each other ever again. If we do, I don't know whether it'll become anything other than friendliness and casual flirting. Don't know if she actually gets you and me, if she could accept the fact that we're a package deal, together for life. Maybe she won't be able to handle knowing that my partner was at one point planning to kill her. I just want the chance to see it though. Does that make sense?" Dee had a wild desperation in his voice, a crushing need for Robbie to understand. It shattered her, knowing that beneath all these thoughts about what might or might not happen with Cassie, Dee was also carrying the worry that Robbie wouldn't support him through it all.

How could he think that? With every wrong turn she'd made lately, Dee had never distanced himself or put his own safety above everything else. He'd supported every bad decision she made. He'd never done anything that made her doubt him. Robbie, on the other hand, had fucked up way worse than she realized. Making a mess of their finances, failing a contract job, befriending a target, she knew all that. But somewhere along the way, she'd fractured the most important relationship in her entire life.

Nicholas didn't have to harm Dee. Robbie had done it all by herself.

She leaned sideways until her shoulder bumped against him, and her head knocked gently into his. She could've said yes, one simple word to push away all those fears and hope it was enough. But there was one surefire way to communicate perfectly with Dee, so instead, softly, just loud enough for the two of them on the empty balcony, she sang. Only a few lines, the chorus from Tegan and Sara's "I Know I Know I Know," a song Dee had introduced her to, simple lyrics about love.

That was enough. He sighed and the physical tension began to melt away.

"I'm going to fix things, Dee. I promise."

Whatever it took, she wasn't going to break that promise.

24

Blame the Full Moon

ROBBIE WASN'T GOING TO BLAME EVERYTHING THAT HAPpened on Sunday night—or more accurately very early on Monday morning—on the full moon. But she wasn't *not* going to blame it on that either. It was possible Julia was onto something.

Around one in the morning, a fight broke out in Coda when two people with a few too many drinks both wanted to sing the same song. It felt a bit excessive, but if five years running this business had taught Robbie anything, it was that people got *extremely* invested in karaoke. Also, drunk people were unpredictable.

Around two in the morning, as she and Dee tidied up just after closing, Dee abruptly threw down his broom, then himself, crashing onto one of the sofas along the back wall. Robbie abandoned her rag and spray bottle and sprinted across the room.

"What's wrong?"

Instead of answering, Dee held out his phone. The voicemail app was open to the auto-transcript of a message left twenty minutes ago from a number Dee had saved as "Cassie" followed by a skull and crossbones emoji and a shrugging emoji.

Robbie didn't bother trying to wade through the lines and squiggles. She hit play and held the phone up to her ear to listen.

It wasn't Cassie's voice. Some nasal, high-pitched stranger. Lots of background noise.

"This is Officer Shapiro calling for, uh, Dee? The owner of this phone was brought in to Reevesburg General about an hour ago. We haven't been able to find any ID, but you're listed as an emergency contact. We would appreciate any information you can provide. You can call back…"

Robbie turned it off.

"*You're* Cassie's emergency contact?"

"How is that what's important here?" Dee snapped.

Right. "It isn't. It's just the first thing that popped into my head. Is there anything incriminating that you or she have texted at any point?"

"*Robbie.*"

"It's a valid question. A cop has her phone. A *cop*, Dee. And not a burner but her actual phone. If there's something on there that's going to link us to anything illegal, we need to know."

"No," Dee said quietly. "There's nothing. I'm not stupid, Robbie."

She sat down next to him, dropping the phone on the cushion next to her and putting an arm around Dee. "I know. I know you're not. I just want to make sure you're safe, okay? A cop calling you is pretty concerning."

"It doesn't matter who made the call. It's the fact that anyone called. And that it wasn't her."

Robbie knew she should've cared more about all that, but Cassie Whitaker or Xavier Landerman coming to harm had never fully made it off the "things that are fine" list in her book. It wasn't that she was actively keeping Cassie there. It was just the default space for anyone beyond herself and Dee, and she hadn't bothered to change things.

What she *did* care about was Dee, and Cassie being harmed was definitely not on Dee's list of "things that are fine."

Nobody in the history of emergencies ever knew how to answer the generic "what do you need?" question, so Robbie went with the trick she'd picked up from Dee, offering specific, if limited, options for support. "Do you want me to call the cop back for you, or do you want me to bring the car around so I can take you over there?"

"Car."

Half an hour later, they walked into the emergency room together. There weren't as many people as Robbie would've expected, maybe ten or so. In her mind, an emergency room at three a.m. should've had more chaos, but she supposed that most normal people were sleeping at this out instead of doing whatever it was that landed people here. Or maybe it *had* been busy, and the hospital had simply already dealt with Julia's plethora of werewolves.

She walked up to the desk. "We got a call from an Officer Shapiro about a patient who was brought in around one-ish. Who do we talk to about that?"

"Presumably Office Shapiro. I think she's still here. Have a seat anywhere. Someone will be out to talk to you."

"Can you tell us what happened?" Dee asked.

"You family?"

"The thing is—"

"Go have a seat."

They sat for twenty minutes before a cop in her midfifties with gray-brown hair pulled into a tight bun and tanned skin that suggested she didn't spend all her waking hours on a night shift came and sat across from them.

"Is one of you Dee?"

"Dee Machado." He raised his hand briefly.

The cop looked to Robbie. "And you are?"

"Robbie McNeil. Friend and driver. And since we're doing names, can I assume yours is Shapiro?"

The woman sat up straighter and tapped the name tag on her uniform. Right. Shapiro. Still, Robbie didn't feel like people with name tags ought to be exempt from the entire social custom of introductions.

The cop's attention was back on Dee. "I expected a phone call, not you showing up here. Here you are anyway, though, so I'd like to ask a few questions. I'm trying to get a response from the phone company, but it's not a quick thing this time of night. Can you tell me your friend's name?"

Okay, they probably should've expected that question.

"Blond hair?" Robbie stalled, then thought of Xavier's defining look. "Punk rock T-shirt?"

"Blond, yes. And I'm not well-versed in punk rock, but I believe the T-shirt had a picture of a blue box from some British TV show my nephew likes. Now, can you please tell me your friend's name?"

"Cassie. Cassandra Whitaker," Dee answered. "What happened?"

"Can you tell me why Ms. Whitaker may have been in the Penny Park area at midnight?"

The Ajax Club. An illegal gambling den. Both Robbie and Dee shook their heads.

"As best we can tell, Ms. Whitaker was the victim of a mugging gone wrong. She was stabbed in the abdomen. No wallet or car keys were found. Her phone was several feet away and badly cracked, so it may have been dropped during a struggle. A patrol car happened to find her, and they were able to get her here in time. Much longer and she would've bled out. She lost a lot of blood as it is. The doctors want to monitor for internal bleeding, but for now, they're saying she's stable."

Some of the tension went out of Dee's shoulders.

"A mugging?" Robbie repeated innocently. "On TV, those are always some guy in a ski mask waving a gun around. But she was stabbed?"

"Don't believe everything you see on TV, Ms. McNeil. While guns are more common, plenty of robberies occur with a knife still. We believe it was a switchblade, not a kitchen knife. Officers canvassing found a switchblade in a gutter two blocks away. Wiped mostly clean, but a bit of blood still. We'll check for prints, but those may have been wiped too." Shapiro shrugged. "It could be unrelated. Lot of crime happens up in that area. We'll know more later."

"I see." Robbie stood. "Dee, I realize in our rush, I forgot to pay for parking. You okay if I leave you here for a few minutes?"

"I can stay with M—your friend," Officer Shapiro said. Robbie was curious whether the cop had been about to go with "Mr. Machado" or "Ms. Machado" since she didn't seem inclined to use first names for Robbie or Cassie.

Robbie hurried out of the building, walking in the general direction of the parking lot. She'd already paid for two hours of parking, which was absolute bullshit at a hospital, so she didn't bother walking all the way to the car. Instead, she pulled out her phone.

Dee wasn't the only one who kept abreast of their colleagues' work. Robbie may not know snipers, but she knew plenty of others. Plenty of hit people specialized in muggings. Fewer routinely left switchblades near the crime scene and might be careless enough to overlook taking the target's phone.

Like Dee, she had to make a few calls to track down a current phone number. Her fourth call was answered by a deep voice and a clear smile. "Robbie McNeil. As I live and breathe. Been a while. I haven't seen you since…"

He trailed off, but Robbie finished for him. "Since the thing in Bermuda. Yeah."

Fucking Bermuda. Never went well, two professionals stepping on each other's toes. Especially not when one of those professionals was Todd Adamson, who had no aversion to messes.

"I'd heard you and Machado are working together now. Wouldn't think your styles meshed."

"Dee and me are both solo. We just share an apartment. It's convenient."

"Sure, sure. Don't you two run a bar for the gays or some shit?"

Robbie took a steadying breath. "Yes, Todd. We run a bar for the gays. We also happen to *be* the gays, if you recall. But that's not what I'm calling about. You're working for Alma now, right?"

Robbie had already been solo when James had his heart attack, but the majority of James's operatives had stayed on, temporarily overseen by Alma. Robbie had considered calling James before anyone else right now. Probably would've gotten the correct number straightaway. But she was doing this for Dee, and he didn't need another thing to be mad about right now. He certainly wouldn't want to hear anything that came from James. And in any case, Robbie was smart enough to get to the bottom of this on her own. Wasn't she?

"Yeah, what about it?"

"Do you know where Dee and I live?"

"Can't say I've kept track."

"Reevesburg, Indiana."

He laughed, all delight. "No flipping way! That's a crazy coincidence. Are you free later? We should get lunch because I'm actually in Reevesburg."

"Work or pleasure?"

"It was work, but totally a pleasure if you want to meet up. Had a real quick job. Client gave me a when and a where and a twenty-four-hour deadline. Said I'm the second person they hired, which is kind of insulting, but I guess the first one botched it. Too many amateurs in this business nowadays if you ask me."

She had not. She bristled a bit at the implication that she was an amateur, especially from someone as second-rate as Todd, but she went with "So that mean you botched it too or..."

"Low blow, McNeil." Was it though? "Course I didn't botch it. I'm sorry about the Bermuda thing, but I do know what I'm doing."

All evidence to the contrary. But Robbie felt tension leech out of her all the same. "Out of curiosity, who was the client?"

"Dude, did I just hear James's precious 'McNeil could've done it better' say she was curious?"

She didn't work for James. She didn't need his approval. But part of her still warmed to know that he thought well enough of her to set a bar for others, even if Todd seemed to have limbo'd under the bar rather than rise to it.

"Figure of speech. I'd heard about someone skipping out on payment recently." Sharing more was risky, but she went ahead. "Blond guy, cocky, enough money that he shouldn't skimp. Has a real obvious alias, but I'm forgetting—"

"Not Mr. Clark?" He sounded a little panicked.

"That's the one!"

"Shit, really? You think I should be worried? I haven't gotten the rest of my payment yet."

At least Robbie could answer that entirely honestly. "I'm sure he'll pay up once you confirm the job's done."

The line crackled with Todd's heavy sigh of relief. "Oh, okay. That'll be fine then."

"I'm sure. Listen, I gotta go. Dee and I have plans today, but maybe next time you're in town, we can do that lunch."

"Yeah, yeah, that'd be great."

"Give Alma my best," she said and hung up before he could realize she'd never said why she was calling him out of the blue.

Dee was still in the waiting room when Robbie returned, although apparently Shapiro hadn't been good to her word about staying with him. He straightened up in his chair as she slumped into the one next to him.

"You paid for parking when we got here. I remember all the complaining. So you find out if this was random bad luck or…"

"Todd Adamson."

"Todd's an ass."

Robbie shrugged. "He got hired. He did the job. It's what we do."

"Oh, I don't mean about that. I wish he hadn't stabbed Cassie, but no, I get it was the job. I meant generally. As a person. Todd's an ass. I never liked him."

"I'm not sure anyone does." Robbie didn't think she was the best judge of that since she didn't like most people, but she was still fairly certain that they weren't the only ones who disliked the guy.

"You didn't tell him she's still alive, did you?"

"Nah, it's his own fault if he couldn't finish a simple job. Yes, I know. Don't look at me like that. But you know how chatty Todd gets. The client called himself Mr. Clark."

"Nicholas Ingram sure gets around."

"That he does." While James had extended his protection to Robbie while she got Nicholas sorted out, obviously he had no reason to put Cassie under that same protection—not the least because James clearly didn't know who Cassie was, or Robbie suspected she would have gotten an even angrier early morning phone call. "I doubt Todd will bother paying any more attention once he gets paid, but hopefully, the fact that his target's still alive stays quiet. We don't know whether he was sent after Xavier or Cassie. And there are plenty of other professionals Nicholas could go to next."

"I don't know who would tell."

"I'm hoping we have a little time to get some answers, but until we do, Cassie can't play Xavier anymore, and best she's not Cassie either. She can't go home. Certainly not to Ajax."

"Yeah, I suppose that'd be best."

Robbie nodded. "Are you waiting on Shapiro or Cassie or anything?"

"No. We're not family so we can't see her right now anyway, and Shapiro is off doing some sort of paperwork now that she knows Cassie's name."

Robbie stood and held out a hand to pull Dee up. "All right then. Your options are we go straight home, or we stop at Lincoln's on Tenth Street on the way and get pancakes. The choice is entirely yours."

"I am kind of hungry."

"Pancakes it is."

Dee nodded firmly, then paused, hesitant. "Robs? Could you drive me to St. Clare's in Larkside first? They, uh, have a meeting in about half an hour."

She draped an arm over his shoulders and steered them both in the direction of the parking lot. "Of course, Dee. Of course I can."

After Dee's meeting, Robbie drove them to the diner. When they were both full up on pancakes drowned in syrup, they went straight home to bed to crash for however long they could manage. Robbie dreamed about the theater, sitting in the balcony with Fletcher Ingram on one side, quiet satisfaction as he watched the show, Cassie or perhaps Xavier on her other side, babbling nonsense she couldn't bother to parse out.

There was more, she was sure, but the pieces of the dream were already scattering when Robbie woke up. The clock read 5:12, which meant she'd been out less than an hour, but she couldn't fall back asleep. The dream felt important, but the harder she tried to remember, the faster the images faded.

Fine. She wouldn't try to remember. Not directly at least. But maybe if she didn't look at it head on, glimpses would still appear in her periphery.

She got up, debated coffee, decided to skip it in hopes of being able to go back to sleep in the near future, and went to the music room. Near the desk covered in recording equipment, she had her keyboard, but right now, she went straight to the glossy black Sauter in the corner. Getting the piano into the apartment had been an absolute nightmare and a half, but it had been worth it. This was the nicest thing Robbie had ever owned in her life. Not that there was much competition. Even if there had been, this still would've been above it all.

She ran her fingers over the keys fondly.

Then she closed her eyes and began to play. She'd never learned to read sheet music—never even tried for fear it would be just like when she tried to read anything else—so she'd always played by ear. By feel? Didn't matter. Her fingers knew the keys, and she didn't have to think, just let her hands move and have faith that the right notes would ensue. She trusted the keys the way Dee trusted his voice, and if it went wrong, well, it wasn't for anyone else anyway.

It felt rather on the nose when trying to remember something, but with no one to judge her, she played "Memory," although maybe a cat trying to win a trip to the afterlife wasn't exactly where her mind needed to be. She tried a few others, but it was possible show tunes weren't the answer. She was going to give up and try going back to bed but started one more, the slow chords of "The Music of the Night," the song Dee had sung that first time Ingram joined Robbie on the balcony during a rehearsal.

It didn't help her remember the dream. It *did* help her remember that rehearsal, that conversation with Ingram. Robbie didn't even finish the song.

She abandoned her poor, beautiful piano and raced back to her room, pulling her phone off the charger on the nightstand. The news article she'd read after Fletcher's emotional sharing session was still buried in her browser's countless open tabs. From her rarely used desk, she grabbed several colors of sticky notes, the ones she usually used to leave herself a thousand reminders of things she'd otherwise forget. This was more or less the same, cues for things she knew but hadn't held together in her mind.

The notes got one word, maybe two. Some sort of intuitive color-coding happened, but Robbie couldn't have articulated exactly what. *Blood* went on a blue one. *Thief* went on yellow. *16yrs* went on green. As she annotated, she scrolled her phone, supplementing her memory with news reports and, better yet, videos of news segments. A *Dateline* episode she didn't watch in full but skipped to three different spots and watched a minute or two on double speed. *Ajax?* went on yellow. A news segment from six years ago got saved on YouTube.

She'd hoped proof Nicholas was behind the sniper attempt on Fletcher's life would give her enough leverage to get him to back off, but without Monty confirming who hired him, she couldn't count on that carrying enough weight. But this? If she could get the whole picture, figure out the full sum of Nicholas's wrongs, that had to add up to enough to threaten him out of their lives. And as a bonus, maybe she could finally get her brain to stop being so fixated on this entire ordeal.

When she'd run through all the information she had, she began arranging things. She started by ordering the sticky notes but stopped partway through that. She didn't need the visuals. Her mind was whirring at full strength again, compiling information, running through possibilities, creating a vision of cause and effect in her mind.

Just shy of an hour later, she burst into Dee's room.

"The hell?" Dee groaned, rolling over and blinking at the light coming in from the hall. He was still in the clothes he'd been in last night—this morning? God, Robbie hated how time worked. The clothes he'd worn for the hospital and pancakes were rather rumpled, and so was he, but he'd get over it.

She thrust her phone at him. "I made a playlist on YouTube."

"You woke me up at"—he squinted at the clock—"six something in the morning to share music with me? Jesus, Robbie."

"It's not music."

"That's even worse. What is it?"

"An idea. Here, I'll text you the link. I can make coffee while you watch, then maybe we can go over to the hospital and see if Cassie is awake, because I have *questions*."

25

A Cat Must Have Three Different Names

HOSPITALS, MUCH TO ROBBIE'S ANNOYANCE, HAD THIS THING called "visiting hours" that meant you couldn't just show up and see a patient, even if you had a *really* important question to ask them.

Robbie and Dee dozed in the car in the parking space they were basically renting by the hour from the hospital, since she'd already paid for it before learning about "visiting hours." Finally, her alarm went off to say it was visit o'clock. And they still had to wait as a nurse informed them that someone would need to make sure Cassie was awake and allowed to receive visitors.

"If I ever end up in a hospital, please kill me," she told Dee as they waited. "Do whatever angel of death shit you gotta do, but for the love of god, don't leave me in here."

"Of course. You know you'd just need to ask for a room with a window, and I'll have my rifle and scope ready to go."

"You're the greatest friend in the world."

"Yes, yes I am." Dee tilted his head toward the nurse who'd made them wait. "Look, he's back."

Reluctantly, the nurse gave them a nod. "Doctor okayed a brief visit. Keep it under half an hour. Room 223. Down that hall, make a right, then the door will be on the left-hand side."

Robbie rushed past while Dee did the nice thing and thanked the man before hurrying to catch up.

As hospitals could be relied on to have an unending supply of hellish things, Room 223 turned out to be a shared room, which meant they didn't even have privacy for a proper conversation. Still, Cassie, in the bed closest to the door, seemed absolutely delighted to see them. Delighted and surprised.

"You're...here. How did you even know I was here?"

"Cop called me," Dee said tersely.

"Oh shit. Why?"

Robbie made herself comfortable in the vinyl-clad chair next to Cassie's bed. "Well, it would appear that someone made Dee an emergency contact in their phone, which allowed the nice officer to call Dee and no one else because your phone was locked."

Cassie turned that shade of pink Dee enjoyed so much. "Right."

As Robbie glanced around the bleak room, she saw a table covered with flowers and cards and garishly bright helium balloons near the window. A similar table was situated behind where Dee was standing at the foot of the bed. It was completely empty.

"Yeah, it's fine," Cassie said, catching Robbie's gaze. "It would've been way weirder if you brought something."

At least they could agree on that. Robbie was fairly certain there wouldn't be a card in the hospital gift shop that said, "Sorry I didn't kill you when I was paid to and now someone else got paid to kill you and failed, but I hope you get well soon and no one else tries to kill you for a while." For starters, it would need a ridiculously small font.

Dee scuffed at the linoleum with his sneaker. "You doing okay?"

"Not great, to be honest, but I've got drugs, so…" Cassie held up a little controller with a push button and smiled weakly.

"Great, great," Robbie said, mindlessly bobbing her head. "Listen, I have a couple questions for you. Actually, a lot of questions, but I'm told we have a time limit for talking to you, so I guess we'll see what we get through, yeah?"

Before Cassie could answer, Dee interjected, "Only if you feel up to it. And if you get tired of Robbie's interrogation, just say so, and I'll haul her out of here."

Robbie glared. Dee shrugged. Cassie said, "It's fine."

"Perfect." Robbie frowned for a moment. She had a torrent of things to ask, but she hadn't put much thought as to the order those questions ought to go in. As far as she could tell, Cassie would be figuring this out as they went along too, so the order of information probably mattered. Robbie didn't have the patience to organize her thoughts, though, so she went with the first one that bubbled up. "When were you adopted?"

"I was eight, I think. Or maybe seven? I think I remember my eighth birthday being with my parents. Adoptive parents, I mean."

"When you were Xavier, you told me you were twenty-five. Is that really how old you are?"

Cassie's nod was hesitant and a bit confused. It was fine. Robbie did the math by counting on her fingers. Seventeen years ago, maybe sixteen depending on when in the year Cassie's birthday was.

"Great. What do you actually remember about your family from before you were eight?"

"Not much, honestly. How much do you remember from that age?"

"Fair enough." Robbie remembered moments: spinning on a tire swing on the oak tree behind the barn, setting up a perfect line of dominoes on the kitchen table that her mother swept off without warning, stuffing herself with hot dogs and gooey ice cream at a county fair. It wasn't the more detailed montages of recent memories. "Tell me what you do remember, however small."

"I remember being a lonely kid more than anything. I was…in foster care for a bit, although I don't remember the details, just that there were lots of different adults looking after me."

"Anything else?"

"I remember music," Cassie added. "A CD player with big bulky speakers. I had a bunk bed at one point, I think. I'd put something on the stereo and climb up to the top to listen."

Lovely but not helpful. Robbie had been so certain earlier with everything mapped out. All she needed to finish the puzzle were a few key pieces. Cassie was giving her fewer of those pieces than she needed.

"Can you tell me what this is about?" Cassie asked, voice full of exhaustion. She raised a hand, carefully avoiding jarring the IV line as she ran her fingers through her dirty, rumpled hair. "Is this to do with who stabbed me?"

"Oh, no, that was Todd," Dee interjected.

"Todd?"

"Don't worry about it."

They might've said more. Robbie wasn't paying attention. In all the times she'd seen Xavier or Cassie, the clothing of choice had been a crew-neck T-shirt, jeans, and Converse. Who knew whether the hospital had tossed Cassie's bloodstained clothes or saved them for her, but in their absence, Cassie had on a grayish hospital gown with a faded triangle print. It tied in the back but loosely, or maybe the knot had come undone altogether.

When Cassie raised her left arm, the right shoulder of the gown slipped. The puzzle piece Robbie was looking for sat on Cassie's collarbone. Part of it anyway. It could've been a rash, maybe even a reaction to all the drugs in her system. Or could be an old scrape not quite healed. The splotch, barely darker than the rest of Cassie's skin, wasn't fully visible, clearly extending farther under the fabric. Robbie could see enough, and she didn't think it was a rash or a scrape.

She knew that birthmark. This one was faded with age, but it wasn't gone. Birthmarks were the sorts of things that went under "distinguishing features" on descriptions of someone people wanted to find. Robbie had read about it weeks ago, and she'd seen another dozen iterations of those descriptions this morning.

"Hey, you got a scar on your back by any chance? Circle-shaped?"

Cassie shrugged. "I don't spend that much time looking at my back. Why?"

Eh, didn't matter. Even if it had been there, it could've faded over time too.

"I'm going to tell you what I think, Cassie," Robbie said carefully, "and it's going to sound utterly absurd, but I'm asking you to listen all the way through, okay? Then you can tell me how ridiculous it all is."

"Sure, all right. Lay it on me."

This time, Robbie did take a moment to put her thoughts in order. She'd come into this whole thing because she'd been curious when she shouldn't have been, but now she'd gone and let that little trickle of curiosity become an entire ocean of speculation. The least she could do was ease Cassie into it instead of taking her to the deepest part and tossing her in.

When she spoke, she kept her voice low, leaning close to Cassie. Dee cocked his head, but Robbie wasn't sure he could fully hear what she was saying. He already knew her harebrained idea though. It wasn't something Robbie was inclined to share with Cassie's roommate on the other side of the hospital's flimsy room dividing curtain.

"I'm fairly certain your adoption wasn't entirely legal. I know." She held up a hand as Cassie seemed about to speak. "If I'm right, you have an older brother. Wide age gap. And until you were born, your older brother was an only child. I'm sorry to say I don't think he was your biggest fan. Not that I'd be upset about that, personally. He seems like an absolutely terrible person, and that's coming from me, a perfect angel, obviously."

Apparently, Dee could hear enough, and his snort made Cassie's hesitant smile turn into something more solid, like it gave her permission to laugh at Robbie. Robbie offered a smirk in return.

"Here's where it gets interesting, and there's a lot of speculation here, so probably I have some details wrong, but think big picture, okay? Your family is rich, like obscenely rich. In the event that something happened to your parents, you and your brother would've been in line to get all that money. When your brother turned eighteen, my guess is he fully realized he could eventually replace his father as head of the company. Maybe even started getting groomed for succession. Plus, I'm certain he got access to a hefty bank account or trust fund. Definitely enough to pay someone quite handsomely to remove his kid sister—or I should say, his fellow heir—from the picture.

"Someone takes the sister—that's you. They demand a ransom. Not sure if they were supposed to do that or if they were supposed to just take your brother's money and go. Either way, your family pays up, but somehow when the exchange is supposed to go down, your kidnappers change everything up, like they've been tipped off about what's going to happen. No one ever hears from you again. An unreasonable amount of your blood is found. The marked bills from the ransom payment never surface. You're dead."

This was actually something of an exciting story to tell, although Cassie did seem like she was enjoying hearing it considerably less than Robbie was enjoying telling it. Dee hadn't been impressed at first either—hadn't believed her at all. Cassie would come around, just like Dee had.

"So," Robbie continued, "you're completely erased. Your kidnapper keeps you, maybe, or dumps you off on someone else. I'm kind of leaning toward dumps you with someone, because if the person who raised you had the kind of money that your ransom supplied, I don't think he would've been a petty thief teaching you to shoplift. He treats you like his child, tells you you're adopted, and I'm sure if you thought you remembered differently, he'd gaslight the fucking hell out of you until you believe you imagined it all."

"Move it along, Robs," Dee said, glancing at his watch. "Let's try not to leave Cassie with a cliff-hanger, all right?"

"Yeah, fine." Robbie met Cassie's wary puppy-dog eyes. "The rest of this is mostly guesswork, but you get the gist. Fast-forward to the present day, or at least sometime relatively recent. Entirely by accident, you are in a place your actual father's been frequenting. Neither of you realized it, but somehow, your brother finds out. My guess is he was following your father. Doesn't matter why. But you're supposed to be gone. He paid good money for that. Possibly you weren't supposed to live at all. But here you are, alive, living under a false name. He does what any rich dick would do. He throws more money at the problem. Specifically, he pays to get rid of you before anyone can find out who you are or what he did. You know the rest from there." She waved a hand vaguely to encompass the whole "I was supposed to kill you" thing. "That's all I've got. Feel free to poke holes in my theory or whatever you'd like to do now."

It was a painfully long and uncomfortable time before Cassie spoke. "Didn't you tell me that the person who hired you was someone named Nicholas Ingram? That he was the son of some very rich and famous political guy?"

"Ah, yes. Yes, I did. Sorry, I didn't include names. I should've mentioned yours. I believe your original name was Alexandria Ingram. I admittedly came up with my theory at five a.m. with less than an hour's sleep and a weird amount of Andrew Lloyd Webber, but I stand by it."

"I think I'd like you to leave now." Her voice managed to be soft and still have a very, very hard edge.

Robbie whipped her head toward Dee. He shrugged and appeared just as bewildered as she felt.

"I wanted you to find actual answers about what's been happening around me, not come up with some absurd fantasy. This is my life. I didn't have a perfect one, sure, but I had a fine enough life before you came into it. If you don't mind, I'd like you to take yourself back out of it." Cassie pressed her lips into a flat line, eyes cold.

Robbie stood. "Yeah, all right. Fair enough. I said you could tell me exactly what you thought after you heard me out, and you did hear me out. You know where to find us if you want to talk more."

She turned and headed for the door, but Dee hesitated. "Cassie—"

"I'd like you to go too, Dee," Cassie said, cutting him off in that firm, detached tone.

"I just—"

Robbie put an arm around him. "She knows where to find us. She has your number. But right now, I think we need to do what she asked, yeah?"

Reluctantly, Dee uncurled his hands from the railing at the foot of the bed and let himself be herded out of the room and back to the car. His mood might not have bothered Robbie so much if not for the fact that she put the radio on as soon as she started driving, and in the twenty minutes it took to get home, Dee didn't sing a single note.

They were both quiet back home. Robbie couldn't stop replaying her story to Cassie, trying to figure out what hadn't made sense, what hadn't been convincing enough. She thought the theory was solid. And Dee, for his part, seemed lost in thought too, although Robbie suspected he was stuck more on Cassie kicking him out than on the story that caused that reaction.

After a few hours of records on Dee's turntable and Robbie glaring at the armada of sticky notes that helped her come up with her theory, Robbie's stomach began a steady growl. She padded out to the living room.

"I think we need shawarma," she announced.

Dee's face lit up. "I think you might be onto something. And I could use the distraction."

"Shawarma isn't a distraction. It's a destination."

He rolled his eyes. "Let me change my shirt, and we can go."

A minute or two later, he emerged from his room wearing what appeared to be the exact same shirt, but Robbie knew he had at least half a dozen of that particular one.

"Let's go," he said. "I'll drive."

She followed him down the back stairs to the alley where they parked. Dee's SUV was down near the pallets where they'd had that first conversation with Xavier Landerman. Robbie couldn't believe that had only been a few weeks ago.

She climbed in the passenger seat and scrolled playlists on her phone as Dee went around to his side. As he started the engine, she switched the Bluetooth from his phone to hers. Dee fidgeted with the air vents until they were to his liking for the current temperature.

And then, "Hey, Robbie?"

His voice was hesitant and deeply concerned.

Robbie snapped her attention to him. "What's wrong?"

"This." He pointed to his right foot and pressed the brake pedal down hard.

"I don't see anything."

"Okay, well, I can't feel anything. I mean, there's no resistance. It just...drops."

"Hop out," Robbie said, already opening her door to hustle around to the other side of the car.

She climbed into the driver's seat, Dee hanging on the open door. She depressed the brake, and...yep, that wasn't right. But she was familiar with this. James had encouraged her to test out her own work as she trained. She'd needed to know how to do this right.

To confirm, she squeezed past Dee and moved around to crouch under the front bumper, searching for—there. A clean cut, a puddle of honey-brown fluid shiny on the asphalt. She would never fully cut the brake lines of a parked car. The brake pedal gave it away immediately, just as Dee had noted. Pressure points, small cuts, weakening the lines so they only went out with sudden sharp pressure, those were the contract killer's ways of tampering. She didn't believe this was a contract killer though. This was desperation and frustration and someone who didn't know better.

Nicholas fucking Ingram.

He hadn't done it well, or maybe he'd only intended it as a threat rather than something effective, but the intent was clear. This was a clear move against Dee.

Getting their liquor license revoked would've devastated Coda's business, but they'd skirted that by virtue of actually running their business properly. Marisol had confirmed the photo of Nicholas looked like the guy who'd followed her, and she'd been beyond freaked out the days she'd been tailed, but he hadn't escalated to any direct action against her or any of Coda's staff.

Hiring Todd to take out Cassie made sense, but Robbie had hoped that would be the end of it. And maybe it was. She couldn't remember when Dee had last driven somewhere, so maybe Nicholas had sabotaged the SUV before Cassie got stabbed, but Robbie couldn't be sure.

This was the closest he'd come to doing real harm, to following through on his threat against Dee and Coda. This was worse than his attempt to take a hit out on her. She didn't like that she needed protection from James, but at least she did have it. The only person to protect Dee like that was Robbie.

It was clear now that Nicholas was still coming for them both. And Robbie needed to find a way to get him out of their lives for good.

26

The Show Goes On

ROBBIE HAD BEEN SO CAUGHT UP IN XAVIER AND MR. CLARK, then Cassie and Nicholas not to mention the threat against Dee, that the realization the show was due to open in a little over a week had her frenzied on all fronts.

Cassie was still in the hospital, which wasn't impenetrable, but not like they had much choice about putting her somewhere safer while she still needed medical care. Nicholas had known her name wasn't Landerman, but they had no idea whether he knew the name Cassandra Whitaker. So far, so good, but Robbie had visited a very weary Cassie to review common means of staging accidental deaths in hospitals. Just in case.

Pointing to Cassie's safety had been the only way Robbie had been granted an audience with her at all. The second Robbie brought up the Alexandria theory, she'd been booted out again. Blackmail was still Robbie's best option against Nicholas, but no matter how many pieces she fit together, she still wanted more. Something utterly damning, the kind of thing that would ruin him.

She needed something, anything, from Cassie to strengthen the claim, to give Robbie some piece of undeniable evidence she could hold over Nicholas's head.

Cassie may have been out of Nicholas's rampaging way now, but Robbie couldn't let go of the feeling that his vendetta against her—and by extension Dee and Coda—was still in full effect. Robbie couldn't be everywhere at once, though, so of the two, she chose Dee. After a single day of her refusing to let him out of her sight, he'd gotten her to cave. She wouldn't let him out of the same building as her, but he was free to roam.

The problem with that strategy was that everyone else in the building—in the Gillespie—needed something from her. Every goddamn minute. If she'd felt useless at rehearsals before, at least all those feelings had been viciously murdered.

A handful of times, she thought she saw a slender figure watching from the balcony, but she was never up there when he arrived, and he left before she could ever talk to him. She desperately wanted to, although she wasn't so clear on what exactly she'd say. "Hi, Fletcher Ingram, wealthy businessman, household name, rising political star. Remember that daughter you thought lost—and by lost, you meant dead, even if you wouldn't say it—some sixteen years ago? Pretty sure your son hired me to kill her last month. What's new with you?"

It was probably good their paths didn't cross.

Despite—or perhaps because of—not having answers from Fletcher or knowing the extent of his involvement in Nicholas's schemes, those sightings sent Robbie swinging wildly between panic that Fletcher was there to pull the stage out from beneath them and relief that Fletcher was still alive, that another sniper hadn't taken out the one person who'd kept this show financed. Who'd made this show happen.

In a shocking turn of events, Monday was followed by Tuesday, which was followed by Wednesday. She wasn't totally sure how that happened, but the days kept progressing from there. Nicholas didn't strike. Robbie didn't either. The tension in her wound tighter every day.

She walked through Coda one night in a rush and could've sworn she saw someone she recognized, one of Alma's people, but when she looked again, he was gone. James's No Killing Robbie rule would run out soon. Maybe she'd imagined that person, but it wouldn't be long before she genuinely started being scoped out as a hit.

But there was dress rehearsal, and another dress rehearsal. Act 1, all the way through, and again. Act 2, all the way through, then repeated. Full run. Robbie wasn't sure how many times she'd seen the show now.

And suddenly they were into tech rehearsals, and holy shit, this wasn't a dream, this was real, her show all real and alive and *happening.*

It was Tuesday again, maybe, when she roused a napping Dee from the green room after everyone else went home. Or she was pretty sure they all had, but as she headed out through the lobby to pull the car around, a figure was sitting on one of the cushioned benches, leaning against the gold-and-white paneled wall.

"Cassie?"

"I was wondering if we could talk," she said stiffly.

Finally.

"Yeah, sure. Here? We were just going home if you want to meet us there." Robbie recalled the time she'd spent following Xavier Landerman and his assorted rideshares. She'd never asked whether that was because Xavier didn't exist enough to have a driver's license or because Cassie Whitaker couldn't drive. "We, um, can also give you a ride if you need it."

"No, I was hoping to catch you here. I won't make it up those stairs of yours."

The exterior stairs up to their apartment were unreasonably steep and only barely up to code. If it were any other time, she'd offer the entire downstairs portion of their building, but the bar was open now, and although weeknights weren't overly crowded, it did tend to be difficult to have a conversation when anyone was singing loudly near you.

"Yeah, all right. Dee's just getting changed. He'll be out in a minute."

"That's fine. You're who I really wanted to talk to. I wanted to ask how much you believe that story of yours."

It was an odd question. Not how much of it was true but how much Robbie believed. "Pretty solidly. At least the current events. The stuff about your childhood, I don't know how many details I got right. I do think this is why Nicholas keeps trying to have you killed though."

Cassie cocked her head. "Keeps?"

"Sorry, with everything going on, I never did fill you in on all the details, did I? The whole stabbing thing? It was another hit. Former colleague of ours. The world of hit people isn't actually that big. Several folks who do the whole mugging gone wrong bit as their MO, one in particular who matched your circumstances. I made some calls and got confirmation."

"Oh. That's... I'm not sure if that's better or worse than being a random victim."

"Probably worse, but I'm not the one who got stabbed, so that's your call."

Gesturing to the space on the bench next to her, Cassie waited until Robbie accepted the invitation, both of them leaning back against the wall, staring out at the dim lobby.

"Let's say absolutely everything you told me is spot-on, completely true. What the hell am I supposed to do with that information?"

"Go claim your inheritance or whatever? You're rich as hell, Cassie, or you could be if you step back into being Alexandria. You'd be able to pay someone else to wash your ridiculous T-shirt collection. And you'd never again have to live somewhere like the Deacon Arms. Plus, if you expose Nicholas, he'd probably not try to kill you again." Robbie hoped she could take care of Nicholas herself before that point, but a backup plan never hurt.

Cassie hung her head. "That sounds great and all, but then what if you're wrong? Which, to be honest, seems more likely."

"Say it was an innocent mistake?" Even to Robbie's ears, she didn't sound particularly convincing.

"Yeah, that'll go well."

They both fell back to their wordless staring. After a few minutes, Cassie said, "I must look like her though. Like Alexandria Ingram might. Even if I'm not actually her, I look enough like her that Nicholas Ingram believed."

"Well, yes."

Robbie expected some sort of follow-up to that statement, but instead Cassie abruptly changed the topic. "Dee said Ingram the Elder is planning to sell this place. It's a beautiful building."

"Sure," Robbie replied hesitantly, unclear where this was going. "Honestly, it's an amazing theater. We are unbelievably lucky to have this space for our show. I hope whoever buys it keeps it going as a functioning theater, even if it's not for little productions like ours. It deserves to have amazing shows, and amazing shows deserve to be in a place like this."

"You say that like yours isn't an amazing show."

"I'm proud of what we've made and all, but it's not like I've created the next Broadway smash hit."

"Maybe not, but you could. You ever do anything like this before? Write a show?"

Robbie shook her head. "I wasn't raised in a household with music. Music was for church choirs, and that was it. Only thing I ever liked about church. I learned to play guitar from a guy I served with in Afghanistan, taught myself piano from endless YouTube videos when I got out, but I've never been some sort of musical prodigy. And I don't think Dee told you, because he doesn't tell anyone without okaying it with me, but I didn't technically write anything for this show."

"I thought you came up with the entire thing."

"Yeah, but I didn't *write* it. My brain doesn't really love writing, and not so much reading either. I had to create the whole thing by narrating the script into a recording app on my phone. Did the music the same way. Dee went through and transcribed all the songs into sheet music, typed up the whole script. But I didn't do any of that. I didn't write the show."

"The hell you didn't," Cassie said with surprising force. "It's just a word, Robbie, something people say. Maybe it's not the strict dictionary definition of the word, but you absolutely wrote this thing, and it is an amazing show."

"Thanks."

"Yeah." They were both silent a moment. "Anyway. What I meant to say was that it would be nice if this place wasn't sold. If it stayed the way it is, kept being available for you and Dee and other people like you who are trying to create something new and brilliant."

"It's a nice idea."

"An Ingram would be able to make that call."

Robbie halfheartedly lifted one shoulder, because a full shrug seemed too much work. "I assume when everything Fletcher owns gets turned over to folks whose sole interest is maximizing profit, something like this isn't exactly going to be a priority."

"Would be nice if it didn't get turned over to them though. Would be nice if maybe it got turned over to Fletcher Ingram's child, one who loved this theater and wanted to keep it alive."

"What are you trying to say?"

Cassie sighed, took a deep breath, sighed again. "Nicholas believed I'm Alexandria. If your theory is right, I mean. But let's assume at least that much is true. Obviously, I'm believable as her. Maybe it doesn't matter whether you're right or wrong. The truth is irrelevant. It's just a matter of belief."

"Possibly."

They both fell silent. Robbie cast her eyes around the gorgeous building, thinking of the incredible luck they'd had in finding this building and getting Fletcher's backing. Financially, of course, but she was certain having the Ingram name highlighted as a sponsor on their show posters was boosting ticket sales.

An idea started to itch at the back of her brain. She let it form, examining it from all angles. Not flawless, but she could make it work, and doing so would land her as much of Fletcher's backing as she and Dee could ever want, for whatever future endeavors they pursued—and perhaps even some measure of protection for them too.

Robbie turned to Cassie. "How would you feel about meeting Fletcher Ingram?"

"I…don't know about that."

Robbie caught a movement out of the corner of her eye that grew into the shape of Dee coming out of the theater, head down as he tried to get the zipper to line up on his bottle-green hoodie. Next to her, Cassie sat up a little straighter—then sucked in a breath, grunted a little like she was in pain, and sank back against the wall. When Dee finally looked up and saw the two of them, he froze.

"I have an idea," Robbie said quickly. She didn't have time to hash out all the details right now. "Look, do you trust me?"

Probably a bold ask given how recently Robbie had intended to kill Cassie, but she felt she'd proven herself since.

"Yeah, I suppose I do. So, what, you set up something like that lunch you and Dee had with him?"

"Actually, I was kind of hoping we could do it on opening night of the show?"

Generally speaking, Robbie avoided situations where there might be witnesses. For this, though, having other people around would be crucial.

When Cassie didn't respond, Robbie darted a glance toward Dee, who was just starting to unfreeze his body, and murmured, "You are coming opening night, aren't you?"

"Of course I am." Cassie shook her head as if clearing it of some unspoken thought. "All right, I'll meet Fletcher Ingram on opening night, if you think that's a good idea."

It certainly was *an* idea.

"Of course. It'll be great," Robbie said confidently as she stood. "You want that ride home? You and Dee can talk on the way?"

"No, that's okay. I'll catch up with him later." It was a bit of a struggle, but Cassie managed to get herself off the bench and upright. She nodded briefly to Dee, then slowly shuffled out of the theater and out of sight.

"Was that…" Dee started when he reached Robbie.

"It was. We had an interesting conversation." She linked her arm through his. "Come on. Let's get you home, and I'll tell you all about this idea I have."

♪

This was a terrible idea.

Everything was a terrible idea.

"Terrible, terrible idea," Robbie muttered to herself.

"Which part?"

She studied Dee in his stage makeup and his black-and-white waiter uniform for the opening scene. "All of it. Making a show. Putting it on here at the Gilly. Inviting Ingram. Arranging for Cassie to meet him."

"All right, maybe that last one was a bad idea. Everything else is just fine."

"What if no one shows up?"

"Did you not see the ticket sales report Janelle emailed us this morning?"

Robbie had seen it, and she had promptly concluded that either she was even worse at reading than usual, or Janelle had made an absurd typo. Before she could tell Dee as much, he had grabbed her hand and was dragging her backstage through shadowy corridors of curtains. He stopped in the wings off stage left.

"Go on. Take a peek."

"I don't want to know."

"Take a goddamn peek, Robbie, or I will shove your face through the curtain myself," he told her in a far more casual tone than the words implied.

Robbie leaned out just far enough to see the theater, the beautiful Gillespie Theater, with all those empty red velvet seats she'd gotten so familiar with. Except they weren't empty. Jesus, there were a lot of people. People had actually come to see their show.

"They're going to be disappointed," she said, shifting to her next worry.

"That's insulting as fuck."

"What?"

Dee gestured to himself with a flourish. "Star of the show. Hello. I can enthrall these people by singing the alphabet if I need to, but I don't need to, because I have a lovely script and beautifully written musical numbers to perform, and I really think it's rather rude of you to claim this will all go poorly when I'm standing right here being absolutely spectacular."

That was…fair, actually. This production was the culmination of many, many people's hard work. It had started in Robbie's head, but they'd collectively grown it into something else. No matter how much she doubted her own abilities, she didn't doubt theirs.

"This is going to be amazing, isn't it?"

Dee nodded with satisfaction. "Yes. Yes, it is."

They made their way back to the green room, and someone grabbed Robbie's arm. "Fletcher Ingram has arrived and asked for you."

Giving Dee a one-armed hug, gently so as not to muss his costume, she murmured to break a leg before heading to the front of the house. She took the stairs two at a time leading up to the box reserved for Ingram on the right-hand side of the theater. Two people stood by the entrance to the box, dressed in matching black suits, standing straight-backed and alert with distinct ex-military vibes.

The one on the left touched their ear as Robbie approached. After a moment, they looked up. "Robin McNeil?"

"That'd be me."

Another touch of the ear. A curt nod. The one on the right stepped forward to pat her down, then pulled the deep-red curtain aside for her and motioned for her to pass.

As she entered, she was surprised to see not one but two of the seats occupied. Shit. Fletcher had been alone every single time he'd come to the theater before.

One was Fletcher, and he looked rather worse for wear. Maybe that was a little uncharitable, but Robbie was nothing if not honest, at least in her own mind. She could relate to the deep sense of exhaustion she read in him, although for different reasons. Probably. His left arm was in a black sling. Monty hadn't missed by much then.

He turned as she came in, still managing to smile warmly at her, even as the smile itself was a little tired. "Robbie. I wanted to give you my congratulations on a wonderful production."

"The show hasn't even started yet."

Fletcher waved a hand like that was a minor detail. "You forget I've seen rehearsals. I've listened to the recordings you sent over—thank you for those, by the way. Don't get me wrong. I am absolutely thrilled to be here for your opening. But I already know that I'm going to be seeing something incredible."

"Thank you," she said, bowing her head slightly. "I appreciate your confidence."

"Ah, and where are my manners!" He tapped the shoulder of the second person in the box, who hadn't looked at Robbie yet or even turned away from the stage. "I must introduce you to my son. Robbie McNeil, this is Nicholas. Nicholas, this is the talented young woman who wrote tonight's show."

She knew. She knew what she was going to see when he turned around, and yet there was still a rush of adrenaline as he stood and moved to face her.

Robbie held out a hand to the man she'd known as Mr. Clark. He'd gotten rid of the beard again, and his features were sharper in full light, but there was no mistaking him. "Lovely to meet you."

"And you," he replied through gritted teeth, gaze darting nervously between her and Fletcher.

Fletcher appeared oblivious as he continued explaining the show to Nicholas, a bare-bones plot summary of how the main character got mistaken for someone else. "And the lead role in the show is actually played by Robbie's business-and-theater partner, Dee."

"Is that so?" Nicholas asked with a bit too much interest for Robbie's taste.

It would be so satisfying to snap back at him to stay the hell away from Dee, but she wasn't about to make a scene in front of the show's angel investor. If she was interpreting those glances right—and her confidence in reading a person had only barely begun to recover—*he* was anxious about *her*. Fletcher didn't know about the hit.

"I should get back to making sure everything is ready to go," she told Fletcher, and only Fletcher. "If you need anything at all, do let one of the ushers know. Mi theater es, well, su theater, obviously." She glanced over at Nicholas. "I hope you enjoy. Dee and I have worked hard to put on an absolutely *killer* show."

His jaw tightened, but he didn't respond. Couldn't. Not in front of his father.

As she pulled aside the curtain to exit the box, she added, "I know you're not here tonight as Fletcher Ingram, candidate for Senate, but a number of our cast and crew are big admirers of yours. Would you mind terribly if I introduced you to a few after the show?"

"That would be absolutely fine, Robbie. I'd love to meet members of your talented company." He gave her his politician smile.

As she left, she had to push her way against the flow of people coming into the theater, but she made it out to the lobby, where Cassie was sitting on the same padded bench where she'd met Robbie a few nights earlier.

"Well?" she asked as Robbie approached. She didn't stand, but her wide eyes grew even rounder.

"Slight snag in the plan. Nicholas is here, and I can confirm he is, without a doubt, our Mr. Clark." Robbie's plan didn't account for Nicholas. He hadn't struck her as the kind of person who attended the theater for fun. She'd figured Fletcher would come alone to see the show he'd helped finance.

"Well, shit. So we're calling this off?"

The images formed in Robbie's mind, multiple mental movies playing at once, just like it did when she was on a job. Unlike with her contract work, she didn't have a whole lot of control over all the factors in play here, but she could adapt.

"I'll do what I can to get him out of the way so you and Fletcher can talk." Before Cassie could respond, Robbie shook her head, wrapping up a different mental scenario. "Actually, no, this is perfect. In fact, this might be exactly what we need."

"Maybe this wasn't such a good idea. I don't need to meet Fletcher Ingram."

"Cassie. We're doing this. Tonight."

Reluctantly, Cassie nodded.

Robbie held out a hand to help Cassie to her feet. "We'll deal with all that after the show. Come on. I'll show you to your seat. You don't want to miss Dee's opening number."

There was that lovely shade of pink. Robbie was really starting to see why Dee found it so amusing to induce. Cassie got to her feet, took Robbie's arm, and let herself be led into the theater.

27

That Went Well

ROBBIE MCNEIL DID NOT CRY.

But if any circumstance was ever going to make her, the applause at the end of the show was pretty damn tempting. People were *standing*. Maybe not all of them, but hell, a single person giving their show a standing ovation was unbelievable.

Not that she heard most of the applause, not with the wild screams from Dee as he grabbed her hands and jumped up and down like an excited teenager. "We did it!"

They had. It had not been a disaster. No one was disappointed, and if they were, fuck them all, because Robbie was so proud in this moment that no one else's opinion mattered. Except the opinions of the people clapping. Those were good opinions.

A stagehand came and whisked Dee away for curtain call. Then another appeared and pulled Robbie along too for reasons she couldn't fathom until Dee took his bow and turned and held a hand out toward her. Reluctantly, she stepped out of the wings and went to meet him at the front of the stage.

"Thank you all for coming to our opening tonight," Dee said, his mic pack apparently switched back on. "I'm sure I'm going to get an earful later for doing this to her, but I wanted to bring out my partner in this endeavor and everything else, Robbie McNeil. She pulled this entire show from the genius of her own mind. Can I get an extra round of applause for her?"

Robbie McNeil *did not* cry.

She *maybe* had a brief bout of severe allergies for a moment. Indoors, in a theater, in late October. Definitely allergies.

The curtain came down, and she turned to Dee. "I'm going to kill you for that."

"I'd like to see you try," he retorted. "But speaking of attempted murder, I believe you have a reunion to orchestrate?"

"That I do." She followed the company backstage. Getting up on top of a chair in the green room, she announced, "First five people to raise their hands—put them down, you don't even know what I'm asking—okay, first five people who raise their hands *when I say so* get to come with me to personally meet Fletcher Ingram. On three. One, two, three."

The chosen few followed her to the stairs. Cassie was waiting, eyeing the steps nervously.

Robbie nodded to her. "You ready?"

"To meet the famous Fletcher Ingram? Sure. To make it up these stairs when I got knifed less than two weeks ago and am not exactly in fighting form? Not especially, but let's do it."

Robbie considered how Dee would feel if Cassie got trampled by the people streaming down the stairs on their way to exit the theater. Shit. She flipped through her mental list of alternate options. The five witnesses she'd brought with her would be okay, but it wouldn't hurt to have more.

She shook her head. "Lobby. Concession stand. I'll meet you there."

Alone, she made it up the stairs quickly. The security outside the box waved her through without hesitation this time.

"Ah, Robbie. I was beginning to wonder whether you'd been carried off by your adoring fans." The warm, actual-human smile.

"Very nearly, but I prevailed." She gestured toward the curtain that enclosed the back of the box. "Speaking of adoring fans, do you still have a few minutes to meet some of yours? I suppose in your case, you'd probably call them constituents, not fans."

"Oh, I have fans too." His fancy gold watch flashed in the low light while Nicholas eyed Robbie warily just out of Fletcher's line of sight. "I'm happy to speak with them."

"Great. Shall we…" She took a step toward the box's exit, and Fletcher moved to leave with her.

"Wait." Nicholas grabbed his father's shoulder, then yanked his hand away when Fletcher flinched and stifled a yelp. Robbie wasn't sure exactly where Fletcher had been hit, but the side with the sling seemed a safe bet. "Sorry. It's just that we—I have other obligations tonight, and you look tired. Maybe this isn't the time for this sort of thing?"

"I'm fine, and your obligations can wait fifteen minutes," Fletcher said with a practiced dismissiveness.

Nicholas radiated a fascinating mix of anger and anxiety. She watched him trying to figure it out. What she was up to. Whether it would affect him.

People started approaching Fletcher before they even got to the lobby. With that fixed politician's smile, Fletcher greeted each of them. Some were cast and crew, mingling with friends or family in the hallways, and he made thoughtful remarks to each with regard to their specific roles. The man really was made of charisma.

By the time they reached the lobby, the crowd was already dispersing. Cassie rested on that same low seat she'd been in earlier. With more stiffness than before, she hauled herself to her feet. Robbie drew in a deep breath. Here went nothing. Or everything.

"Over here," she called to Fletcher. "Come meet some friends of mine."

Cassie stepped forward, and Robbie was glad they were here, not high up in the box where Fletcher could've toppled over the railing as all the blood drained from his face and he swayed on his feet. Still, she filed away falling from a theater box to her bucket list of staged accidents.

"Hi, Mr. Ingram," Cassie said smoothly. "I'm a huge fan. Thank you so much for letting Robbie introduce us."

"Cynthia," Fletcher whispered. His wife's name, Robbie recalled. She did a mental chef's kiss. This was going to be perfect.

Nicholas, a few steps behind, caught up. His sullen glare transformed into a snarl. All right, not *perfect*.

"Who is this woman? She's obviously not cast or crew, and she's upsetting my father. Please have her removed."

Cassie held up her hands. "I'm so sorry. I didn't mean to cause any upset. I was part of the backstage crew until I was injured recently. Robbie was nice enough to invite me to—"

"My father is quite unwell. I must insist you give us our privacy." Each word Nicholas spoke was angrier and louder than the last. He tugged at Fletcher, trying to hurry him to the front doors, but Fletcher didn't budge.

"Really, I'm so sorry," Cassie repeated. "I can go."

That wasn't the line Robbie had mentally written for Cassie. Stepping forward, Robbie directed her toward coat check, for lack of a better place, thinking how to salvage this off-script improvisation.

Fletcher rasped, "Stay."

They both froze. The word wasn't meant for Robbie though.

"Father, please. We should go."

His protesting was only drawing more attention. More people from the lobby turned for a show they didn't even need tickets for. But to Fletcher, Nicholas might as well not have been there. In fact, the whole lobby could be deserted, and he wouldn't notice. Fletcher's gray eyes were locked on Cassie.

"What's your name?"

"Cassie, sir. Cassie Whitaker." The *sir* was a nice touch.

"Cassie," Fletcher murmured. Some of the blood was returning to his face, and he seemed a little steadier on his feet. "Cassandra, like Alexandria."

Just what Xavier Landerman/Cassie Whitaker needed. Another name.

"I suppose," Cassie said hesitantly.

"How old are you?"

"I'm… Well, the thing is, I was adopted, and there were some issues with my paperwork. Best as I know, though, I'm twenty-five." Oh, the girl was clever. She could've just given exactly how old Alexandria Ingram ought to be, but slipping in the adoption bit there… Robbie wished it were appropriate to clap.

She did not clap.

She shifted, stepping out of scene, making herself as unobtrusive as possible until she bumped into the concession counter.

Just as Fletcher couldn't break his gaze away from Cassie, Nicholas hadn't broken from Robbie, his eyes tracking her retreat.

Fletcher's mouth moved, but from here, she couldn't hear what he was muttering to himself. Abruptly, he seized Nicholas's arm. "Don't you recognize her, Nicky?"

"It's Nicholas," his son corrected, as if that were at all the most important thing going on right now.

"Look at her, Nicky. Don't you see? Of course you do. You couldn't possibly not."

Obviously, he had, or none of this would be happening, but he shook his head, murmuring something about his father's poor health, blaming whatever was happening on imagination and poor memory and whatever else he could come up with.

Robbie moved her attention from them to Cassie, who, with no one observing her, cut Robbie a knowing smile. When Robbie'd had to revise her plan to include their surprise guest, Robbie had cast Nicholas in this exact role, making a scene, publicly positioning himself against Fletcher. She'd wanted this dispute to happen, and Cassie knew it.

"She looks just like your mother."

"A coincidence, I'm sure. Perhaps a bit of a resemblance, but not even a strong one."

The images of Fletcher's late wife had been one of the tipping points for Robbie when she came up with her theory. Cassie was a dead ringer for the dead wife. That wispy blond hair, the wide puppy eyes, the rounded nose, the narrow mouth. There had even been an old news clip where someone made a joke that made Cynthia Ingram blush, and oh man, had that looked familiar.

"I was married to your mother for twenty-four years before we lost her," Fletcher snapped, surprisingly harshly. "I have not forgotten a single thing about her. And I haven't forgotten Alexandria either. You pretend they never existed, but I remember them every single day."

"You have to stop clinging to the past, Father. Let it go."

"I'm not clinging. The past walked right over to shake my hand." He turned to address Cassie, who slipped from smug satisfaction to wide-eyed alarm, eyes darting between the two men. "Ms. Whitaker. I apologize for subjecting you to this little family dispute. Nicholas, perhaps you and Robbie could give us a moment?"

Nicholas looked like he'd rather set himself on fire, but Fletcher's tone had not been a request. Grabbing Robbie's arm hard enough to bruise, Nicholas dragged her aside and shoved her against the beautiful white-and-gold molding of the walls.

She ducked just in time for his fist to crash into the wall where her face had been. He gripped the front of her shirt to yank her back upright. She could always scream, but fuck it. If he wanted to do this, they were doing this.

Robbie crossed her arms, forcing his hand away, and lifted her chin defiantly.

"What did you do?" he hissed.

"I didn't *do* anything." She tried for a careless shrug. "Or don't you remember?"

He flung an arm in Cassie's direction. "She's supposed to be dead."

"Seems like a personal problem." If her heart rate went any higher, she wasn't sure she'd survive. She kept her voice as steady as she could. "Did Todd tell you he got the job done?"

Nicholas huffed. He recognized the name. "Now you and he both owe me money for failing."

"Just me and him? Does Monty owe you money, or was he supposed to miss all along?"

"How—" The shock only lasted half a second before turning into stony defiance, but Robbie caught it all the same. "I don't know who that is."

Oh, Robbie understood the sense of triumph Dee must feel when he hit a target with a perfect shot. "Like you don't know me and you don't know Todd?"

Nicholas snarled, an animal caught in a trap but still trying to fight.

"You can't solve every problem in your life with contracted hits," she murmured.

Before he could reply, he flew backward. Dee hadn't thought security guards were a necessary part of the theater, but Janelle had insisted, for liability and insurance reasons.

Robbie was going to buy Janelle the world's largest gift basket.

"You okay?" asked—oh, she knew this. She'd memorized their names just a few days ago.

"I'm fine. Thanks, Brandon."

"You want us to call the cops or let him go?"

Chances were he could easily pay his way out of a minor assault charge. Physically accosting Robbie was far from the worst thing he'd done, but it was the most visible.

She took a deep breath and used those seconds to run her options. Bringing up Monty hadn't been quite as impactful as she'd hoped, but he knew she had something on him now. Would that be enough to keep him away from Dee and Coda, to keep everything she loved safe?

All the noise in her head went silent, letting that question hang in the air.

No.

It wouldn't be enough. Not with someone as unhinged as Nicholas, who might keep quiet for a little while but couldn't be trusted not to set himself on fire to burn her life down at some point in the future. She knew what she needed to do, and she knew how to do it.

It wasn't a sentence she'd ever expected to cross her lips, but she said, "Yeah, I think maybe cops would be best."

28

Unexpected Connections

NICHOLAS HAD ALREADY TAKEN UP ENOUGH OF THE SPOT-light tonight. Robbie instructed the guards to hold him somewhere quiet while she got his father. Robbie watched them drag Nicholas toward the staff-only door behind the coat-check desk, then turned and drifted toward Cassie and Fletcher, who were now sitting on Cassie's bench. Ought to engrave her name on it at this point.

"—wanting to create my own shows," Cassie was saying. Ah, the musicals bit. Robbie had told her about that conversation with Fletcher. But she hadn't told her the next part. "I liked to get my stuffed animals and set them all up to be my audience sometimes. I had this bright-green elephant I'd always put front and center, because in my mind, she clapped the loudest. I left her at the park once, and we never found her again. I was so devastated. Tammy, I think was her name."

Fletcher's gasp was so sharp Robbie was sure it must have cut his throat going down.

Cassie kept right on talking as if she hadn't even noticed, moving smoothly into an anecdote about Sunday's dress rehearsal, which absolutely never happened. She chattered for several more minutes, then stopped self-consciously. "I'm so sorry. I have been rambling on forever. I didn't mean to dominate the conversation."

"Not at all," Fletcher said softly. His voice was thick, his eyes glistening. "I'd like to show you a picture if I may."

He struggled around his sling to pull a wallet from inside his suit jacket. With a bit more struggle, he pulled out a battered, folded photo. Robbie edged around to the wall and stood on tiptoes so she could spy over Cassie's shoulder. Cassie took the photo and casually held it up like she was trying to see it in better lighting. Robbie dropped the heels of her boots back to the floor.

A woman and a little girl sat on a bench, half of a wooden sign behind them. A park, maybe, or a zoo. The woman was perhaps in her forties, the girl maybe five or six. The resemblance between them was strong, the girl being a miniature version of her mother, who Robbie recognized as Cynthia Ingram. The two of them weren't paying any attention to whoever was taking the picture, instead both looking at each other, laughing hard. And beside them on the bench, clutched in the little girl's hand, was a lime-green stuffed elephant.

Cassie stared at it hard for a long time before looking up at Fletcher with a frown. "I don't understand."

She was good. She was very good.

"I used to have a daughter," he said slowly. "Her name was Alexandria Jaqueline Margaux Ingram."

Robbie pitied the poor child who'd had to learn to write out *that* full name. Way to burden a kid.

"When she was eight years old, she was taken from a park one day in the summer. We never saw her again. We never found a body, although there was circumstantial evidence that led us to believe she'd been killed."

"I'm so sorry for your loss," Cassie murmured.

"I know this will sound strange, but I believe you may be my Alexandria."

Cassie choked, and Robbie wasn't sure whether that was real or part of her act. What wasn't an act was the sharp collective intake of breath coming from several onlookers still loitering in the lobby.

Well, not onlookers. Witnesses.

Maybe Cassie's identity as Alexandria would fall apart eventually, although Robbie had seen how completely Cassie could disappear into a role. But Fletcher publicly claiming her was exactly what Robbie had hoped. No backing down now. At least one of the people holding their phone up had caught his statement on video, and that would be going viral the second it was uploaded anywhere.

And all she and Dee owed Fletcher for his support making the show happen was nothing compared to the eternal debt he would owe her for reuniting him with his long-lost daughter. If the poll numbers were right, Fletcher was fully on track to become a senator, and Robbie couldn't think of anything more useful than having a senator owe them this much. Though she'd probably tarnish that goodwill a little by having his son arrested. Hopefully, the balance would come out in her favor.

"I'm going to need some time to process this." Cassie's voice was faint and distant with disbelief.

"Of course. I understand. I realize that to you, this must just seem the daft imaginings of an old man. I would be happy to tell you more about my Alexandria if that would help you. Or I would, of course, be more than willing to have a DNA test done to show you that you're truly my daughter."

Well, that was unexpected. The most likely outcome of the reunion would've been in Cassie trying to convince Fletcher, asking for a way to prove herself truly the heir to a multimillion-dollar fortune. Somehow, she had *him* begging. Of course, a DNA test could make this all come crashing down hard. Robbie cringed. How much faith did she truly have in this wild theory of hers?

But Cassie was already nodding. "Yeah, okay. I guess we can do that."

"Thank you." It sounded completely heartfelt. "I'll leave you be. Whenever you're ready to talk more, Robbie knows how to reach me."

He rose slowly, casting a final lingering glance at Cassie. Then political Ingram snapped back into place. He smiled the slightly fake smile and shook a few hands. He seemed to be murmuring "I'm afraid I can't comment" a few times as people lobbed questions about Cassie and about Nicholas attacking Robbie. After a minute, he excused himself and came to shake Robbie's hand.

"I'm terribly sorry for any trouble Nicky caused."

Not as sorry as *Nicky* was going to be for fucking with Robbie's life.

"And I apologize if it seemed I was upstaging your show, if you'll forgive the pun. Though I can't imagine I did that. I'm not sure anything could upstage your incredible production."

Politician voice, but who cared. Robbie took the compliment. "Thanks."

"No, I should be thanking you. For introducing me to your friend there. That might be the greatest thing anyone has done for me in my life."

Perfect. Senator in her pocket. Check. She sent a prayer out to the universe that his gratitude wouldn't entirely vanish when he heard her next words. "I'm glad I could help, but I'm afraid I can't bring myself to let Nicholas off the hook. Security has already called the police."

He took a deep breath.

This was it. This was when he would boot them from the theater, bring the show to a crashing halt. But Robbie had gotten her opening night. She'd gotten a standing fucking ovation. It was all about to go to hell, but no one could take that away from her, and at least this way, she could keep everything else she loved safe.

But instead, his breath turned into a weighty sigh as he looked over at Nicholas with the air of a man who'd had to deal with his wayward son and law enforcement more than once. "If you don't mind, I'd like a word with him before he's taken in."

Robbie nodded, watching him go. Could it be that simple? He'd let one child go as long as she provided a replacement? Then again, he probably thought he'd get Nicholas off easily. Robbie wasn't going to let that happen.

"So that was a surprise."

Robbie startled at the thief who'd silently snuck right up beside her. "Everything went exactly according to plan," she lied breezily.

"Including Nicholas grabbing you? I figured he might make a scene shouting and carrying on, but I didn't expect that."

Robbie shrugged. "It all worked out. I'm not worried about it."

"Oh, what are you two worried about that isn't you not coming backstage to tell me I was awesome?"

Robbie hadn't heard Dee's approach either. He stood with his duffel over his shoulder. His hair was still parted and slicked in the

1920s show style, and some of the stage makeup still ringed his eyes, but he'd changed into street clothes. Cassie, looking absolutely beat at this point, gestured for Dee to sit, and she gave him a one-armed hug, gushing about the show and his performance.

He let her go on for longer than Robbie thought was necessary before holding up his hand. "All right, my ego is satisfied. Now, I assume you had a damn good reason for not meeting me, so let's hear it."

When Cassie's recap reached the bit about the photo, Robbie interrupted.

"Ingram was absolutely stunned when you mentioned your elephant toy. I never told you that. How did you even know to bring it up?"

"I, uh, broke into the Ingram house yesterday."

"You did *what?*"

Cassie held up her hands and waggled her fingers. "Thief. Remember? Except I didn't steal anything. Not tangible things anyway. I just poked around. I saw a picture on his desk in his office. Not that exact one, but same child, same elephant. Incidentally, his office also has a very nice painting on the wall that I stole."

"You just said you didn't steal anything," Dee pointed out.

"Oh, sorry, I didn't mean I stole it yesterday. I stole it about six months ago, as Landerman, from a private gallery in Texas of all places. Part of my audition with Lucky."

"You're saying the illustrious Fletcher Ingram, millionaire investor, front-runner for the Senate, and patron saint of our show…bought stolen art from some shady guy in the back room of an illegal gambling operation in Penny Park?" Dee sounded about as skeptical as Robbie felt.

"Not sure. All I know is that piece definitely passed through the Ajax Club."

"Could've been a bribe," Dee suggested. "He didn't buy the art so much as had it casually donated to him in exchange for not coming down on Ajax or any other operations of Lucky's once he's elected?"

Robbie nodded. She found it reassuring, the idea that he took bribes like a normal person. Like a proper politician. As much as she liked him, she didn't think she could ever fully trust someone who couldn't be bought. And now she'd bought him with an unpayable debt. Excellent.

"So everything played out like you planned," Dee said to Robbie.

"More or less. But credit where credit's due, this couldn't have worked without Cassie playing the star."

"What can I say?" Cassie shrugged. "Whether or not I'm actually Alexandria Ingram, I'm pretty damn good at pretending to be someone other than myself."

Robbie nodded. "Yes, Xavier Landerman, I suppose you are."

Robbie insisted Dee head home while she gave her statement about the Nicholas incident to, of all people, Officer Shapiro. The cop did not look thrilled to see Robbie. The feeling was mutual, but at least Shapiro's curt demeanor worked in both their favor, moving the whole mess along promptly. Watching Shapiro cuff Nicholas wasn't quite the same high as earning a standing ovation, but damn, it wasn't bad. Not bad at all.

What truly mattered was what came next.

The success of her plan to get Ingram to publicly claim Cassie as Alexandria had done wonders for her confidence. She could take puzzle pieces and arrange them exactly as she needed. This was what she was best at, and it felt good to remember.

Now she needed to arrange the next pieces, slot everything into place for the perfect hit. Nicholas was where Robbie wanted him: contained in a known location, at least for the next few hours.

Robbie needed him gone, but no fucking way was she putting her own neck on the line if anything went wrong now. God, she'd never wanted it to come to this, but she'd tried everything else she could think of to deal with Nicholas. But she'd exhausted all her options, and there was only one left.

She dropped into a café chair near the concession stand and pulled out her phone. Scrolling through her call log, she found the day Cassie had been stabbed and dialed the unsaved number.

"McNeil?" Todd sounded confused but not unpleasantly so.

"Got it in one," she replied. "You remember the job you did last time we talked?"

"Reevesburg! Home of the gays and shit!"

Robbie would love to see that slogan on the city welcome signs. "Right. The Reevesburg job. This is my city, and I hear a lot of things. You know your target survived?"

This was the riskiest part of her plan, but she was counting on Todd, one of the most self-centered people she'd ever met, putting his own interests first and not going after Cassie again.

"No way. Dude, that target's totally smashing crates for all the extra hit points, because I was only hired 'cause the first hit didn't stick."

"Sure," Robbie said, hoping to move this along. Todd seemed full of energy, but Robbie was exhausted beyond measure. She didn't want to say this next part, but she hadn't been able to come up with an alternative. "Here's the thing, Todd. The contractor who didn't get the job done the first time? That was me."

His gasp was dramatic as fuck but seemed genuine.

"I have my reasons I wasn't able to complete the job," she continued before he could comment. "But when I didn't, the client took out a hit on me."

"Ohhh," Todd said as if a circuit in his brain finally connected. "I heard about that and James blocking it for a bit."

"Do you think James will do the same for you?"

"What do you mean?"

"Well, you also didn't finish the job. So when the client puts out an open hit on you, do you think James will protect you?"

He was silent long enough for her to know her question landed.

Now was not the time to focus on how special James thought she was or the way that warmed something in her belly. "That client is currently being held for something else at the Reevesburg jail, at least for tonight. And he knows you failed. If you take him out, you wouldn't even need protection from someone like James or Alma. No one would need to know. And I wouldn't tell a soul you failed a job."

"Why don't you do it?"

A fair question, although she'd hoped he wouldn't think to ask. Robbie sighed. "Above my threshold for risk. He's in on an assault and battery charge, and I'm the one he assaulted."

"Shit," Todd breathed.

"Yep. So you gonna be able to handle this?" She paused, then added, "And actually complete the job this time?"

The leverage of Todd's failed job worked to her advantage in terms of getting him hooked in, but it did have the drawback of being proof of how sloppy he could be. Still, this was her best bet, and when she'd told the security guards to have the cops come take Nicholas, she'd been counting on Todd coming through. It wasn't a great idea for him to be involved, for the same reasons she'd turned down Cassie's offer to hire her to take out Nicholas, but whether it was oblivious short-sightedness or differing levels of what they considered acceptable personal risk, Robbie had a feeling Todd wouldn't draw the line in the same place she would.

"You want radio silence, or do you wanna know when it's done?"

A thrill of success, blended with relief, raced up her spine. "I'd like to know."

"I'll take care of it. Thanks for the heads-up, McNeil. You're a good one."

"Gotta look out for each other, right?" Robbie didn't give a shit about looking out for anyone other than her and Dee, but the words sounded nice.

"For sure, dude. For sure."

They hung up, and Robbie knocked her head back into the wall, letting herself breathe properly for the first time in hours. After a moment, she hauled herself to her feet and headed for her car.

"Better not fuck this up, Todd," she murmured to the night air.

Robbie woke to the sensation of her hand vibrating. She'd fallen asleep clutching her phone, and now she bolted upright in bed to look at it. A little after five in the morning.

She had one text message from an unknown number.

> **UNKNOWN**
> Done

And a second later, another message from the same number.

> **UNKNOWN**
> For real this time

Robbie tossed her phone to the side and flopped back into her pillows. She'd check for confirmation in the morning, make sure Todd truly did get the job done. But she had a feeling her faith in his sense of self-preservation hadn't been misplaced.

The weight that had been draped around her shoulders since Mr. Clark showed up to '80s night crumbled away. She closed her eyes and slept better than she had in weeks.

29

The Cat Herself Knows

MOVING TO THE GILLESPIE HAD SHIFTED THE DATES OF THE show so that it was due to close the first weekend in November rather than the originally planned mid-October, which meant Dee had three shows the entire weekend leading up to Halloween. In general, Coda was well run with a limited staff and help from Robbie and Dee as needed. It turned out they had six employees now, thanks to a round of hiring that took place while they were occupied in the weeks leading up to the show. Six ought to have been plenty sufficient most of the year, but the way queer people turned out for Halloween made for one of those times when Robbie wished they had an entire battalion of people on payroll.

Asha was on desk duty near the stage to take sign-ups and run the karaoke system, but Robbie tagged her out for a break as a drag queen Marilyn Monroe started in on Madonna's "Rebel Heart."

A cluster of movement by the door caught Robbie's eye. The crowd shifted, moving away from a pack of four people in black clothing. A boring costume if ever she saw one, but then the light hit just right for her to recognize one of the faces. It took her a moment to place them—from outside the Ajax Club, that was it. Fletcher Ingram's bodyguard. She scanned the other faces. One was entirely unfamiliar. The other two she recognized from opening night at the theater.

The four newcomers dispersed into the crowd. As Marilyn finished off her song, Robbie caught a glimpse again of one of the bodyguards going back out the front door. A couple dressed as Poison Ivy and Harley Quinn stepped up to do a duet. Robbie got the screen queued up for them, started the music, then looked back up in time to see Cassie step into the bar, followed closely by Fletcher Ingram.

It was an odd sight: a presumably straight, white, male politician with gray hair and a thousand-dollar three-piece suit in the middle of a bar full of queer people in a wild array of costumes. She wished she could get a picture.

Instead, she stayed where she was, watching from a distance as Cassie got drinks for the both of them before winning the Coda-in-full-swing lottery by finding two available seats. Fletcher's posture was slumped in a way it never had been before, but the fact that he'd come at all impressed Robbie. He'd made a public statement about his son's death a few days after the news broke, and he'd looked ready to collapse then, although he'd stated he wouldn't drop out of the Senate race. While he still didn't seem fully his previous confident self, he seemed a little better tonight.

After a few songs, Cassie got up and made her way over to Robbie.

"Interesting company tonight, Cassie," Robbie half shouted, leaning toward Cassie to be heard over the speakers directly behind her.

"Oh, I'm sorry, you must have me mistaken for someone else." Cassie winked. "My name is Alexandria."

"I have so many questions."

"You gonna shout them all at me?"

Robbie shook her head. "Later. Right now, you going to sing? For the illustrious Alexandria Ingram, I have any song you want."

Cassie wavered her head in thought, then replied, "Why not? Do you have anything by Queen?"

"Oh, you sweet child," Robbie said with a laugh. "We have every Queen song ever or we would've failed at the karaoke business a long time ago. Anything in particular?"

"Can I do 'Don't Stop Me Now'?"

"You happen to be in luck that no one's sung that already tonight. There's a lot of people in queue though. It'll be about half an hour."

"No worries," Cassie said before turning and heading back to her seat with Fletcher. With her father, apparently. Weird.

Robbie ran the next several people through their songs before finally calling up…Lexi, according to her sign-up. Of course.

Lexi/Cassie/Xavier/whoever else she was took the microphone, grinning a little nervously, and stepped up onto the stage. She began to sing and…she was good. She was very good. Robbie tried not to look too surprised, but she was certain she couldn't entirely conceal it. Everybody loved Queen for karaoke, but no one realized how tricky the vocals could be. "Lexi" barely glanced at the screen, singing the lyrics from memory and still getting the timing right.

Fletcher was at his seat across the bar, smiling that warm smile and looking happier than Robbie had ever seen him. Entirely reasonable. She'd be pretty damn pleased if she had a long-lost child who reappeared and could actually hit every note in a karaoke song. Well, she was sure he would've been pleased with an entirely off-key performance too, but Robbie had standards.

Out of the corner of her eye, she caught motion near the bar as Dee slipped in from the back, eyes still heavy with stage makeup, staring past Robbie with a pleased sort of surprise, like he'd been given an early birthday present.

As Cassie finished the song, Fletcher made his way over. "You have a lovely business, Robbie. A very lively crowd."

"It's not usually quite this…" She waved a hand at the chaos. For a moment, she considered offering her condolences on the loss of his son, but somehow, shouting over said chaos seemed like it would make her insincere apology come across even more so.

"Nevertheless, I enjoyed seeing it." He glanced up as *his daughter* stepped off the stage. "And I enjoyed getting to see my Alexandria perform. You were fantastic."

"Thanks." Cassie blushed a bit, although not her full flare.

"I'm going to head home, but why don't you stay here, hang out with your friends. You have a key, so just come home whenever." There was a note of satisfaction in his voice as he said the word *home*.

The next singer had made it to the front, and Robbie had to turn her attention to setting them up. By the time she turned back, Fletcher was already halfway across the bar, his bodyguards appearing out of nowhere to flank him as he headed for the door. Cassie was making her way to the bar where Dee was now helping serve the wild masses.

Robbie checked the clock and did some math that definitely did not involve counting on her fingers. Roughly…sixty more songs to go before closing? Hopefully the newest Ingram would stay long enough to answer questions at the end of the night. Robbie wasn't sure she could stand it if she had to wait much longer.

If the floor hadn't been so disgustingly sticky, Robbie would've been tempted to collapse onto it and sleep for the next week. Instead, she dutifully got out the cleaning supplies and went to work helping set the club to rights. It was nearly three in the morning when their employees shuffled out the door, and she and Dee dragged themselves up the back stairs to stumble into their living room.

A heaping lump of blanket lay on Dee's couch, a bit of blond hair visible near the pillow. At the sound of their heavy footfalls, the blanket shifted and fell away, Cassie sitting up and blinking at them drowsily.

"I told her she could wait up here for us," Dee explained from behind Robbie, shoving her to keep her moving forward. The two of them fell clumsily onto Robbie's love seat.

"Busy night?"

Robbie eyed Cassie. "No, not at all. Totally dead. We barely had a single person come through the bar all night."

Dee halfheartedly smacked her on the shoulder, presumably for her tone, although he didn't say anything.

"Mm. Seemed like it."

Robbie pulled a blanket from the back of her seat and draped it over herself and Dee. She couldn't quite remember when the oppressive summer heat had turned into this crisp autumn chill, but fall had definitely arrived.

"All right, *Alexandria*. Spill."

Their guest grinned, eyes sparking mischievously. "As you may recall, at our eventful first encounter, Fletcher offered a DNA test to prove he was related to me."

"Have I mentioned how smooth that was?"

"Several times, Robbie, several times. So we went ahead with that, and the results came back on Friday. According to the papers that arrived at the Ingram house, I am definitely his biological daughter. Of course, Cynthia Ingram is long dead, so technically, we didn't establish me as Alexandria specifically, only as Fletcher's daughter. If he had an affair or something, I could be the product of that, but he says it's absolutely impossible that I'm anyone other than Alexandria, and who am I to argue?"

"So that's it?" Dee asked. "You're just…an Ingram now?"

"That's it."

"What do we call you? Because I kind of liked Cassie."

"Fletcher—sorry, *Dad* is going to make a statement to the press next week officially sharing the news of my return. He wanted to wait a bit after the Nicholas thing." She shrugged. Robbie hadn't explained directly, and she wasn't sure how much Dee had told Cassie about how "the Nicholas thing" was orchestrated. "I told him I'm in no rush, but he wants to go ahead. I'll be Alexandria to everyone then. But you can call me whatever you want."

Dee rested his head on Robbie's shoulder and pulled the blanket closer to his chin. "Maybe we just call you X and cover it all."

"If you'd like."

Robbie had been contemplating the blue rug. She tugged her attention up to the newly minted Alexandria. "You said 'according to the papers that arrived at the Ingram house.' That's an interesting choice of words. I feel like the normal thing to say would simply be 'according to the test results' or something like that."

"And?"

"And I'm wondering if the papers that arrived at the Ingram house were quite the same as the ones that left the lab."

Dee sat up a bit, looking between the two of them in curiosity.

Their guest cocked her head. "Are you suggesting I tampered with the results in some way?"

She didn't sound offended, more amused.

"You broke into Fletcher's house and found all those details about his daughter. You stole an incredibly valuable painting from a museum without leaving a trace. I don't think it's an unreasonable suggestion to say you interfered with the test or the results in some way."

"An Ingram would never do such a thing," Alexandria Ingram said haughtily.

It wasn't an answer.

Robbie didn't care enough to pursue it further though. What difference did it make to her life whether the long-lost Alexandria was a fraud?

"So," she asked Alexandria now, "are you just going to pretend everything with Nicholas never happened?"

"For now. I don't see the point of dragging it all up. Fletcher has enough going on right now. Might as well let him mourn the son he thought he had, not the one he *actually* had. Besides, I can't talk about his hit on me without risking exposing you, Robbie, and the original kidnapping sixteen years ago is an even harder case to prove."

Robbie nodded. "Thanks for leaving us out of it."

It would been utterly naive to think there wasn't any risk at all.

She and Dee had talked about it several times since she'd gotten the confirmation text from Todd. If things went south, they each had a bag in the hidden room with clothes, cash, and the very best of their fake ID documents ready and waiting. But then that was nothing new.

"Yeah, no problem." Alexandria ran a hand through her hair, leaving it ruffled and very Xavier-esque. "Thank you both. I'm so grateful for everything you did to make this happen. And, Robbie, once again, thank you for not killing me. Much appreciated."

Robbie grumbled something, but even she wasn't sure what the words were meant to be. No one had ever thanked her for not killing them before, presumably because, well, they'd been dead. Given how this whole business had gone down, she would be happy if no one else ever thanked her for such a thing again.

"Oh!" Alexandria exclaimed abruptly. "Speaking of not killing me… How did I almost forget?"

She grabbed a shoulder bag that had been slumped against the coffee table and rummaged around before producing… Was that a check? She held it out to Robbie.

"I know I never paid you what I owed you for our deal."

Robbie was certain she wasn't reading the check right. She passed it to Dee, who confirmed she had indeed read it correctly when he said, "This is three times what you owed."

"Right, well, it turns out that at the time of Alexandria's—of *my* kidnapping, a reward was offered for anyone who provided information that led to my safe return. Despite how long it's been since that was offered, you did exactly that." She paused. "Also, um, Dee has told me a bit about what you two did to finance the show. With Coda money and whatnot. He said everything was settled between Nicholas's money and Fletcher's, but I thought this might help you build back some buffer in Coda's accounts, just to be safe."

"And then some." Robbie wasn't sure a handshake was the appropriate response here, but she had to do something, and she wasn't about to hug someone who wasn't Dee. Alexandria accepted the handshake. "Thanks."

"Of course. Now, you two look exhausted. I should get home." There was a certain bit of delight in that word that mirrored Fletcher's earlier.

"You need a ride?" Robbie offered.

"Oh, no, I'm an Ingram now." Alexandria laughed. "I can't believe just a few weeks ago, I was living in that shitty apartment at the Deacon Arms, and now I have a private chauffeur on call to take me back to my family estate."

As far as changed circumstances went, she'd pretty much won the jackpot. Robbie nodded and murmured some congratulations, because what else did you say to something like this?

Dee stood to walk Alexandria out.

Robbie tilted her head back against the couch cushions. James had always taught her to keep things neat and tidy. No messes, no curiosity. She hadn't handled any of this the way he would have liked, but hey, James wasn't here, and Robbie was. As Dee liked to point out, they'd gone solo, and that meant operating without James's oversight. She could handle things any damn way she liked.

Dragging herself to her feet, Robbie shuffled off to crash into her lovely, lovely bed.

CODA

A FEW DAYS BEFORE THANKSGIVING, ROBBIE AND DEE HAD their long overdue brunch of killer French toast. A TV was playing on the far wall, and Robbie caught a glimpse of a familiar face. She nudged Dee and pointed.

"It's something about the Ingrams," he said, squinting as he read off the closed captioning. He shook his head and pulled out his phone. Through a few moments scrolling, Robbie got to see his facial expressions—surprise, a frown, a satisfied little smirk—but she had to wait for context. Finally, he looked up. "Well, well. Looks like rumors about Nicholas's involvement in Alexandria's kidnapping have started to reach news outlets. Legit ones, not just conspiracy sites."

That had to have originated with X, although who knew which identity started it. She'd intentionally waited until after the election. Robbie knew that much. Tragedy helped poll numbers, but a whiff of scandal could demolish any chance of winning. So she'd stayed silent, waiting until Senator Fletcher Ingram became a reality. Robbie couldn't guess why X leaked the info now, but Xavier had been clever, and so had Cassie. If Alexandria wanted the rumors out there, she had her reasons.

Robbie sat back, considering. "Nicholas really was a piece of work, wasn't he?"

"Kidnapped his sister who stood to split his inheritance. Maybe offed his mother to get at her share. Tried to have his sister killed when she resurfaced and threatened his place in the Ingram legacy. Orchestrated a sniper to shoot at his father. Do you think there's anyone he's related to who he hasn't tried to harm?" Dee shook his head. After a moment, he leaned forward. "You know who would've probably loved him?"

Robbie had had the same thought. "James."

"You think we're like Nicholas?"

"Nah. He was petty and reckless. We're clever and professional." It was a somewhat fuzzy line, but Robbie was quite certain she and Dee didn't belong in the same category as Nicholas Ingram. And they didn't belong to James's ilk anymore either. They were their own category altogether.

"That we are." Dee took the bill from the waiter, pulling out his wallet and beginning to count out cash. "You take that job in Montreal?"

"Yeah, I head up on Monday." Robbie had just taken on a new contract the night before. "It'll be nice to get out of town. No more local work for me for a while. Maybe never again. Too messy."

"You worried you're going to get hired to kill another person who doesn't exist and turns out to be the long-lost heiress to a multimillion-dollar fortune?"

Robbie laughed as she stood and pulled on her jacket. "Please don't jinx it."

They headed out into the chilly morning. As soon as Robbie started the car, Dee had his hands on the stereo. He chose "Put Your Records On," settling back in his seat and managing to let Corinne Bailey Rae sing almost a whole verse before he let his voice harmonize with hers. And after a moment, Robbie joined in too, letting the music take over.

Reading Group Guide

1. Robbie is recruited as a contract killer because she lacks curiosity, but her pursuit of Xavier is driven by it. How do you think her history and experiences shaped her sense of curiosity? Do you feel curiosity is an innate human trait or something learned?

2. Robbie believes James truly cares about her, but Dee doubts James's motivations. Who do you think is right? Is it more important to know the truth or to hold onto beliefs that help them in some way?

3. The term *queerplatonic* originates with aromantic and asexual individuals and a need to describe something deeper than friendship but not a romantic and/or sexual relationship. How do you feel Robbie and Dee embody this deeper relationship? What aspects of traditional friendship and traditional romantic relationships are blended in theirs? What differs?

4. Like many queer people, Robbie is estranged from her birth family. How has she built family on her own? How does creating that for herself provide support to others searching for family and belonging?

5. Robbie doesn't have formal diagnoses, but her history highlights challenges stemming from learning disabilities and attention problems. How do her views of this change over time, and how does that impact her confidence? Does having strengths or advantages from the way her brain works negate the challenges it gives her?

6. Playing the role of Xavier brings up questions about gender for Cassie, and Dee compares this to theater. How do activities like theater or role-playing games provide space to explore identity? How have different roles in your life helped you better understand your own identity?

7. Robbie tries to find every alternate solution she can rather than outright killing Nicholas, drawing a line between killing for money and killing for personal reasons. What do you think of this moral separation? Do you think it's a true difference or a false dichotomy Robbie has created for herself? How does this reflect society's views about acceptable or unacceptable killing?

8. Part of Robbie's job as a contract killer is setting a price on a human life. What factors do you think would be most important to her in that calculation? How might her approach differ from other ways a value is placed on a person in our society?

9. Robbie and Dee treat contract killing as just another part of their existence while living full, joyful lives and being integral members of their community. How does this reflect the ways we cognitively distance ourselves from how our own behaviors may support unethical or immoral practices? What truths of your own life do you distance yourself from?

10. When talking to Robbie about being Alexandria, Cassie says, "The truth is irrelevant. It's just a matter of belief." Do you believe Cassie truly is Alexandria? What do you think happened to Alexandria after she was kidnapped? Was Nicholas really involved?

11. Music is an integral part of Robbie's and Dee's lives and serves to help them understand and process the world. How did music serve to support or parallel the story? How did songs give you insight into characters or clues to the mystery?

A Conversation with the Author

What inspired *Robbie McNeil's Hit List*?

A joke. This was all a joke! One of my best friends had shared a playlist with an odd combination of songs, and we were coming up with who that mix would appeal to. They joked it was perfect for "artistic lesbians in karaoke bars doing murder." I joked that I could totally make that concept into a book and I'd "see where this goes."

Best. Joke. Ever.

Three and a half weeks later, I completed the first draft of this book! As for seeing where this idea could go, well, this is far further than either of us could've imagined.

Music is such an integral part of this book and to Robbie and Dee as characters. Would you say music is just as important to you? What music has shaped you and your life?

I grew up in a musical family, surrounded by music. In my late teens, I met someone who never listened to music, and their family didn't have a single musical instrument in their home. I was utterly baffled. I couldn't (and still can't) even comprehend living that way!

After writing Robbie and her love of playing piano and guitar, I decided to learn to play guitar and reteach myself piano as an adult (after decades of not playing). Like her, I'm terrible at reading and writing music, so I mostly play by ear and I have so much fun with it! For many years, I was also a dancer. I did ballet, jazz, swing, contemporary, and others. Even now, I tend to conceptualize music in terms of shapes and body movements in my mind.

Music has always influenced and supported me. For every big moment and every "phase" of my life, I can point to the music that went with it. I could fill another entire book just listing out songs that have impacted or held some meaning for me. In the interest of space though, here's four great hits:

"Blackbird" by The Beatles is one of the earliest songs I remember hearing my dad play on guitar, so I always associate it with feeling happy and loved.

"Vienna" by Billy Joel was a counterbalance for my overly ambitious speeding-through-life teen self.

"She Keeps Me Warm" by Mary Lambert came out right when I was figuring out my own queer identity and felt so validating.

"Laughter Lines" by Bastille is a comfort song that never fails to calm me down when I get stressed.

Every character here feels so distinct and real. Is there a character you've written who you relate to the most? The least?

Characters are the heart of my writing process. If my characters don't feel real to me, I can't write a story. Period. (And I've tried!)

In the process of creating realistic and nuanced characters, they inevitably end up with some pieces of me and often pieces of other people I know too. Robbie has my sense of humor, my sticky interest, and to be honest, probably some of my less admirable emotional coping skills. Dee's history of depression and his sobriety as a means of protecting his mental health also come from my own experiences. But while this is my debut novel in terms of publishing, it's far from the only one I've written, and I have to say the characters who are persnickety and a bit neurotic are probably the ones I relate to the most. Robbie is way more easygoing than me! (The scene where she's wired and Dee teases her about not being chill? That's probably the version of Robbie most like me.)

The characters I relate to least usually end up being my villains/antagonists, but even then, I still build from a basis of realistic and relatable experiences. I'd obviously never make the choices Nicholas does, but I have experience with being driven by ambition and making choices to your own self-detriment in the single-minded pursuit of a goal.

Robbie spends a lot of time reckoning with the consequences of her curiosity or lack thereof. Would you consider yourself to be a curious person? Do you think curiosity is an important trait to have?

I am insatiably curious! One of my favorite things about being a writer is the excuse to go deep dive into topics I might never encounter or learn about otherwise. But even when I'm not in writer mode, I am a scientist, and I deeply believe that is not something accomplished by degrees or letters after your name but at its core is about being someone driven by curiosity and discovery. I have journals from when I was six or seven where I compiled lists of questions and countless things I was curious about.

Throughout my life, I've pretty much always worked with kids in some capacity or another. Kids ask "why" about the wildest things (and can often stump adults!). I think we can learn so much from that innate curiosity children have before social expectations and pressures often smother it—and before we develop egos that make us think we already know everything we need to know!

Years ago, I read the book *Station Eleven* by Emily St. John Mandel, and there's a part that has stuck with me ever since. The story takes place in a postapocalyptic world. A young person born after the end of modern civilization asks someone who lived in the "before times" why, in the age of the internet and libraries and constant, freely available information, didn't everyone spend all their time learning everything they possibly could. So why don't we? Why not follow that curiosity you had as a kid to learn as many new and amazing things as you can?

What does the future look like for Robbie and Dee? Do you think they stay contract killers forever?

I love the idea of Robbie and Dee in their eighties singing karaoke in a retirement home and sneaking off to kill someone once in a while… Really though, I'm not sure they'd stay contract killers forever. I don't think they would actively retire from killing so much as just wake up one day to realize it's been ages since they last took contract jobs because they've been so busy with all the other things going on in this life they've built together. I would love to see them make more music together—not just musical theater, but I think with Robbie writing and Dee singing, they could produce a killer LP of their own!

I think they'd try to expand Coda's role in the community too. Bars are hubs for queer community, often the only hubs some people have access to. But substance abuse is significantly higher among LGBTQ+ individuals compared to the general population. There's a huge need for safe and inclusive places for queer people to gather that aren't centered around alcohol. Especially with Dee's sobriety, I think Robbie and Dee would be very on board with creating that kind of space however they could, whether that's through daytime events or mocktail-only nights or something else.

And no matter what directions their future takes them in, it will absolutely have the two of them, together, always.

What do you hope readers take away from this story?

There are a lot of things I could say for this. I hope readers who've never heard of aromantic identities or queerplatonic relationships come away with more understanding and compassion for an experience that may be very different from their own. The same goes for people who don't understand or know much about neurodivergent experiences. I hope readers who identify in any of those ways feel seen and valued.

There is so much more in the book about belonging, identity, cognitive dissonance, truth, and other themes that I'm sure I have some big important message in there somewhere… But this book started because my friend told a joke. It exists because an idea made us laugh. So, at the end of the day, I really just want readers to have fun. If someone comes away having smiled or laughed while they read, my work here is done.

Do you have a go-to karaoke song?

Like Robbie, I don't love singing in front of people, so I do karaoke very rarely and only in private spaces with family and friends. If you feel awkward singing in front of people though, my best tip/trick is to pick a song everyone will know and feel compelled to sing along with. It makes it feel less like all the attention is on you and more about everyone having fun with the music. Two songs I think are great for this are "Pompeii" by Bastille and "Dreams" by Fleetwood Mac!

Music in *Robbie McNeil's Hit List*

Within this book, twenty-seven songs are referenced in the text. Some of these are there for vibes. Some contain hints about the mystery or foreshadow later events. I'll leave it up to astute readers to figure out which are which!

Robbie also has her own playlist of music she listens to while on a contract job (her Hit List!). While this was originally something referred to only on page, I ended up putting together a real playlist of the songs Robbie would have on her Hit List. Whenever I returned to working on this book after taking a break from it, I would put on her Hit List and find myself right back in Robbie's head.

The tracks for Robbie's Hit List are included below. Links to this playlist and the playlist of in-book references can be found at briannaheath.com/playlists.

Songs on Robbie's Hit List:

1. "When the Lights Go Out" by The Black Keys

2. "God's Gonna Cut You Down" by Johnny Cash

3. "I'm Gonna Do My Thing" by Royal Deluxe

4. "Red Right Hand" by Nick Cave & The Bad Seeds

5. "Seven Devils" by Florence + The Machine

6. "Control" by Halsey

7. "you should see me in a crown" by Billie Eilish

8. "Kill of the Night" by Gin Wigmore

9. "Hell's Comin' with Me" by Poor Man's Poison

10. "Bad Things" by Jace Everett

11. "Seven Nation Army" by The White Stripes

12. "Ain't No Rest for the Wicked" by Cage the Elephant

13. "99 Problems" by Hugo

14. "Black Betty" by Larkin Poe

15. "Supermassive Black Hole" by Muse

16. "Can't Go to Hell" by Sin Shake Sin

17. "Whatever Doesn't Kill Me (Better Run)" by Benj Heard

18. "Raise Hell" by Brandi Carlile

19. "Wicked Ones" by Dorothy

20. "Trouble Finds You" by Juliet Simms

21. "Tell That Devil" by Jill Andrews

22. "Ain't No Grave" by Crooked Still

23. "Sinister Kid" by The Black Keys

24. "bad guy" by Billie Eilish

25. "Dangerous" by Danger Twins

26. "Gasoline" by Halsey

27. "Hellfire" by Barns Courtney

28. "Don't Stop the Devil" by Dead Posey

29. "Glitter & Gold" by Barns Courtney

30. "Bottom of the River" by Delta Rae

31. "Hunt You Down" by The Hit House ft. Ruby Friedman

32. "Graves" by Whiskey Shivers

Acknowledgments

I wrote the first draft of this book in twenty-four days, alone in a hammock, but since then, so many people have become part of its journey, and I am beyond grateful for their support.

The book would not exist at all without my friend Teryn, who made a casual offhand joke that I decided to turn into an entire book. Please continue to make weird jokes forever.

Endless and enormous gratitude to Jenna Satterthwaite, my absolutely incredible agent. Thank you for being my guide and advocate in this strange industry, encouraging and reassuring me every step of the way and always believing in me and Robbie. I could not have a better champion for this book or myself.

To my editor MJ Johnston, I knew you were going to be perfect for this book when we hopped on a call and one of the first things you said to me was "I've been wanting a karaoke murder forever." I'm so grateful to you, Nia, and the whole Sourcebooks team for believing in this book and turning the karaoke murder dream into a reality!

To my mentor, Jackson Ford, thank you for helping me build

the story into something I was proud of. At a point when I was ready to give up on this book, you gave me renewed faith that it could and should make it out into the world.

Mom, thank you for your eternal support, for all the phone calls listening to me stress about publishing, and for truly instilling in me a "you can do anything you set your mind to" approach to life. I set my mind to writing and publishing a book—and here we are! Dad, Shannon, Brian, Corri, James, Jeremy, Cathy, Marin, Weston, and Max: Thank you for always supporting every new adventure I pursue. (I know there are many!) I love you all!

My Baguettes, my com-breads in arms: Thank you for helping me rise. This book making it all the way to publication is as much your accomplishment as it is mine. It would not have happened without you. Gingko, thank you for always having such thoughtful, insightful feedback and always, always having a kind word to say (and some choice words for Brian). Mango, my pub twin, thank you for sharing this weird and wonderful journey with me. And to all my co-breads: I cannot wait for our books to share a shelf together!

My wonderful agent sibs of Team Jenna, you have become an unexpected but wonderful and uplifting family, and I'm so grateful to have you all on this wild publishing roller coaster with me.

Baby Giraffe, you have always had a passion for words that I admire so much. Every scrap of creative writing I've done as an adult exists because you reminded me how to find joy in writing again.

Alexa and Kali, thank you for reading and loving early versions of Robbie and Dee.

Beau, my life, my love, my joy.

A thank you to Microsoft Excel, without which I would never

write any books or do a lot of other things in life. (For anyone who thinks this acknowledgment is weird, wait until you hear about the seventeen spreadsheets I made just to write this one book.)

And to aro, ace, and other queer people who don't always feel like they fit in, thank you for showing me how much it matters to tell our stories. *You* matter. You belong here. If this book accomplishes nothing else, I hope it helps you feel seen and loved.

About the Author

Brianna Heath is queer and neurodivergent but definitely not a contract killer. She writes stories that can be broadly described as "Be Gay, Do Crime" with queer millennials. She aims to put stories out in the world that reflect the lives and experiences of people who don't always see themselves represented in media. This is her debut novel.

In her nonwriting life, she works as a program manager for autism research and teaches seminars on neurodiversity, disability advocacy, and inclusion.

Brianna lives in Northern California with Beau, her rescued border collie/gremlin, who, like her, has absolutely no chill. She can be found at briannaheath.com and @BriannaHWrites on Instagram.